Crazy Busy Guilty

LAUREN SAMS

Legend Press Ltd, 107-111 Fleet Street, London, EC4A 2AB
info@legend-paperbooks.co.uk | www.legendpress.co.uk

Contents © Lauren Sams 2017
Originally published in Australia by Nero, an imprint of Schwartz Publishing
Pty Ltd, Level 1, 221 Drummond Street, Carlton Victoria 3053, Australia
www.nerobooks.com
The right of the above author to be identified as the author of this work has
been asserted in accordance with the Copyright, Designs and Patents Act
1988. British Library Cataloguing in Publication Data available.

Print ISBN 978-1-7895501-0-8
Ebook ISBN 978-1-7895500-9-2
Set in Times. Printing managed by Jellyfish Solutions Ltd.
Cover design by Gudrun Jobst | www.yotedesign.com

Lauren Sams is a writer whose work has appeared in *ELLE*, *marie claire*, *Cosmopolitan*, *Good Food*, *delicious*, *Sunday Style* and *Daily Life*. She lives in Sydney with her husband, daughter and two dogs. She first introduced readers to Georgie and her friends in *She's Having Her Baby*.

Visit Lauren at
www.laurensams.com
or follow her
@laurenssams

For my mum, who always made it look easy,
even when I know it wasn't.
Thank you for all that you did for me, and all that you do.

Prologue

What kind of mum are you?

Are you Foodie Mum? Do you make nutritious, delicious meals for your children, often at a moment's notice? Do you swear it's 'the same old thing' every night? (When actually it's homegrown kale – painstakingly, lovingly massaged with extra virgin olive oil – and pearl barley 'risotto', liberally sprinkled with nutritional yeast – the new parmesan! – from Nigella's latest.) Do you spend the six weeks prior to your child's birthday scouring back issues of the *Donna Hay* kids' edition for sausage roll inspiration? Do you make your kids themed birthday cakes every year, from scratch, from a dog-eared copy of *The Women's Weekly Children's Birthday Cake Book* (the updated edition, without all the artificial food colouring and potato chips for ducks' bills)? Is your freezer stocked with balanced meals and brownies made from sweet potatoes and agave syrup (white sugar being, of course, off limits)? Is your freezer decidedly *not filled with gin*?

Or maybe you're Patient Mum. You never begrudge another story at bedtime, another song in the car, another five minutes in the bath at night. In fact, you usually read *several* books before tucking your children in, calmly, without a fuss.

You don't mind if the kids get up to go to the toilet five times. They're only little once, Patient Mums say, smiling as they fetch their four-year-old a seventh glass of lukewarm water.

You might be Martyr Mum. Did you insist on a natural birth, without intervention? Did you feel like your body was about to implode, collapsing in on itself like a punctured lung or a basketball that's lost its pep, because you were so goddamn sore and tired? You got through it, though. Martyr Mums do – they just keep buggering on. You feel – quite understandably – very proud of this achievement, wondering if maybe there's a space to add it to your LinkedIn profile. You also breastfeed. Like, a lot. Are you breastfeeding now? Not just in general, but right now, as you read this? Did you stick with it even though you struggled at first and no matter how much it hurt, because you knew that breast was best? Do you love it now? Are you, perhaps, not quite sure when – or possibly if – you'll give up? Do you co-sleep? Are you careful to tell only other confirmed co-sleepers, lest you be judged by society and its misguided insistence on sole-sleeping? You might be Martyr Mum.

Are you Stylish Mum? Stylish Mum looks good. Obviously. She does not wear a crumpled t-shirt, stained with last night's dinner and possibly this morning's breakfast, to the park. She Instagrams her outfit – an Être Cécile t-shirt (ironed, of course) with an ironic slogan emblazoned across the front, her Frame jeans (the ones she fits into again thanks to her thrice-a-week Pilates habit) and Repetto flats – cold brew / green juice / child optional. Stylish Mum blow-dries her hair, manicures her nails and would not think twice about wearing white jeans. Because Stylish Mums beget Stylish Children, who have a very adult respect for pale denim (and their shoes, too – Stylish Children would never dream of kicking off their sandals in the park, befouling their naked feet with dirt. Stylish Children are too busy reading *Madeline* and sipping their babycinos).

Then there's Organised Mum. Organised Mum knows the exact date of her child's next vaccination and precisely how much Panadol can be given to an eighteen-month-old with an ear infection, without so much as looking at the bottle. She remembers the contents of the fridge with a precision that borders on militant. Organised Mum takes her children to the park, and to playgroup, and to Rhyme Time, and to Gymboree, and to the pool. She knows what, specifically, to pack for each of these different events. She never forgets sunscreen or wet wipes or water or snacks or her child's hat. Organised Mum fills her schedule with child-centric activities and enjoys catching up with all the other Organised Mums she meets there.

Are you Involved Mum? Do you volunteer at playgroup, preschool, and school and weekend sports (not as a coach, mind you – that's a job for Involved Dad)? Can you hear the words 'canteen duty' without shuddering, wincing and choking on your sav blanc? Do you have your kids' Halloween outfits sorted before the Christmas tree comes down? Have you ever attended a Mums'n'Bubs ballet class?

Or are you Hipster Mum? Hipster Mum feeds her kids organic chia seed milk but has sort of forgotten why. Her kids are called Arlo or Edie. She thinks it's important that kids learn a second language – and that's the only reason *Dora the Explorer* is allowed to be screened in her house. If you're a Hipster Mum, you'd sooner strangle yourself with your fair-trade organic cotton scarf than buy your kid a toy from Kmart. You don't know what canned soup tastes like, and neither do your kids. They prefer bone broth, anyway.

Or maybe you're not any of these mums. Well. *Are* you? I didn't think so.

None of these mums actually exist. But for some reason we tell ourselves they do: these perfect mums who are different in their methods but similar in their madness for their kids. We tell ourselves that we should seek to be one of these mothers, these mothers who think of nothing but their children, day in and day out. Whose worlds revolve entirely around their kids, to the exclusion of everything else. We tell ourselves that is what motherhood really is. But it isn't.

We all know what motherhood's really like. Nobody has the energy to make sugar-free muesli bars for lunch boxes and compost every single scrap of vegetable and make a Sunday roast every week without fail. Nobody does it all the time. Nobody plans playdough fun crafternoons every single day, without ever resorting to plopping their kids down in front of a *Ben and Holly* DVD and sneaking off to the kitchen for a glug of wine from the bottle.

My bet is that you're Just Trying to Keep Everyone Happy Mum. You have a child – or children – and a job. A husband, maybe a wife. Friends. Mothers. Fathers. Sisters. Brothers. A boss. Employees. Your own interests. Your life is full, which you like but also find terrifying because if one ball drops the rest may come crashing down soon after. You are perpetually tired in a way that is very hard to articulate (mainly because you're so very, very tired). You want to keep everyone happy and do everything properly and be in many, many places at once. You are very sick of people telling you to 'slow down', 'meditate' and 'get a dog, the kids would love it!' (you do not have time for a dog!). You are sick of answering questions – like 'How do you do it?' – as if you are some sort of superwoman. You know what the real answer is: by missing out on other things. You are late to the Easter hat parade every single year, despite all your best efforts. Best efforts like choosing your employer based on their 'flexible working policies' and 'support of working parents', only to find that this equates to an annual family picnic to which you must bring your own booze. You have heard of 'me time' and think it is ridiculous bullshit that women have to justify simply doing something for themselves for once. You're tired of having to explain how much you do for others in order to 'earn' said 'me time' (still, you nick off for a pedicure once in a while under this guise – because why the hell not?). You send emails while singing to your kids in the bath and cooking tomorrow night's dinner. You braid your kid's hair while memorising a speech you have to give later. You tuck your kids into bed and race away after the final kiss to finish a report that's due in the morning. Sometimes, in dark moments, you feel that 'Cat's in the Cradle' was written with you in mind. You know it is supremely audacious to love both your child and your job.

And you sometimes wonder if your life is about to reel right out of your control.

I mean, *what the hell were you thinking?*

Chapter 1

There's life Before Baby, and life After Baby: that's pretty obvious. Any idiot knows that.

I knew that.

Except I didn't know what life After Baby would really be like.

Before Baby, life was full of statements. *I'm going to do this. I'm not going to do that. I'll go to bed now. I'll wake up now. I'll eat this. I'll go here. I'll see this. I won't see that.* Easy. Simple.

After Baby, life was full of questions – from the moment I woke up to the lovely, luxurious second I laid my head on a cool, firm pillow, ready for a shallow but desperately needed rest, if not exactly sleep, because who knew when I'd have to get up again?

The questions were more or less the same every day.

What time is it? 5 am. *Oh Jesus, really, only 5 am? Still, it was 4 am yesterday, wasn't it? Was it? Who knows?*

In this new reality, it was difficult to remember how many fingers and toes I had, let alone when Pip had woken the day before.

Maybe this is what progress looks like? Maybe tomorrow it will be 6 am! What a beautiful, crazy dream. Wait, what day is it? God, who cares? It's not like I have anywhere to be. No, wait, that mother's group thing is today, isn't it? I need a diary. Do they still make diaries?

Wow, she's getting heavier. How has she grown so much in such a short space of time? Is that good? Bad? Healthy? Do I have an obese baby? No, I have a gorgeous baby, I have the best baby. Don't I?

Right, is she hungry? She's hungry. OK, she's hungry, so why isn't she latching on? Why is she still crying? Shh, baby, shh. It's OK. Here's the boob. You love the boob, right? Maybe she can't smell me. Ellie says it's important the baby can smell you so she knows who you are. But Pip knows who I am, doesn't she? After all, I feed her with my own body. Still, maybe I should shower less: pheromones and all that. Ugh. No. Not doing that. Who would have thought I'd become so preoccupied with my own smell?

She's latching! She's officially latched! She's drinking. Why is it so wet on my stomach, though? Wait, is she... right, OK, so I'm leaking. Why? Too much milk? Not enough latching? Maybe both? (Again: who cares? Who's going to come in, the cast of *Magic Mike*?)

Good job, Pip, good job, keep drinking. I'll just rest my eyes for a second.

Shit, did I just fall asleep?

Is she alive? Have I fallen asleep on her? Oh my god. No, she's good. Very much alive.

Phew.

She's stopped drinking. Why? Have you had enough to eat? Let me check the app. Fuck, I didn't press start. Now I don't know how long she fed for. How long did she feed? Why did I fall asleep?

Now she's crying. Why are you crying? What's wrong? Are you too hot? Too cold? Hungry? I knew you didn't have enough to eat. Drink? Eat? What are you supposed to call it? Technically it's drinking, but it's the only sustenance you get. So it's eating. But that's weird.

Do you need a cuddle? Do you need space? Has there ever been a baby who has needed space? Maybe you're that baby? Just tell me, and we can be cool about it. NBD.

Should I put you down for a nap? Will you even sleep, if I do? What if I lay you down next to me? Just like that, verrrrry gently. You won't even notice. There, like that. Is that OK? Want me to pat your tummy? Stroke your forehead? What is it, exactly (truly: the precise, actual thing) that will make you fall asleep every single time I put you down for a nap? If you could tell me, I would be so grateful. I feel like it would vastly improve our relationship.

She's asleep! Yes, yes, yes, she's asleep! HURRAH! I did it! ASLEEP, ASLEEP, ASLEEP, ASLEEP. Just going to rest my eyes again, just very briefly, not for...

Fuck, did I fall asleep again? Is she... yep, she's alive.

And still asleep.

Should I wake her up? Has she slept too long? I've heard other mothers talk about sleeping too long. Sounded crazy at first, but maybe they're onto something. Should I wake her up? Will she hate me if I do? What would *I* do if someone woke me from a lovely restful sleep? I'd probably be pretty grumpy – just like I am when Pip wakes me up ten times a night.

God, I'm hungry.

Can I move yet?

I need breakfast.

Do we have milk?

Could I use breast milk in my coffee, and just pretend it's cow's milk?

No, no, I can't. Not even I could stoop so grossly low.

Could I?

NO!

Right then. Maybe we could go to a cafe?

That might be nice.

Is a cafe even open right now?

Probably not.

But maybe when Pippa wakes up, it will be? We could go to Ruby's. Have the pancakes with rhubarb compote and double cream. Or the bacon and egg roll on brioche?

(Breastfeeding burns through calories like a flame to a tissue. It was both the easiest and most time-consuming diet I had ever been on. I planned to do it until Pip was at least twenty-five.)

I'd need to have a shower first, clean off all this milk. Too early to wake Nina up. Maybe I can bring Pip into the shower with me? Maybe she'll like it. I love showers – maybe it's genetic? But maybe she'll hate it and start screaming and then Nina will wake up and be rightfully annoyed with the two of us.

Maybe I won't have a shower. Maybe I'll just pat myself down with a damp washcloth, like a soldier at war. That sounds OK, doesn't it? No, it doesn't. It sounds awful.

Right, Ruby's. Bacon. Eggs. Aioli. Some sort of breakfast dessert, definitely. I'll need to pack things – what? Nappies? Wet wipes? A wrap? Toys? A book? (For me, not Pip.) But am I even capable of reading more than one page at a time? What if she cries, and someone – someone like me Before Baby – tells me to leave with a withering glare? What if Pip shits all over me? What if she throws up? How much do you tip if your kid regurgitates breast milk all over the cafe floor?

Fuck it, I'm going back to sleep.

Annnnnd... of course, she's awake.

(If you ever want to see magic performed live, ask a mother to make herself a cup of tea or lay down for a nap and see how quickly her baby wakes up. Better than David Blaine.)

What time is it?

5.58. *Jesus Christ*.

*

So Pip and I got up and began our morning routine: I fed her (again), and after a shower and a half-arsed attempt at making myself look like I had slept more than five consecutive hours, we ventured out into the world.

I thought about waking Nina up but it was only 6.30. She had plenty of time to get ready for work. Plus, I knew she'd been out the night before. These days, she'd always been out the night before.

Somehow it was easier to face the day outside, with coffee and sunshine and crisp clean air, than it was to stay inside, cosy in my pyjamas. Off we went, down Redfern Street and across to our favourite cafe (by which, of course, I mean the one with the most high chairs and the least disdainful wait staff).

All around us sat men in business suits, women clutching expensive handbags and takeaway coffees. I tried not to stare. These people – they looked just like me, but our lives were so different now. They were heading to their offices, their city skyscrapers, their desk salads, and I was going home. I shouldn't have been jealous of them, but I was.

We made our way back home – and found Nina at the front door, letting herself in. It was 8 am on a school day. She should have been at work.

'Hey,' I said, cocking my head to the side. 'Where have you been?'

'Hey,' Nina whispered back to me, clocking Pip's covered pram. We had become used to talking in hushed tones and stage whispers over the last six months. We weren't into attachment parenting or child-led parenting or nappy-free parenting. Our motto was simple: keep the baby asleep at all costs.

'It's OK. She's not asleep. Tried to get her to nap in the pram but I don't think it's happening.'

Nina opened the door and I pushed the pram in. Nina lifted the cover and picked Pippa up, holding her close and breathing in her milky baby scent.

'Hey, little munchkin! How are you today?'

I sat down, trying to let all the fatigue roll right off me, trying to breathe some energy in. Instead, the exhaustion wrapped itself around me like a heavy blanket, with all the weight of the sleep I wasn't getting. It's hard to convey exactly how tired and grumpy and abrupt a person can be after nine months of pregnancy, followed immediately by six months of caring for a newborn. Honestly, evolution has this one all wrong – how is it possible that we have to follow something as exhausting and physically taxing as pregnancy with something as exhausting and physically taxing as caring for a newborn? Sometimes I needed to see Nina getting such warmth and pleasure from Pippa to remind me that I felt that, too. It could be hard to remember that when it seemed like my sole function was to be a walking milk bar.

I was still constantly surprised by the engulfing, overwhelming love I felt for Pippa. I'd been worried that I wouldn't connect with her, that having been so adamant in not wanting children and then so hastily changing my mind, I'd be deficient in love for her, that I wouldn't have enough.

But six months into this new gig, I knew I did have enough. It manifested in ways I hadn't expected. I felt it when I fed her, when I heard her crying, when I set her down for a nap. Burst! Bam! There it was, the love. It was different to romantic love, but it was all-consuming in the same way. I'd always fallen in love quickly, and then just as soon felt it fade away. But with Pippa, the love kept growing. I saw it like a sapling in my mind, getting stronger and bigger every day.

The thing was, though, I loved Pippa but I wasn't very good at being her mum. I had assumed that in the first few weeks after birth when you're essentially quarantined at home, every new mother was hapless and helpless. But then I started to meet women with babies the same age as Pip, and they knew exactly what they were doing. Their babies were on schedules and listened to classical music – some even slept through the night. Their babies did not need to be encouraged to latch. These women were relaxed and at ease with their babies in a way I was desperately jealous of. If life After Baby was full of questions, the most pressing was this: what am I doing wrong?

I used to be someone. I mean, I wasn't Beyoncé, but you know, I did OK. I had a job. A good job. For which I was paid quite a decent salary. I edited a popular women's magazine called *Jolie*. It was smart and funny and cool and showed you exactly what to spend your salary on (mainly makeup brushes and scarves). I had some semblance – maybe not much, but some – of power. I had a team, I made decisions, I worked hard. I was respected.

And then I got fired. And replaced by a 22-year-old.

Well, I quit, but I was about to be fired. So it was a bit like telling people you were becoming a 'minimalist' when really you were just broke.

Now I spent my days doing nothing more than trying to get a baby to nap and feed. Most days, I was not successful at either.

Nina sat down next to me, cradling Pip. She gave her a tight squeeze.

'Not too tight, OK?'

Pip hadn't reacted at all. She was almost asleep. But still, Nina knew she didn't like to be held too tightly. At least, she *should* know.

Nina raised her eyebrows. 'I know,' she said, an edge to her voice. 'I know she doesn't like it too tight. Geez.'

I shook my head. 'Neen, that's not what I meant. It's just... I'm tired. Start over?'

She nodded, giving Pippa another unnecessarily tight squeeze. I closed my eyes and let it go. I was so grateful to Neen for being here. Really, I was. When Pip was born, I'd suggested that she move in with us. Well, I'd asked her. Less a suggestion, more a very enthusiastic challenge. I had expected Nina to say no. I'd just had a baby; she had just lost her final chance of having one. I thought it would be too painful for her to be around us. And then there was that whole thing where I'd agreed to be her surrogate and ended up getting accidentally

19

knocked up by my ex instead. Standard stuff, really. But to my surprise and delight, she had said yes. And so far, we were doing great.

But every so often, there would be a small but noticeable reminder that Nina was not Pip's mother; I was. I had told myself many, many times not to one-up Nina or tell her she was doing the wrong thing, but sometimes I forgot. The other day I had pulled her up for bouncing Pip 'too vigorously'. Today she had squeezed her too tight. I made another internal memo to cool it with Nina. She was helping me raise the child that should have been hers.

'So, you're home late. How was last night?' I asked, changing the subject. Nina had been out with some work friends, I vaguely remembered. She must have slept at one of their places. Maybe it had been late when they'd finished up and she hadn't wanted to wake us up.

Nina's eyes lit up. 'It was great. Like, really great. I probably drank a bit too much, but it was such a good night. You should come next time.'

Here's a little tip. When talking to a new parent, don't tell them about hot new restaurants they 'have to try'. Don't tell them about the movie you saw that 'will definitely win an Oscar'. Don't tell them about the bar you went to that served a cocktail made with some cool new hipster spirit you pretend to be able to pronounce. Don't tell them about the music festival you went to or the comedy show that changed your life or the new shop that is literally redefining retail. Don't tell them about the new yoga class you're loving or the new coffee shop that only sells double-shot espressos because that's a thing now. Just shut up about all of it. We do not want to hear it.

We're not going to restaurants anytime soon. Ditto cinemas, comedy clubs, music festivals, yoga classes or cool new cafes. So just be quiet. Pretend, please, that your lives are as monotonous and repetitive as ours, and then we can still be friends.

'Right. So you had fun?'

Nina nodded. 'Yeah. I actually went home with someone.'
Whoa. OK.

'Wow. Really?'

More nodding, accompanied by a wide, cheeky grin. 'Yep. I did it. *It*,' she added, for emphasis that was not strictly necessary.

'It? *It-it*?'

Nina nodded proudly.

I had assumed that Nina, who had recently separated from her high-school sweetheart Matt, would be lonely and sad after her break-up. I was wrong. I had thought that, after years of trying to have a baby and not succeeding, she'd be depressed. Again, wrong. Nina had taken to her new life eagerly. She was on Tinder. She was meeting people. She was drinking things other than pinot grigio, the white wine of choice for all women over thirty-one. I was taken aback by all of this until I realised that the last time Nina had dated, R. Kelly was not a convicted criminal. Times had changed. Now all you needed was a jpeg and a location, and bam, you were dating! She had gone on a swipe-right spree recently, but this was the first time she'd actually gone home with anyone.

'You... wow. That was fast.'

Nina scoffed. 'I don't think so. You know Matt's probably dating someone already, he's such a serial monogamist.'

'He was only a serial monogamist because he was with you for seventeen years,' I countered.

Nina shrugged, stroking Pippa's tiny nose and cooing into her face. 'That's beside the point. Anyway, don't you want to hear about it? All the gory details?'

Did I? Maybe I did. The last time I'd had sex was... actually, the last time I'd had sex, I got knocked up.

'Sure, whatever. Just don't corrupt Pippa, OK? I don't have enough money for therapy.'

Nina laughed. 'Don't worry, it's not that scandalous.'

'So who was it? Another teacher?'

Nina made a face. 'Oh god no, I would never date a teacher.'

'Really? Why?'

She shook her head. 'They're the worst. Self-righteous. Preachy. Know-it-all. You know the type.'

I did.

'No, this guy's a bartender,' Nina continued, eyes ablaze with excitement. 'Jed. He's so hot. Let me show you a photo.'

I tried to remember the last time I'd slept with a bartender. I'd been, what, twenty-two? Twenty-three? In other words, a perfectly acceptable age to sleep with a bartender, because he'd had as few prospects and responsibilities as I did – not to mention access to free booze. I made a mental note to google 'early midlife crisis' to see if Nina was having one.

'Right... so... where did you meet him?'

'Tinder,' she replied. 'He was working at the bar, but I didn't actually see him because I was with the girls from school and we were in the restaurant part. But anyway, they all needed to leave because they have, you know, husbands and kids–' here, she made a face, as if she had forgotten that, up until very recently, she too had had a husband and was desperate to have a child, 'but it was only 11, so I stayed, obviously.' Obviously. Like it was the most obvious thing in the world that 11 pm was an extremely lame time to go home on a Tuesday night. What was I doing at 11 pm last night? Cleaning up spilled breast milk from the kitchen floor and trying desperately not to cry, if I recall correctly.

'Anyway,' she went on, 'I got another drink and went on Tinder, and bam! There he was. And he was just finishing his shift, so it was perfect. We hung out and he was so funny – like, really funny, George, you'd love him' – this, I doubted – 'and then he said, "Do you want to come back to mine?" and obviously I did and then... we did it.'

Nina finished with an actual flourish of her hand.

In less than a calendar year, Nina had gone from a married school teacher who wanted to have a baby more than anything, to a Tinder-swiping, hard liquor-drinking gal about town. I couldn't blame her, of course, but it was still strange. After a month or so of coming home morose and mournful from the support group meetings her therapist had recommended, she had just stopped going. 'I don't know how sitting in a room listening to a bunch of women wail about how they can't get pregnant is going to help me get over this,' she'd said. 'I need to move on. How can I move on from wanting a baby when all I do is talk about how much I wanted a baby? It's pointless.'

So now, instead of leaning on other women to help her move on, she was leaning into a bartender called Jed.

'And... how was it?'

'Well,' she started, with a sigh that I think was happy, 'it was good. It was... different? Like, are guys different now?' She directed the question at me, as if I had any idea.

'Um... I don't know. Are they?'

'Well, yeah. I mean, he was young... -er. Younger. Than me. Than us. So maybe that's why he seemed so, um, up for everything?'

My eyes widened, I couldn't help it. 'Like what?'

Nina lowered her head and covered Pippa's ears. 'Everything,' she whispered dramatically.

'Not... that? Not that?'

'That.' She raised her eyebrows, punctuating the statement.

I laughed out loud. I could just imagine Nina's reaction. Nina, who had slept with three guys her whole life (marrying your post-high-school sweetheart will do that to a person). Nina, who once asked me, after reading a *Jolie* article, if fisting was 'what it sounded like'.

'Well, that would have gone down well.'

'It was OK, actually.'

'What do you mean?'

Nina grinned sheepishly.

'You did it?' I couldn't believe it.

She shrugged, nodding. 'It hurt, but... I didn't mind it. Maybe something to add to the menu.'

I felt my jaw unhinge. 'It's not roast chicken, Neen. It's anal sex.'

She shrugged again. 'Don't knock it–'

'Oh, I will. I will knock it because I'm not trying it.'

I couldn't believe it. Nina was a 35-year-old woman who'd just come out of a 17-year relationship. The last time she'd had casual sex was in a German nightclub in 1996. This Jed guy was probably watching Bonita sing with Big Ted in 1996.

Right on cue, Pip started crying.

'Is she OK?' Nina asked, giving Pip's leg a little rub.

I nodded. 'She probably just needs a feed. She didn't have a lot this morning when she first woke up.'

'Yeah, what happened in here? It smells like old milk.'

'I leaked. I leak now. My body is broken. Or maybe her mouth is too big? Are my nipples too small?'

'Your nipples are fine. I think you're just blessed with an almighty flow.'

'I don't know that "blessed" is the word I'd use...'

Nina smiled. 'No, it's good. Better than not enough right? Remember how freaked out Ellie was when she had trouble feeding Lucas?'

'Remember it? She hasn't shut up about it in four years.'

Nina flashed a placating teacher smile and I immediately regretted being nasty about our friend. Ellie had taken to motherhood the way Nina had taken to anal sex – with surprising eagerness. A reformed party girl who once spent her nights being thrown out of clubs, Ellie now spent her evenings reading *French Children Don't Throw Food* and nursing a solitary glass of red wine. But she had also taken me in after Jase and I broke up last year, when Nina couldn't bring herself to talk to me because I was suddenly pregnant with the baby she was meant to have. So I had made a vow to go easier on Ellie. She was a good mum. Not just to her four-year-old, Lucas, but to me, too.

'Anyway, what have you two got on today?' Nina asked.

I sighed and gritted my teeth. 'Mother's group. Last one before I go back to work.'

Pippa sucked away contentedly this time, blissed out in her own small world, where the only things that mattered were milk and sleep. It sounded lovely. I wanted to go to there. Badly.

While I was still at *Jolie*, I'd been approached to work for a newspaper supplement called *The Weekend*. It was a new launch; very exciting, lots of money behind it. Lee, the editor, had three Walkleys and a no-BS attitude. She wooed me, told me I could write what I wanted to write, there'd be no advertiser promises, none of the usual malarkey that comes with editing a glossy. So when I left *Jolie*, I immediately called Lee. I wanted in. Some people dream of marrying their true love, all that Disney BS, but what I always wanted was a brilliant career.

Then two months ago, Lee told me she was leaving. Did I want to be editor again? The prospect was thrilling. I'd have creative control, she said. Over everything. Editors were trusted at Live Now Media, Lee said. Respected. They held the brand's reins and went forth, doing what they thought was best. Publishers and ad teams acquiesced to the editor's power. I was awed. And what's more, Lee said, it was a family-friendly company. All the top brass were women. They knew the score, they knew they had to keep mothers in the workforce – they knew that if they didn't, all their editors would be spoiled 25-year-olds from Rose Bay who couldn't figure out what DPS stood for. So I didn't need to worry about how it would affect Pip, Lee said. The work stuff would fit in around the two of us.

And the truth was, I needed to go back to work. I'd been unemployed for over seven months. My severance pay had been decent, but it wouldn't last forever, and it was hard to cover the cost of nappies and Farex and bottles and three coffees a day on the government's paid parental leave, aka minimum wage. A regular salary would be a good thing. A very good thing.

'How are you feeling about it? Are you ready?'

I shrugged. Another question to add to my list: was I ready to go back to work? What kind of mum did it make me? 'Yes. No. Part of me is excited. The other part is... freaked out. It's hard enough getting everything done when I'm at home all day with Pip. How will I feed her and bathe her and play with her when I go back to work?'

Nina smiled and squeezed my hand again. 'You'll be fine. I'm going to do pick-ups, OK? It's easier for me.'

I shook my head. 'No, you don't have to do that. It's not fair on you. It's too much.'

Nina rolled her eyes. 'I would never offer if I didn't really want to do it, OK? Please just let me.'

I smiled back, non-committal. I should be able to do this by myself. It's not like I'm the first single mother in history. My own mother was a single mother, and she managed just fine.

Then again, she hadn't gone back to work when her daughter was six months old. Or ever.

*

I had wanted to go to mother's group about as much as I wanted to eat my own placenta.

Mother's groups were not for me.

They were for mothers who dressed their babies in colour-coordinated outfits, with proper shoes (mini Nike Air Maxes, preferably) and handmade cardigans and bonnets. Pippa owned zero cardigans, and certainly zero bonnets, hand-knitted or otherwise.

Mother's groups were for women who knew how to fold down Bugaboos properly and waited patiently as their babies drifted off to sleep (instead of mentally clocking the minutes till they could get back to their Netflix-ed Swedish thriller and a cold glass of pinot G). Mother's groups were for women who took photos of their babies constantly and knew exactly the right hashtags to use (#baby #sosweet #newborn #mylife #blessed). They weren't for women who swore like sailors as they wrestled with baby equipment and really, really wanted to swear like sailors as their babies fought sleep. They weren't for women who used Instagram exclusively to see if Liam and Miley were back on. Women at mother's groups were already reading to their babies in a second language, sleep deprivation be damned. Mother's groups were for lactating warriors, for women who wore their mum badges with so much pride you could see it coming off them in comic-book-style waves.

Mother's groups, in short, were for the Ellies of the world.

And, of course, that's who had sent me here in the first place.

'You know, I think you're really going to love it,' Ellie had said, picking up Lucas's errant Lego pieces and throwing them haphazardly into a giant plastic tub. Lucas himself had long since vacated the area, and Ellie was making the slow pilgrimage that is Cleaning Up After a Four-Year-Old. Who knew what fresh trouble Lucas could be making as Ellie attempted to deal with the debris of his last adventure?

'Why, exactly, do you think that?' I'd asked, a single eyebrow raised in exasperation. Ellie was one of my oldest friends, and to be fair, she really was a great friend, but she was still the kind of mother who assumed that what was right for her was right for everyone. I already had a friend like that – her – so why did I need to go to mother's group?

Right before I went into labour with Pip, we'd gotten into a huge argument and I'd told Ellie that I wasn't going to be the kind of mother she was – that is, totally consumed by her child. I still felt guilty about saying it, but as each day passed it became increasingly true. I loved Pip but she couldn't be the only way I marked myself in the world. She couldn't be the only thing that said, *look at me*, *here I am*. It was unfair to her and it was a lie. It wasn't that she wasn't enough to define me, she just wasn't the only thing that did. And that's OK. That's normal.

Isn't it?

'It's good to have a community, George. Having a newborn can be isolating. The days are long, and they're repetitive. I mean, it's amazing, don't get me wrong, but it can be tough.'

There is a list of unspoken rules about mothering that everybody seemed to know – except me. The number one rule of the Motherhood Code was to never be outright negative about parenting. Sure, you could say that there were tough times, or that you had a shitty morning, but it always had to be tempered in some way. 'Sure, he threw up on me seven times in a row before 7 am today, but you should have seen his face – soooo sweet! Makes you realise that it's all worth it.'

'I have a community – you. And Neen. And my mum. Jase. Kevin?' Kevin, my mum's husband (it felt odd to call him my stepfather – they got married when I was twenty-six) had welled up with tears when he'd laid eyes on my little girl, and planted a rose bush in her honour. At first I'd found that creepy – it was like she'd died – but now I thought of it as sweet.

Ellie nodded, staring intently at a hair-covered sultana she'd found on the carpet. 'What is this? We've been off sugar for months. I can't even remember the last time I bought sultanas...' She glanced up at me and focused. 'Look, it's all well and good to have us, George, but you need people on your schedule. You need people who don't work, who can hang out with you between naps. Because those days are going to be really, really long, George. They can be lonely. And you don't want to turn into one of those women who does nothing but breastfeed and watch TV all day.'

'That sounds amazing, Ellie. I would love to be one of those women.'

Ellie rolled her eyes. 'No, you wouldn't. Maybe for the first few weeks, but after that, you need structure. Naptimes. Bedtimes. Breastfeeding schedules. You can't just laze around and wait for Nina to get home.'

So I went to mother's group, and truth be told, it was not quite the seventh circle of hell I had imagined it to be.

The mothers were nice. But they all knew the Motherhood Code, and the main thing I felt when I was there was envy. They all seemed to have their mum personalities figured out. There was Organised Mum and Hipster Mum and Foodie Mum and Stylish Mum. They had opinions on co-sleeping and formula feeding and even private versus public school. They talked about discipline tactics they would use in the future and they knew how they felt about smacking and outdoor play and organic food. I didn't understand it; they had been doing this for as little time as I had – how had they figured it out already? I didn't feel comforted, like Ellie had said I would, or part of a community. I felt judged and inferior, and I couldn't for the life of me figure out how these women had cracked the code of something I found so bloody hard.

I was jealous of the young mums because, god, it had to be easier doing all this in your twenties, right? It would make the sleepless nights more restful, the never-ending days seem less like work. At the very least, they'd have to be less jaded.

I was jealous, for obvious reasons, of the women who wore activewear almost exclusively and made it look good. I was still in my maternity clothes, mainly out of laziness but also because of a pouch of flub that refused to budge. What was their secret? Drugs? Surgery? Some sort of powerful laxative tea made from illegal substances like rhino horns? I was willing to at least read a pamphlet about whatever it was.

I was jealous of the mums, no more experienced than I was, who seemed far more at ease with their new role. I doubt any of them had to be taught, by a nurse, how to hold their new baby. I mean, what could come more naturally than holding your own child? A lot of things, apparently, if you are me.

But now, it was over. This was my last mother's group. Next week, when the mums sat down to coffee and banana bread, I'd be in a meeting or checking my emails or editing copy. I couldn't wait.

We'd started mother's group in the local clinic, with a tall, excessively confident woman named Sharon who, by way of introduction, got us to share our birth stories not five minutes after we had met. Another commandment of the Motherhood Code: never abbreviate a birth story. That particular meeting went for three hours as twenty women described, in excruciating detail, the journey their babies made from uterus to hospital bed.

Now we were on our own, and met at a cafe every Wednesday morning for decaf lattes and attempted conversation.

'Hey, George!' they all sing-songed as I rushed in, late as usual. I waved back and forced my biggest smile. How did they all manage to get out the door so easily? To me, it was an obstacle course, my own mini-Tough Mudder (with similar amounts of disgusting fluids) to be reckoned with daily.

I sat down next to Harriet, my favourite, who signalled to the waitress that I would need a coffee. Like me, Harriet was making it up as she went along. She was sort of Hot Mess Mum. The difference was, Harriet rolled with it with unbreakable chirpiness. She was a bubble that could not be burst. She didn't worry about what other people thought, which was confusing and refreshing. It also defied the Motherhood Code, which I loved.

'Hey! How are you? Hi, Pippa!' Harriet peered down at my chest, where Pippa was lying, strapped into the Ergobaby. Six months in and it still took me ten minutes to do it up.

Pippa cooed back at Harriet, her gummy smile sending rivulets of spit down her chin and onto my top. There were no two ways about it, I had given birth to a dribbler. The first couple of times Pip had released a torrent of her own saliva on me, I'd committed to changing my shirt. But then it started to happen five times a day and I ran out of tops. So now I just stuck the blow-dryer on it and went about my business. I had officially become disgusting. Worse, I didn't even care.

'Hi, Harriet,' I said, wiping Pippa's chin with a napkin. 'How are you?'

'Great, thanks,' she smiled. 'Well, you know. I was up all night with this one, but what can you do? I think he might be teething.'

Harriet's baby, Charlie, was the biggest baby I had ever seen. You know how some people can estimate how big dogs will grow to be from the size of their feet as pups? Well, you knew Charlie was going to be a bruiser when you saw the size of his head. He totally owned his Giant Baby status, too. Charlie was the noisiest one, the one who needed to touch all the things, to be seen and heard. I liked him a lot.

'Oh no. God, I hope Pip never gets teeth. I am not prepared for all that,' I said. 'Strong decaf flat white, please,' I added, to the waitress.

'Strong decaf?' She raised a single brow, her pen hovering hesitantly over her little notebook.

I nodded. 'Yes please. I need decaf–' I pointed to Pip by way of explanation '– but I really like the taste. Strong decaf, please.'

She nodded grudgingly – how dare I come up with my own coffee order, just like everybody else did, every single day?

'I hate this place,' I whispered to Harriet. 'Why do we come here? It's so overpriced and the staff are such hipster shitheads.'

She laughed and nodded. 'That is why we come here,' she said, cocking her head towards Jane, the self-appointed president of mother's group.

Jane. Jane was Organised Mum and Involved Mum and Stylish Mum, all rolled into one. Jane was to mothering what Kobe Bryant was to basketball: she just did it better than anyone else. There wasn't much point trying to keep up with her – she was far and away more competent than I'd ever be. I could picture Jane, ten years from now, running the P&C and hand-sewing her kids' ballet costumes and Instagramming their nutritionally-balanced-but-still-delicious lunch boxes. Jane was born to be a mother, born to lead the other mums, born to choose where we all drank overpriced coffee.

31

I didn't dislike Jane. She was really lovely, if I'm honest, and had, on more than one occasion, given me exceptionally useful (if unsolicited) advice. She taught me how to settle Pippa after a feed (newsflash: babies cannot burp on their own) and how to swaddle her so her arms wouldn't come out ten seconds after I put her down.

But like decaf coffee or Zooey Deschanel's music career, there was something about her I just couldn't fully embrace.

I rolled my eyes at Harriet and smiled.

'Hey, my mother-in-law bought me these cute little bibs for Charlie. I'll give you one for Pip, it'll help with the dribbling.' She reached down into her bag and fished around, producing a triangular floral bib. 'Not sure why she bought flowers for a boy – here you go.'

'Are you sure?'

Harriet nodded vehemently. 'Of course. Think of it as a back-to-work present.'

I smiled gratefully. 'Thanks, love.'

As the waitress deposited my coffee on the table, Jane tapped her empty cup with a spoon, bringing the mums (and some of the more alert babies) to attention.

She cleared her throat and looked my way. Oh geez.

'George and Pip, we know this is your last day with us at the best mother's group in the world –' pause for smiles and laughter '– and we are so sad that you have to go back to work. But we will all keep in touch because we need to see this little one –' she pointed to Pip '– and when we can all have a glass of wine again, we'll need to organise a mummas' night out!'

More smiles, laughter, nodding of heads. I stifled an uncharitable groan.

'Anyway, we will definitely miss you, George. You've become a really great friend–' had I? '– and we wanted to give you a little something to make going back to work easier.'

I smiled. I had to admit, the world needed women like Jane. Women who remembered to buy the presents and celebrate the occasions and maintain friendships in real ways.

'Thanks, guys... you didn't need to do that. It's so sweet, but, honestly, I didn't expect anything at all.'

'Don't be silly!' said Min, her teeny-tiny premmie strapped to her chest. 'It's the least we could do. We feel awful about you having to go back!' The words stung like a slap – why did they feel awful about me going back to work? All of their husbands were back at work, why couldn't I work, too?

Next to her, Irish Katie (a nickname I had given her on the first day, when I struggled to remember my own child's name, let alone anyone else's), nodded. 'It's not going to be the same without you, George. We'll miss you and wee Pip.'

Jane beamed as she handed me a beautifully wrapped box.

'Thanks, everyone, this is so lovely,' I said, unwrapping it. Inside were bags and bags of... tea?

'It's lactation tea,' Jane offered. 'In case your supply goes down when you go back to work. Just a little something to make life easier.'

I forced a smile. 'Wow, great idea. Thank you. Thanks, guys, this is a really thoughtful gift.'

And it was. But I couldn't help but think that this thoughtful gift also came with a side serving of guilt.

'How're you feeling about going back?' Katie asked.

'I feel OK. It'll be hard, I think, but manageable,' I said, lying through my teeth. I felt ecstatic. But I couldn't admit that here – major breach of the Motherhood Code.

I love Pip. Of course I do. (Motherhood Code: anything remotely negative must be prefaced by 'I love my child'.) But as I suspected long before having a child of my own to take care of, I did not love the monotony of being with her every single day. Each day was exactly the same as the one before it, give or take an explosive poo. I hated the struggle of getting her down for her naps, a twice-daily routine that set my teeth on edge and my heart racing as Pip screamed for me to pick her up. I had no idea what I was doing, and yet I had to be in control – I had a baby to take care of, for god's sake.

There were moments of brightness, of course. Moments

that made the drudgery less dreary, like when Pip would suddenly stop in the middle of a screaming fit, open her eyes wide as if to say, 'What the hell is going on here?', smile and nestle into me, falling asleep instantly. Or when she would reach out and tenderly touch the pages of *Guess How Much I Love You*, as if she understood the words. (Genius!) Or when she would gurgle at me through a porridge-y mouth, or bang on her high chair with her tiny fat fists as I walked away – only to break into a grin when I turned back. When her personality shone through, I was captivated. *I made this? How?*

But those moments were like full moons – I knew they would come around eventually, but they sure did take their sweet time. You had to go through the entire gamut of emotions, hours and hours and hours of them – before those shiny baubles of beauty arrived. I was sick of cleaning up spit and coughed-up milk. I was sick of feeling my arm grow leaden as I rubbed Pip's back so she would finally (finally, please!) go down for her morning nap. I was sick of tiptoeing into my own bedroom with the stealth and panic of a mouse for fear of waking her.

I needed a break.

So I was going back to work.

'Will Jason help out much?' asked Jane. *Good question, Jane. Good question.*

My ex-boyfriend had responded to fatherhood much as I knew he would: with limited-time-only enthusiasm. His biggest contribution so far had been dressing Pip up in a yellow Tour de France onesie and staging a photo shoot with her. He couldn't quite believe it when, after twenty minutes of having a DSLR in her face, she started bawling and would not stop. Until that moment, I think Jase believed his daughter was an actual doll. He had the gall to ask me, 'Has she ever done this before?'

'He's going to help with daycare pick-ups,' I lied, 'and when Pip gets a little older she might spend a day a week with him.'

Harriet cocked her head in confusion, knowing the truth. I shrugged. Jase had not offered to help at all, but it was easier for people to think he was being the father I needed him to be.

The truth was, I didn't trust Jase to do much. While I had been learning a new language, acquiring the skills I needed to take care of Pippa, Jase had been living exactly as he had before. My life had experienced a seismic shift, but Jase's had barely been nudged. He had scoffed at me when I suggested I might need to go to Tresillian with Pip because she didn't seem to have an off switch. 'It can't be that bad, George. Just ride it out,' he had said, as if raising a newborn was one of his bloody cool-downs, blithely unaware of the flare of my nostrils. He had no idea how difficult life with a baby could be.

'That's great!' said Jane. 'You've got it all figured out, George. I honestly don't know how you're doing it. You're so calm. I'd be a complete wreck.' She was lying and we all knew it. Jane had never once been a wreck, not a single time in her life.

I shrugged again.

'It's true!' said Min. 'I'd be stressed out of my mind. But you're just so on top of everything, George. I mean, I haven't even read a book since Alex was born, and you're starting this amazing new job. You're our Sheryl Sandberg.'

The whole table laughed and I joined in. I wasn't Sheryl Sandberg, of course, but maybe I was the closest thing they had. I didn't understand their collective lack of ambition, the way they desired nothing more than to stay at home with their babies. Weren't they bored? Weren't they tempted to run for the nearest bus every time they heard the *Yo Gabba Gabba* theme song? Weren't they ready for a glass of wine by 11 every morning?

They weren't. But I was. So what was wrong with me?

Chapter 2

The crying was the worst part. Of course I knew that babies cry, but I didn't realise you couldn't block it out. I didn't realise how long they could cry for (forever, seemingly) or how loud their cries could be (somewhere between monster truck and Kris Jenner shouting at Rob). I didn't realise there were different types of cries for different shades of rage, or that there were times when absolutely nothing would calm them. For the first brief, few glorious days of Pip's life, she had (quite unfairly, I feel) lulled me into a false sense of hope and not cried once. Now, any time I attempted to settle her, she screamed and screamed like she'd just seen Donald Trump take his weave out. I was baffled. What had happened? What had I done wrong? How did anyone put up with this long enough to get to the 'out' part of 'cry it out'?

I was running out of analogies to describe how I felt about the whole thing. It was a puzzle I couldn't find all the pieces for. It was a marathon I hadn't trained for. An obstacle course that never ended. An exam without answers.

The second – the very, actual second – I began to feel that I was finally getting a handle on just one aspect of this gig, something would change. I'd finally perfect the way I held Pip as I fed her, only to find her wriggling away from me the next moment. I'd manage to put her down for her morning nap without a struggle, but as soon as I crossed the threshold of the door, she'd be wide awake, as if she'd successfully micronapped for, oh, point-ten-of-a-second and didn't need to sleep any longer. I would figure out the intricate origami of swaddling her only to see her little fist pump out, Jesse Owens-style, ten seconds later. It was a game I could not win.

I'd lost count of how many people told me to 'sleep when the baby sleeps'. As if. It's the second biggest lie you can tell a mother. (The first is 'don't worry, you can't break them'. What a lie! They didn't know that. I might break Pip. What about that plant they told me wouldn't die? Dutifully, I never watered it – and it withered away to crumbly brown tendrils.)

Sleep? I had shit to do when my baby finally napped. Life had not stopped because I had given birth. In fact, it had sped up. But every time I counted on Pippa to sleep through something – coffee with Harriet and Irish Katie, a walk to the shops, a phone call with Mum – she'd invariably pick that one nap time as the one she was deadset on skipping. And not just skipping – she'd wail through, puncturing the air with her screams, making conversation – not to mention dignity – impossible. It made organising anything a struggle of mind-bending proportions. I'd always have to sift through the various scenarios: if she slept, I'd need to put her in her pram, bring a blanket and try to avoid noise. So I'd have to walk the long way to the shops, where you couldn't hear the roadworks, and then I'd have to choose the stores that didn't blare muzac at you as you decided how many mandarins you could afford that week. If she didn't sleep, I could get there quicker but I'd have to find things to entertain her. I'd have to pack a buggy book and maybe a rattle for her to throw on the floor approximately every ten seconds. And if she got hungry before we got home, we'd have to find a place to feed, somewhere quiet so she wouldn't jerk her head back every time someone ordered a skim latte, revealing to everyone to the exact circumference and shade of my post-partum nipples (larger than a 50-cent piece and the exact shade of Ribena).

I was not Olivia Pope. I was not handling it.

By stark and ironic contrast, Nina handled it beautifully. In between nightly Tinder dates and swiping right on essentially any man under forty without facial hair, Nina settled Pip as she wailed, patting her tummy gently and knowingly, running on pure instinct. She talked to her easily, something I found odd and difficult. What was I meant to say to a six-month-old? What did we have in common? Did she really want to hear about *Lemonade*? Nina effortlessly narrated her actions to Pip: 'I'm just going to pop your nappy on now,' 'Let Aunty Nina put a bit of Sudocrem on your bottom,' 'OK, I'm wrapping you up nice and cosy for bedtime.' She knew what she was doing and I had no idea how. It felt like the day I'd been sick in primary school and missed the lesson on long division. Now I was thirty-five and still didn't know how to divide 450 by 7.

Even Jase, when he was there, seemed to be, at the very least, comfortable with Pip. He picked her up with ease, held her close and rocked her as he sang from the Vampire Weekend oeuvre. A few times she had drifted off to a deep, peaceful sleep as he did this, leaving me slack-jawed and overwhelmed with jealousy. I had to put Pip to sleep twice a day, every day, and even now, most of the time I gave up and just lay down with Pip until she fell into slumber.

And the worst part was, everyone could see how at ease Jase was with Pip. Of course I wanted him to feel comfortable with her, but I felt like it was happening at my expense. At her 'head-wetting', every guest just about masturbated over how 'great' Jase was, how 'hands-on' he seemed, how 'lucky' I was to have him.

It was Jase's idea, of course, to 'wet the head'.

'What?' I asked, confused. Pip's head was already wet; she never stopped bloody dribbling.

'Wet the head, George. It's a tradition. You got a baby shower, so the dad gets to wet the head.'

'Actually, I didn't have a baby shower.'

He paused.

'Well... we can do it together. Wet the head together.'

'Mmm... what is it, exactly?'

'I don't know. A piss-up, I think.'

'Alright.'

So we invited our friends and family (including Jase's mum, who insisted on calling Pip 'Phil' for reasons entirely unknown to us) to the pub down the road and Jase raised a teary toast to his firstborn. It was quite sweet, but I was infuriated by what the toast implied: that Jase had done more than buy a pram and help Nina build a cot for Pip (and truth be told, Nina did most of the building). That he was there, night in and out, to help settle her. That he knew what it was like to listen to her cry for close to an hour and feel helpless because he couldn't calm her down. Everyone but me cheered as he recounted Pip's birth story – which he only knew second-hand – and raised a glass as he talked about the way he fell for her instantly and how much he loved being a dad.

Of course he loves being a dad, I thought. He gets all the fun bits. The easy stuff.

Afterwards, in between Jase's mum Tracey asking me approximately every 2.5 seconds when we were going to baptise 'Phil' (never), almost every guest made a special trip my way to tell me how great Jase was. Actually, they didn't tell me: they asked me, then expected me to agree.

'Isn't he great?'

'Wasn't that a great speech?'

'He's such a great dad, isn't he?'

Nobody told me I was such a great mum.

Even the other mums at mother's group, who had only been mothers as long as I had, were better at it. Harriet was so relaxed and at ease with Charlie, it was like she had been his mum her whole life. Nothing was a bother, nothing was too much trouble. Charlie was a baby like any other, in that he frequently spewed and often cried and sometimes shat his pants, but Harriet just dealt with it. I wouldn't have been surprised to hear that she'd given birth to Charlie with nary more than a sneeze, after which bluebirds flew down to sit on her shoulder.

And while nobody could call Jane relaxed, at least she knew what she was doing. If Harriet's parenting was defined by calm, Jane's was about assertion. Jane was a pack leader, determined to steer Evie away from any danger and mould her into an organic food-eating, Tchaikovsky-listening, Margaret Atwood-reading adult (who happened to have a medical degree and an MBA). She had memorised *What to Expect in the First Year*. She knew the safest way to feed, hold, sleep, walk. It was Jane who'd explained to me how to check rashes for signs of meningitis and how to tell a normal cough from whooping cough. She'd told me about the night GP and the breastfeeding hotline and Tresillian. She knew everything, I knew nothing.

I had never been so bad at a job before. If I was getting paid, I'd have been fired by now. Maybe I had some potential, but I certainly wasn't living up to it. I was putting in the hours, sure, but I wasn't getting results.

On Pip's four-month-birthday, the pressure valve cracked. Like every day that had preceded it, it had been very long. But it wasn't a bad day, not entirely. The house was a mess but I had grown used to that. Pip had had two short, fitful naps, but at least she had slept. She'd thrown up on my clothes twice but I'd managed to handle it. Things would get better, I kept telling myself. It's not always going to be like this. I didn't quite believe it but I couldn't afford to contemplate the alternative.

While Pip was down for her afternoon nap, I threw piles of washing in the machine and then hung them out. I washed the dishes and tidied the piles of magazines that covered the kitchen table. I straightened corners and put away the general detritus that Nina managed to ignore by virtue of almost always being on a date. I made a cup of tea and drank it when it was still a little bit warm. It was forty-five minutes of victory and it felt good.

It was Wednesday: bin night. I calculated Pip's nap time – I probably had five minutes to throw the recycling in the bin and take it to the street. Then everything would be done. The house would be clean – in a relative sense, anyway. I could not control anything about my child, but I could control this.

I listened for any sound of Pip rousing. Nothing. Phew. Maybe – maybe – when I got back from doing the recycling, I'd be able to sit down by myself for a few minutes. The thought was both tantalising and ridiculous. How had I got to the point where sitting on my arse for more than sixty seconds was something to get excited about?

The bin was close to full with baby-product packaging and the bottles of wine Nina had begun to plough through with astonishing speed. I added some old magazines – 'Bruce and Kris more in love than ever!' – and a few more wine bottles. When had Nina found the time to drink these?

Eileen's bin, however, was near empty. Eileen was our neighbour, the kind you could count on to know exactly who'd been walking down our street at 3.37 pm the previous day. She'd add little details like what they were wearing and carrying and if they looked 'a bit shifty'. She would have made an ace reporter. Or private eye.

Of course Eileen's bin was empty, because Eileen must have been eighty if she was a day. How many bottles of blackberry nip could you get through at that point? I snuck round to her bin and shoved our surplus cardboard in. Done. I might get my few minutes of peace.

'Georgina?'

I spun around. 'Hello, Eileen! How are you?'

She raised her very thin eyebrows at me. 'What are you doing, Georgina?'

'Um, just putting the recycling out. Bin night!'

She narrowed her eyes as her mouth became a slit. 'I can see that. You're using my bin.'

'Oh, well.' I paused. Did it matter? How could it? Eileen crossed her arms and stared at me, awaiting a response. Scratch the reporter vibe – she was a high-school principal through and through. 'Yes, but...'

'But what?'

'But... it's bin night. And ours is full. So–'

'I know what your bin is full of,' she said, her voice sharp and high. 'Alcohol.'

I cleared my throat. My time on the couch was slipping away. If I didn't leave now, I wouldn't get it. Not today, and maybe not for a long time. I had to seize this opportunity.

I began to back away.

'Yes, there are a few bottles in there,' I said, trying to be playful and casual. *Ha ha ha, Eileen, we're all friends here.* 'But, um... the bins are going out tonight, so it's no big deal. Thanks Eileen! Let me know if you need anything from the shops tomorrow! Happy to pop down for you.'

'It's a big deal to me. Get your rubbish out of my bin.'

'Are you serious?'

Eileen stared.

'You want me to take my rubbish out of your bin?'

More staring.

'You're serious.'

She nodded, motioning towards the bin as if to say, 'Get a move on.'

'Why?'

'Because it's not your bin. It's mine. It's for my rubbish.'

Now I stared. She couldn't be serious. It was fucking rubbish, for fuck's sake.

'But... your bin is empty and our bin is full. And technically, the bins belong to the council, so... I think it's fine. And they're going out tonight anyway. I really don't see what the big deal is, Eileen.'

She scoffed. 'I pay my council rates, it's my bin. Not yours. Kindly take your rubbish and leave.'

I felt my chest begin to tighten. Was this woman serious?

I was doing all the right things – I cleaned the house, I did the washing, I was *recycling* for god's sake – and all I wanted was 120 seconds of silence and alone time. And this woman was taking it away from me.

'No.'

Eileen's mouth formed a shocked O.

'Excuse me, young lady?'

Secretly thrilled at being called a young lady for the first time in fifteen years, I nonetheless rolled my eyes. 'Eileen, it's rubbish. It will be gone by tomorrow morning. Calm down. I'm not taking it out. I have to go back to my baby now. Goodbye.'

'Now you listen to me!' she yelled. 'Get back here and take that rubbish out!'

'Or what?' I snapped, exasperated. 'It's just bloody rubbish, Eileen. I need to get back to Pip.'

'Don't you swear at me, young lady.'

I gritted my teeth. 'I'm not a young lady, Eileen. And you're not in charge of me, or anyone. It's rubbish.'

I heard her huff with indignation. 'You are a very, very rude young lady, Georgina. If this happens again I'll have no choice but to call the police.'

From inside, I heard Pip begin to cry. It was all over. Two minutes. That was all I'd wanted. Just two minutes that were just for me, that weren't hijacked by another tiny person's needs. And now my two minutes were gone.

I spun around. 'You know what, Eileen? Go–' I was vertiginously close to telling an eighty-year-old woman to go fuck herself. *What was wrong with me?*

Eileen peered at me, ready to pounce on whatever came out of my mouth next.

'Yes, Georgina? What was it you were saying? Because to my mind, the only acceptable thing for you to do now is to apologise. Your behaviour is completely uncalled for.'

I groaned, hearing Pip cry from inside again. Sod it. 'No, Eileen. I'm not apologising. I couldn't give a fuck that I upset

43

you.' I turned to leave but as soon as the words left my mouth, prickles of heat made a rash across my body, covering me in shame. Oh my God. I swore at an eighty-year-old woman. Next stop: *A Current Affair*.

I turned back.

'I'm sorry, Eileen. I didn't mean that. I'm really sorry.'

Eileen just shook her head and turned around, hobbling away as fast as her Zimmer frame would take her.

Oh my god.

'Eileen!' I called out, as Pip's cries grew louder. 'I'm so sorry, Eileen! I didn't mean it. I won't use your bin again! I'm sorry!'

She didn't look back, but it did take her a good three minutes to shuffle back inside.

I headed inside and cuddled Pip into me as if she were a salve for the horrible words I'd said. I couldn't do this. I was – pardon the pun – rubbish at this. I hated being home all day. I'd had a romantic notion of walking Pip to the park, spreading out a picnic blanket and lying in the sunshine in mother-daughter bliss. The last – and only – time we had attempted that, a couple of stoners from Sydney Uni came over and asked if they could share some of Pip's rusks. It took every shred of my remaining dignity not to ask if I could share one of their blunts.

The monotony of daily life with a baby was about as romantic as watching the footy finals. I loved Pip, I felt it with all of my body, but I also felt like she was a stranger. I didn't know what she wanted from me, and even if I managed to figure it out, I didn't feel like I could give it to her.

Sometimes, in darker moments, I suspected I had been right all along. I had never wanted to be pregnant. I didn't want to be a mother. I was no good at it.

A few days later, I got the reprieve I'd been so desperately waiting for.

'You're *leaving*?' I was shocked. Lee loved being at *The*

Weekend. She was the founding editor. She'd shaped it into the clever, snappy read it was. And now she was going?

'Yep. John got a job offer in Washington.'

'DC?'

'Yeah. It's pretty exciting. It's a once-in-a-lifetime thing, you know?'

'How long are you going for?'

'I'm not sure. Six months at minimum. Probably longer.'

'Wow.' I wasn't sure what to say.

'I want you to be editor, George. I've talked to Meredith and she's keen, too. You can do this.'

'Who's Meredith?'

Lee paused. 'Hold on.'

I heard the click of what I assumed to be a door shutting. 'You there?'

'Yes,' I said, dangling a teether in front of Pip to distract her from gnawing on my earlobes. I wish I could say it worked.

'Meredith's the publisher. She's... she's got a big personality.'

'She's crazy,' I translated.

'Well... she's very good at what she does.'

'And also crazy?'

Lee laughed, but it sounded high and thin. A little like Meredith herself, I suspected.

'Not... "crazy", per se. More like... interesting. She has a lot of ideas. She's very hands-on.'

'Uh-huh,' I said, reading between the lines. Lots of ideas = do this absolutely impossible thing immediately and ask no questions. Hands-on = extreme micromanagement.

Pip stuck a curious finger in my ear and I tried not to yelp.

'Look, I'm not meant to start for another six months—' I said, phone wedged against one ear as Pip literally chewed the other. At two months, the chewing had been cute. At four, with a tooth edging its way down her gum, it was pretty bloody painful.

'I know, I know. But look, this is the job you've dreamed about, George. The team here is great. I'm biased, of course,

45

but it's a great brand. All the hard work – the initial stuff – is done. You just have to keep it ticking.' She paused. 'Or not, of course. You'll be the editor, you can do what you want.'

'You want me to be the editor?' It was like I'd only just heard what Lee was saying. 'Of *The Weekend*?' I tried not to let too much hope show in my voice. I had dreamed of working for a magazine like *The Weekend* my whole life. Smart, witty, topical, ahead-of-the-curve, it was a Saturday supplement that car advertisers loved and readers genuinely looked forward to. It was that excellent mix of insightful profile, hilarious essay, in-depth reporting and, of course, a recipe or two at the back. I loved it. I was meant to be going back as features director – this was much bigger.

'Yep. George, I really think you're the right person for the job. The only person, truth be told. I know you'll be able to handle Meredith and the advertisers and the bloody freelancers who never turn in their copy on time. You can do all that. And hey, the money is good. You'll even get a car spot,' she added.

'I can't drive.'

'Oh.'

'Will they give me a driver?'

'Sure. What else? Personal trainer? Chef? Stylist? Maid? Someone to massage your cuticles at whim?'

'Just whatever Anna Wintour gets.'

Lee laughed, for real this time. 'Done. Look, George, I know you can do this. And don't worry, you'll be able to leave on time and do all the stuff you need to do with Pip. It's a really family-friendly place. They've just run this big HR campaign about leaving on time and taking lunch breaks and there's even a breastfeeding room. So you can keep feeding Pip! I promise, you can work it all around Pip. She'll still come first. And I mean... don't you want to be an editor again?'

I did. I really did. I missed working. I missed being part of a team, firing off ideas and fixing things and making stuff. I had always loved the day the mag went on sale. I'd walk past the newsagent near my office and feel my heart skip as

I saw shiny copies of *Jolie* on the stands, waiting for readers to dive in.

There was definitely something tantalising about returning to work. About getting on the bus without having to wrangle the pram on, too, and using the commute to read a book for ten uninterrupted minutes. Wearing pants that weren't described as 'lounge wear'. Talking to adults about things other than where to buy the rumoured-to-be-sold-out Sophie the bloody Giraffe. Returning to deadlines and meetings and interviews and expectations might improve my sanity somewhat, I suspected. I'd always thrived on that stuff.

As Lee told me about the team and what I'd be doing, I counted the daycare centres within walking distance and wondered whether Jase could help with pick-ups. I fantasised about buying a new outfit. Putting on makeup. Using social media for something other than comparing myself to celebrity mothers who ran on the treadmill as their babies napped beside them (I liked to accompany this particular exercise in masochism with a large bowl of Doritos).

And if I was honest with myself, I didn't know how much longer I could exist in this day-to-day way, without some promise of a life that was more stable, more routine. More like... my old life. I could handle my old life. It was predictable, but not boring. Now it was boring, but unpredictable. I could never be sure when I could leave the house because I never knew when Pip would sleep, or for how long. I dreaded being out in public when she had a meltdown. I was tired right down to my bones. In a few months our house had become oppressively small and I craved the outside world. I needed to get away from the dirty washing and the piles of dishes in the sink and the smell – the smell of milk and poo and stale air that took days to be flushed out in winter. On top of all that, the exhaustion had aged me ten years, give or take. My skin had taken on the grey pallor of a sickly child in an English period movie. I wore tracksuit pants almost exclusively – I even had a 'nice' pair. It made me sad just thinking about that. I had memories of wearing makeup, once, but even they seemed distant and uncharacteristic. Now, putting on moisturiser was Victoria's Secret model-level maintenance.

'Yep, I'll do it,' I found myself saying.

'Really?' Lee seemed surprised.

I paused. 'Yep. I'm not a stay-at-home mum. It's just not my bag.'

She repeated me, word for word. 'Right! You're not a stay-at-home mum. Of course you're not! This is such great news, George! I'm going to tell Meredith right away, she'll be so excited.'

I wasn't a stay-at-home mum. That was the whole problem. I didn't know what kind of mum I was.

Chapter 3

Pop!
'Cheers to you, George!' said Nina, pouring me a glass of bubbles. Real ones. I'd insisted on French, owing to both my recent pregnancy sobriety and my new job. I deserved real champagne. It hadn't been difficult to twist Nina's arm. In fact, she'd bought two bottles. I added 'early signs of alcoholism' to my Nina-related googling.

'Thank you!' I settled Pip on her tummy – tummy time, apparently, separated the genius wheat babies from the chaff – and took a glass, raising it to meet Nina's.

'To new beginnings,' she announced brightly. I smiled and our glasses clinked, but I did wonder if perhaps it was slightly too soon for Nina to be toasting a new beginning. Her divorce hadn't even gone through. Her high-school artwork was still at the old house, with Matt. She still had a faint tan line where her wedding rings used to be.

I brushed the thought aside. If anyone deserved a new beginning, it was Neen. The last year had pummelled her pretty mercilessly. She needed a reprieve, a new start. A life where she wasn't married to Matt or trying to get pregnant. A life where she could just be Nina.

'To new beginnings,' I repeated.

'Are you excited?' Nina looked excited for me. So far, she was the only one. I'd told Jase earlier that week and he'd nodded, looking confused.

'Who'll look after the baby?' he'd asked.

'The *baby*? Her name is Pip.'

He rolled his eyes. 'Don't be silly, George, I didn't mean anything by it. I was just wondering, that's all.'

I crossed my arms against my chest. 'She's enrolled in daycare.'

'Oh.' He looked confused.

I raised my eyebrows. 'Why? Have you got any better ideas?'

'Hey! What's all the attitude for?'

I sighed. 'Nothing. It's... nothing. Do you have a problem with her going to daycare?'

He paused. 'No,' he said eventually. 'No. I just...' Here, I assumed he would put up his hand and offer to help. 'I just thought your mum might pitch in and do a few days. Pip's still so little, that's all.'

Ellie and my mum had similar reactions. Mum wondered why on earth I wanted to go back to work so soon, 'if at *all*, Georgina!' and had promptly written me a cheque for $5000.

'Mum! I don't need this. It's not about money.' Well. It was a little bit about money. I certainly wasn't working for free. But I didn't want my mum bankrolling my life, especially now that I was a mother myself.

'Well, why would you possibly want to go back to work now, Georgina, if not for the money? Look at this beautiful little baby. She needs you at home.'

I briefly wondered where I might dump Mum's body if I committed murder right there before snapping back to reality. 'Mum. That is a really outdated – not to mention totally sexist – idea. Most women go back to work now. We're all leaning in these days.'

'What?'

'Leaning in. You've got to have a seat at the table, Mum.'

She pursed her lips. 'And who is going to make dinner to put on that table, Georgina?'

Ellie had been much the same, only more passive in her aggression. 'I wonder–' she mused, bouncing Pip up and down, trying to settle her after I hadn't been able to, 'if a nanny isn't a better idea than childcare,' she said, giving 'childcare' the same tone as she might have used for 'gulag'. 'A nanny is less disruptive. More attentive. Some of them even make your dinner!'

A nanny did seem like a good idea. Especially one who'd serve you a steak dinner as you walked through the door after a long day. But I couldn't get right with the idea of another woman in my apartment, taking care of Pip all day. It was ridiculous and selfish, and yet I couldn't shake the fear that Pip would grow to love a nanny more than she loved me. We were hanging by a thread as it was.

'Um, yeah, I am excited, actually,' I told Nina. 'Bought a new outfit and everything.' Pip squealed. She was making more noises lately. Unfortunately for me, many of them were quite high-pitched and tended to be emitted between the hours of 2 and 3 am.

'How was your last mother's group?'

I laughed. 'Yeah, it was fine. They're nice. They gave me lactation tea.'

Nina furrowed her brow. 'Oh. Interesting choice. As, like, a present?'

I nodded.

'They don't know you very well, do they?'

'No, sir.'

'Should I tell them a bottle of wine will do just fine in the future?'

'Sure,' I said, reaching for a wedge of sun-warmed brie. 'Could you also tell them to stop asking me if Pip is sleeping through yet? Seriously, that shit is getting old.'

Nina pulled a face. 'It's totally fine that she's not sleeping through the night.'

'I know. It's fine. She's a baby. They're not meant to sleep through the night right away,' I said, repeating the mantra I had memorised. The problem was pretty much every other mother in my group had managed to get their baby to sleep through. I didn't know how. I didn't have the heart to let her cry it out, but I wasn't hippie enough for co-sleeping. So instead Pip and I waged a nightly battle in which she would cry, I would tell myself this was going to be the night I would let her whimper until she finally fell asleep again, and then approximately two minutes later I would be picking her up and feeding her because it was the easiest way to get her back to sleep. It happened again the next hour, and the next, and the next.

'Anyway, we're not here to talk about sleeping. We're here to celebrate this new chapter! It's so great, George, you really deserve this. They really made a mess of things over at *Jolie*. I'm so glad you got this job.'

'Thanks, Neen.'

She smiled and her phone pinged. The smile grew bigger.

'Jed?' I guessed.

She looked up, coy.

'He's been texting a lot,' I said.

At first, Tinder had been a fun distraction for Nina. After dinner, the two of us would sit down with a glass of wine and Nina's phone, giggling as we swiped dismissively left or gleefully right. It was like free, sexy shopping. But soon it became clear that Nina actually wanted to date one of these guys, and that just felt inherently weird to me. I was so used to Nina being with Matt that the idea of her being with someone else was bizarre. I'd assumed the phase would pass, like ombre highlights or the ice-bucket challenge, that she'd find a rebound guy and be done with it. And then she'd found Jed.

Jed wasn't the first guy she'd met on Tinder, but he was the first she'd had a second date – and adult sleepover – with. There had been other guys, and they were all striking in their similarities. Their profile pictures were all either suit and sunnies or bare chests on the beach. What were they interested in? 'Marathons – the 42-kilometre kind, and the *Breaking Bad* kind.' 'Working hard... and playing hard.' 'Healthy living – and the odd bottle of Mumm.' Grooooooooaaaaaaaan. Without exception, they were younger than Nina, sometimes by more than ten years.

She put the phone down. 'Yeah. I think we're... dating,' she said, smiling bashfully.

'Oh.' Dating? That seemed sudden. 'Well, that's... good. Right?'

As Nina's best friend, I didn't really know how I was meant to feel about this turn of events. Was I supposed to be protective of her heart, and warn her that a rebound guy might not be the answer she was looking for? Was I supposed to support this clearly silly, sex-fuelled relationship with a minor (let's call a spade a spade) because it was what Nina needed right now? Was I supposed to be loyal to Matt, in case they got back together?

'Yeah! Definitely. I really like him.'

I smiled. 'You got a crush, Nina Doherty?'

'Um...' Nina reached for the bottle, pursed her lips and smiled. 'Yep. I do. A big fat one.' She poured us both another glass, even though mine was still half-full.

'Wow. Well, I think that's... very cool,' I said, trying to convince myself.

'What?' Nina asked, in the withering tone you use when your parents ask if there'll be boys at the party.

'Nothing,' I said. 'I think it's good. I do. It's good to have a rebound.'

'Really?' asked Neen, sceptical.

I nodded, far too fast. 'Absolutely. Yes. Yes,' I said, really emphasising the last yes. I skolled the newly full glass and reached for the bottle again. Nina raised an eyebrow.

'Good. I'm glad you're supportive of this. It means a lot.'

I gulped down half a glass. 'Sure. Of course.'

'Because the thing is, well, he might not just be a rebound. I like him.'

53

Pip squealed again, and in the distance, I swear I heard a dog howl. Nina picked her up for a cuddle, and Pip cooed into her neck. For the briefest of seconds, I saw Neen close her eyes and breathe in the embrace, before she laid Pip down on the rug again. I'd seen her do this more than a few times before. It broke my heart.

'He might not just be a break-up bone, you know?'

I said nothing.

Nina matched my silence.

'Isn't that –'

'A bit quick?' Nina interrupted. 'Maybe. But you know, maybe not. When you think about it, I've really wasted a lot of my life. I have a lot of stuff to catch up on.'

I baulked. 'Like what?'

Nina shrugged. 'Everything! I need to travel. I need to meet people. I need to be... be more me. I mean... that's really what it boils down to: who am I? I feel like I don't even know anymore.'

I was suddenly grateful for the extra bottle of booze.

Nina was in the gesticulation phase of her sermon now, hands in the air like an evangelical pastor. 'Do I even want to be a teacher anymore? Part of me was only there for the school holidays, you know, for when I had a kid. And now... well, that's not going to happen.'

I took a breath. What was Nina on about? Tinder was one thing – changing her career was something else entirely. I knew she was hurting, of course, and I knew life had fucked her over, but I'd never heard Nina talk like this before.

'Really? But you love teaching.'

She shrugged. 'I did. Well, I do. But I never even stopped to think that there might be something else I want to do.'

'Like what?' Pip had rolled over onto her back and I picked her up, attaching her to my boob on autopilot, wondering what passersby glancing in the window thought of the chick with a baby on her left boob and a glass of champagne in her right hand.

Nina threw her hands up. 'I don't know! Maybe I'd be a good... lawyer? Or... architect? Maybe I could be a writer? A baker? Yeah... I mean, why not go to culinary school and become a pastry chef?'

I stared at her.

'Neen, you don't want to be a pastry chef. You've never even made a cake.'

'Because I never thought I could! But what if I can? What if there's a whole other me, just dying to get out, and I've never given it the chance? Maybe I could start one of those... what are they called? Start-ups! Maybe I could be a DJ. Or a wedding celebrant. Or a comedian.'

What could I say to that? The answer, it turns out, is nothing... but laughter. I couldn't help it.

'Why are you laughing? It's not funny,' Nina said. She looked hurt.

'Hon... sorry. I didn't mean to laugh. It's just... this is all so out of the blue. For me, at least.'

Nina crossed her arms. 'Well, I've been thinking about it for a few months. OK, so maybe technically I haven't "wasted" anything, but George... I have to make some changes. My life has done a complete 180. I need to figure out –' she threw her hands up again '– all this.' By the time she'd finished speaking, her voice was whisper-soft and her eyes were fixed on me, needing me to understand. I set down my glass and put my hand on hers.

'Look, hon, I know everything is weird right now. That's to be expected – so much has changed. But try not to make any rash decisions, OK? Trust me, you have not wasted your life.'

She flashed a small, tight smile and sipped her champagne. I knew she was all over the place – hello, 25-year-old bartender! – but she had to understand that this was all normal, considering what she'd just been through. She had wanted me to have her baby. Instead, I'd had my own. She'd broken up with her husband, her high-school sweetheart. She'd moved in with me and Pippa. A lot of shit had gone down. So yeah, she had a bit of soul-searching to do. But she was still Nina.

Wasn't she?

Because if Nina wasn't Nina, who did that make me?

*

In my mind, I was ready to go back to work. Apprehensive, maybe, but ready. I had psyched myself up for it. I had planned for every eventuality. If Pip was stricken with a dreaded daycare lurgy – which Ellie had warned me about so frequently, I fully expected Pip to fall victim to whooping cough before the week was out – I had a back-up plan (her name was Mum). Nina had promised to pick Pippa up, but if she couldn't, I'd arranged with Meredith, my new boss, to leave early. It wouldn't happen often, I'd promised. I could count on Nina. I'd found the fastest route to the station from our house, and Pip and I had even practised it. I was ready. I could do this.

Meeting with Meredith had confirmed that yes, I was meant to take this job. Tall, thin and expensive-looking, Meredith had her shit firmly together. She smiled warmly and shook my hand. 'Georgina?'

'George is fine,' I said. 'Meredith?' The question was redundant. I'd been up half the night googling Meredith Parker. I knew exactly what she looked like.

'Ms Parker,' she said, looking serious. I paused, and she burst into high-pitched laughter. 'Meredith! It's Meredith! I'm kidding, I'm kidding.'

'Oh, OK.'

'Sit down,' she said, gesturing to the chair opposite hers. Her office looked like an ad – pens sat upright in a stylish gold jar; laptop closed on the desk, thin and flat. Typographical posters screamed witty entrepreneurial inspiration from behind her desk. A mug emblazoned with 'But first, coffee' sat clean and seemingly unused next to a stack of books that included *Lean In* and *Thrive*. I liked Meredith already. 'So,' she said, smiling broadly, 'are you ready to be editor again?' It wasn't a challenge: it was an invitation.

'Yes,' I said, perfectly confident. 'Yes, I am.'

And I was ready to work with this woman. Meredith Parker was a publishing legend. In my baby brain fog, I somehow hadn't recognised her name when Lee had first told me about the job. But a quick search and I suddenly realised: holy shit, this is *the* Meredith Parker. At twenty-four, she became the youngest editor – worldwide – of *gisele*, a smart, sassy magazine for smart, sassy ladies. At the time, it was tanking, but in less than two years Meredith turned the ship around and made the magazine a powerhouse. She was friends with the celebrities she put on the covers and the advertisers who bought pages. At thirty, she became the magazine's publisher – unprecedented at the time – and soon took on even more titles, showing a knack for reviving the particularly profitless. When *gisele* famously ran out of inventory – meaning that all the ads were sold, for the entire year – she dreamed up spin-off titles: *gisele girl*, *gisele guy*, *gisele home* and *gisele at work*. All but *gisele guy* were runaway successes (perhaps male magazine readers were not quite so smart and sassy?).

After all that, Meredith had been lured to New York to head up a new network of websites. It was the mid-2000s and everyone was excited about this crazy new thing called 'The Internet'. Anyone who was anyone had a MySpace page. But the idea of getting information online? Getting your *news* online? Still preposterous. Nobody could have imagined, at the time, the octopus-like reach of the Lurker network. Soon Lurker, a NY gossip site, spawned more sites: TechBible (geeks), HunterGatherer (food geeks) and Capitol (political geeks). And Meredith had been there from the beginning, convincing people that the internet was here to stay, and that there was no need to be afraid.

Two years ago, she'd arrived home to publish *The Weekend*. I couldn't figure out Meredith's exact age – forty... -ish? – but whatever the number, one thing was clear: the woman was a dynamo. She could make hay even if the sun had set.

'And you have a baby, Lee was saying?'

I nodded. 'Uh-huh. Pip. Philippa.' I didn't know why I felt compelled to explain my child's name every bloody time I said it. 'She's five months old.'

Meredith nodded. 'And in terms of care for her...?'

'It's all been sorted,' I assured her. 'But if I need to leave or be flexible – will that be OK?'

Meredith shrugged. 'Of course. We all have lives outside of work. It's not a problem.'

'Great! What a relief.'

Meredith smiled. 'In saying that, we have a lot of work to do. I have big plans for this brand, George. *The Weekend* is doing very well. Very, very well. So what we need to do now is capitalise on that success. Seize the day. We'll go up a book size, definitely. Hire some new writers, maybe do a redesign. I'm talking podcast, TV show – I want you to have a presence in the main newspaper as well, to drive readership. Your own column.'

My own column?

These days, the only people who got regular columns in the newspaper were retired athletes and the wives of active athletes. It was practically unheard of for an actual writer to score her own column, unless she also had 100,000 followers on Instagram and a headshot in which she wore a tasteful bikini.

'Yes! That sounds incredible. I'd love that.'

'Excellent,' she said crisply. 'Now George, I know what went on at *Jolie*.'

I opened my mouth to speak, but Meredith went on before I could start.

'And I don't care. I've spent the past ten years working in digital, but I do think there's life in print – just not all print. A magazine like *Jolie*? It won't survive. But a magazine like *The Weekend*? Yes. By the time Saturday rolls around people are sick of looking at screens. There's still a place for the weekend paper; for lots of people, it's romantic, it's nostalgic. That's why I chose you; great print editors are a dying breed. You're a great print editor. I want you on my team.'

'Oh,' I said, brightening. 'Well, thank you.'

Meredith smiled curtly. 'Don't be too flattered. That's probably the last compliment you'll receive from me for some time.'

I smiled uncertainly. Then Meredith laughed – a little maniacally, but still, a laugh. I joined in.

'I'm only kidding,' she said, reaching over to pat my hand.

I nodded and kept laughing, quite sure she was not kidding. Still, I could handle Meredith. I wasn't young or naive enough anymore to think that my work had to serve some higher purpose; I just wanted to do a good job, produce a good magazine, and head home.

I was ready.

I knew exactly how each morning would start. I rehearsed it over and over in my mind during those endless breastfeeds that ate up entire afternoons. The ones that lasted from the end of lunch to the start of dinner.

I would get up around 6.30, early enough to get shit done but not so early that my eyes were in danger of falling out of their sockets. Sun streaming through the shutters, I would nurse Pip as I made a pot of coffee, then breastfeed her as I read the news on my phone, getting a head start on the day. Yes, all at the same time. This is how I would do things from now on: all at the same time. Ha! Younger, childless colleagues would have nothing on me. I used my time purposefully because I must. No faffing about looking at pictures of overhyped milkshakes on Instagram for me. Nope. I could feed a child with my very own body *and* stay on top of current affairs.

The important thing about being a working mother, I knew, was to behave as if you were not, in fact, a working mother. So yes, you could go to work and have a career and contribute to society, but you should never, ever forget that your number-one priority is your child, and that as well as leaning in and kicking arse and smashing glass ceilings, you also needed to ensure your child never ate sulphates (note to self: google sulphates) or was monolingual. Yes, you could go back to work, but if you did, you needed to really step it up at home so nobody thought you were a Bad Mother. I needed to get over feeling confused and underprepared for this motherhood caper. If I was going to go back to work, I needed to step it up like never before. So I needed to ensure that Pippa only ate locally sourced, organic food. I needed to make sure she was breastfed for... forever? That seemed to be the amount of time experts agreed on these days. I needed to make sure she got adequate tummy time and language play and outdoor activity. In order to be a Working Mum, I would need to devote all the time I wasn't at work entirely to Pip's wellbeing. No problem at all.

When Pip had her final suck, she'd peacefully drift away from me and go... somewhere (the lounge? to watch *Baby Einstein*? down to the shops for a loaf of bread?), and I'd be free to have my shower. Now that I was a working mother, the pressure would be on to look like I had *not* given birth in the last six months or been up several times in the night, even though both were true. I would have a long, hot shower during which I would shampoo and condition with the expensive stuff (leaving the conditioner in for the recommended three minutes, to allow full moisture lock), cleanse and exfoliate, shave legs and underarms and wash bits with pistachio-honey body balm. I would feel like dessert warmed up.

Exit shower feeling ready to start the day, not to mention gorgeous. Apply toner and moisturiser to face and let them sink in for recommended minute. Apply primer. Rub thick globs of moisturiser over scaly legs until they appear silky and luminous, like Pip's (youth: always wasted on the young). Twist wet hair into loose curls, dab ends with argan oil and spray with the proper curling spray stuff that I would definitely find before I had to go back to work. Undies and bra on (both clean!), silk dressing gown over the top.

Check on Pip. Still fine. Loves *Baby Einstein*. Clearly becoming a baby genius.

Dot foundation over face and blend with sponge. Do the contouring thingy with blush and bronzer and choose from a selection of eyeshadow shades. Settle on 'nude bronze', which sounds like something they keep at the British Museum but is also perfect for your eyes. Pencil in eyebrows (men are allowed to have their natural, wayward, homeless-cat eyebrows but women have to wax theirs off and *then* pencil them back in so they look normal) and flick mascara over lashes. One swipe of lipstick and a few minutes of a cool blow dryer and I'm done.

Almost.

Pick up Pip and tear her away from her beloved *Baby Einstein* DVD. She lets out a small cry but somehow, in this new fantasy, I can assuage her tears with nothing more than a soothing 'shh' and a series of gentle pats to the head. Cuddling her close, I feel her crying slow down and then stop. Looking up at me, she smiles. Good girl.

Take off her pastel pink pyjamas and nappy and put her in her daycare outfit – cheap (for obvious reasons), brightly coloured (so I can spot her in the photos they email out each day), ready to be spat on, torn and covered in spilled milk and stewed vegetables (see above). She will giggle as I smooth cream over her nappy rash and coo to her, remembering the importance of speaking to your child NO MATTER HOW YOUNG THEY ARE. How else will Pip become a High Court judge or even a judge on *MasterChef*?

Nina will call out to me from downstairs, 'Want some breakfast? I'm putting toast on.' Downstairs we'll go, Pip and I, to a plate of hot buttered toast and another coffee. When I'm finished, I'll hand the baby to Nina and head upstairs to don the outfit that I ironed the previous night and have laid out in readiness, shoes and all.

Then it's out the door.

I'll strap Pip into her Bugaboo and she'll happily flick through the *Paddington* board book I've hinged to the side. How I loved *Paddington* as a little girl! How thrilled I am that Pip inherited that same love! We truly belong to each other. Evolution is at work, right before my eyes. Amazing. I am so fulfilled.

We'll walk to the train station and find our platform. Strangers will make way for us and even offer to help us down the stairs. *Thank you, thank you, that would be lovely.* The train pulls up and on we get. I sit and whip my phone out once more, eager to see what has been tweeted in the fifty-six minutes since I last checked. Pip is still ensconced in *Paddington*, page three of four.

Town Hall is here before we know it and off we get, walking briskly through the crowds to the brand-new, progressive-learning-style daycare I managed to get Pip into. An eager young teacher will take Pip from me and engage her in some French language play as I make her cot for the day (these people can teach infants French but cannot be expected to pull a fitted sheet over a cot mattress?) and finally, give her a firm squeeze and a pash on the cheek before I dash out the door, leaving a smiling Pip gurgling as the daycare teacher sings, '*Je peux chanter un arc-en-ciel*'.

A quick pit stop at the cafe downstairs for another coffee (because even in my fantasy life, I am tired) and I'm almost there. I'll swipe my card over the security gate, send a beaming smile to the doorman and bingo, I'm in.

A productive eight hours will whiz right by and then it's time to head home, where I will make dinner, bathe Pip and put her to bed, and then settle down in front of the TV, totally satisfied with how the day went.

Except that's not exactly how it goes.

The first day back was fine. Everything (basically) went according to my extreme fantasy plan. OK, so Pip threw up on my first outfit and I had to change into my back-up dress, but hey, I *had* a back-up dress. I was ready. And yes, she cried on the train instead of becoming engrossed in the adventures of a charming, marmalade-obsessed bear, but that's OK, right? Babies cry. It's sort of their thing.

It was the day after that when it got hard. And the day after that, it got even harder. And so on. It was a grotesque bell curve – the days went on and things got exponentially worse. Every day I would think, 'Once I get X done, things will be fine,' but even if X got done, there'd still be Y. And Z. And if we're being really honest, I usually never got around to doing X in the first place, so...

When we woke, it wasn't for a restful twenty minutes of catching up on the overnight news and a quick boob session. It was more like armed battle, where my arms were intent on holding my phone and scrolling through headlines and Pip's were determined to push mine away at any cost. She was focused, and she wanted me to be, too. For the first few days, I attempted a sort of breastfeeding yoga thing and twisted my body so Pip couldn't see the offending phone and I could read in peace. Well, if you call peace lying with one leg at half-mast, a baby attached to your left nipple and your right arm stretched comically away from said baby so you can read '10 Reasons Lucy Turnbull is Ready for a Makeover' (after which I would definitely get cracking on the *New York Times* profile of Edward Snowden). But no matter what position I pretzelled myself into, Pip found me out. She was like the world's tiniest, most adorable MI5 agent. So in the end I sat there, staring at the blank wall in front of me, trying to remember the coming day's to-do list and reminding myself to please put some photos up soon so I could at least stare at my baby girl and try to feel something other than sheer boredom as I feed her.

Post-feed, it would be time for my coffee. None of this 'feed yourself before you feed the baby' nonsense. Pip would never allow such a thing. The second she rose, she was ready for food, ravenous for it. So I waited until she had finished with my boobs and then I headed to the kitchen. Once I got there,

I played an exhausting game of 'Pick Up Put Down', which involved me putting Pippa down for a matter of microseconds as I deftly filled the kettle with water and switched it on, and then picking her up again because, during that time, she'd become so distressed that I had dared put her down that she'd started to cry with the insistence of a sorority girl fresh outta lip gloss. Then, when I needed my hands again, it was time for Put Down. Pick Up. Put Down. You get the drift.

Getting myself ready – having a shower, applying makeup, putting on clothes – was another game entirely. It was called Fast Fast Fast. The first morning, I had followed the fantasy plan and plopped Pippa in front of a Wiggles DVD (turns out we don't even own any *Baby Einstein*) and plopped myself into the shower. Ten minutes later, I could hardly believe my luck – it had worked! I'd shaved, I'd washed, I'd shampooed and conditioned! Hurrah! Then I turned off the water and realised it had been masking Pippa's devastated cries the whole time.

So I took her into the shower with me – like, all in. It took more time this way, yes, and it wasn't convenient for me, but it was easier than listening to Pip crying for ten minutes. Essentially, this was parenthood: figuring out a way to get through the day that will least upset your child.

After I did a thirty-second wash/condition-the-ends-only/ cleanse-face routine, I dried us both and slapped on some moisturiser, and, if I remembered, a dab of eye cream for which I'd paid about the same amount as a week of daycare, in some distant past I wasn't even sure existed now.

Then the real fun began.

Nina made me toast, like in the fantasy plan, but instead of eating it hot, as wisps of steam rose from it and the butter formed tiny scattered pools of yellow, I ate it cold, the fat of the butter having congealed in a greasy mess on the plate. By the time I got Pip and myself downstairs, Nina could have made and served a three-course breakfast. But I wouldn't know, because she was gone before I even saw her most days.

Clothes on (mine clean, Pip's only very, very lightly stained) and hair still wet (both), I strapped Pip into the pram as I sang 'The Wheels on the Bus' to calm her down.

How entirely inconvenient it is to have a child who hates their pram. At seven kilos already, Pip needs to love the pram. For the love of sciatica, Pip needs to love the pram.

But she doesn't, so I mime an elaborate version of 'Wheels' every morning in a valiant attempt to soothe her, desperately hoping that one day she'll magically become so entranced by my off-key rendition that she'll forget all about the straps tightening over her chest and legs, start giggling and then, God willing, fall asleep.

Because Pip doesn't like trains, either. Every time the doors close and open, she cries. Every time there's an announcement over the loudspeaker, she cries. Every time a person sits down next to me, she cries. So I get her out of the pram, sit her on my lap and cuddle her into calmness. And then I remember, *oh Lord give me strength, now I have to strap her back in*.

We make it to daycare. It's not the shiny bilingual baby's paradise from my dreams. Apparently you have to put your baby's name down at *that* one the minute you get your first period. The one daycare in our area that did have a free spot was housed in a somewhat rundown workers' cottage that I truly hoped was not overly diseased with asbestos. Faded paintings of gardens and sunshine marked the walls, and while every intention was unquestionably good, it was sorely in need of some sort of renovation rescue reality show situation. The teacher, whose name I could never quite remember (Janine? Jane? Jean? Jen?), comes towards us, arms outstretched. She is lovely, Jen (?), she really is. But Pip can't stand her. She burrows her head into my shoulder when Jen approaches, and makes a whimpering sound. I then begin a round of 'Let's Have a Look,' where I take Pip around the room to show her all the toys and books. 'Ooh look, Pip, a dinosaur! Roar!' I say, holding a soft pink toy up and shaking it in my daughter's face. 'Oh, look, they have Dr Seuss! Oh Pip, you'll love that!

So fun!' I say, wondering if any other parent expects their six-month-old child to understand a single thing that they are saying. I have to believe it, because how else will I be able to go to work unless I think Pip has understood me when I say, 'I love you and I will be back very soon'?

My hair still wet, my shoulder now covered in a slimy epaulette of Pip's saliva, I make a break for it. On the way out, another mother catches me.

'Hello, Georgia!' she says, holding little Harry (Henry?) on her hip and carrying his water bottle. Shit. I forgot Pip's water bottle. Again. Now my child will have to use the 'spare' bottle, and risk cryptosporidium/Ebola.

'Hi... mate,' I said, blanking on the woman's name. 'Call me George. How are you?' I sing-song as I attempt to sidle past her towards the gate. She steps in front of me.

'Great! Just wondering, are you around for a playdate on the weekend? I thought it might be nice for the kids to get to know each other outside the daycare environment.'

NOPE. Bad Mum.

'Oh... this weekend?' I ask, feigning disappointment, as if there might be another, more convenient weekend for us to get together. 'Gosh, we're not, actually.' OK, the 'gosh' might have been too much. 'Off to, uh... Palm Beach.' We are not, and never will be, off to Palm Beach, but Henry's (?) mother does not need to know that. All she needs to know is that I suddenly have a convenient, weekend-long excuse not to spend time with her.

'How lovely!' she smiles. She looks at Harrison (pretty sure it's Harrison) and tickles him under the chin. 'Do you want to go to the beach like lucky Pippa? Do you? Pippa's mum is a clever clogs, isn't she?'

I wince and smile at the same time, like I am sucking a lemon or watching an acoustic performance of 'Everybody Hurts' at an open mic night. The only beach Pip will be visiting this weekend is Laguna, when we watch *The Real Housewives of Orange County* as I nurse her.

'Maybe some other time,' I say, attempting to move again. I am now ten minutes late for work. I start working on excuses in my head.

'I'll give you my number! Then we can work out a better day.' She is smiling so much I am afraid her mouth will just burst right open, spilling teeth and tongue everywhere.

'OK, sure... mine is 04 —'

'Wait! I've got a better idea. I'll friend you on Facebook. And then I can add you to the group.'

'The group?'

'It's a group just for the daycare parents. So we can organise meetings and discuss what's going on here. I mean, it all seems fine so far, but there is a new staff member coming on board in a few weeks, so...'

'There is?'

'Yes, didn't you get the newsletter?'

I shake my head. 'Look, I'm really running quite late, I do have to run. But thanks, er...'

'Jen,' she says. 'I'll friend you. Then you won't forget!'

I run for the gate, laughing in that big, loud, pretend way I do when something is not actually funny but I need to save face. I sprint for the office. Sweat patches start to form under my arms.

If Jen is Harrison's mum, who the hell is Pip's teacher?

When I finally make it to the office, the line for coffee is twenty deep. I check my phone. 9.20. Fuck. I swipe my card and run for the elevator. By the time I have made it to my desk (9.23), I am what the kids would call a 'hot mess', only I am literally hot, not metaphorically. Sweating profusely, I switch on my computer and breathe.

Time to start the day.

*

At midday, my boobs began to throb, my own milky alarm clock going off just as it would at home. Only this time, there was no baby to feed.

67

I dug out my breast pump then realised I had no idea where I could use it. The kitchen seemed too clean. The bathroom seemed too dirty. I considered shutting the door to my office, but the giant glass windows could prove problematic. Then I remembered: Lee told me there was a breastfeeding room.

So I knocked on Meredith's door.

'Hello, George! How's it all going?' Meredith looked up from her knife and fork, poised over a plate at her desk.

Meredith had launched *The Weekend* just over a year ago, to great acclaim. The industry loved it, advertisers were buying and readers had given great feedback. It was, by all accounts, a huge success, which was quite something in these days of declining circulation and incessant talk of 'the end of print'. It was heartening to know that people still wanted to read something that wasn't condensed to 140 characters.

'Oh, I'm so sorry, I interrupted your lunch. I'll come back.' I could feel my boobs hardening like a concrete sidewalk. Someone had better stick a handprint in me, quick.

'No, no! I'm just eating, not stopping. Come in.'

Meredith continued eating the... thing on her plate. It was a flat brown disc, dry and lonely.

'OK, if that's alright.'

She nodded as she finished the disc. 'Right, that's over.'

'What was that?'

'What?' Meredith looked up at me.

'Um, what were you eating?'

'Veggie patty. I'm on a diet.'

Meredith was one of the thinnest women I had ever seen, and I used to edit a women's fashion magazine.

'You're on a diet?'

She nodded.

'But... Why are you on a diet?'

She stared at me as if she hadn't understood the question. 'What do you mean?'

It was my turn to stare. 'I mean... why are you on a diet? You seem very... healthy to me.'

'I seem healthy?' She repeated the word 'healthy' as if I had actually said 'gastric bypass candidate'.

'Thin. You seem thin,' I corrected myself.

'Oh,' she said, relaxing into a smile. 'Thank you.'

'You don't look like you need to be on a diet, that's what I mean,' I said, and she brightened.

'Thank you. But that's why I'm on a diet. I don't ever want anyone to think I *should* go on a diet.'

'So you're just always on a diet?'

'Uh-huh.' Meredith nodded and smiled. 'So how's it all going out there? Everyone being nice to you? Not scaring you away in your first week?'

So far it was a pretty standard mix of media types. The food writer, Neil, with the teensiest paunch and the most gargantuan ego. The young writer, Anna, who, by virtue of having wealthy parents, had managed to intern for years before she finally got a paying job. It was the unspoken *Hunger Games* of publishing: whose parents' finances were robust enough to sponsor their fashion-obsessed offspring through the dry years of an internship? There were the hard-working subs who never seemed to leave their desks. The fashion team who flitted in and out between appointments and had, within my first three hours on the job, asked me if they could get another $5000 for the photographer they really, really wanted for an upcoming shoot. (Short answer: no.) The older, more harried writers who had barely looked up from their phone interviews as Meredith paraded around me the office.

'Yeah, everyone seems great. It looks like a very well-oiled machine.'

It was true. The flat plan was done weeks in advance, there were plenty of ad bookings, covers had been secured.

'Well, I keep an eye on everything. I like to know what's going on with everyone in the team.'

I nodded enthusiastically.

'Have you had a chance to think about the podcast?'

I squinted. Was I meant to have thought about the podcast?

I'd been here a week and Meredith hadn't mentioned it since our first meeting, before I'd started. Shit.

'Um... not in any specific sense, no.'

Meredith frowned. 'Well, that's your first priority.' *It was? Since when?* 'Have a think about what it should be about, what we might call it, who'll be on it – topline stuff.'

'Uh, OK. I was sort of thinking that I should spend the first month or so just getting the lay of the land.'

Meredith blinked. 'I'm sure you'll figure it all out quite quickly. The podcast is of particular importance, so please do prioritise it. We'll have a meeting on Monday to discuss your ideas.'

'This Monday?'

Meredith nodded.

'And change these cover lines,' she said, pushing a mock-up of next week's cover towards me.

'They're weak,' she went on. '"15 essential pieces" – it doesn't tell me anything. Pieces of what?'

'Right,' I said, a little confused. I mean, obviously when you put the word 'essential' next to the word 'pieces' it meant clothing. That was basic magazine speak. Like tresses meant hair and pins meant legs. You'd never say those things in real life, but you could get away with it in mags.

'Oh, OK. Sure. No problem.'

'George?' Meredith asked, cocking her head ever so slightly.

'Yes?' I smiled, hoping my expression was enthusiastic rather than exhausted, which is how I already felt.

'You need to hit the ground running, OK? I don't have time for people who don't want to put in the work. *The Weekend* is very, very important to me and my career. And it could define yours. I have big plans for you, and I want to see you succeed. Do you want to succeed?'

I nodded.

'Good,' she said, smiling tightly. 'I'm very glad to hear it. I think you and I will get along very well.'

'Yeah, I think so too. I'm so excited to be here. This is my dream job, it really is. I'm ready to work hard. But, uh, I need to ask you something first – where can I pump?'

'What?' Meredith's smile faded.

'I need to express. I'm still breastfeeding,' I explained.

'A child?'

No, a dog.

I stared at her. 'Yes. My baby. P—' Before I could say Pip's name, Meredith cut me off.

'I don't know,' she said, flatly, her eyes flicking back to her computer.

'You don't know where I can express?'

'No.'

'OK. Is there a common room? A breastfeeding room? Lee said there was...'

She didn't take her eyes off the screen. A second ago, we'd been a team, working towards global domination – or at least, a podcast. Now she didn't want anything to do with me.

Meredith shrugged. 'I'm really not sure. Nobody has ever asked that before.' Meredith stared at her computer, tapping at her keyboard as if I wasn't there.

'Really?'

She turned to me, apparently surprised that I was still there. 'Really what?'

'Really... nobody has ever asked about breastfeeding?'

She flashed a tight smile. 'No. Why don't you go ask Bea?' she said, gesturing to her assistant, whose desk sat outside her office.

'Ah, OK. Sure.'

Another forced smile and Meredith turned back to her computer.

What just happened?

Chapter 4

'I can't believe you're dating, Nina – this is so exciting!' said Ellie.

I raised a sceptical eyebrow at her.

'I know!' Nina said, her eyes switching on like the Griswolds' Christmas lights. 'Jed is amazing. I can't wait for you to meet him, El. You're really going to like him.'

I stared at Ellie in shock. There was no universe in which my most sensible friend would 'really like' Jed, the schoolboy bartender boning our recently separated, borderline depressed friend.

Nina and Jed had been dating for about a month, and in the brief snatches of time I got to talk to my friend, it was all Jed, all the time. I'd heard all about the Kickstarter Jed was running to fund his 'research trip' to Canada (what this research entailed, Jed could not yet say) and the varying shades of his hair at dusk. I'd heard about the 'amazing' bar he worked at, how it was 'so different' because the bartenders refused to serve beer, wine or cocktails. 'What can you drink, then?' I'd asked. 'Whisky,' said Nina, who then rhapsodised about whisky for a good fifteen minutes. She didn't even like whisky! *Nobody* liked whisky until two years ago!

But Ellie just smiled right back, her eyes also alight with

the thrill of it all. These women had been married for way too long, I thought, if this was what got their rocks off.

'I can't wait to meet him!' she said, and the two of them started giggling like 15-year-olds. Nina was all lilting vowels and upspeak now. Soon she would start shopping at Sportsgirl. Then, she'd get a cutesy cover for her phone. It would have a doughnut or a pineapple on it. Or some stupid saying like, 'Dance like nobody's watching'. My head hurt just thinking about it.

Nina's promise to help me with Pip was all but forgotten (by everyone except me, that is). She'd told me she would pick Pip up every day, but so far I'd had to step in at least three times a week. I hadn't brought it up, but I was rounding the corner of Frustrated and on my way to Pissed. I really needed Neen, and she seemed totally oblivious.

I focused on helping Lucas finish his toast, zooming it into his gob like an aeroplane, as Nina and Ellie twittered about Jed. Lucas giggled, his mouth full, and crumbs sprayed onto the table. Since staying at Ellie's house last year, Lucas and I had become firm buddies. I really liked spending time with him. It was easy. At four, he was genuinely funny and laughed easily. Nothing made Lucas happier than a fart joke. I could work with that.

By the time I tuned back in to Nina and Ellie's conversation, they'd moved on to Nina's second-favourite topic, The Reinvention of Nina Doherty.

'So where do you think you'll go?' Ellie was asking, hailing the waiter for another cup of coffee. I glanced down at Pip. Could I have another one? Better not chance it. She hadn't been taking the bottle at daycare, so I had to feed her more often when I was around. As soon as she woke up, she'd be ready for a boob. Decaf, please.

'Not sure. I mean, I'd love to go to the Middle East. I've always found it so fascinating.'

'What?' I squinted at Neen. 'You're going to the Middle East? Are we talking Dubai or Beirut?'

Nina shrugged. 'I really just want to go somewhere different, you know? I've never really travelled. All my holidays with Matt were to islands where all we did was drink cocktails by the pool. We could have been anywhere.'

Ellie beamed and nodded. 'That sounds amazing.'

'I'll probably take next year off work, maybe do a bit of travelling then. Jed's heading to Canada for a while, maybe I'll start there with him.'

I stared at Nina. She was talking about all this like it was no big deal.

'You're taking a year off work?'

Nina nodded and continued to munch on her granola. 'Yeah.'

'Seriously?' Nina had mentioned a change in career, but I hadn't imagined she'd actually follow through with it. 'Why?'

'Lots of reasons. I don't love it anymore. Maybe I never did.'

While Ellie nodded in sympathy and agreement, I pressed on. This was ridiculous. Nina loved being a teacher. She was throwing everything away. She was only thirty-five, she wasn't old enough for a mid-life crisis.

'So you'll just *travel* for a year?'

She nodded, smiling. She looked excited. 'Yeah. Jed has a YHA membership, so I'll probably hang out with him for a while. Save some money.'

'YHA? As in... youth hostels?'

She nodded again.

Even Ellie was disturbed now. 'Nina. You can't stay in a hostel. You'll be mugged. You'll end up on *Foreign Correspondent*.'

'Or *Today Tonight*,' I added, finishing the last of Lucas's toast.

'Guys, enough. Nothing has been decided yet. And if and when I stay in a hostel, I'll be absolutely fine. OK?'

Nina crossed her arms and sat back.

I said nothing, and Ellie, god bless her, had the good sense to change the subject.

'And what about you, George? How's work?'

I took a deep breath and thought about the first two weeks. It had been like running a marathon every single day, with no training, over and over. Every time I felt like I had a handle on things, or could stop or slow down, some obstacle would appear out of nowhere and I'd be running again, just trying to keep up. I had done everything and I'd done nothing.

But the work itself wasn't the problem. I liked the work, the pace of it, the team. I was excited to have a challenge ahead of me. I'd thought up some cool podcast ideas and Meredith seemed to like them. (After the weird breastfeeding episode, Meredith had returned to her normal, if slightly neurotic, self. I made a note to keep talk of Pip to a minimum around her.) It was getting all the other stuff – my life, essentially – figured out that was the hard bit. It didn't help that Nina wasn't pitching in the way she'd assured me she would.

I started to answer when Ellie noticed that Lucas had run away.

'Lucas! Lucas! Get back here. Lucas! Get. Down. Now. I'm counting to three. Are you ready? One...' Lucas had hoisted himself up on his chair, then climbed onto the fence behind us. By the time Ellie had counted to two, he was three tables down. The kid was quick. Like, celebrity-in-drug-scandal-needs-to-flee-the-country quick.

'I'll get him,' said Neen.

When she was gone, I whispered to Ellie, 'What are you doing? Don't encourage this!'

'Huh?'

Pippa started to mewl in her pram and Ellie and I both instinctively reached out to rock it.

'Don't encourage this ridiculous thing with Jed. Or being a bloody pastry chef. Or going to sodding Beirut, for that matter. This is not right. I thought Nina would sleep with this Jed guy once and that would be it! It's gone on too long now.'

Ellie shook her head. 'Don't be crazy. She needs a rebound.

If we don't encourage it, if we tell her how stupid it is, she'll just run off with him and we'll never see her again.'

'She's not sixteen, El. She's not going to run away with her boyfriend.'

'Just give her space. And time. She's getting divorced. She needs to be reckless and crazy for a while.'

Nina had never been reckless or crazy. She was inherently sensible. It was in her DNA; it was what made her Nina. *I* was the reckless one, the one who'd made Nina and Matt sit through countless dinners with dickhead boyfriends who would drink all their expensive wine and then bring out pingers at the end of the meal in the same way other people brought out Michel's Patisserie mud cake for dessert. The craziest thing she'd done before this was the life-drawing class we organised for her hen's party in the mid-2000s.

So I sat back and ate the rest of my omelette. Fine. I would let her be reckless and crazy. Surely it wouldn't last long. This was Nina: responsible, clever, got-her-shit-together Nina. She was thirty-five, for Christ's sake. I could just imagine all the venereal diseases Jed might pass on to her. I knew this much: I was too old to comb crabs out of my best friend's pubes.

Then there was the question of Nina's crazy career 180. Pastry chef? That was a joke, surely... but there was some level of earnestness to Nina's sudden search for meaning. I needed to put a stop to her soul search before it got out of hand. Before she started reading *The Prophet* or planning to visit a yoga retreat in Bali. Before she started posting motivational quotes to Instagram. Before she went on a 'wellness journey'.

'Here he is, the runaway fugitive!' said Neen, returning triumphant with Lucas tucked under one arm in the football hold. He tried to squirm away, but you could tell he loved it. He loved Nina. She was fantastic with kids, always meeting them at their level, never expecting too much of them. She was a natural. Which was exactly why she had chosen to be a school teacher. And exactly why she loved it. And why she should not, under any circumstances, move to Beirut to become a pastry chef.

'Thanks, Neen,' said Ellie. 'Lucas, sit down and finish your babycino,' she continued, her voice hardening. 'Honestly.' She tsktsked and then lowered her voice to speak to Nina and I. 'He's been... difficult lately.'

Mmm. He didn't look difficult. Lucas sat down obediently and began playing with the wooden toy train Ellie had packed for him.

But then, out of nowhere, Lucas started to cry. Big, fat toddler tears made their way down his cheeks.

'What's wrong?' Nina asked, lowering herself to Lucas's eye level. He couldn't speak, he was sobbing so hard.

'My... my...'

Before Ellie could move to Lucas's side of the table and figure out what was wrong, an older woman appeared, turning her attention to Nina.

'Your son dropped this,' she said, handing Nina the front of the train.

Lucas stared at it, as if he couldn't quite believe that this toy, which he'd lost all but sixty seconds ago, could possibly have been found. Then he snatched it back, embarrassing Ellie by ignoring her pleas that he say thank you.

Nina said nothing, but I could tell she was rattled by the woman assuming she was Lucas's mum. It was hard enough for her to hang out with a couple of breeders like Ellie and I, without having her lack of motherhood rubbed in her face.

'So how about a man for you, George?' Ellie asked, her voice shrill with the urgent need to change the subject.

'Huh? Me? I don't think so.' As if on cue, to remind me of my perennial undateability, Pip started to cry. I picked her up with a little trepidation. This past week, she had clung to me before I'd left her at daycare, but when I'd returned, she didn't want me near her. Which was difficult, seeing as I was literally feeding her with my own body.

Nina clapped her hands. 'Yes! That is such a good idea.

You need to get back out there.' She nodded sagely, as if seven months back on the market had made her an expert.

I shook my head, flipping my boob out of my bra and trying to get Pip to latch. 'No, thanks.' Pip squirmed and scrunched up her tiny face. Sometimes I swear she was looking at my boob as if to say, 'Really? Milk again? Is that all you have?'

'What happened to that Colin guy?' Ellie asked.

I held the back of Pip's head and manoeuvred her into position. Finally, she found my nipple – as if I had been hiding it from her – and let out a sigh of relief as she started to feed. I sighed too. Breastfeeding had started to become painful, since Pip wouldn't feed as often. I pumped twice a day at work, reading emails and taking calls over the wheezing push-pull of the manual pump, telling anyone who asked that there was construction going on outside. What I really needed was an electric pump, but every time I thought of buying one online, I'd be interrupted by some work crisis that needed sorting immediately, and then I'd forget. By 4 pm, my boobs were hard and full and bloody painful. I had to wear two sets of nursing pads as insurance against leaks. I was over it, but I knew I wouldn't give up feeding. Good mums breastfeed their babies. They don't give up because it hurts.

'Colin?' I shrugged. 'It just fizzled out.' I had met Colin when I was pregnant with Pip and, despite my gestative state, we had made plans for a date. Owing to a commitment I couldn't really get out of (labour), I had to cancel. We'd texted a few times after I had Pip, but one day he just stopped replying. That was that.

'Right. Time to find a new one!' Nina said, grinning.

I shook my head again. 'Seriously, guys, I really don't need a boyfriend.'

Men were the furthest thing from my mind. How would I ever find time to date someone? I didn't have time to masturbate, let alone have actual sex with another person.

'It's not a boyfriend,' Nina said. 'It's a date. And you need a date. It'll be fun, come on!'

I grimaced.

'No. I don't think so.'

Nina tut-tutted. 'Anyone at work you want to date?'

'Like I said, I don't want to date anyone. And the only guy at work is Neil.'

'Ooh!' they both sang simultaneously. 'Neil!'

'No.'

'Who's Neil?' Ellie demanded.

I rolled my eyes. 'The food writer.'

'Ooh!' Nina said again. 'What a cool job.'

Ugh. It was not a cool job. Or at least, it might have been, but Neil was not a cool person. Neil the Fucking Food Writer, as I had taken to calling him (so far, only to myself) was cute, in a scruffy facial hair sort of way, but pretentious in the extreme. He scoffed at my pronunciation of pho, forbade anyone from touching the Aeropress coffee maker on his desk and told me he was going to write a five-part series on offal, which I put a swift stop to.

'No. Not Neil.'

Nina wasn't discouraged. 'Come on, George. Think about it. When was the last time you did something fun? Something just for you?'

I thought about it. For too long. I couldn't remember.

Nina and Ellie both shot me knowing smirks.

Maybe it would be kind of fun to go on a date. I could go to a restaurant. Drink a glass of wine. Maybe two.

'Who's going to look after Pip?'

Nina put her hand up. 'OK, so obviously I will, but let's find the date first. We'll cross that bridge later.'

Ellie leaned over and grabbed my phone from my bag.

'Hey!' I said. 'What are you doing?'

'Who's Meredith?'

'Can I have my phone back please? What are you doing?'

'Getting you a date. Who's Meredith? You've got seven missed calls from her.'

'What?' My phone had been on silent. Actually, my phone had been on silent since the day I brought Pip home from hospital.

I reached over and Ellie handed it back, with some reluctance.

Urgent. Call me pls.

It was 11.30 on a Saturday. What could be so urgent? A copy of *The Weekend* lay on the table next to us. I grabbed it and took a quick look before I dialled Meredith's number. It looked fine to me.

'Hello?'

'Meredith?'

'George?'

'Yeah, hi. What's up? Is everything alright?'

My mind raced over the possibilities. A defamation suit? Disgruntled advertiser? Staff resignation?

Meredith sighed. 'Not really. I think we should fire Celeste.'

Celeste was *The Weekend*'s beauty editor. She was quiet and got her work done: everything I wanted in an employee.

'Oh my god. Why?'

'Mmm... she's just not really working out.' I heard the low hum of muzak in the background. She was shopping. Alone, probably. I couldn't conceive of a time when I'd be able to do that in the next, say, eighteen years.

'Why? I think she's great.' I also thought it was supremely odd to call someone seven times on a Saturday to talk about firing an employee for no specific reason. Couldn't this wait until Monday?

'Well, the thing is, I had a friend of mine come in and do some aura readings the other week, and... Celeste's aura is showing a lot of green.'

Ellie and Nina stared at me. I waved them off. What on earth was Meredith talking about?

'Uh. OK. Look, I think Celeste is really good. And don't

you have to give people warnings before you fire them? Has Celeste done anything wrong? I mean... apart from her... aura?'

Nina started to laugh. I put my finger to my mouth to silence her, but she kept going.

'Well, not technically, no. But a green aura... it's not good. Celeste has a tendency to be jealous. She lacks personal responsibility. Very insecure.'

'Oh. Well... do you really believe in all that?'

'Yes! Of course I do. You can't get by in business without having a developed sense of spirituality, George. Everyone knows that. That's what Martha says, anyway.'

'Martha?'

'Martha *Stewart*. She's a friend.'

'Oh. Of course. But Meredith... do you think Celeste really is irresponsible? Has she done anything to make you think that? Or is it... the aura?'

Meredith huffed. I heard the click of clothes hangers being pushed along a rack. 'The point is, Celeste is not working out.'

I cleared my throat. 'Right. OK. Look, Meredith, I'm sure we can work this out. Can we talk on Monday?'

'Is now not a good time?'

I paused, trying to decide how to respond.

'Uh... well, no, not really. I'm with my... friends.' And my baby, I thought. My baby, who I have hardly seen all week.

Meredith didn't say anything.

'So, um, enjoy your weekend, and I'll talk to you on Monday.'

'Email me with some ideas for a new beauty editor, OK? Once you're done with your... friends.'

'Uh... as in, today?'

'Yes! We'll need to get started on hiring right away. Thank you, George,' she said, in the clipped tone she used to signal that a conversation was over. She hung up.

'Who the fuck was that?' Nina asked, as Ellie shot her a look. 'Sorry!' she said, glancing at Lucas. 'I mean, George, who was that?'

81

'Meredith. My new boss, remember?'

I had, of course, told Neen all about Meredith, but it seemed listening was optional for her these days.

'Why is she calling you on a Saturday?'

'I have no idea. It's weird, right?'

Nina and Ellie nodded.

'Right, can we get back to finding you a date, please?' Nina asked, brightening again. She snatched my phone and the two of them got to work while I simultaneously breastfed Pip and played 'Round and Round the Garden' with Lucas.

Nina looked over Ellie's shoulder and giggled, nodding. I tried to see what they were doing but I was tethered to Pip and could only lean so far.

'Guys. What are you doing?' Nina looked up and giggled. 'Here you go.'

Ellie handed my phone back, fresh with a new Tinder profile.

'Are you kidding? How did you do that so quickly? I didn't even have the app.'

Nina rolled her eyes. 'It's easy. Now pick someone.'

I looked at my profile. They'd chosen a photo from four New Year's Eves ago, when I'd been skinny and had time to blow-dry my hair into submission and wore clothes that were actually purchased in the same year I was wearing them.

'Isn't this a bit... misleading?'

Nina and Ellie shook their heads in unison. 'No!' Ellie said. 'You still look great.' That's what friends are for – blatantly lying to you when you need it most.

I raised my eyebrows. 'Mmm. Yeah, I feel like–'

Nina cut me off. 'Can you just choose a guy please? Come on! Get to the fun part!'

I swiped to the first round of guys.

'How are you meant to find a date based only on their age and face?'

Nina looked at me like I'd asked her why the sun was hot. 'That's all you need. Just choose. Come on!'

Jordan, thirty. Blonde hair. Strumming a guitar. *No*.

Steve, twenty-four. Which of the two guys in the photo was Steve – the one administering the headlock, or the one receiving it? *No*.

Jonathan, forty. Hair greying at the temples. Wearing a wetsuit, standing beside a surfboard. *Too much pressure. No*.

Alfie, twenty-one. *No*.

Alex, thirty-eight. Wearing a business suit. Smiling. Looks relatively normal. *Bingo*.

'How about this guy?' I showed them my phone, feeling Pip drift off to sleep on my boob.

Nina scrunched up her face. 'He looks a bit–'

'He looks great!' said Ellie. She snatched my phone from me and swiped right.

'Hey!'

Ellie shrugged. 'You have to make a move. Don't worry, you're not marrying the guy.'

'Since when did you get so fast and loose with my love life?'

She smiled. 'Since I decided you could do with having one.' Suddenly she spied Lucas making off again, zooming his toy train along the garden bed and running after it. 'Lucas! Lucas, get back here! I'm counting to–' Ellie ran after him.

I sighed. The idea of having a love life again was completely weird. How would I tell a date I had a kid? What was the right moment? Before dinner? While we were paying the bill? Just before we got married? 'Oh, PS, I know someone who'd make a great flower girl!'

'So what do I do now?'

'Wait,' said Nina gravely, hands up like a stop sign. 'You wait for him to swipe right on you, and then don't say anything until he messages you, OK? Don't be too eager. Let him work for you.'

'OK, OK.'

'And in the meantime,' she said, 'you should find some more guys.' She wiggled her eyebrows at me.

'For what?'

'For dates. Keep your options open. Who knows what this Alex is like? He could be a serial killer.'

'Aren't you trying to encourage this?'

She threw her hands up. 'I'm joking,' she said with a wry smile. 'Get out there, George. Life is short. What's the worst that could happen?'

I gritted my teeth. 'Uh, he could be a serial killer.'

Nina smiled. 'Well, I'll really miss you if he is. And I promise to take care of Pip.'

'Oh, that's a relief, thank you so much.'

'Go on, George. I never thought I'd be single at thirty-five, but here I am. And you know what? It's not as bad as I thought it would be.'

'What, dating?' I looked down at Pip. I certainly never thought I'd be single at thirty-five... with a baby.

'Yeah, the whole thing. I thought I would have a breakdown last year, I really did. When you got pregnant and I didn't... I told Matt I thought I was going crazy. I would wake up in the middle of the night and lie awake for hours. It got to the point where I didn't trust myself to drive, because I just wasn't there, you know? I couldn't focus on anything.'

Holding Pip in the crook of one arm, I leaned over and grabbed Nina's hand. 'You never told me that.'

She smiled wryly. 'It's OK. I'm OK. Look, George, I know what you think about Jed and... everything else.'

I started to protest but Nina cut me off.

'It's OK. I get it. But I chased this thing for years. It was my whole life. And now... I have to work on accepting that it's not going to happen.' She bit her lip and stared in the distance, not quite looking at me. 'I'm not there yet but I'm really trying. I like Jed. I want to take a year off. I need to figure out who I am now.'

'Can't you figure out who you are in Sydney? Why do you have to quit your job and go travelling?'

Nina sighed. 'I don't know. I just do. I have to do something different, you know? I can't keep doing the things Married Nina would do. I'm not her anymore.'

I laughed a little, but Nina's expression was serious. 'I'm not, George,' she said, quietly. 'And you're not the old George, either. It's time for you to figure out what you want, too.'

I started to laugh at her earnestness again, before I cut myself off. What did Nina mean? Hadn't I already figured out what I wanted?

And if I hadn't, how the bloody hell was I supposed to?

Chapter 5

Not a morning person? No problem! Instead of hauling yourself out of bed at 5 am every day, why not do a Power Prep the night before? Laura, thirty-six, drives to her local cafe just before closing time to grab her favourite cold brew. 'I put it in the fridge,' says Laura, 'so it's there when I wake up in the morning. It saves so much time.' Yvette, twenty-nine, drafts important emails for clients just before she heads to bed. 'I have clients all over the world,' she says, 'so I need to stay on top of things. By drafting emails just before bed, all I need to do is quickly skim them and hit "send" in the morning. I'm not lying when I say this has revolutionised the way I work.'

I'd become obsessed with organisation. Before I had Pip, and certainly even before I went back to work, 'organised' meant 'I can probably find the iron if I need to'. It didn't mean buying my coldpressed coffee the night before so it was ready when I woke up at 6 am. It didn't mean drafting emails at 11 pm. And yet, I was seriously contemplating these things now. I had so much to do.

'Knock, knock,' came a voice at the door, accompanied by two sharp raps.

I looked up. Neil.

I forced a smile. Neil and I hadn't exactly got off to a flying start. I could tell he preferred Lee's style – he'd made several quips about her and I definitely got the sense that she was missed around the office. I was trying not to let it get to me – I had too much to do – but it stung nonetheless.

'Hi, Neil. What's up?'

'Just checking on the review this week. You want me to do McCool's?'

I screwed up my face and flicked through the stack of papers on my desk. 'Which one is that again?'

He rolled his eyes. 'Hot dogs, burgers, cheap American beer served, for some inexplicable reason, in school mugs they found at an estate auction.'

'Which school?'

He smirked. 'Shore.'

'The private boys' school?'

He nodded. 'That's the one.'

'So who goes to this McCool's place?' I asked.

'Who do you think? Private school boys, I'd say.'

'Former.'

He shrugged. 'Do they ever really leave?'

I couldn't help it; I smiled. 'Right. Well, what do you think, should we review it?'

He squinted at me and cocked his head. 'Um... well, normally you would tell me what to review.'

'Oh. Is that what Lee did?'

He nodded. 'Yeah, that's the way Meredith wants it. I think Meredith chooses the places; Lee just filters it through to me.'

'Oh.' I paused for a second. Why would I tell Neil which restaurant to review? He was the food editor – surely it was up to him. 'Look, I trust your judgement. Just find one that's right for our readers – sounds like McCool's isn't – and go there. And stick to the budget, OK? I saw that bill for Gigli. No more lobster.'

He smirked again.

'I mean it. Don't take the piss.'

Neil held up his hands in defeat. 'OK, OK. The lobster's their signature dish, so–'

I glanced up from my raft of papers. 'It's not, actually. I checked, when I got the $600 bill. The Moreton Bay bug ravioli is their specialty. Like I said, don't take the piss.'

He nodded slowly, the smirk dissolved.

I raised my eyebrows suggestively – suggesting he vacate my office. Neil took the hint.

- Don't check your emails in the morning! Set aside an hour a day to respond to emails, and don't look at your inbox outside of this time.
- Meditate as soon as you wake up: a clear mind is the best way to start the day.
- Don't just sit on the couch when you get home – TV drains your energy and productivity. Instead, schedule a walk with a friend or go to a yoga class.

I wondered if anyone else reacted to these time management tips with anything more than an overwhelming sense of defeat. I couldn't do any of these things. And yet I kept reading. I was particularly fixated on reading interviews with successful women who had kids. How did they do it? There must be some secret, something I didn't know about. I was determined to figure it out.

There were secrets, it turned out, but most of them involved nannies or husbands, neither of which I had. Several mentioned wine, which was more promising. But mostly the tips were exhausting. The women all got up early and went to bed late. They were organised to the point of military precision. They shopped online and had little alerts set up for when they needed more toilet paper or milk. They cut up vegetables and laid out school uniforms and even put bread in the toaster, ready for the next morning's breakfast, the night before. They had back-up plans for their back-up plans.

It was bamboozling just reading about these women, let alone trying to put their tips into practice. Why didn't any of the articles just say: *Do less. Pick a few things you don't like and stop doing them.* Imagine! Nope, don't like going for a run, not gonna do it. Nope, not into meditating, that's out.

The whole point of these articles seemed to be to reassure the reader that as long as you still did all the motherly things that were expected (read bedtime stories, cut veggies, mend school clothes), you were allowed to have a career as well. But you couldn't be a sub-par mum *and* have a job. After all, if you worked fulltime, you were already a sub-par mother.

I closed my browser and opened the window. Fresh air blew in and I felt the sun on my face. What was Pip doing right now? Was she outside in this loveliness? I hoped so. I closed my eyes and repeated the words I'd been telling myself for the past few days: it'll all be worth it.

*

'Where's my beautiful girl at?'
  Shit.
Jase's voice echoed through our tiny apartment, instantly waking his beautiful girl.

I gritted my teeth and vowed to at least try not to be too passive-aggressive about it. To his credit, Jase was helping out. Not much, but I had to remind myself that as much as parenting had been thrust on me, it had basically been dumped on Jase's head like an 80-tonne piano dropped from the top of Centrepoint.

'Shh!' I whispered redundantly as Pippa's cries filled the apartment.

How long had she slept? I checked my phone. Thirty-five minutes. Great.

'Sorry, did I wake her?' Jase asked, just as redundantly. I nodded, glaring at him. 'Sorry, George.' He had the good grace to look sheepish, at least. 'I brought coffee!' He held up two Campos cups and my eyes widened like saucers. 'And... doughnuts!' A paper bag appeared, stained greasily by the yeasty confections inside.

'My hero,' I deadpanned. 'Come inside, I'll go get her.'

In the dark of our bedroom, Pippa was, miraculously, still neatly wrapped in her adorable pastel yellow sleeping bag, munching on her fingers and staring up at me like, 'Where the fuck have you been?' I gave her a smile and she returned it.

There she was – my little lady. Sometimes, through the fog of sleeplessness and busyness, I forgot that I was meant to be enjoying all this. How many times had someone – my mum, usually – told me 'they're only little once'? At first I had mentally followed that up with, 'And thank god for that, because I couldn't handle her being this needy and helpless twice', but now I could see that the days really did fly by. These little moments when I could hold my head above water long enough to really see Pip smile at me were like nature's version of inspirational Instagram quotes.

I de-swaddled Pip and carried her downstairs. Jase had flung himself onto the lounge. Gosh, he must be *so* exhausted with all of his zero commitments.

'How come you're here so early? I didn't expect you until after lunch.'

'I had an early ride this morning. Figured I'd kill two birds.'

Jase and I had dated for a year. We broke up for the same old reasons everyone does – I had agreed to carry my best friend's baby without telling him. Typical. Then I found out I was – *whoops!* – pregnant. I don't think Jase ever really bargained on me keeping the baby – in a lot of ways, I hadn't either – but when I told him I was going through with it, to his credit he was totally fine with it. Until he decided we should get married and I had to talk him down off the ledge.

'Here you go,' he said, handing me a coffee. We had reached a decent place now, Jase and I. We could stand to be in the same room. We got along. And though I knew that Jase was, deep down, kind of lazy about everything except his precious bloody cycling, I wished he could see that I needed more help with Pip. He'd be dining out on this token effort for months. No matter that he had never – not once – woken in the middle of the night to feed Pip, or puréed mountains of fruit or wiped shit from a wall (often things I had done all in the one half-hour). He'd brought doughnuts and coffee? What a guy.

I took the coffee, snatched a doughnut and sat down, cradling Pip with one arm. I unclipped my maternity bra and let an eggplant-shaped, vaguely eggplant-coloured boob flop out. I'm not exaggerating, it flopped. One minute it wasn't there, the next second – flop! – it was. It was about as sexy as Margie and Tony Abbott's wedding night.

'I shouldn't be eating these,' he said, brushing away doughnut crumbs as he picked up a second. A smear of jam clung to his top lip. 'Gotta get down to eighty-five kay-gees for the ride next weekend,' he said. 'I'm at eighty-seven now, so I think I can do it, but it's going to be tough.'

I paused for a second to remember that Jase's life hadn't been entirely re-calibrated like mine had. He still had space and time and energy to devote to something outside Pip. I didn't. He had a part to play in Pip's life, of course, but the expectations were so vastly different. All Jase had to do was show up occasionally. I felt the gulf between us stretch further.

'Where's the ride?'

'Wollongong. Saskia's coming, actually. It's our, uh... our first weekend away together.'

'Oh yeah? That sounds nice.'

Saskia was Jase's girlfriend. He had wanted us to meet months ago, but so far I'd been able to dodge that particular event. I didn't know when would be a good time to meet the girlfriend of the father of my baby, but I imagined it should be sometime after my episiotomy stitches had dissolved.

'Yeah. She's really great, George.' I almost breathed a sigh of relief when he didn't follow it up with that old chestnut, 'I think you'd really like her.'

'That's good, Jase,' I said, trying to keep my voice light, matter-of-fact, normal. 'That's good to hear.'

'Thanks George, that's nice of you. I think she's going to be... part of my life.'

I nodded.

He went on. 'So, you know, at some stage–' I raised my eyebrows, daring him to continue. I knew what he was going to say. '...I guess I'd like to introduce her to Pippa. If that's OK with you,' he added hastily.

I cleared my throat. 'Sure. Someday. Not yet.'

God, I couldn't believe him. Pippa was barely on solids and Jase wanted her to have a stepmother.

He nodded quickly. 'Sure. Just, uh, let me know when you're ready. Anyway, how's our girl?'

I pushed my lips out and breathed loudly. 'Well... I'm not sure if I'm any closer to figuring out the instructions, but... she's fine. We're fine,' I lied.

Jase did not like hearing uncomfortable truths any more than I liked telling them. I wasn't fine, but I wasn't about to admit that. How could I complain about the rush rush rush of my life with a baby when Nina couldn't have one? How could I properly explain the madness of working and parenting without seeming ungrateful and selfish? I bottled up the broken sleep and the gravel rash nipples and the persistent ache in my lower back. I already felt bad enough for not loving motherhood the way I was supposed to, there was no way I was actually going to confess to it.

Life had become a blur of near-missed deadlines. I ran to the train station every night, leaving just enough time to sprint from the office to the platform. Meredith did not like people leaving 'early'. And Meredith's definition of 'early' was 'before 7 pm'. I fed Pip her dinner as I cradled a tumbler of wine, careful not to gulp it down too quickly. When I had finally finished the dinnerbath-bed routine I would tidy the house and pay bills and answer the seventeen text messages that Meredith would have sent, and then about twenty minutes after that I would realise I'd forgotten to have dinner, so I'd pull out a packet of chips and pour myself another glass of wine and fall asleep in front of *Real Housewives*. But nobody else needed to know that. I'd gotten pretty good at pretending that this mothering caper was no biggie. I knew exactly which boxes to tick on the Edinburgh test to make sure I didn't end up medicated or in therapy. I didn't have time for either.

Jase smiled and nodded, taking a stab at an understanding facial expression. What I would have really liked to hear was, 'Anything I can do to help?' But he didn't say that.

'That's great, George. I guess it helps that you have a lot of help.'

I couldn't help it. My mouth fell open like a hinge. 'What?'

'Well, you have me, Nina, your mum. Ellie. I mean, she's like, the world's best wife. It's harder for Claire, you know? Being a stay-at-home mum. She does everything herself.' Claire was Jase's sister-in-law, and yes, a stay-at-home mum. But she was also married to the father of her child, so I highly doubted she 'did everything herself'. Maybe everything between the hours of 9 am and 5 pm. Maybe.

I laughed. 'Mmm, but Ellie's not my wife,' I snapped, trying to make it sound like a joke. 'Ouch!' Pippa bit her gummy mouth down on my left nipple. I pulled my boob back and she looked up at me, as if to say, 'What the hell?'

'You OK?' Jase asked, and I swear he had one eye on his phone.

'Mmm. Fine. Anyway, what I mean is, Ellie's not my wife. Nobody is my wife. So I don't know if I'd say I have "a lot of help". I mean... I do everything around here.'

Jase looked at me, took a breath and presumably decided against saying anything more. *Good move*.

I felt Pippa detach and I folded my boob up and clipped my bra closed. I'd always had such a love–hate relationship with my boobs – they always felt unnecessarily big, never right for spaghetti straps or halter-neck tops or (god forbid) anything strapless (the main reason I'd never agreed to be a bridesmaid).

But now they were... flat. Empty. Still big, but without shape. Like a bean bag without the filling. Instead of rounding at the top and finishing in neat, bouncy spheres, they began – and continued – in planes that went straight down, towards my ankles. Of course, they were still massive, thanks to a rather large and constant influx of milk, but it was an uncomfortable size, not in any way sexy. And throughout the day they alternated between feeling rock-hard and jelly-soft, thanks to the ebb and flow of milk. It made me want to write an obituary for them, or at the very least, some sort of commemorative haiku.

Too big, too bouncy,
No more of that now. Gone forever
Lest we forget.

Or maybe:

Deflated balloons
You fed a child, thank you,
But what of bikinis?

'Do you want to have a hold?' I asked Jase, motioning towards Pippa. He nodded eagerly.

'Yes, please! Come here, baby girl.' Jase sat down next to me on the orange sofa he'd despised when we lived together and delicately took Pippa from me, still careful not to let her head drop back, even though she'd been holding it up by herself for months now. I took for granted all the little details I knew about Pip. I hadn't worried about her neck for ages.

Pippa settled in to Jase's embrace and I felt the now-familiar tug of hormonally-charged love. It pulled at me every time I saw her with someone else. It was like I needed that bit of distance to remind myself of everything I felt for her.

Jase peered down at her, his eyes passing over her features slowly, as if he was looking for something.

'Whose eyelashes do you think she has?' he asked quietly, almost reverently, as Pippa's lashes fluttered with the onset of sleep.

I shrugged. 'I don't know. I haven't given it much thought, to be honest.'

'I think she has mine. Don't you think they look a bit like mine?' He closed his eyes and leaned towards me, showing me the ancestral eyelashes.

'I guess,' I said, slowly. 'They're both very... fair?'

'That's what I mean.' He smiled and continued to assess Pip. 'She looks so peaceful when she's asleep. Like nothing would ever wake her.'

'Except you, twenty minutes ago. You've got to be quieter when you come in, Jase.'

He frowned. 'Sorry. I thought you said nothing wakes her.'

'No, I didn't.'

I had heard – from Ellie, font of maternal wisdom that she is – that babies were capable of sleeping through jackhammers drilling and helicopters taking off, but not mine. Pip could be woken by a cotton ball touching a piece of felt three rooms over. Seven months of having a kid had trained me in the art of cat burglary, if nothing else.

Jase offered me a wry smile. 'Sorry, George. Won't happen again. But you seem like you're doing really well. Are you?' His tone was kind. I could have told him, right then, that being a single mother was not the endless love-in I had so naively imagined it would be. I could have told him that sometimes I cried in the shower, where I knew nobody would see or hear me. I could have told him that exactly once I had allowed myself to wonder if I had made a huge mistake.

But I didn't.

'I am. I'm doing really well.' Lies. 'I'm just... tired.' True. Very true. 'Would you mind if I... if I had a nap?'

He shook his head. 'No! Not at all. We'll just hang out here. You just tell me what I need to do and I'll do it. No problem at all. I do need to go pick Saskia up from work at some point, but...'

It was too late. I was already asleep.

*

By the following week, Meredith had forgotten all about Celeste and her aura. She was waging a new battle.

'All of these covers have to go,' she said, walking into my office and pulling a pile of mock covers from my desk. She threw them all in the bin.

'Good morning,' I said, trying to keep my voice level. Those covers – six of them, to be exact – had required weeks of negotiating. They'd all been retouched. Designed. The cover stories had been written. It was like setting $100,000 on fire.

'Morning,' she said. 'So – the covers. I hate them. Get rid of them.'

'What's wrong with the stories as they are?'

'It's not the stories, it's the covers. They're too...' Meredith threw her hands in the air. 'I don't know. I don't like them, though. They don't fit with the rebrand.'

Meredith didn't like a lot of things about this magazine she had created. She didn't like Celeste's aura. She didn't like the fashion team using the in-house photographer, even though we were meant to, to cut down on costs. She didn't like her assistant, Bea, wearing culottes. She didn't like the length of our profiles and had sat with me, red-penning thousands of words away. She didn't like anyone over forty on the cover but she didn't want anyone under twenty-five, either. She didn't like the tone of our social media accounts but couldn't quite put her finger on why. Every sixteen minutes or so, she'd rush into my office in a flap, teetering on her stacked heels, informing me of a new problem that had to be dealt with 'right away'. Yesterday, it had been the horoscopes. Scorpio and Capricorn were 'too negative'. Sixteen minutes later, there was a new crisis. I had learnt to take Meredith's 'emergencies' with a grain of salt, considering there was sure to be a new one within the half-hour. But throwing out six covers? That *was* an emergency.

'Ohhhhhhh-kayyyyy,' I said, as she sat down opposite me. 'There are six covers here. We've spent a lot of money on these. We have the stories. We've retouched them all. A lot of them are already laid out. And if you throw out this week's, what are we going to replace it with?'

Meredith shrugged and shook her head. 'I don't know. You'll figure it out. Have you got any ideas?'

I didn't, as it happened, because I had assumed – wrongly, naively – that the next six covers were locked in. And I'd been too busy coming up with ideas for the million and seven new things Meredith wanted to launch immediately, if not sooner. And when I wasn't coming up with those ideas, I was putting out the tiny but dangerous fires she created approximately every sixteen minutes. So, no: no ideas.

'Uh, no, I don't, not off the top of my head, but... let's see. How about Freya Knight?'

Meredith stared at me blankly. 'Who?'

'Freya Knight? She's, uh, a news anchor at ABC. She might be good. She did that speech recently about refugee women and FGM?'

Still blank.

'So she's quite topical. It could be good to explore that further. I mean... we'd have to pull it together quite quickly, but–'

Meredith see-sawed her head. 'Mmm. I'm lukewarm. Who else?'

'OK. Right. What about a man? We haven't run a man for a while. How about that chef who's doing all the root-to-stalk stuff? He's cool.' I couldn't remember his name, but Neil had mentioned this chef guy in one of our daily stand-up meetings. I mined my brain for more information.

'A chef could be good,' Meredith said, nodding. 'Chefs are really big. People like food, don't they?'

'Yes!' I said, as if I was personally confirming that people liked to eat. 'OK. Well, this guy... Daniel... Something,' I guessed, 'he has this no-waste philosophy.' I tried to remember exactly what Neil the Fucking Food Writer had told us. Neil usually went on at such length that, after the second sentence or so, I tried to have a microsleep. 'And, uh, he... makes this pasta out of broccoli stems.'

Meredith's lip curled. 'What?'

'Yeah, apparently it's amazing. He's in Brisbane. I think it could be cool.'

'Brisbane? Ugh. No. Get me someone in Sydney or Melbourne.'

'Why not Brisbane?'

Meredith smirked. 'Nobody cares about Brisbane. Advertisers don't care about Brisbane.'

'What if Miranda Kerr moved to Brisbane?'

Meredith let out a peal of laughter. 'Oh, George! This is what I love about you. You've got such a good sense of humour.'

'Right. So, uh... is that a no to Daniel?'

Meredith furrowed her brow. 'Yes. That's a no. But I like the chef idea. Get someone from *MasterChef*.'

'Oh, it's not on TV right now–'

'Doesn't matter. Get the hot one. The one who made the chocolate mousse. Blonde. Starts with a... You know him.'

I squinted, as if this might help me work out who she was talking about, but I had no idea.

'Uh, I'm not sure–'

Meredith pushed her chair out. 'He's great. Get him.'

'Uh, OK. I'll ask the team,' I said, as Meredith headed for the door. 'Wait – what about the rest of these covers?'

She kept walking. 'You'll figure it out, George.'

*

'Hey, Neil,' I said, sidling up to his desk. He took his headphones out and leaned back.

'What's up?'

'Listen, Meredith wants to do a cover story on *MasterChef*. Some guy who was on it – blonde? He made chocolate mousse?'

He frowned. 'I don't watch it.'

'Oh.' I took a breath. 'But aren't you... the food writer? Isn't that sort of your beat?'

He raised one cynical brow. 'I am the food writer. But I don't consider watching *MasterChef* part of my beat.'

'OK. So you don't know who he is?'

He shook his head, smirking. 'Maybe ask Valerie. She's mad for Gary, I hear.'

I forced a tight smile and turned away. 'Thanks.'

'Hey,' he called as I walked away. 'What'd you think of that pitch I sent you?'

I turned back. 'Which one?'

Neil sent me at least seven pitches daily, mostly forwarded ideas from PRs who wanted to send him on fully-funded trips to Turks and Caicos or Casablanca or Nashville to sample the local food. So he was fine with PR-funded trips, just not reality TV. The line had to be drawn somewhere.

'Manchester. It's really pumping right now.'

'Manchester? In England?'

He nodded, smiling. He was quite handsome, really, once you got over the fact that he was a massive wanker.

'It's amazing. You know Jonas Silberhorn has opened there?'

I stared back and, after a beat, began nodding, as if I knew exactly who or what Jonas Silberhorn was.

'Three Michelin stars. Runs Stront, in Copenhagen? Recently voted best restaurant in the world...?'

'So he's a big deal?'

Neil paused. 'The biggest. It's a great story. I'll get to spend a whole day with him, I can do a profile.'

'Right. And you want to go to Manchester for this?'

He nodded slowly. 'Yeah, it'd make a great story.'

'I'll think about it.'

'Well, don't think too long. I need to go in May.'

'Why?'

He grinned. 'Premier League Grand Final.'

I blinked. 'Huh?'

'Premier League. Soccer. Football.' He cocked his head. 'David Beckham?' he added, not even trying to hide his disdain.

'I know what soccer is, Neil. So – is there really anything going on in Manchester or do you just want a free trip to the soccer?'

'Well... Jonas Silberhorn is there.' He had the nerve to look playfully affronted. What was he doing? He was humiliating me in front of everyone. I'd only just started and he was dressing me down, stripping me of authority.

'Do you have an interview with him, or not?'

He paused again. 'I can line one up.'

'May, was it?' I shot him a shit-eating grin. 'What a shame you can't go. That's when *MasterChef* starts again.' I turned on my heel and left.

Chapter 6

'Hello! Anyone home?' I heard Nina call softly. Even when Pip was awake, we'd taken to speaking in stage whispers. It had become so normal, we often did it when we were out, too. Nothing says 'I live with a newborn baby' quite like ordering your pancakes so quietly that you actually get served a croque madame.

'Hey!' I whispered. 'In here!'

I set Pippa down gently on the couch, hoping she wouldn't stir. She'd been asleep on my chest for the last forty minutes, which was nice, but the Holy Grail of naps, I'd discovered, was when your baby slept and you were not attached to her in any way, allowing you to go about your business as you please. So liberating! So useful! Time had been reconfigured entirely in this new world, and a period of twenty minutes spent like this, with Pippa asleep in her cot or on the couch, could basically be used to solve world hunger.

Yesterday I'd put a load of washing on, got the dry washing in, folded it, chopped vegetables for dinner, cleared my inbox and made myself a cup of tea in the precious half-hour I had. It astounded me that nobody had thought to involve the mothers of newborns in Israel and Palestine to sort their problems out.

Honestly, a week of nap times could do more for the Middle East crisis than any UN accord.

When I got to the kitchen, Nina was packing the groceries away. I bent to help her and noticed new muscles bulging in her arms. I pointed to them.

'What are these?' I asked, teasing.

Nina smiled. 'I've been doing Bikram with Jed.'

'You look good. Have you lost weight?' Nina had always been slim, but now she looked thin. Proper Hollywood thin. The kind of thin that had people on the verge of asking if you were OK. The kind of thin we all bitched about but wished we were.

Nina nodded back. 'A bit, I think. I've been running a lot, too. Clears my head.'

I bent to pick up a box of wine. 'Whoa, how many bottles are in here?'

Nina ignored me. 'It's OK, let me do it,' she said. 'You must be exhausted. I heard Pippa waking last night.' I put the box down and let Nina's newfound upper-body strength take the weight.

'Yeah, I think she's teething.'

I didn't really know if Pip was teething or not, but it seemed like a possibility. I'd heard Jane, leader of the mother's group, talk about teething as if it were an affliction on par with, say, the plague. She'd said that every child went through it, so it could be true. I had to cling to the idea that there was a reason my child was fucking with me.

Nina flashed a supportive smile. 'That's tough. You OK?'

'Yeah, I'm alright.'

I felt better with Nina home. She was hardly ever here now – occasionally she'd pop home for breakfast and a shower before heading to work, but most of the time she was with Jed. It was like living with a flight attendant. I was lonely. At work, I felt old. I didn't know if I was the only one with a kid, but it felt like it nobody else ever mentioned children. They all seemed so young. Meredith's assistant, Bea, had laughed when I'd asked how Snapchat worked, then her face dropped when she realised I was serious. She laid a comforting hand on mine and said, 'Oh my god, I had no idea,' as if she'd just found out that my mother had died. And at home, I was just alone. I had imagined that Nina and I living together would be one long Netflix session. But I spent most nights on the couch by myself, flicking through TV shows I knew I wouldn't stay awake for, one eye on the door. When Nina did come home, it was great. Most of the time. When she wasn't banging on about quitting her job or dating a foetus or becoming a yoga instructor (I sensed it was coming), Nina was still Nina. My best mate, my confidante, the one person I could rely on to get me.

Nina crouched down to load the fridge with cheese, milk, yoghurt. 'So there's heaps of stuff for dinner in here. I picked up some of those meatballs we had last week from the butcher.'

'Great, thank you. I will heat up a jar of sauce and pour it over them and call it cooking.'

'Sounds delicious.'

'And you, Miss Wino Forever, can open the red,' I said, trying to address Nina's recent surge in drinking without, you know, accusing her of a recent surge in drinking.

She stared up at me. 'Huh?'

I shrugged. 'I just noticed that the recycling bin tends to fill up a lot quicker these days.'

She laughed. 'Oh, well, I'm making up for lost time, aren't I? Hey, speaking of which, did you see Eileen's recycling bin?'

'No,' I said, panicking. 'Why?'

Nina laughed. 'She's got this funny sign on the top of it. "Property of Eileen McGilvray. No foreign objects." Hand me those mushrooms, will you?'

I exhaled and laughed nervously. Every time I had seen Eileen since The Incident, she had dramatically turned away as if the very sight of me was too much for her to bear. 'Oh, right. You know,' I said, turning away from Neen so she wouldn't catch me in a lie, 'I think Eileen might be a bit of a drinker. Blackberry nip.' I mimed a drinking motion.

'Really?' Neen asked, looking up from the fridge. 'Geez, wouldn't have picked it.'

Oh good. First I swore at this poor woman and now I'm accusing her of having a drinking problem. What an excellent example I'm providing for my daughter.

I veered back on course, desperately hoping Nina Doherty, Social Justice Warrior, wouldn't try to 'help' Eileen with her 'problem'. 'Anyway, dinner sounds great. It'll be nice to have a chance to catch up.'

'Oh, I won't be here,' she said, her head in the fridge again. 'I'm going out with Jed.'

Of course.

I raised an eyebrow behind Nina's back. I knew I'd probably be going nuts with my 25-year-old boyfriend, too, if I'd just gotten divorced after almost two decades with my high-school sweetheart. But I definitely would not fall for him. And neither should Nina. I mean, she couldn't meet the next love of her life on a hook-up app. Could she?

'Oh, cool.' I feigned interest as best I could. 'What's the plan?'

'Don't know. Food, probably. Drinks. He said he's broke so nothing fancy.'

Gee, what a catch. I rolled my eyes inwardly. Nina was about to get divorced for *this*? What had become of romance? Or at least a decent bottle of red? I prayed – somewhat redundantly, I suspected – that Nina wouldn't be funding this date herself. Obviously I'm a card-carrying, abortion-granting, Tina-and-Amy-shipping feminist, but for Christ's sake, couldn't Jed fork out for a couple of burgers?

'Great.'

So tonight, like every other night this week, there'd be nobody to help me bathe Pippa. Nobody to ask if I needed a glass of water as I settled down to feed her before bed. Nobody to call out to for help if she spewed all over me as

I fed her. Nobody to take over if (let's be real: *when*) she just wouldn't go to sleep. Nobody to talk to when she finally drifted off, nobody to take the edge off the day with. Nobody to watch *Orange is the New Black* with. Nobody to bitch to about what a bitch Piper is.

I ducked my head around the corner to check on Pip. *Miraculous*. Still asleep.

'Neen,' I said, gesturing for her to join me. 'Come here.'

She stood beside me. 'What's up?'

'Look at her.' I pointed to Pip, her eyes blissfully closed, her little fists resting next to her head, her mouth slightly open, her steady breath making her chest rise and fall with slow grace. She was perfect. 'Isn't she amazing?'

'Yep.' Nina promptly turned around and walked back to the fridge.

'Are you OK?'

Nina said nothing.

'Neen? You alright?'

'Yep,' she said, her voice tight. 'Hey, um... whatever ended up happening with that guy?'

'Huh?'

Nina stood and turned to me. She looked perfectly normal, as if nothing had happened. Maybe nothing had happened. 'Alex. That's his name, right? The Tinder guy?'

'Oh. Yeah. I'd forgotten about him.'

Nina rolled her eyes. 'George! Come on. Where's your phone?'

'Upstairs.'

She stared at me. 'Go get it. He probably messaged you back last week.'

'Yeah... I'm not interested. Let's just leave it.'

'George. Go and get the phone. Now.'

I sighed. 'Why?'

Nina shot me a withering look. 'Because you need some fun.'

I do! I wanted to say. I do need some fun! With my best

friend. Who is right here, and who shouldn't leave me alone. Again.

'Alright.'

So I went to retrieve the phone. No missed calls or messages from Meredith. Another miracle.

'Here you go.' I handed the phone to Nina.

'What?'

'Have a look. See if he's messaged.'

She stared at me, confused. 'Are you serious? You don't know how to do this?'

I shook my head. 'No.'

'Did you only use Tinder that time in the cafe with Ellie and me?'

I nodded.

'Oh my god, George. You are so lucky you have me.'

Nina tapped at the screen then let out a triumphant 'ha!'

'It's a maaa-aaatch!' she said, Oprah-style. 'He messaged you. Oh my god, he messaged you three days ago. This is actually so perfect. You've got the upper hand.'

For once, my inability to get my shit together had worked in my favour. Nice.

'What did he say?'

She glanced down. '"Hi."'

'That's it?'

'That's it. OK, now you say "hi" back.' She handed me the phone.

I typed dutifully.

'Isn't this exciting?'

I raised my eyebrows. 'For some.'

Nina frowned, arranging fruit into the bowl. 'Do you not want to do this?'

I took the bowl from her and removed the fruit, pointing to the sticky sap of an uneaten pear making a well in the bottom of the bowl. 'Gross, Neen. Can you please clean the bowl before you put the fruit in it?'

'OK, Martha Stewart, calm down, I'll wash it.'

What had happened to me? I had never been the person worried about the fruit bowl. I had never even owned a fruit bowl.

Nina looked over from the sink as she washed the offending bowl. 'Are you annoyed with me?'

I shook my head. 'No.' *Yes*.

'Do you want me to stay home?' she asked.

'No! Definitely not. Of course not.' *Lies, lies, lies*. Of course I wanted Neen to stay home. 'No, don't be silly. You don't need to be home on my account. Go out, be young, see the world.' It wasn't a genuine offer. It was a 'Look what a good friend I am, now please stay home with me' offer. I needed her here.

'I feel bad. I should be here with you.'

'No, I'm fine,' I lied.

'Maybe you should get Jase to babysit soon and come out with us,' she said, her voice hopeful. Who was this 'us'? 'Us' used to be me and Nina. 'Why don't you see if he can babysit next weekend? A bunch of Jed's friends are going to Oxford Art Factory for this gig on Saturday. I think you'd be into it. Something about a contortionist who's also a rapper?'

'Huh?'

'I don't know, it's probably not my thing, but... it should be fun. You should come. We never go to stuff like that.'

Yeah. We never go to stuff like that because it's nonsense hipster bullshit.

'Right. Yeah. Maybe.'

'Come on, George, you need a night out. Let's do it!'

I stared at the back of Nina's head as she tetrised the contents of the fridge. Did she really think I would be able to go out? That Jase would be willing and able to look after – not babysit, it's not *babysitting* when it's your own kid – Pip? It wasn't possible. And besides all that, I didn't need a night out, I needed a best friend.

*

It was the nights that were really lonely. After I'd finally settled Pip (much patting, rocking and shushing ensued; Tizzie would be appalled), and cleaned the kitchen and vegetable-smeared highchair and soaked her dirty clothes and ironed my dress for the morning, I sat down with a glass of wine and called Ellie. I needed an adult to talk to; someone who understood that I'd just put in a 21-hour shift and needed to decompress.

But tonight, Ellie was the one who needed to decompress.

'Something happened,' she said as soon as I said hello.

Immediately, and for no good reason, my mind raced right to 'affair'. *Simon's having an affair?*

'What?'

'It's Lucas.'

'Oh my god, is he OK?' Lucas was the only kid I had ever really connected with; he was the only person I knew who considered it socially acceptable to eat Dunkaroos while sitting in the aisle of a grocery store, and you have to hold on to people like that.

'No.' Ellie said the word with such finality that I honestly believed Lucas had been diagnosed with some horrible disease.

'Ellie! What happened?'

'He's...' I could hear her crying now, and tears sprang to my eyes as well. From nowhere, little white dots of milk formed on my chest – now I cried from my boobs, too, apparently.

'He's what, love? What happened?'

I heard a few more sobs as Ellie tried to get herself together. 'He's... developmentally delayed.' More tears.

'What?'

'He can't... he can't read. He can't read anything.' Ellie said it as if she really meant, 'His white cell count is zero.'

'But... he's four.'

'Exactly!'

'Wait, El, I'm so confused. Do you mean that he'll never read? Or just not right now?'

She didn't answer. Could she hear me over her crying?

'Ellie? Is Lucas, like, actually... slow? Or can he just not read right now? Ellie?'

'He's...' *sobs*, 'he's...' *sobs*, 'he can't read yet. All the other kids can read, Georgie. What have I done?'

'Hon... what other kids?'

'All the kids at his preschool. He's the only one who can't. My child is a dummy, George, and it's all my fault.'

I tried hard to take Ellie seriously, but come on: a four-year-old who couldn't read? It was like a Republican who didn't believe in gun control – hardly newsworthy. 'Is he even meant to be reading now? It seems kind of early. Isn't that what school's for?'

I could hear Ellie gulp down tears as she bravely told me how all the kids at Lucas's preschool had been studying their 'Reading Eggs' (what?) for a full year now – except Lucas. And how the teacher had gently encouraged Ellie to download the app and she'd had to admit she'd never heard of it.

And that wasn't all.

'He can't count past ten. He doesn't know how to tell the time. He can't tie his shoelaces. He doesn't play even one musical instrument. Leo plays two!'

'Who's Leo?'

Ellie sighed. 'His best friend.'

'Oh. OK. Ellie, I need you to repeat something after me. You ready?'

She sighed again. 'No.'

'Ellie–'

'Alright. What?'

'Repeat after me. "I, Eleanor Hughes–"'

'I, Eleanor Hughes.'

'Am a good mother.'

Third sigh. 'Am a good mother.'

'And I understand–'

'And I understand–' I could practically hear the eyerolling at this point.

'That it is completely ridiculous–'

'That it is completely ridiculous–'

'To expect a four-year-old–'

'To expect a four-year-old–'

'To read, write or tie his own shoelaces.'

'To read, write or tie his own shoelaces.'

'Much less learn a musical instrument.'

'Much less learn a musical instrument.'

'Much less two musical instruments.'

'Much less two musical instruments.'

'Because he is four.'

'George–'

'Ellie! Repeat. "Because he is four."'

'Because he is four.'

I heard a deep sigh on the other end.

'Feel better?'

'Kind of,' she said. Then Ellie's voice quietened. 'Do *you* think Lucas is... developmentally delayed?'

'No! Of course he's not. Ellie, he's a smart kid. He taught me how to use your DVR!'

'Ugh! That just means he spends too much time watching TV!'

'Oh, it does not. And he's four. He's allowed to watch TV. He's not watching *Entourage*, for god's sake.'

'I know.' She paused.

'Ellie?'

'Yeah?'

'You're a good mum.'

Silence.

'Ellie?'

'What?'

'I mean it.'

'I know.' A pause and then, 'Thanks. But... you know this is your fault, right?'

'What?!'

'It is! After our fight just before Pip was born, when you told me that Lucas didn't need to go to Mandarin lessons or Kids Who Kode, I backed off a bit. I let him watch non-education-based TV. I let him ride his bike without knee pads. I let him drink a popper. And here we are.'

'Ellie!'

She laughed. 'It's OK, I'm just joking. I did need to calm down a bit. But do you think I'm not doing enough? I mean, how could I not have known about Reading Eggs? Leo's mum says he's been doing them since he was two. Two!'

'So what?'

'So... maybe I don't read enough books to Lucas. His teacher said his vocabulary isn't as developed as it should be. Maybe we should enrol him in a language immersion program. Leo's mum did that last summer and she said it really helped.'

'What language?'

'English.'

'Ellie, Lucas's *home* is an English language immersion program. Calm down. Lucas is fine. He speaks in full sentences, he says please and thank you, he has a healthy love of Emma Wiggle. He's *four*. Don't worry so much. He's a great kid.'

'Yeah, but Leo–'

I sighed. 'Ellie, isn't Leo the one who got his penis caught between the toilet seat and the lid?'

'Yes.' She giggled. 'It's mean to laugh at kids, George.'

'Yeah, but... come on. Leo might be reading, but at least Lucas can piss in the bowl, you know?'

*

'Shh! Shh! Be really quiet, OK?'

Footsteps. Not especially quiet ones. Coming down the hall. I heard the clomp-clomp of heels on wooden floorboards, followed closely by the definitive thud of men's shoes.

Nina.

And Jed.

Nina and Jed.

I pulled the blankets up and snuggled into them, actually crossing my fingers that Pippa wouldn't wake. How long had it been since she'd gone back to sleep? Unlike Jane, who went to sleep school before her baby was even born, I was no baby sleep expert. But the past seven months had taught me that babies needed at least forty-five minutes to get into a deep, unwakeable sleep. The kind of sleep that would not be interrupted by the clomping of drunken idiots. I checked my phone. 2.34 am. I had a vague memory of putting Pip back into her bassinet sometime around 1.50 am. I started to go over the lines I repeated in my head every time a plane passed overhead or the neighbours turned their music up.

Please don't wake up, please don't wake up, please don't wake up, please don't wake up.

It always felt vaguely ludicrous, but sadly, part of me actually believed this would work.

I needed it to work. I needed it to work so I could have a break from the office and Meredith, and from Pip, so it could just be me. Just for a few hours.

'Whose pram is that?' Jed asked in a stage whisper.

'Shh!'

'What? I *am* whispering!'

'It's my friend's.'

Friend? I was her *best* friend.

'Do you live with her?'

'Shh!'

'I'm being quiet! Who do you live with?'

I could practically see Nina rolling her eyes at this moron. Or was she? The Nina I knew wouldn't bring a random guy home to the house she shared with her best friend and newborn baby, so maybe I was wrong.

'George. I live with my best friend, Georgie. And her baby.'

Nina hadn't even told him about me? What had they been talking about for the past six weeks? How had she never mentioned me? Or Pip?

I heard them take their shoes off and chuck them on the floor with loud thuds. It felt weird, lying in the dark, being able to hear everything they said. But it was unintentional eavesdropping. Totally not my fault.

'Wow. A baby.'

And the award for Most Redundant Statement goes to... Jed! (Also the award for Stupidest Name. Also probably the award for Worst Person.)

'Shh! Come out to the kitchen. Do you want a drink?'

'What do you have?'

'Shh! Could you please just be quiet? Just come out the – SHIT!' There was a loud crash, followed by an even louder cry from Neen.

I shot out of bed.

'What happened?' I asked, pulling my t-shirt down and feeling the wetness at my chest. I would never, ever get used to my boobs leaking. I turned on the light and saw Nina, facedown, clutching at her ankle. Jed stood next to her, doing exactly nothing.

'Ouch. Shit a brick, that hurts,' said Neen.

'What happened?' I asked again.

She looked up at me.

'Sorry, George. I didn't mean to wake you. I fell, that's all. I didn't turn the light on and I slipped.'

'Are you OK?' I asked the question Jed should have asked.

She nodded. 'Yeah, I'm OK. Uh... this is Jed.'

I looked at Jed, all six-foot-four of him. He stared directly at my milk-soaked nips. I cleared my throat and did the only thing I could think of: stuck out my hand. He stared at it for a second before shaking it.

'Hey. You must be Georgie.'

I nodded. He was handsome, I'd give Nina that. Scruffy, almost curly hair that could do with some VO5. Chin stubble. Swimmer's shoulders. Alright, alright: I would have slept with him, too.

'Sorry, George, go back to bed. I hope I didn't wake Pippa.

We'll be really quiet.' Nina smiled at me indulgently, no doubt hoping that all would be forgotten by morning. Which, for her, meant sometime between 9 and 11. For me, it was closer to 5. As in two-and-a-half hours from now.

'Have a drink with us!' Jed boomed, forgetting to whisper.

'Shh!' Nina and I said in unison.

'Sorry, sorry!'

I rolled my eyes.

'Keep it down, OK?' I snapped. Nina glared at me, but Jed had the good sense to at least appear chagrined. He looked like he was about to be sent to the principal's office. Ugh. I hated that Nina had made me the nag. I felt like her mum, busting her for being out on a school night. I didn't know what else to say that wasn't passive-aggressive or just plain aggressive, so I padded back to the bedroom and shut the door slowly so it wouldn't slam. It let out a high-pitched squeak though, made worse by the fact that I was closing it so goddamn slowly.

And then Pippa started crying.

Chapter 7

Here's what it's like to get ready for a date when you have a baby: totally shit. I used to look forward to getting ready for dates: glass of wine in hand, Sophie B. Hawkins cranked up, spending an hour on my eye makeup (mainly because I kept fucking it up, but still).

This was different.

After a few days of messaging Alex, with some coaching from Nina, he asked me out to lunch. He seemed nice. Normal. He worked in marketing, had recently been to Spain and now had a thing for cava. Cool, me too. I bought mine from Liquorland, but still.

I was excited. Exhausted, sure, but maybe Ellie and Nina were right. Maybe dating would be good for me. I needed to at least give it a go. And Alex seemed like a decent guy. He was better than 98 per cent of the other guys on Tinder, and I wasn't likely to meet someone offline, either. The only place I ever went was work, so unless you counted Neil, which I most definitely did not, Tinder was where it was at.

As a self-appointed Tinder expert, Nina took it upon herself to train me in how to respond to Alex's messages, as if I hadn't spent the last fifteen years dating. The irony that she found time to be around when something fun was going on, like this date, but was nowhere to be seen when I needed help with Pip was not lost on me. Since I had started work three weeks ago, Nina had picked Pip up from daycare exactly five times. Every other day, she'd messaged me at 4.30 to tell me something had come up and she couldn't make it. Then I'd be left to make an excuse to Meredith about why I had to leave – picking up one's infant not being a sufficiently vital reason – and fly out the door just in time to make the train.

But Nina's interest in my dating life did mean she'd agreed to babysit Pip while Alex and I went out for lunch, so that was something. A glimpse of the old Nina. I didn't know how long her enthusiasm would last (two dates? three?) so I decided to be grateful for it and let her help.

Getting ready for a date while also looking after a baby should be one of those psychological exercises Google makes its employees do when they're interviewing for jobs.

Here's how it goes.

You put the baby down for a nap and pray (*please! please!*) that it's a long one, because you have some serious work to do before you're show-ready again. There's leg-shaving, hair-washing and face-masking. And that's all before you even get out of the shower.

As you turn to leave the room, you thank all the heavens and gods et cetera (even though you question their existence) for Nina, who will be here to babysit Pippa while you leave the house for what will probably amount to no more than two hours. But what glorious hours they'll be! You'll see the sun! You'll eat a meal! You'll talk to an adult! You'll drink wine! You might be kissed!

OK. Maybe not. You force yourself to calm down.

The baby cries for a bit. You attempt to placate her but, like a dog who knows you're afraid, she can sense your tension, your need to get away quickly. So she cries more. You look around, wondering what will soothe her. You turn on the mobile above her cot, which twirls slowly while playing its repetitive song. She is entranced – for a second. Then she realises what you're doing – she's clever, this child of yours – and she resumes wailing.

Right. Plan B.

You pick her up. There, there, it will all be OK. No need to worry. Mummy's here. Mummy's here. Does she sense that you're leaving? Is that possible? Maybe she's super-smart. Maybe she's a genius. In your slightly hyper, I'm-going-on-a-date state of excitement, anything seems possible. You pat her back and as the sobs start to ebb, your breathing slows too. Now she just needs to fall asleep, and then after that you can gently – so, so gently – lay her down in her cot and quietly tiptoe out of the room like this was all a dream. Then you can start getting ready. And you really need to start getting ready, because you've already spent ten minutes longer in here than you planned.

Bugger.

You feel her start to relax against you, snuggling in, and for a second, you forget what you're meant to be doing – *retreat, retreat, retreat!* – because it feels so lovely to cuddle her like this. Maybe you should become a co-sleeper? This feels quite nice, right? Maybe all those weirdo co-sleepers are onto something.

No. Focus! You have a date – with a man – very soon. Get it together.

But first, you must gauge whether she's asleep *enough*. Simply being asleep will not do. She has to be deeply, deeply asleep. If you put her down now, will she wake up? That's what happened last night. Remember last night? She snuggles against you some more and you feel a little bit more guilt about having to put her down, just to add to all the other guilt you have sloshing around in your brain. Guilt soup.

You turn – ever so slightly – back towards the cot, hoping you can angle her just so and then set her down slowly. It'll be easy. A cinch. Right? You can do this. You're the adult. You're in charge. You're not her slave.

Hahahahahahahahhaahhaahahaha. Wrong.

You gently pry her away from you, one centimetre at a time. Slowly, slowly, that's the key here. She lets out a little baby groan.

Shit.

You pull her back and cuddle her gently and she settles again.

You start to wonder where the phrase 'sleeping like a baby' came from, because your baby seems to sleep very lightly indeed. Who are these babies who sleep through lawnmowers and earth-quakes and tornados, and where can you order one?

Time is passing. How long has it been now? Twenty minutes. Twenty minutes? That can't be right. You have to go in half an hour. Half an hour! Fuck. You won't be able to wash your hair now. You'll have to wear it up. Dry shampoo. You can dry shampoo it.

OK, so: shower, dry shampoo, hair up, quick makeup job, out the door.

Ooh, and get dressed. Don't forget to get dressed.

You can't wear your jeans. The only pair that still fits you has regurgitated milk down one leg, remember? You could wear a dress, but then you'd have to shave your legs, and if you did that, you probably wouldn't have time to do your makeup. Nope. No deal. Makeup is way more important at this point. Your eye bags have eye bags.

You bob up and down, careful to fade the tempo of your rocking ever so slowly, so that you can put your baby down soon. Like, five minutes ago.

You find your silk pants – OK, polyester copy, but whatever – and they're not too crushed. OK, so silk/polyester pants. And a top... maybe that nice wrap top that makes your boobs look great? The pale pink one? Yes. Except... do you have the right bra to wear with it? Remember, your boobs are basically separate entities from you now. Your nipples might actually be able to give you a manicure at this point, they hang so low. Trying to fit your inflated bosom back into a normal, pre-pregnancy bra is going to be like stuffing sausage meat back into the casing – really fucking messy. You'll have to wear a maternity bra.

Which means you can't wear the lovely boob top.

OK. So you'll wear a jumper. A nice one. It's no big deal. The one Neen bought you for your birthday – yep. It's perfect.

Meanwhile, where *is* Nina? She should be here by now.

Oh, and don't forget the nursing pads. Nothing says, 'I am not suitable to sleep with' like leaking breast milk.

Alright. How's Pip going with this sleeping thing? Good? It's gotta be good by now, right? It's been... argh, how has it been half an hour? Now you only have twenty minutes left. Is there even time for a shower now? You have to shower. It's non-negotiable. You smell like stale milk and sweat and sleep deprivation.

OK, Pip, time is ticking. Mama's gotta go. You start to lift her from your chest again, trying to keep calm. Don't panic, don't panic, your internal voice says as you completely wig out. You're close now. She's off you. She's suspended over the cot as you lower her, inch by inch, to the sheets. You pray that she's warm enough because putting a blanket on, at this stage, is a fool's game. It'll surely wake her up and you can't have that. You have to go.

She's down! *She's down, she's down, she's down!* PHEW. You back away slowly, like a jewel thief after a heist. You're amazing. You did it.

See? Proof! You *can* have it all!

Fifteen minutes left. OK, time to get real. No shower, no way.

Nina, where are you?

You run to the bathroom and scrub your face with a baby wet wipe. Then you do your pits and ladybits, followed by a liberal dousing of deodorant and Narciso Rodriguez. No time for primer, it's straight on with the foundation. It's been so long since you've applied anything but SPF15. God, you look so different with foundation on. Like you may have actually eaten a green vegetable in the past three months.

You find the blush and sweep it over your cheeks and see the life come back into your face. It's you! It's you again! You exist.

A quick flick of mascara, eyeliner and a slick of lipstick. You look like you jumped out of the pages of *Jolie*. No, really. You do. You lose track of what you're doing for a second and stop to admire yourself in the mirror. Wow. You're, like, really pretty when you're not wearing tracksuit pants.

You pull your hair up into a loose, messy pony and give your head a decent spray of Elnett. You look good. You look really good.

You wonder where Nina is for the thousandth time. She should be here by now.

En route to the bedroom, you grab your phone. A text from Alex, saying he's running ten minutes late, which is the best thing you've heard since McDonald's started doing all-day breakfast. Thank god. Now you have a little extra time.

Nothing from Nina.

You call her. No answer.

OK, time to get dressed. Nina will be here before you know it.

You grab your clothes, realise the jumper isn't ironed but who cares? It's a goddamn jumper. You undress and briefly see yourself naked, and let out an involuntary shudder. What has happened to your body? Why does it still look so strange? Why are your boobs so full and round but also saggy and vaguely purple? What are these tense blue lines stretching across them – can they please hurry up and leave? Why does your stomach still look like a balloon that's had the air kicked out of it by a small, impatient and unreasonably strong child? When will your body come back? Yes, some things have returned to normal – you're skinny again (basically), because you're a human cow. You no longer have cankles. You can, in fact, see your toes again. These are huge victories. But you still want your old body back, thank you very much. You're not asking for Gisele's

120

body, or J.Lo's or anything like that. Just yours. It is not too much to ask.

You remember what you're meant to be doing and pull on the unironed jumper, searching for a pair of heels.

Heels. You haven't worn heels in a long time. This is going to hurt.

You find the heels and place them by the front door, ready to go.

You get your bag, and quickly pull out all the old wet wipes and tissues and rusk wrappers. Wow. The lining is super-cute. You haven't seen it in a long time.

You're ready. You're so ready.

You're going to go to a restaurant. With an adult! You're going to order anything you want because it's highly unlikely that anyone will pull your plate towards you and dump its contents on your lap, accidentally or not. You're free! This is better than any celebrity hall pass. You'd trade in both Hemsworth brothers for this moment, right here, right now.

OK, stop dreaming. You've really got to go now. Where is Nina? You've got to make that bus, and it leaves in three minutes. You calculate. If she gets here in the next minute, you can still make it fairly comfortably. Any later than that and you'll have to run for it.

She's not here.

Where the fuck is she?

You text her.

Where are you? About to
be late, please call.

Nothing.

Then: 'Message read 12.47.'

Then, the seductive ellipsis that means she's typing.

Great! She's typing, this is good. Maybe she's just running late. There's another bus. And remember, Alex is running late, too, so don't sweat it.

Except you are sweating it, and quite literally at that. You can feel patches of warm sweat begin to bloom under your arms. You wave your arms frantically, trying to air-dry them. You feel like an idiot. You're quite sure you *look* like an idiot.

Then you see that the ellipsis is gone. She's not typing. Nina is not typing.

If she's not typing, what is she doing?

Come on, come on, come on.

Ping! A message.

George is your date today?!?! I
had it down as tomorrow. We're
on our way to Jed's parents'
holiday house in Avalon for
the day. I'll make it up to you.

You sit down and try very hard not to cry.

You do not succeed.

*

I had been at *The Weekend* for just over six weeks when Meredith approached me about my column again. It was exactly what I needed to hear. Even though it seemed like it took hours to get out the door every day, and even though it was frantic and stressful and Meredith quite enjoyed texting me at midnight to see if I had 'any ideas' (just, like, in general), I somehow felt like I belonged there. I knew what to do, I knew what my purpose was. And when Meredith pushed me for ideas about my column, I knew I must be doing something right.

Meredith and I were working on a redesign together, an entire overhaul of the brand. It was challenging but exhilarating, the way I imagined abseiling or making a soufflé might be. I relished the familiar, seductive feeling of being someone whose opinions were sought. The pace was quicker than any other mag I'd worked on, but I didn'tmind. On Thursday nights I took the whole thing home, and after I put Pip to bed I painstakingly studied every word, every image, every comma, to make sure it was all perfect. There was something uniquely satisfying about seeing the mag come out on Saturday and knowing that I captained the team that made it. I felt useful again.

'How about this column idea, George? Are you ready to write for The Big Paper?'

We always referred to *The News* as The Big Paper. It was a big deal to write for The Big Paper. Over the years, I'd submitted a few story ideas and had a few chats with editors, but I'd never actually seen my work in print there. To have my own column wasn't just a pinch-me moment, it was a knock-me-out moment.

'Yes! Definitely.'

The idea was to cross-promote the brand. My column would drum up interest in *The Weekend* and make sure readers opened it, the way our advertisers expected them to.

Meredith clapped her hands together, as she was wont to do when she got excited. 'Great! I knew you'd say that, George. You're such a go-getter. That's what I love about you. You never stop!'

I smiled and laughed, a little nervously.

'Well... I love my job.'

Meredith patted me on the shoulder. 'Have some ideas on my desk tomorrow morning. I can't wait to read them.'

As I settled into work, though, home became a battleground. Pip refused to go to bed. She wouldn't let me nurse her. She spat her puréed vegies right back at me and tipped her bowl on the floor. The only time we seemed able to relax with each other was in the bath, where she would begrudgingly let me sponge her down as she played with a rubber ducky. It was the best fifteen minutes of my day.

The mornings were a blur of sticky porridge and spilled water bottles and leaking nappies and other various disasters that threatened to derail us. It was triage, every morning. By the time we rolled into daycare, I was ready for a nap. Or hard liquor.

'Hi, Georgie!' yelled one of the daycare mums, waving madly at me. The daycare mums were a funny bunch. I'm not sure why their children were in daycare because they never seemed in a rush to be anywhere. With the exception of one or two harriedlooking, pencil skirt-wearing women who speedily dumped nappies and bottles and gave their kids a quick kiss goodbye, most of the mums wore activewear and looked as though the biggest decision they'd have to make that day would be choosing between almond milk or soy.

'Hi... love!' I said, racking my brain. Claudia? Kristy? No, they were members of *The Baby-Sitters Club*. Right. Kirsten? Christine?

I bundled Pip's nappies into her locker and noticed she was the only kid who wore the cheap Aldi ones. Everyone else's nappies bore the telltale signs of nappy wealth: Disney characters. Bad mum. Pip was also the only baby who was dropped off just after the centre opened and picked up just before they closed. Very bad mum. And she was the youngest baby by far. Most were around a year old – the second youngest was nine months.

'How are you? I haven't seen you in a while. I've been dropping Archie off a little bit later because he just wants to sleep in so much now. Don't you, Archie? Don't you?' Daycare Mum squeezed Archie's cheeks and he let out a delighted little squeal. The kind of squeal I would probably make if I'd had a nice, long lie-in.

'Oh yeah, right,' I said, like I myself had a baby who just slept and slept and slept.

'Are you coming to the working bee this weekend? I'm making brownies.'

'Working bee?'

Daycare Mum (Christina? Chrissy?) nodded. 'Mmm. It was in the newsletter. And we've been talking about it on the Facebook page.'

I had joined the daycare parents' Facebook group and, an hour later, turned off the notifications. In just sixty minutes I'd been flooded with concerns about the new teacher, the snacks they were serving for morning tea and an invitation to a 'MUMS ONLY!!!!!!!' wine-tasting night.

'What newsletter?' I asked, confused.

She stared at me. 'The newsletter. They drop it in your locker. There's one every week.'

Pip tugged at my hair and I tried to wrangle the curl out of her fingers. Impossible. A chunk of hair came away and I winced. Daycare Mum gasped. 'I'm fine,' I lied. 'Do you mean Pip's locker? I've never seen a newsletter in there.'

A smile curled on Daycare Mum's face. 'No, silly – *your* locker. Hasn't anyone ever showed you? Come with me.'

She sat Archie down on the mat and he crawled over to a pile of board books and began happily chewing on one. When I plopped Pip down, her face crumpled into a cry as she reached her chubby little arms up towards me. Ellie had advised me not to pick her up again, as it would only give her mixed signals. Instead, I was meant to firmly tell Pip that I loved her and that I would be back to pick her up at the end of the day. But I couldn't do it. Every time she flung her hands up, red-faced and sobbing, I'd be down on the floor cuddling her and starting the process all over again.

But this time Vanessa, Pip's carer, swooped in and picked her up. It was like turning off an alarm. No more crying. It was brilliant and awful all at once. I didn't want Pip to be upset, but I was jealous that I hadn't been the one to comfort her. I attempted a smile as Vanessa lifted Pip's little hand and waved it for her, singing, 'Bye-bye Mummy!' I lifted my own limp hand and waved goodbye.

Daycare Mum walked me to the parents' lockers. There were about fifty of them, in a room I had never seen before. It was Daycare Narnia.

'So every parent has a locker?'

Daycare Mum nodded. 'Look, this is mine,' she said,

pointing. *Dana Alexiou. Archie, Babies Room.* Dana! Kristen/Christine was... not even close. 'And here's yours!' she said, with a flourish of her hand.

There it was. *Georgina Henderson. Philippa, Babies Room.* Ah.

'Is there a key or something?'

Dana shook her head. 'You have a code.' God, first a secret locker, now a secret code?

'OK, right. Gee, you learn something new every day, don't you?'

Dana nodded. 'Subeta will have your code. You can ask her.'

'OK, thanks, I will. But, uh... not right now, I have to get to work.'

Dana smiled. 'Gosh, I don't know how you do it, Georgie. I see you rush in and out of here and I think, "That woman has got it together." You're on top of it all!'

I suppressed a laugh and thought about how the only thing I would like to be on top of at that moment is a hotel bed – and maybe that guy from *Suits*. I was not on top of everything. Or anything.

By the time the office was in sight, I was running, milk-full boobs bouncing like the least sexy *Sports Illustrated* model ever. I made it to the office just in time to start the daily stand-up meeting. The stand-up meetings were Meredith's idea, of course. 'Buzzfeed do it!' she'd told me with great excitement, and that was that. If it was good enough for the site that produced '27 Signs You're Becoming Your Cat', it was good enough for us.

'Right!' Meredith barked. 'What brilliant ideas do we have today?'

At stand-up, everyone had to have a brilliant idea. Neil often had 'brilliant ideas' involving long investigative pieces on single ingredients that interested absolutely nobody but him. He often suggested being flown over to Brazil or Sweden or Peru to check out 'the world's most experimental chef' on *The Weekend*'s dime. Today was no different.

'There's a new Pacojet on the market, and they're offering to fly me over to have a look. Huge story,' said Neil, barely glancing up from his newspaper.

'Really?' I asked, not bothering to disguise my scepticism. 'In what way is this a huge story to anyone but you?'

He glanced at me, a smirk beginning to form. 'Do you know how influential the Pacojet has been in revolutionising modern dining? Everyone uses one.'

I scoffed. 'Could you do me a favour, please? When you come to these meetings, make sure your ideas are fully formed, OK? I don't have time to listen to your sweeping statements and decide if they're worth pursuing.'

The smirk broadened into a smile. 'No problem, boss,' he said, and I realised all eyes were on me.

I cleared my throat. 'OK, well, good. Anyone else?' I asked, trying to hurry the meeting along. Meredith liked to ask a thousand questions about every idea, even if it was clear from the get-go that it'd never make it into the mag. She bought a coffee especially for the meeting, as if we were all just hanging out and having brunch and we didn't have to, you know, make a magazine at some point.

The ideas kept coming – something about the Federal budget, why is autism on the rise, something about start-up culture.

'George!' Meredith never simply said your name, she announced it. 'How about you?'

'Oh,' I said, trying to remember some of the ideas I had written down at 4.32 that morning, while feeding Pip for the third time. The early hours were the only time Pip was content to be fed – no thrashing, no crying, no biting. Thank god, no biting.

I drew a blank.

'Um, actually, I thought maybe we could get Richard–' humour writer '– to do a field guide to daycare mums. You know, the ones who only feed their kids superfoods, the ones who volunteer for everything, the ones who harass you to buy a Thermomix. It could be funny.'

Meredith paused for a second before erupting into laughter. 'Yes! Love it. We'll get it illustrated.'

Another thousand questions later and it was time to get a coffee and sit down. Sitting at my desk was like a little holiday sometimes. I studied the flat plan. *The Weekend* was a good read. It had substance, and the writing was solid. It was nice to be part of something that had nothing to do with babies and talcum powder and the merits of Annabel Karmel's cookbooks. Harriet had messaged me with frequent updates from mother's group – Charlie was bigger than ever, Evie had sprouted fine red hair, which quietly mortified Jane – but I didn't miss it. At home I was completely out of my depth, struggling to keep my head above water. Here, I could handle things. Meredith may have been her own unique brand of crazy, but at least she didn't cry for fifty-six minutes straight.

When the daycare mums and mother's group mums told me they weren't going back to work, I couldn't help but judge them. I was all for women having choices, and sure, feminism was about doing whatever you wanted with your life... but I just wasn't sure Gloria Steinem anticipated how many women would devote their lives to sorting the laundry and ensuring sandwiches were crust-free.

How had these women lost their ambition in just nine months? How had they forgotten that they had jobs they liked and were good at? I didn't want to be like that. I needed more in my life. I *needed* to have a career. Bad mum.

I fired off an email to the daycare centre about my secret code. Why hadn't anyone told me? Then, on a whim, I opened my junk folder. Ah – 398 emails, approximately 346 of them from daycare. Yes, there was the email about the working bee. And Book Week. And the secret code. Right.

After I'd gone through the junk emails and marked the safe ones (daycare and ASOS), I went back to emails I actually had to reply to.

Fuck. The column ideas. I only had one and I sensed Meredith wouldn't go for it. Ever since I'd started to read – almost to the point of exclusivity, really – all these time-management and working-mother how-tos, I desperately wanted to write about what it was really like to juggle a career and a baby. I wanted to write about how sometimes you looked in the mirror and wondered who the old lady was, staring back at you. I wanted to write about how there was no time to make bloody bliss balls or bone broth or organic chicken nuggets and how any mother who said she did was doing us all a great big disservice. Shut up! Let us buy our jars of Heinz! Leave us alone! I wanted to write about the joy of sitting on the toilet for three uninterrupted minutes, or the relief that washes over you when you hear your baby go to sleep after a midnight crying jag. I wanted to write about doing online grocery shopping at your desk while running a meeting because otherwise nobody would eat that week, and how you used your commute time to ring and book your pap smear and had forgotten to care if anyone overheard.

I wrote a quick email to Meredith outlining the idea, bracing myself for a definitive no.

I glanced at the photo of Pippa on my desk – at just two weeks old, she looked both supremely young and also as if she'd lived forever. Larval yet wrinkled. Newborn but wise. I'd set it up on my first day in the office, proud to display it where I could see Pip's gurgling face, and where visitors might be able to glimpse her too. But slowly I'd been shifting the frame further towards me, where only I could see it. Nobody had said anything, of course, but I gradually realised there were no other photos of kids in the office.

I deleted more emails, despite all those warnings from productivity experts to only check them once a day. There was one from Ellie, who was concerned that Lucas might have a lisp after mispronouncing *The X Factor* last night (she was also concerned about Simon letting him watch *The X Factor*, and noted that Simon only watched it for the Dannii Minogue factor), and one from my mum, who had apparently found a sleeping bag that Pippa would not be able to thrash her way out of sometime between 2.35 and 2.38 am, every single night.

And one from Nina, apologising again for making me miss my date.

I was furious with her. After a flurry of 'Shit, I can't believe it's today' messages, Nina had now emailed me with, 'George, I'm sorry, but I've got something up my sleeve for you, OK? I'll make it up to you and you can reschedule the date with Alex.' I didn't want to reschedule the date. I'd messaged Alex and told him what had happened, and he hadn't replied. I didn't blame him. There's nothing sexy or romantic about the babysitter not showing up.

'Morning, George!'

I looked up and saw Neil walking into my office with Anna Cantwell-Hart. I sighed. Hadn't Neil pushed my buttons enough for one day? And Anna. Ugh. The daughter of Robert and Helena Cantwell-Hart, both former state politicians turned art gallery board members, Anna wasn't born with a silver spoon in her mouth, she was born with the whole damn cutlery set. Splades and all. For someone who only grew up ten kays away from where we sat, her voice was plummier than Christmas cake.

Anna was our junior features writer, which was a funny title for someone who did absolutely no writing. She couldn't be trusted to write, of course, because she could barely string a sentence together. She got the job because her father had some complex arrangement with the paper's CFO and as such, she was my cross to bear.

'Neil, Anna. How are you?' I kept my tone even, determined not to stoop to her level.

Neil said nothing. Anna chirped along for both of them.

'Yeah, great. Just finishing off some research for the upfront pages.'

'Right.' I smiled tightly. 'Sounds like a lot of work.'

Anna nodded knowingly, as if she had ever worked for more than fifteen consecutive minutes without checking Instagram.

'Yeah. I'm snowed. So listen, Neil and I were just talking and... we need to sort something out with you. Meredith wants me to do the Free Chef profile, but –' She sighed dramatically. I wondered how having two assignments in the one week would interfere with Anna's two-hour lunch breaks and frequent eyelash extension appointments.

Neil shook his head emphatically. 'No. We shouldn't be doing this at all. I told Anna we needed to talk it through with you.' He looked at me expectantly.

'Wait, I've never heard of this story. The Free Chef? It's not on the flat plan.'

Anna smiled sweetly, like, 'Aren't you an idiot?'

'The Free Chef. George, you must know about her. She's amazing. All my friends are, like, in love with her.'

Neil rolled his eyes.

I shook my head and turned back to my emails. 'Never heard of her. And I've never heard of the story.'

'She owns this restaurant in Bondi, where everything is free.'

'Free? Completely free?' I looked up.

Anna nodded. 'It's amazing.'

'It's not,' said Neil. I glanced at him. Maybe I liked Neil. Or at least this side of him, the side that gave Anna Cantwell-Hart what for.

'How does she make money?'

'What do you mean?'

I flashed her my own 'Aren't you an idiot?' look. 'I mean, if nobody pays for their food, how does this woman make any money? How is she keeping her business afloat?'

Neil smirked and crossed his arms against his chest.

Anna stared at me. 'No. You pay for your food, George. It's a restaurant.'

'You just said everything was free.'

'Free of gluten. And dairy. And wheat. And sugar. And meat.' Anna gave me an 'I'm-being-very-patient-with-you-even-though-you're-clearly-not-very-smart' smile. Neil laughed.

'Right. So what do you eat there?'

'Mainly fruit salad. And dairy-free chia puddings. Like I said, my friends are *so* into it.'

I nodded. 'Yeah, right. Look, I'm not running a feature on someone who cuts up kiwifruit and calls it lunch. Did Meredith tell you to do this?'

Anna nodded. 'Yep. Well, I told her about it, and she was really interested–' pause for emphasis '– and I've done all the interviews, so we can run it soon.'

'Let me say again,' said Neil, quite emphatically, 'we should not run this story.'

'Yeah, listen, I think I'll have to take Neil's side on this one, Anna. It sounds silly. Too much of a fad. I'll take a look at it, but... I wouldn't hold your breath.'

Neil smiled, pleased with himself.

Anna pursed her lips and attempted a smile. 'Well, I'm not sure I'll have time to write the story if there's no guarantee it'll run–'

'Fine. You just do what you can, Anna,' I said, and turned back to my monitor. When I looked up again, Neil was still there. A cheeky smile played across his face. I raised my eyebrows.

'What?'

He shook his head. Then he started laughing. 'I just love

seeing you put Anna in her place. Nobody's ever done it before. Could become a new hobby of mine, I think.'

I furrowed my brow.

'Yeah, well, I don't have time to sit here and listen to her bang on about stories that will never run.'

He nodded.

'Well, I liked it. It was... it was cool.'

I furrowed my brow. 'I think you must be confusing me with someone else. I'm not cool. I'm not even in the orbit of cool.'

He smiled, and it seemed genuine. 'Anyone who has the guts to shut Miss Eastern Suburbs down is cool. Meredith thinks the sun shines out of Anna's arse, and Lee mostly went along with whatever Meredith wanted. It's nice to find someone who's not afraid to be Anna's boss.'

I cleared my throat. 'Right. Well. I have a lot to do. Why don't you go work on the Pacojet brief?'

He nodded, smiling. 'Sure. You gonna send me to Sweden? Big ice-hockey game there soon.'

I studied him. The smirk was back on his face. Who did this guy think he was?

'Really? Big hockey fan, are you?'

He nodded and smiled, like a kid at Christmas. 'Yeah, I love ice hockey. Played a bit myself when I was younger. Buggered up my knees. Still love watching it, though.'

'Is everything a joke to you?'

He stopped smiling. 'Pardon?'

'Is everything a joke? I'm your boss, Neil. When you pitch me a story, pitch a real story. Not an all-expenses-paid trip to watch an ice hockey game or a soccer match. I don't have time for this.'

He opened his mouth to speak, looking as contrite as his obnoxious face would allow.

'That'll be all,' I said, turning to my emails, glancing up only briefly to watch him walk out the door.

Chapter 8

'Do you want sugar?' I called out to Mum.

No answer. The kettle finished boiling and I stuck my head around the corner of the kitchen so I could see out to the livingmeets-dining-meets-everything-else room.

To say our flat was small was a little bit like saying Miley Cyrus was outgoing: both obvious and a huge understatement. While everything worked and there were no leaks or even any rising damp (a Sydney miracle), it was, to put it mildly, a tiny little shithole. The kitchen hadn't seen a paint job since John Howard was prime minister – the first term – and it wore a shocking shade of green that didn't exactly scream 'let's eat!' There was only one window in the living room, which let in just enough light for, say, a mouse to read his tiny mouse-sized book by. And speaking of mice, I was pretty sure there was a whole family of them living in the walls, Stuart Little–style. It was near a busy intersection, which meant people walked past at all hours of the day, occasionally dropping fast-food wrappers or beer bottles over the fence, as if our entire balcony was a bin. But it was the cheapest place we'd been able to find that was also vaguely inhabitable, and one of the bedrooms had a walk-in closet – which I intended to use as Pippa's bedroom. Bad mum.

'Mum?'

Sitting on the lounge, Mum held Pippa on her lap and appeared to be talking to her. Quite intently, in fact. About what, I had no clue. But Pip was chewing on Mum's bracelet, entranced by the jangling of its charms.

'Mum!'

She looked over to me. 'What's up, darling?'

'She's chewing on your bracelet.'

'Oh, she's fine. I don't mind.'

'She could choke.'

Mum shot me an exasperated look. 'Darling, she doesn't have any teeth. She's hardly going to chew through my bracelet.'

'What if one of the charms falls off and she chokes? Just take it off her, please.'

She shot me a look and tut-tutted under her breath. 'If you say so.'

'I do. Thank you. Do you want sugar in your tea?'

She shook her head, eyes still on Pippa. 'No, darling, sugar is so bad for you. Don't you know that? You shouldn't have it in the house.'

'Why? Will it come and attack me when I'm sleeping?'

'No... Don't be silly, Georgina. But it's rusting your insides. And you know it's in everything, don't you? You should have seen Kevin's face when I told him how many tablespoons of sugar were in a bottle of tomato sauce! He near died.' She paused. 'Which is what will happen, I don't doubt, if he doesn't stop eating so much sugar.'

'Mum, Kevin is almost seventy. Let him have his tomato sauce,' I called from the kitchen, adding half a sugar to my Earl Grey for the hell of it.

I took the mugs and joined Mum and Pip on the lounge. Pip, who seemed to have grown about five centimetres overnight – actually, she seemed to do that every night – was staring up at Mum, smirking adorably.

'She is the most beautiful baby in the world. She truly is.' Mum beamed.

'She's pretty special,' I agreed.

She was. When she wasn't screaming in my face or vomiting, *Exorcist*-style, she was my beautiful little girl. She had a tuft of Jase's dark hair right in the middle of her head. It was forever sticking up or out, or to her head in a sort of baby comb-over effect. It was hilariously endearing and I was already ruing the day it grew long enough to behave itself and sit down properly. She had pale blue eyes that I'd been told by approximately one million strangers would change colour as she got older, because 'all babies are born with blue eyes', by which I assumed they meant all white babies. She had doll-like features – a nose that turned up slightly at the tip, eyes shaped large and round, a little cleft in her chin.

But the best part was that she was so deliciously chubby. Her fat rolls had fat rolls. Her legs looked like croissants. She had a quadruple chin. Her arm fat ended in neat little bracelets, as if someone had put a rubber band around her wrists. Her belly was delightfully distended. Harriet once joked that my boobs delivered cream, not milk. I worried about everything else in Pip's life – how much sleep she was getting, how many books we should be reading each day, whether I was setting her up for a lifetime of abandonment issues by sending her to daycare so early – but I did not worry about her fading away. The kid could go on a three-year hunger strike and she'd be fine.

'Where's Nina?' asked Mum, momentarily pulling her focus away from Pip.

'I'm not sure, actually. I haven't seen her this morning.' Or any morning for the past week, I wanted to add. But Mum loved Nina. I didn't want to tell her what was happening. And by now, I was used to not seeing Nina. The only evidence she lived here was the occasional bill that arrived bearing her name. Sometimes I'd get downstairs in the morning and there'd be a half-drunk mug of coffee in the kitchen, waiting for some sort of magical fairy – *me?* – to wash it up.

'How is she? I've been thinking of her. This must be very tough on her.'

I suppressed a laugh. Tough? Nina was having the time of her life.

'No, she's fine. I wouldn't worry too much.'

Mum looked surprised. 'Really? Gosh, darling... I would have thought that –' She gestured around the living room. 'All this. You and Pippa. No more Matthew. Trying to make sense of everything. I would have thought it would be very, very hard on her. And all without her mum.' Mum paused with a heavy sigh. 'And that father of hers... he's no use. Neither's the sister. And don't get me started on Leanne.' Mum shook her head with a disappointed glare.

I might have been angry with Nina, but even I could admit that Mum was right: Nina's family were hopeless. Her sister, Jill, who had moved to London years ago and rarely visited, was the kind of person who thought it was cute to sing 'I Touch Myself' at office karaoke.

'I know, they're not the most supportive.'

When Nina moved out of the house she'd shared with Matt, her Dad hadn't even offered to help her move. In fact, he hadn't called at all.

Mum raised her eyebrows in solidarity. 'They're hopeless. All of them, but especially her father. Jan did everything for him, and when she passed away, he never learnt to pick himself up and get on with life. He just got another wife and expected her to do it all. Happens all the time.'

'What do you mean?'

Mum nodded in that self-satisfied way that mothers of a certain age have down pat, bouncing Pippa, now safely charm-free, gently on her knee. 'I've seen it many times before, Georgie. Men lose their wives and they can barely cook themselves dinner, but instead of learning to do it themselves – like a woman would – they just find someone else to cook and clean and iron their shirts. Look at Glen Hastings, when Francine died – he married that awful Geraldine six months later!' Mum looked cross now, the way she does when she finds out she's missed the sale at Katies. 'And we all know what Geraldine is like.'

I didn't, actually, because I hadn't met her. Mum made sweeping statements about her circle of friends all the time, as if I was intimately acquainted with Geraldine and Glen and Hildy and Jack and Grace and Robert. But I had a hunch Geraldine wasn't keen on playing couples golf or going to the club for badge draw night – two highly criminal offences in Mum's eyes.

She was right about Nina's dad, though. He'd remarried just eighteen months after Jan died, and I knew, even though she would never admit it, that it had nearly broken Nina's heart. It was one of the reasons she'd fled to Europe as soon as she finished high school – she couldn't wait to be out of there.

My phone pinged. Meredith.

Richie loved column idea!!!!!!!
Wants to see first three on desk
by Monday. Go George! MP xxx

My heart jumped a little. He liked my idea. Richie liked my idea!

'Who's MP?' Mum asked, peering over my shoulder.

'My boss, Meredith.'

'Why is she calling you on the weekend?'

'She's not calling me, it's just a message.'

'It hardly matters. It's your day off.'

I thought about explaining that Meredith did not take days off, and that she didn't really believe anyone else should, either. But Mum wouldn't understand. She'd never had a job, let alone a career.

'It's one message. I'll just reply quickly.'

I tapped out a message in reply.

Great! Looking forward to
writing them. Monday is
absolute latest deadline?

Also, did you approve a profile
of someone called the Free
Chef? With Anna C-H? GH.

I put my phone down.
   Ping!
   'What's that?' Mum asked, her eyes sharpening.
   'Nothing. Just a message.'

Yes. Free Chef very cool.
And she's gorgeous, pics
will be great. Re: column –
yes. Richie planning to run
first one next week.

Ugh. I loved *The Weekend* and I knew that Meredith was great
at what she did. But she increasingly asked me to include
celebrities and features that had about as much substance as
cat memes. I got that she wanted to broaden the appeal of the
mag, but, well... did it have to be quite so broad?

   'Do you want to go out for lunch?' Mum asked, doing
'Round and Round the Garden' on Pip's palm. 'I noticed
a new cafe down on the corner. They're selling something
called quinoa.' She pronounced it *kwin-oh-ah* and I suddenly
had a glimpse of what it must be like to be Neil. Neil, who
had knocked on my door yesterday afternoon and delivered
a cold glass of wine.

   'Hey,' he'd said, placing the wine on my desk.

   'Hey yourself,' I said, wondering immediately if I sounded
too flirtatious. I didn't want to be any level of flirtatious with
Neil. If the Alex/Tinder debacle had taught me anything, it
was that I wasn't ready for a relationship. At this stage, I
couldn't see myself dating before Kanye became president,
at the very least.

   'Happy hour.' He smiled at me – a real, open smile, not the
smirk he usually wore.

'Thank you.' I never joined in happy hour on Friday afternoon. As Meredith led the rest of the office in cracking open bottles of bubbly and beer, I frantically tried to wrap things up for the week then took the opportunity to pick up Pip a little earlier. It was easier to sneak out of the office when Meredith was getting sloshed.

'You never come out for it, so... I thought I'd bring it to you.'

'Oh. Thanks.' I took a sip, wondering which exotic locale Neil wanted to travel to this time. He was clearly buttering me up for a reason. 'I have to go in a second, that's why I'm not out there. Daycare pick-up.'

Neil nodded. 'Uh, look,' he said, hands in pockets, swaying a little on his toes. 'I wanted to say sorry. I think we... I think we might have gotten off on the wrong foot. And that's my fault.'

Well. This was unexpected.

'Right,' I said, unsure how to proceed.

'I didn't mean to make a joke out of the pitch or offend you with the stuff about Anna—'

'George!' Meredith barged in, bottle of Mumm in one hand and two glasses in the other. 'Oh. Neil. What are you doing in here?'

'I was just offering George a glass of wine.'

Meredith's eyes blazed with happiness. 'Great! That's what I was going to do. Come on, George, time to drink up! It's been a long week.'

'Actually, Meredith, George said she can't,' said Neil, taking the bottle of Mumm from her and expertly opening it without even a pop. 'She's off to meet with a... contributor.'

Meredith frowned. 'On a Friday?'

I nodded quickly, getting into the rhythm. Neil was covering for me? 'Yeah, we're meeting for a drink.'

Meredith seemed impressed. 'Don't give that corporate card too much of a workout, will you?'

I laughed, uneasy with the lie. 'Not a chance, Meredith.'

140

Half listening to Mum, I tapped out another message. *OK. Will make sure Anna gets started on Free Chef. Will get cracking on columns. Already written one! GH.*

Lie. Huge lie.

'Have you ever had it?' Mum asked.

'What?'

'Kwin-oh-ah. What is it? A type of meat?'

'No, it's a... a grain. Or a seed. I don't really know. They put it in salad.'

'Oh. Very interesting. Well, let's go, shall we?'

'Go where?'

'To the cafe.'

'What cafe?'

Mum stared at me. 'Have you been listening, Georgina?' *Ping!*

I picked up my phone and Mum snatched it out of my hands.

'That's enough,' she said, and stood up.

'Where are you taking my phone? I need to message my boss.'

'Not on a Saturday you don't.' She glared at me in a way I hadn't seen since the time I came home drunk from my 'HSC study group'.

'Mum, there is no "Saturday" anymore. We live in a 24/7 culture. Everyone is on, all the time. And if you're not, you fall behind.' I repeated the words Meredith had used in an advertising presentation a few days ago. 'You can't afford to not take calls or be unresponsive.'

She raised her eyebrows, lips pursed in disagreement. 'I'm going to change Pip's nappy. When I come back downstairs, we're leaving for lunch. No phone. I mean it.'

I was about to scoff and roll my eyes and answer back when I remembered I was thirty-five and a mother myself, and that was probably not the right thing to do. I wondered how many other women my age needed reminding that they were actually adults.

'Fine. Can I have my phone back, please, so I can finish this?'

Mum took a breath, like the heroine of some tragic play. 'Yes,' she said, giving the phone back. She took Pip upstairs and I unlocked my phone.

That's my George! Such a
go-getter. So great to work
with someone so invested
in the brand. Cannot
wait to read. MP xxx

'Georgie!' Mum called from upstairs. 'These nappies don't fit Pip. Where are the ones in the next size up?'

The next size up? I hadn't *bought* any in the next size up. Pip didn't need it yet.

'I think they fit, Mum. Just pull the tab over a little more.'

A pause. 'No, Georgie, it's too tight. It'll give her a rash. Where are the ones in the next size up?'

'Hold on.'

I went upstairs. Pip, bare-bottomed, kicked her legs and laughed as Mum blew raspberries on her belly. Mental note: blow more raspberries.

'Here,' I said, hoisting the nappy on Pip's bottom and pulling the tab around to meet its sticky mate. It didn't reach. I pulled more. Still no.

'Don't hurt her,' Mum cautioned.

'I'm not, I'm not. It's OK.' I gave the tab another tug and – *rip* – off it came.

'It doesn't fit, Georgina. Do you have any in the next size?'

'No.'

'Why not?'

'Um... because... hold on. Maybe I do,' I lied. Again. It was so much easier to lie, to pretend I was on top of everything – the column, the nappies – than to admit that if I really wanted

142

to get everything done I'd need another seven hours in the day. Every day.

I made a big display of rummaging around, trying to find these nappies that I knew did not exist, making little tsk-tsk noises, like, *gosh, where can they be?*

I came up for air.

'Nope. Can't find them.'

Mum gave a little tsk-tsk herself.

'You have to get more organised, Georgina. Now poor little Pip doesn't have a nappy to wear.'

'Mum, Pip will be fine. It's only a nappy. We can get some when we go down the street for lunch. Honestly. This is not a disaster.' My tone became more withering with every syllable. How could she possibly understand? Mum's idea of a working parent was one who made sandwiches at the school canteen.

Mum glared at me. 'She might wet her pants by the time we get them. Or worse.'

'Yes, but...' I had no answer for that. If we took Pip down the street without a nappy, it was a surety that she'd shit her pants. Murphy's Law had always kept a close eye on me. 'Oh! I know! Swim nappies!'

Mum raised an eyebrow.

'Here!' I said, rummaging around for the swim nappies I'd bought last week before an aborted attempt to actually go swimming. Who knew you had to pack so many things to go swimming with a seven-month-old? By the time I'd rounded up her tiny goggles, cossie, rashie, hat, baby sunscreen, toys and the aforementioned nappy, not to mention my own stuff, Pip had fallen asleep, so I poured myself a gin and tonic instead. It was, after all, going to be 5 pm in three hours' time.

I pulled the nappy over her bottom and – presto! – it fit. I looked over at Mum triumphantly.

'OK,' she said, conceding defeat. 'Let's go, then.'

We made our way down the road to the kwin-oh-ah cafe

Mum was so desperate to try. Pip was crying by the time we reached our table. Lunch time.

'What are you doing?' Mum whispered frantically as I pulled out my boob and began to feed Pip.

'I'm just organising a rally for Sudanese refugees, Mum,' I deadpanned. 'What does it look like I'm doing?'

'You can't feed Pip here. You should have told me before we left. You could have done it at home.'

'Excuse me?'

'You can't just... you can't just breastfeed your child in a public cafe, Georgina!' she hissed.

'Yes, I can, Mum. It's 2017. Look–' I said, gesturing to the other customers, all of whom were engrossed in their phones '– nobody cares. It's just a boob.'

'We're going to get kicked out.'

I sighed. 'No, we're not, Mum. Can you please just calm down? Nobody cares about this but you. Please be quiet.'

Mum had the nerve to look hurt. 'Well,' she said huffily, clearly wounded. She began studying the menu, no doubt looking for the kwin-oh-ah.

'Can I get you ladies a coffee to start?' the waitress asked. 'Oh! Look at that little beauty,' she said, reaching down and giving Pip's cheek – a mere two centimetres from my nipple – a pat. 'She's gorgeous,' she said.

'Thank you,' I said, shooting Mum an 'I told you so' look. 'I'll have a strong decaf flat white.'

'Sure. And for you?'

'Uh... I'll have a mug of cino, thank you.'

'Pardon?'

'A mug. Of cino.'

The waitress stared, her pen poised over her little notebook. 'Uh-huh. And that is–'

'She just wants a big cappuccino,' I said.

'Ah,' the waitress said, flashing me a look that said she, too, had tried to explain to her mother how Facebook worked.

'What did your boss want?' Mum asked as soon as the waitress had gone.

'Nothing,' I shrugged, glancing down at Pip, who'd stopped sucking and was instead staring at the ceiling, leaving my nipple exposed. As soon as I had covered up, Pip began crying. I unclipped my bra again and she went straight back to it. This happened approximately five times a feed nowadays. Like most of us, Pip didn't know what she had till it was gone.

'She called quite a few times for nothing.'

'Messaged, Mum. There's a difference.'

Mum frowned.

I took a deep breath. Why was she being so mean? Couldn't she see I was doing my best? Who cared about nappies and breastfeeding in public and taking a call from my boss on the weekend? Anyone could see I loved Pip, and that was the most important thing. Wasn't it?

'How's Kevin?' I asked, keen to move the conversation away from Exactly How Fucked Is Georgie's Life on a Scale of One to Britney Circa 2007?

'Good,' said Mum. 'Not happy about quitting sugar, obviously, but it's for his own good. Did you know there are three tablespoons of sugar in a packet of chips? Chips!'

I made my best 'You don't say' face and rubbed Pip's cheek, trying to get her to actually feed, instead of just lying with her mouth around my nipple, staring at it. I could feel milk beginning to dribble down the front of my shirt.

Mum rabbited on about the annual flower show and a holiday her friend Noreen had taken to China ('awful, darling, just awful – did you know about the pollution there?') and the various grandchildren of various friends.

I felt myself gradually zone out and slip away from the conversation as she droned on and on ('Lucia came second in the cello recital and she's only been playing for a year!' she said, as I wondered, 'Who the hell is Lucia?').

'Georgina! Did you hear me?'

I snapped to attention. 'Yes, it's a great idea.'

She furrowed her brow. 'What's a great idea?'

'Um... you know. What you were... talking about.'

Mum let out a huffy little sigh. 'What is wrong with you? Why are you always so distracted? Honestly, Georgina... I just don't know where your head's at.'

I stared at her blankly. I didn't know either.

She let out another little sigh, as if I was exhausting her. 'I have to ask you, Georgina – are you sure this job is right for you? It seems awfully... complicated. You don't seem to have much time to concentrate on – well, anything else.'

I tried not to let the pain register, but I felt my eyes bulge with disbelief. She meant I didn't have time for Pip. And I knew what that implied: that I wasn't a good mum. But what more could I be doing? How many more times could I wake up in the middle of the night, rocking Pip back to sleep as I stood by her cot, trying not to crumple onto the floor and sleep too? How many more times could I run to the station every afternoon just in the nick of time to get the last train before daycare closed? If I wasn't being a good mother now, what more would it take?

Mum sensed nothing. She barrelled on, quite oblivious to the possibility that she had hurt my feelings. Or maybe that was the whole point.

'I just don't understand why you'd want to go back to work right now, darling. Having a child is a commitment,' she said, as though I thought having a child was like having a Tamagotchi. 'You don't want to be one of those women...' She trailed off, as if I knew exactly what she meant by 'those women'.

The problem was, I did. Those women who had children *and* worked – the nerve of them. How dare they? My rational self knew Mum was wrong. I knew it was ridiculous to subscribe to such old-fashioned thinking – especially when I had always intended to go back to work. So why did her comment sting so much? Why did I believe, deep down, that I really was doing the wrong thing by going back to work? Doing so had added another layer of complication to our lives – actually, it had added about thirty extra layers of complication to our lives – so why did it feel like I was somehow taking the easy way out? Why did it make me feel like such a shitty mother?

This wasn't how it was meant to be. Was it? I'd known it would be hard. I'd known it would be thankless. I'd known it would be all-consuming. But I hadn't known it would be so lonely, so complicated. I'd had no idea that every decision would have so many ramifications, such a strong possibility of completely fucking everything up.

I blinked back tears and stared at Pip's sweet little face as Mum banged on about her friend Nancy's daughter who went back to work when her child was two, and six weeks later, he was diagnosed with autism, as if the two were somehow definitively linked. I ate my kwin-oh-ah in silence and nodded at the appropriate pauses as Pip fell asleep at the boob.

Wasn't motherhood meant to be blissful and serene and help you see the beauty in everyday moments? Wasn't I meant to acquire an entirely new perspective on life as soon as Pip exited my body? Weren't we meant to bond immediately and start binge-watching the same shows while eating our favourite Ben & Jerry's flavour? What was wrong with me? Why couldn't I just enjoy this? Wasn't I supposed to be #grateful for every small moment with Pip, every step towards independence, every gurgle and smile and suck of the boob? The women on the Facebook groups Ellie had me join were #grateful. They documented their children's every move, meticulously curated it for social media and were rewarded with about 6,000 likes every time they did. They took selfies with their babies and captioned them 'my little prince/princess' or 'matchymatchy' or 'baby love' or 'baby bliss' or... you get the gist. I was exhausted by their zest for parenting, these women who propped their babies up against little paddles that read 'Day 37' when I could barely remember to take a photo a week.

'And how's Jason handling all of this?'

I blinked. How was *Jase* handling all of this? Mainly by being absent. Mainly by texting me pictures of onesies Saskia had found online. Mainly by asking when Pip could meet Saskia. Mainly by not doing anything that resembled actual help.

I shrugged. 'What do you mean by "all of this"?'

She gave me a withering look. '*Tone*, Georgina. You should try to be more positive. You know, my friend Noreen says that just smiling more makes her feel happier. You should try it.'

I pursed my lips and gave her what I certainly hoped was the universal expression for 'Please fuck off'.

'Anyway,' she went on, totally undeterred. 'What I mean is, how is Jason handling being a father? I mean, it certainly took him by surprise, didn't it?'

'Sorry?'

'Well, Jason was hardly expecting to be a father so soon. How's he dealing with it all?'

I thought back carefully over the morning, trying to work out if there was any chance I had somehow been thrust into a parallel universe where Jase's life had been disrupted, but not mine.

'Yeah... well, I wasn't exactly expecting to be a mother, either.'

Mum gave a little shake of her head. 'No, but–'

'But what?'

'But... but this must be quite a lot for Jason to... to digest. That's all. You don't have to take everything so personally, Georgina. Sometimes a question is just a question.'

Cradling Pip in one arm, I let my head sink into my other hand. I could not handle this right now. I could not handle *her* right now. Sometimes a lunch should just be a lunch, I wanted to say. No talking. Just superfoods you cannot pronounce.

'Fine,' I said. 'Jase is coping just fine. He has a girlfriend. He's cycling to Wollongong or something.'

'To meet the girlfriend?'

'No. With the girlfriend.'

'Oh.' She seemed disappointed. 'Such a shame he's moved on so quickly. I always hoped–' She let the sentence hang wide open, like a door that just wouldn't close.

'Mum,' I said, becoming more pissed off by the second. 'Enough. During the half-hour that we've been here, you've told me off for feeding my kid, made me order a salad, had a go at me for working and praised my ex for the actually quite shitty job he's been doing taking care of our kid. So maybe for the next half-hour, you could just order me a piece of cake and stop talking about how much of a screw-up I am. Could you manage that?'

A flash of annoyance shot across Mum's face, but then it softened. 'Darling. I'm sorry.'

I was taken aback. It was rare for me to call Mum out on her special brand of passive-aggression, but it was even rarer for her to apologise for it.

She reached across the table and took my free hand. 'I know this must be hard.' She gave me a rueful smile. 'I know exactly how hard it is.'

Part of me wanted to interrupt and say, 'No, you don't. You don't know exactly how hard it is because the world in which you were a single mum was infinitely cheaper. You weren't a single mum and a full-time employee. You were twenty-three, not thirty-five. You were married. You planned to be pregnant. I was recently dumped when I got pregnant, completely by surprise (the pregnancy *and* the dumping). So... you don't know "exactly how hard it is".'

But I didn't say any of that.

'So – how about we clean up that house of yours?' Mum asked cheerily, back to picking at her kwin-oh-ah, which she hadn't enjoyed as much as *Prevention* magazine had promised. 'I don't know how you can relax in there, it looks like a bomb's hit it. And the kitchen... Haven't you been using the Enjo I gave you?'

'The hair removal thing?'

Mum tsk-tsked again. 'It's an anti-bacterial cloth, Georgina.

149

Lord knows your kitchen could do with a wipe down. When was the last time you cleaned your oven?'

'This oven? In this house? Or any oven?' I laughed.

Mum stared at me, completely serious. This was a woman who bought a laminating machine so she could laminate her cleaning schedule and stick it to the fridge. She probably doused herself in Purell every time she left my house. 'What do you mean?'

I shrugged, sighing. 'I've never cleaned the oven, Mum. Like, I've never cleaned any oven. Can't really see the point when I don't cook.'

Mum's eyes widened. 'Right. We need to do some serious cleaning. I can't have Pip living in a... in a petri dish of a house! It's not right. Honestly, Georgina. When I was your age –'

'What? What were you doing when you were my age? Getting married... again? Dropping me off at school, doing nothing for six hours and then picking me up? What were you doing that was so much better than what I'm doing? Honestly, Mum,' I said, mimicking her sing-song tone, 'I'm sick of you being so self-righteous. I'm doing the best I can. The house is clean, even if it's not up to your military standards. Pip is fine. So I forgot to buy the nappies. Big deal. I have so much to do. I have so much to remember. I'm doing *everything*. You wouldn't know anything about that because you've never had a job in your life. And you're meant to be here helping me, but for the last two hours all you've done is tell me what a shit job I'm doing. And I'm not apologising for swearing, because I'm really... I'm really bloody angry with you, Mum.'

I drew a deep breath. I had never sworn at Mum before.

'Oh, darling,' she said, her face softening. 'What's going on?' She reached across the table to take my hand again. 'Have you got the post-natal thing? Depression?'

I shook my head. 'No, Mum. I'm not depressed, I'm just... busy. I'm trying to do everything and it's really hard. So I can't take it when you tell me I'm a bad mum, or my house is filthy, or that I need to quit my job. Why can't you just give me a break?'

She nodded. 'You do need a break. I'm sorry, darling. I just don't want Pip–'

'What? You don't want Pip to what?' I was exhausted. Exasperated. What personal failing would she reveal now?

'Nothing, darling. Why don't you and Pip take a walk and I'll head back to the house, spruce things up a bit. Have you got dinner ready?'

It was midday. Of course I didn't have dinner ready. I took a deep breath and weighed my options. Head back home with Pip and stare at the mound of washing that beckoned as I tried to watch *Jessica Jones*. Or go for a walk in the sunshine and let my 60-year-old mother clean my house for me while I window shopped.

'I actually don't have dinner sorted. Nor do I have groceries in the fridge. I would love some help, thank you.' I sighed.

Mum smiled. Pip burped.

Chapter 9

Another raging Saturday night in, waiting for Pip to wake up and feed. I was limp with fatigue, stretched on the couch like a starfish – only I don't think starfish guzzle wine for dinner.

And I shouldn't, either. I had been drinking way too much – for a normal person, even, and especially for a breastfeeding mum. While my GP had told me it was fine to have the occasional drink while I was nursing Pip, I knew I had taken her liberal allowance way too far. It didn't help that Meredith popped bottles of champagne for achievements as slight as sending a viral GIF around the office. It also didn't help that the only thing that calmed me after a day with Meredith, and then with Pip, was a glass of pinot noir.

With my laptop in front of me, I tried to think of three distinct ideas for columns. I had – by my calculations – about sixteen hours of Pip-free time to come up with something and get them all done, and that didn't include time for sleep. Thank god for Mum's herculean efforts. Our furniture was no longer covered by detritus; amazingly, you could actually see the floor (and, even better, it had been vacuumed and mopped). The fridge was stocked and Mum had made an exceptionally large and delicious pot of bolognaise. The shower glass was transparent again. Dirty clothes had not merely been washed, but folded, too. Mum had played 'Round and Round the Garden' with Pip (a game she never seemed to tire of) while I'd had a shower, one that lasted longer than two minutes, and actually managed to shampoo and condition my hair. I'd even had time to exfoliate, even though I knew I'd spend the next day undoing all the good work because I wouldn't be able to stop touching my unusually soft skin. Whatever. I felt like I'd been in Maui for two weeks.

So now I had nothing to do but finish my work. And also start my work. But what should I write about? The column had been my idea, but now that I actually had to write it – of course – I was stuck. Every time I began to type I felt that familiar stab of writers' stage fright and deleted it all.

I checked Instagram. Nina, who hadn't been home in days, had checked into a place called Sandwich, which appeared to be some sort of nightclub–florist hybrid. She and Jed were probably contemplating exactly when they'd go home to have wild anal sex. Ugh.

Fuck it. I switched on the TV.

Half-watching an episode of *Friends* I'd seen about 4000 times, I felt myself drift into sleep. Every so often I'd open my eyes in alarm, sure I'd heard Pip stir, but discover it was only the sweet sounds of Joey and Phoebe bantering.

I must have drifted off entirely, because when I woke up, god knows how long later, it was because of The Pain. What was happening? I was freezing. I pulled the lounge throw over me, but I barely felt the change – it was like putting cling wrap on a mammoth. Then I felt it: my chest. It was on fire. More specifically, my nipple was on fire. I tore my shirt away from it – too quickly, it turned out, as a small plug of semi-dried milk came away with the fabric, making me screech. This was worse than the first time I'd gotten my toes waxed.

'Ohhhhhhhhh my god,' I groaned. I went to touch the offending tit, but the lightest brush felt like burning steel ripping into my skin. I was dying. I must be.

I called Nina. It was what I'd always done during medical emergencies (though, before this, my medical emergencies had amounted to the odd ingrown toenail and a bout of indigestion after too many cruffins).

It rang out. I felt my heart, so close to my burning nip, sink. I typed a message instead.

Neen. My boob is on
fire. Something is really
wrong. I need you to come
home. Please. G x

I waited. The fire blazed, and quickly spread over my whole chest. I tried to calm down, to slow my breathing and be zen and hope for the best. If I had ever paid attention during shavasana at yoga class, maybe I would have been more prepared for this moment. If I could meditate through the pain, I'd be fine. Instead, I was pacing the room, practically hopping from foot to foot like a cartoon rabbit, clutching at my overgrown, overheated right breast. I always thought I'd die in some dramatic way – a plane crash in a celebrity's private jet, botched plastic surgery. But now I knew I would die looking like Bugs Bunny with an inflamed tit.

I checked my phone, frantic now. I needed Nina. A hot tear landed on the screen and it took me a moment to realise it was mine. Where was she? I couldn't die alone. What about Pippa?

Nina, where the fuck are you? I typed furiously, panicking now.

Should I google my symptoms? I wondered what would come up if I typed 'burning tit'.

The pain intensified.

I was going to die alone.

And then, suddenly, I knew what I had to do.

El, boob is on fire. I feel
like I'm dying. Help.

Seconds later, I saw the screen light up.

Mastitis. I'll be there in a minute.

*

Three hours later, I woke to find Ellie in full-on *Grey's Anatomy* mode.

'You OK?' she asked as she applied a cold washcloth to my naked boob, as if it was the most normal thing in the world.

I stared at her blankly and mustered a small nod. I remembered Ellie arriving, grabbing Pippa from her cot and placing her on my boob, and then only heat. So much heat. It had felt like my nipple had been picked up with sharp tongs and flung on the barbie, like a piece of meat.

Then there was some Panadol and Nurofen, carefully administered and followed by lots of water and clucks of concern from Ellie, who wasn't sure 'chemicals in the bloodstream' were such a good idea while I was breastfeeding, but conceded that pain relief was more than necessary. I didn't even have the energy to roll my eyes at her. And then I fell asleep.

Pippa was in the portable bassinet, the one that followed me all around the house like a silent R2D2, and the lights were dimmed. Ellie sat next to me, making *shh* sounds and gently pressing the face washer to my boob, which still felt intensely warm – unlike the rest of me, which was icy to the touch.

'I think you passed out for a minute,' she whispered. 'Or–' she checked her watch, 'maybe an hour.'

I raised my eyebrows as high as I could and blinked.

'Are you OK?' she asked again.

I nodded, more determined this time. I still felt as if I might die sometime in the next forty-eight hours, but at least if I did, I had a friend with me now.

'What's mastitis?' I asked. 'You said mastitis, right?'

Ellie nodded. 'You poor thing. I had it twice with Lucas.

Hurts like a motherfucker, doesn't it?' The last time I'd heard Ellie swear was when they'd run out of Grey Goose at her hen's party, an eon before Lucas. Mastitis must be serious.

'Why does it hurt so much?' I asked weakly.

El shrugged. 'It's an infection. As if breastfeeding isn't hard enough, they throw this in the mix, too. And then you have to breastfeed through it...'

I opened my eyes in alarm. 'What?'

Ellie nodded. 'Sorry, George. It's the only way to drain the breast.'

Drain the Breast. Wasn't that a riot girl band from the '90s?

'How long will it last?' I sank back down into the pillows behind me, wanting to sleep but not quite sure if that was allowed. Maybe having mastitis was like being concussed?

'Not long,' Ellie said, too hastily for my liking. Seeing my face, she shook her head. 'No, I mean it. It should be cleared up by tomorrow afternoon. Really. One time I went to sleep and when I woke up, it was completely gone. It's like a weird medieval disease, honestly. Like something that should have been eradicated by now.'

I nodded weakly. 'Like scarlet fever.'

'Or smallpox,' Ellie added. 'Which, I believe, was gone until the anti-vaxxers brought it back.' I didn't say anything. It wasn't wise to get Ellie started on anti-vaxxers (or, as she calls them, 'medical terrorists'). She was a member of at least three pro-vaccination, anti-anti-vaccination Facebook groups. She'd weeded out all the anti-vaxxers in her own mother's group by going undercover and convincing the likely suspects that *she* was anti-vax, catching them out and forcing them to leave the group. Ellie might use two types of fabric softener on Lucas's flannelette sheets, but she was hard as a helmet on this matter.

'Is there a vaccine for mastitis?'

Ellie raised a sceptical eyebrow. 'Honey, if men got it,

there'd be a vaccine. And you could download it or something, that's how quick it would be.'

'So, no?'

She shook her head.

'How did I get it? Does Pip have it?'

Ellie stared at me quizzically. 'Have you really never heard of mastitis? It's pretty common.'

I shrugged. 'No.'

'OK. It's just an infection. Don't worry. Pip won't have it, just you. It usually happens either right at the start of breastfeeding, when your boobs produce heaps of milk, or at the end, when your boobs don't know how much milk to make anymore.'

'Ah.' I thought of all the feeds Pip had refused, the expressing at work with my stupid manual hand pump, the hour-long feeds in the middle of the night. I thought of the lactation tea Jane and the other mother's group mums had bought me, the box that I'd dutifully taken to work and never opened. Was this my terrible penance for being a bad mother? 'It's my fault.'

Ellie shook her head. 'Of course it's not. Don't be silly. Almost everyone I know who breastfed has had it. It's just one of those things.'

I grimaced. 'If I hadn't gone back to work, I wouldn't have got it.'

'You don't know that.'

'As soon as I went back to work, Pip just refused to feed – until 2 am, that is, when she feeds for an hour. And I've been using that bloody pump at work. I bet that's how this all happened.'

'Hey, hey,' Ellie said, in her best Soothing Mum voice. 'That's not true. Babies go through different feeding needs – sometimes they're hungry and sometimes they're not. It's not your fault.'

'You don't know that.' I felt myself creep closer to the verge of tears.

'Well, you don't know it either. Maybe –' she looked at me hopefully. 'Maybe it's time to stop breastfeeding.'

'No.'

'She's eight months old. It's OK to switch to formula. She'll be on cow's milk before you know it.'

'No.'

Ellie sighed. 'If it's causing you all this grief... maybe it would just be easier to stop.'

'No,' I said, trying to hold back a sob in my throat. 'No. I have to keep breastfeeding.'

I didn't go to Rhyme Time. I didn't go to playgroup. I didn't have time to read books with Pip or help her practise her pincer grip or give her a baby massage. The only thing I had was breastfeeding. I couldn't stop.

We sat there in silence for a few minutes before I remembered Nina.

'Did Nina call? I messaged her. And called.'

'No, not that I know of. Let me check.'

Ellie grabbed her phone, and mine too – but there was nothing from Nina. I had thought I was dying, and she was having too much fun to even call me back. Sure, we'd had a fight, but... that was all her fault. If *she'd* messaged *me*, afraid she was going to die, I'd have been there in a flash. I mean... I had been ready to have a fucking baby for Nina, and she couldn't even text me back? An awful, selfish part of me felt, for a brief moment, that everything had turned out for the best. How could Nina be trusted with a baby when she couldn't even return a text message?

'Where is she tonight?' Ellie asked.

I shrugged, not ready to put into words how furious I was with Nina.

'You're pretty annoyed with her, huh?'

I grimaced. 'Yeah. Understatement. Huge.'

Ellie smiled and stroked my forehead, the way I imagined she might when Lucas was sick. Ellie was such a good mum. She always knew exactly what to do, and how to make things better. She had so much love to give. And she got shit done. She didn't obsess over her stupid best friend (like I did), or worry about how she was going to fit everything in (me again): she just kept buggering on and did it all. It was amazing. I needed to be more like Ellie.

'She said she'd help me out... but she's never here. She didn't even turn up to look after Pip when I was supposed to go on that Tinder date. But –' a shot of pain interrupted me, 'it's not even that. It's more... I thought we'd do this together. I know Pip is mine, and she's my responsibility, but... I guess I thought Nina would want to be like another mum to her. I mean, she wanted to be a mum so badly she asked me to get pregnant for her. And now it's like she wants nothing to do with any of it. She just wants to go out with... Jed.'

Ellie left the washcloth on my boob and sat back. 'It's been a big year for Neen.'

I rolled my eyes. 'I'm a bit sick of people telling me that,' I said.

'George... look, I know what you're saying, but Nina is grieving. She lost her husband and her baby. I mean, not an actual baby, but... the idea of one. She thought she was going to have a baby, and now she has to come to terms with the fact that it probably won't happen. Her whole life is out of whack.'

'I know all that,' I whispered, like a sooky teenager. 'But I thought that Pip would make it better for her. That she might forget some of the sad stuff and feel happy when she's here. But she's never here.'

Ellie scrunched up her face. 'Would you want to be here, if you were Neen?'

I sighed. Would I? Would I want my best friend's fertility flaunted in front of me, day in and out? OK. Maybe not.

'Give her time,' said Ellie. 'It's like we said – she needs to get all of this out of her system. Right?'

I nodded. 'Right.'

'And you –' she said, her tone becoming more serious '– need to take better care of yourself. You look exhausted.'

'I have a baby. This is just my face now.'

'What's going on?'

'Nothing. Everything.' I felt tears stream down my cheeks as Ellie pulled me in for a cuddle, careful of my boobs. 'I'm so shit at this, Ellie. I didn't even know what mastitis was. I'm such a shit mum. Nina can't even have a baby and I can and I'm so bad at it. I don't know anything.'

Ellie pushed me away and held me by the shoulders. 'That's enough. You're not a shit mum. I don't ever want to hear you say that again. You're busy and you're tired. But you are not a shit mum. Do you understand me?'

I nodded.

'George... are you coping?'

I closed my eyes and nodded.

'Really? I'm a bit worried about you. You look so tired. You're back at work, you're a single mum, your mum lives an hour away. And she's, you know... your mum. It's OK to admit you're not coping. It's really hard. Pip is still really little.'

'I'm fine.'

Ellie sat in silence for a minute or so. 'OK,' she said eventually. 'But if you want to talk about it later, we can. And George?'

I looked up. 'Mmm?'

'You're a good mum.'

I sniffed back tears.

'But you don't have to be everything to everyone, OK? I know you love your job, and I know you're good at it. But you can pull back a little, if you need to. Nobody will think any less of you. Nobody will think you're not capable.'

I stifled a laugh. 'I can't pull back now. I'm getting a column.'

Ellie looked surprised. 'A column?'

I nodded, plastering on a weak smile. 'Yeah. In the paper. Every week.'

'Oh. Are you sure... are you sure you'll be able to handle that?'

'Of course!' I said, my voice as inflamed as my boob. Of course I could handle the column. I had to. It was part of the dream. Anyone who's ever had a Pinterest board knows that you never give up on your dreams.

'OK. But in that case, if you're taking on more at work, I really think you should ask for more flexibility. I mean, you're doing more for them, they need to help you out too.'

I laughed. 'Mmm. I don't know about that.'

Ellie frowned. 'George, this boss of yours... she has to understand you have a family. Pip comes first. It's OK to tell her you need some time off, or more flexibility. Parents do it at Simon's office all the time.'

'Yeah, but Simon works at one of those cool tech companies with rollercoasters instead of desks. He could just do his work by Snapchat or whatever and it would be OK.'

She rolled her eyes. 'People know now that there has to be balance and flexibility. Just talk to her. Give it a go. I think you'll be surprised.' I must have looked dubious, because she added, 'What's the worst that could happen?'

I literally could not imagine the worst thing Meredith could do. I was both in awe and slightly terrified of her. She'd wanted to fire Celeste for her 'aura'. What would she do to me if I asked for a few hours a week to spend with my child? I couldn't risk it.

Ellie smiled. 'Promise me you'll talk to her? I think it'll make a really big difference.'

'OK. I will.' *Lie*.

'I mean it. I'm going to ask you about it. And I'll know if you're lying.'

'I know you will,' I answered drily.

Ellie sat back. 'You OK?' she asked after a minute of silence.

'Yeah, I think I am.'

'Good. Want to watch something? This is, like, the most exciting Saturday night I've had in months.'

'Glad to be of service, but... it's the middle of the night.'

And I was tired in a way that was near impossible to describe. I couldn't keep my head from falling back against the couch.

'You have Netflix.'

I looked at El, my party-girl-turned-earth-mother friend. She smiled at me. Who else could I have messaged in the middle of the night, begging for help? Who else would have come running to my side and known exactly what to do? I couldn't think of anyone else. Certainly not Nina.

'Alright then.'

*

Blessedly, Ellie turned out to be right. By the time I woke up next morning, I felt better. Not 100 per cent, but somewhere in the 60 to 70 per cent region, which felt almost as good.

A trip to the GP and a dose of antibiotics later, I was basically back to normal, with only the occasional stab of molten heat shooting from my nipple. Maybe that was the girl band I was thinking of: Shoot from the Nip.

My brief brush with – if not exactly death, then death-like feelings – had strengthened my resolve to Get My Shit Together. I would ask Meredith for some flexibility – I was well within my rights, just like Ellie had said. I needed to be more like Ellie. I could do this. Pip needed me to do this. She deserved a good mum – the kind of mum who could deal with mastitis without legitimately thinking she was going to die. Ellie would have known about mastitis from the minute she was pregnant, and she would have recognised all the warning signs. There was no way mastitis could sneak up on her, like a cat without a bell.

Nina came home in a flap, barely looking up from her phone to ask if I was OK.

I blinked at her, then turned away, disgusted. 'Yep. Fine. Now.'

'What happened?' When I didn't answer, she looked up

from her screen, her thumbs hovering above it, mid-message. 'George?'

'I have mastitis.'

'Oh,' she said, sighing, visibly relieved. 'Mastitis! Is that all? Phew! Glad you called Ellie, she would have known what to do.'

That's all? Phew?

'I mean, I'm glad you're better, George. But from your texts... honestly, I thought something terrible had happened.'

'Something terrible did happen,' I said flatly. Not waiting to hear Nina's response, I walked upstairs to my room, where Pip was sleeping, and shut the door.

When Jase turned up later that morning, he was marginally more supportive.

'Ohhh shit, mastitis?' he said. 'Claire had that after Thomas. You OK?'

I nodded, picking up the rest of the offending clutter. Claire, Jase's sister-in-law, was a Martyr Mum. She was an attachment parent, the first I'd ever met. She and Thomas co-slept, and she planned to breastfeed him until he graduated from Harvard Business School, I believe. Claire never complained about the all-consuming nature of motherhood, she just got on with it. Maybe I needed to be more like Claire – though perhaps not with quite so much... attaching.

Jase picked Pip up and plopped down on the couch.

'You feeling OK?' he asked.

'Yeah, much better. On antibiotics now.'

He nodded. 'Well... I'm exhausted,' he said. Apparently while I had contracted mastitis, Jase had come down with a case of Deep Irony.

'I know the feeling.'

Silence.

'How's work?' he asked after a pause. 'I saw the magazine yesterday. Looks good. Saskia really liked the article on the mining wives.'

'Oh, right. Great.'

'So work's good?'

I shrugged. 'Yeah. It's good. I really like it.'

Jase dangled Sophie the Giraffe in front of Pip, who squealed with delight.

'Great. Glad to hear it's working out, that it's all worth it.'

I winced. 'Worth it?'

Jase nodded, still dangling Sophie.

'What does that mean?'

'Nothing,' he said, 'Just, you know, I'm glad it's worth being... at work. That's all.'

'As opposed to...?'

Jase sighed and looked up. 'Come on, George. You know I didn't mean anything by it. You know I want you to be happy. I just don't want you to feel like you're missing out on anything. That's all.'

I felt my teeth set on edge. 'What,' I began slowly, 'would I be missing out on?'

As Pip gummed on Sophie, Jase ploughed on, mansplaining my life to me.

'George, you don't have to make a big deal about this. You know I'm on your side. All I'm saying is, it's important that women make sure their jobs are worth it. I'm only repeating what Claire says, anyway. Apparently quite a few of her mothers' group friends went back to work and now they're miserable because it just didn't work out. But it doesn't sound like you're feeling that way, which is good. Right?'

I just blinked and stared back at him.

'It's not a big deal, George. OK? I just know that sometimes, for some women – not you! – it's just not worth being away from your baby. Like, unless you're the CEO or something.'

Since when had Jase been so obsessed with something being 'worth it'? He sounded like a L'Oréal commercial.

'So women are only allowed to go back to work after having kids if they're CEOs?'

Jase opened his mouth but nothing came out. He did a

halfshake of his head. 'No, that's not what I meant. You're putting words in my mouth–'

He trailed off, but I said nothing. I couldn't wait to hear what he said next.

Jase was squirming. 'I just mean, um... you've got to be careful, you know? You don't want to become one of those women who never see their kids. Saskia works with a few of them, and... well, they're not very happy.'

I shot him an ingratiating smile. 'How many times have you seen Pip in the last eight months, Jase?'

Jase's eyes bugged. 'What?'

'I said, how many times have you seen Pip in the last eight months? I'm just asking because I don't want you to become one of those dads who never sees his kid, that's all. They're not very happy.'

Jase laughed nervously. 'George! Don't be silly. I'm just trying to help you, that's all. I think you're doing a great job, you know that.'

I got up and went to the kitchen, leaving Jase to dangle Sophie in front of Pip. Good. He could dangle that thing for hours and never get near the amount of time I'd spent shoving it under Pip's nose.

I poured water in the empty kettle and turned it on, using the hissing noise as cover as I reached into the fridge and pulled a swig from a bottle of white wine. Bad mum. I was breastfeeding *and* on antibiotics. Sometimes I used to do this when Jase and I were together. Why had it never occurred to me, then, that if I needed alcohol to deal with this man, well... maybe we weren't exactly love's young dream?

'Do you want a cup of tea?' I sang out. May as well fulfil at least one female stereotype for poor misunderstood Jase.

'No thanks,' he called back. 'I'm off caffeine now. For the ride.'

Taking full advantage of the fact that there was a room between us, I rolled my eyes with glorious temerity and spooned espresso powder into my cup, just for the hell of it.

'I'll take a milk, if you've got it,' he said. 'Full-fat.'

'You sure? Aren't you trying to get down to eighty-five kay gees?' I asked, teasing him.

'Ha! I'm at eighty-three, I'll have you know.'

I took a deep breath and walked back in with the drinks. Jase must have been hard up for a latte, because his eyes lit up like Christmas as he took in the scent of the Moccona.

He shook his head. 'God, I really miss coffee.' He swallowed half the glass of milk in one go, wiping his mouth with the back of his hand. 'But when you want something, you really have to go all in, you know? You have to commit.' As he said this last word, he chopped the air.

'Mmm.'

'And I won't lie.' He shrugged with an insouciant air of arrogance. 'I won't. It's been hard. Really hard. But –' and here, I fear Jase may have suffered severe memory loss '– it'll be worth it.'

Something snapped.

'You've got to start looking after Pip. Alone,' I blurted out.

Jase's neck snapped back like I'd shot him. 'Huh?'

'You have to start looking after Pip. On your own. She's old enough now. You're her dad, you need to start taking care of her. Like... starting right now,' I said, remembering, quite startled, that I needed to file three columns before tomorrow morning. Maybe one could be about mastitis? At least all the research was done.

His neck remained retracted, giving him an extra chin. 'Uh... OK.'

'I mean, if you want to be part of her life–'

Jase's eyes grew large as he nodded. 'Of course I do! Of course. Of course.'

'Good.' I swallowed and smiled, trying to appear as confident as I sounded. 'So, seriously, can you take her now? No time like the present, hey?'

'Um–' Jase looked uncertain. I stared at him. He wasn't getting out of this easily. 'Why now?'

'I have work to do. I have to write three columns by tomorrow.'

'Oh.'

'And I haven't started.'

'Oh.'

'Yeah.' I looked at him hopefully. 'So...?'

'Well... is it OK for me to take Pip to my house?' He looked doubtful.

I took a breath. 'Is it baby-proofed?'

Jase shot me a simpering smile. 'Well, I got rid of all the shotguns, and the hand grenades are locked away safely. So I think we'll be OK.'

I shot my own smile back. 'Do you have surge protectors on every outlet? Covers on every outlet? Locks on the cupboards? Corner protectors? Slipmats? Where do you keep your bleach?'

'Ummm... I don't even think we have bleach.'

It took a beat, but the sentence settled. 'We?'

Jase nodded. 'Saskia moved in.'

'Oh.'

'About a month ago.'

'Oh.'

Jase smiled, the smile you give to your ex when you've moved on and they haven't. The 'so sorry you're not there yet' smile. The 'I wish you had moved on too, so this would be less awkward for me' smile.

'That's not weird, is it?'

'No!' I said, way too quickly, shaking my head vigorously. 'No, it's not weird at all.' It was weird. It was really weird. Less than a year ago I had been pregnant with this guy's child. Now he lived with someone else. What was this, *The Bold and the Beautiful: Inner West Edition*?

'So, uh, Saskia will be there when Pip is there. Most likely, anyway,' said Jase.

'Yeah,' I replied, trying to sound nonchalant. 'Of course. She's your girlfriend. She lives with you. Of course she'll be there.'

'Are you OK?'

'Yeah,' I said, scratching the back of my head. 'I'm just going to pop out for some air.'

I retraced my steps back through the kitchen – one more sip of wine for good measure – and out the back door. Leaning against the rickety wooden frame, I closed my eyes and took a breath. Everybody had someone but me.

Chapter 10

'I love it, I love it, I love it!' Meredith was standing on a crate, leading the daily stand-up. She'd taken to doing this over the past few weeks, ostensibly to keep everyone in order but really so that everyone knew she was The Boss. The crate had nothing to do with height; Meredith was supermodel tall. But during one standup, Bea had had the nerve to ask my opinion on a story. I could sense Meredith's bruised ego as soon as Bea turned her attention to me. The next day, the crate made its first appearance.

'Thanks, Meredith! I'll get working on it right away,' Anna said, all plummy vowels.

'Got that, George? Add it to the plan,' Meredith barked at me.

I nodded, snapping to attention. I had no idea what the story was. I could barely keep my eyes open.

In addition to recently recovering from possibly life-threatening mastitis, I had also contracted a mild dose of Romantic Jealousy, as a result of my ex (and the father of my child) announcing he had Officially Moved On. And moved in. Saskia was probably purging his bookshelves right now to make way for her trove of Bradley Trevor Grieve books, or maybe having wild sex with Jase. It took me a second to remember that wild sex wasn't really Jase's thing. He was more of an 'Oh, it's Tuesday night at 9.30? Better have sex!' kind of guy. Spontaneity wasn't really in his repertoire.

To my surprise – and Jase's, I think – his first outing with Pip had gone well. He changed multiple nappies. He pushed her down the slide – gingerly, with caution at first, and then when they'd both gotten the hang of it, like hell for leather. He proudly showed me photos of Pip demolishing her first babycino (quite literally – she threw it off the table, smashing it to smithereens) and I didn't have the heart to tell him she wasn't meant to have cow's milk yet. I just smiled and patted his arm. He'd done it. His proud smile was brighter than if he'd racked up 20,000 steps on his FitBit.

I had scrambled and drafted and deleted and, OK, yes, procrastinated a little bit, but I had managed to get two columns done. Which was pretty good, considering I'd had a Genuine Medical Emergency over the weekend. I'd just explain that to Meredith. Ellie was right: she had to understand that sometimes the shit hit the fan. And Meredith herself had told me, when we'd first met, that she could be flexible.

But after I had finished my two columns, I'd stayed up late – even later than usual – scrolling through Tinder. The thought of Jase moving on when I so clearly hadn't was... well, it was annoying. I wanted to move on, too. I knew I was being ridiculous but that hadn't stopped me from swiping right on so many guys I'd practically given myself RSI. When I woke up this morning to see who I'd been matched with, I saw that I'd taken quite the open-door, scattergun approach. There were fat guys and thin guys and short guys and tall guys and guys whose profile pics featured dead pigs and wide grins and sawn-off shotguns and guys who enjoyed the music of Nickelback. There were too many matches for me to even scroll through – it was like I'd simply swiped right on everyone, regardless of profile pic or musical taste or whether they'd misspelled their own suburb. When I woke up and saw the damage, I deleted the whole app immediately and vowed to stop being so bloody silly.

When the meeting was finally over, I trudged back to my office, hoping to perhaps have a nappuccino, a world-class approach to beating fatigue: you drink a coffee, have a little nap and then wake up twenty minutes later feeling how I imagine Leonardo DiCaprio does when he sexts Brazilian supermodels.

I was just about to close the door when Neil walked in.

'Late night, hey?'

I cleared my throat. *Jesus, do I look that bad? Also: how dare he?*

'Uh, I guess so. I was, uh, up late working.' I walked back to my desk and began shuffling papers.

'Really? On what?'

'Hmm?' *Shuffle shuffle. Very busy.*

'I asked what you were working on. Last night.' He had that bloody smirk on his face again. Couldn't he just smile normally for once? Why did he have to look so smug all the time?

'Oh. Um. A, uh... a story.' Oh my god. I was like Hillary in the Benghazi trials. I had nothing to hide, so why was I acting like I did?

Neil shot me a bemused smile. 'Great. Hey, uh, I really like your hair straight.'

I furrowed my brow. 'What?'

'In your profile pic. It's straight. I've only ever seen it wavy – which is nice, too – but it looks good when it's straight.'

I looked up from the papers and glared at him. 'Neil. I am your boss. This is completely inappropriate.'

He looked confused. 'Oh. I thought it would be OK now, seeing as you picked me on Tinder.'

I dropped the papers. 'What?'

'Yeah. We're a match.'

Gulp. 'Oh, well...' *Fuuuuuck*. I swiped right on Neil? My heart began to race. Oh my god. What if Meredith found out? I'd surely be fired.

He smiled again, not teasing this time. 'So... when do you want to go out?'

'What's that?' I asked, as if I hadn't heard him.

'When... would... you... like... to... go... out?' he asked slowly, playfully.

'Um... That's not a good idea.'

He frowned. 'Why?'

'Well... we work together. I have a baby. They're kind of the two big reasons, I guess.'

Neil shrugged. 'But *you* picked *me*.'

'Yes.' He gave me a look like, 'Your move, Henderson.' 'However... that was an accident.'

He nodded slowly, like he was trying to fit the puzzle pieces together. 'So you accidentally found me on Tinder, and then swiped right on me, but we can't date because we work together and you have a baby?'

'That is correct.'

He whistled, long and slow. 'What a shame.'

I shrugged, trying to find an expression that was both contrite and firm.

'But...' he started again, 'you are single, correct?'

I nodded. 'Yep.' Very.

'Well... for the record, I don't mind about the work thing. Or the baby thing.' He waggled his eyebrows at me and despite myself, I laughed.

'OK, OK,' I said, holding my hands up. 'Listen, I'm sorry. I know I sound like a weirdo, and this is – obviously – off the record in terms of our... um, working relationship, but it really was an accident that I matched you on Tinder. I think you're a lovely guy–' *wait, did I?* '– but I was a bit down last night and I was on Tinder and I sort of went on a swiping spree. I didn't even realise I'd matched with you. I'm sorry. It was an accident.'

'What happened?'

I arched a brow. 'What do you mean?'

'Why were you feeling down?'

172

'Oh. Um, that's really–'

'Off the record?' he guessed.

I nodded. 'It's not a big deal, really. My ex is moving in with his new girlfriend.' Why was I telling him this? I found myself looking at the two of us, as if I was an objective outsider. The man – young-ish, tall, a bit handsome but not terribly so, his cocky grin disappearing after the woman handed over her emotional card. And the woman, also young-ish but never feeling like it, trying to keep it together but not quite managing.

'Oh,' he nodded, giving me an understanding smile. 'That's hard. How long were you married?'

I let out a defeated little laugh. 'We weren't. We didn't get married.'

'Thank god for that.'

I raised my eyebrows.

He bit his lip and I tried very hard not to be charmed by it. 'Sorry. All I meant was, it's a good thing this isn't harder than it already is. That's all.'

I shrugged. 'I know, it's OK.' I sat down at my desk, an indication, I thought, that our conversation was over. Neil didn't get the memo. He sat down opposite me.

'Uh, anyway,' I began, clearing my throat and trying to reestablish some sort of professional boundary between us, 'so you see, matching with you on Tinder was really just a silly mistake. I'm sorry about that.'

He smiled. 'Sure. I get it.'

I breathed a sigh of relief. 'It was just a misunderstanding.'

He nodded. 'Yep.'

'Thanks, Neil.'

'No problem,' he said, standing. 'But don't misunderstand this: I want to take you on a date. I know we work together. And I know you have a baby. And I still want to take you on a date. So... you just let me know.'

173

'Hello you two! My favourite ladies! Here you are!'

Nina swept in, as if it wasn't at all unusual for her to be home on a Tuesday night. As if she were here all the time, with Pip and me. As if nothing had changed.

I didn't know how to respond, so I didn't.

Pippa and I were sitting on the couch and I was feeding her as we watched *In the Night Garden*. The clinic nurse had told me that TV exposure in kids under two years led to behavioural problems, but the clinic nurse didn't have to put an eight-month-old to bed every single night by herself, did she? Over to you, Upsy-Daisy.

While balancing Pip with one hand, I was replying to a text from Meredith using my Pip-free hand.

Only two columns?
What happened? Richie
needs three. MP xxx

It was beginning to grate a little that Meredith sent such aggressive texts and ended them so passively, with kisses.

I had a medical emergency
over the weekend. Next one
coming tomorrow. GH

'Hi girls!' Nina said, again.

I glanced at her. 'Hi. How are you?'

'Great! How are you?'

I stared at her. How was I? Seriously? I was really fucking pissed, that's what I was.

'Tired,' I replied, my voice clipped.

'I bought you a present! Want to see?'

'You bought me a present?' I kept my voice flat, even.

I couldn't believe her. Nina was acting like a divorced dad waltzing in at Christmas when you hadn't seen him all year.

'Mmm-mmm. Want to see?' She was giddy, like a game show host just about to reveal the big prize.

'Sure.'

She picked up a large plastic bag and set it on the opposite couch, pulling the bag down to reveal... a breast pump.

'Is that a...?'

'It's a breast puuuuuuump!' she said, adding a few extra, unnecessary syllables. Now she both looked and sounded like a game show host – she was practically doing jazz hands.

A breast pump? This was how she apologised for not being there when I had mastitis? It was like giving a deaf person an iPod.

'For me?'

Nina scoffed. 'Of course for you. Who else?'

I shrugged.

'Don't you love it? It's the best kind. I looked online, did all the research, and this brand kept coming up, over and over. It'll be so much better than the manual one. You'll have a lot more free time. Plus, I asked Ellie – it's the one she used, so you know it's good, right?'

I felt my brows knit together. I didn't try to unstitch them.

'Thank you...?'

Nina widened her eyes. 'Don't you like it?' she asked.

'Um... I don't know why you bought it. I don't need a breast pump. I already have one.'

A brief flash of annoyance passed across Nina's face, but she quickly recovered her composure. 'You have a second-hand manual pump that you complain about all the time,' she said, her voice straining. She had me there. Milking myself at work was giving me RSI. But I didn't want Nina buying me off. She needed to apologise. A breast pump was not an apology.

'You told me pumping at work takes too long. That's probably why you got mastitis! So this will help,' she said, a hint of vexation stirring in her voice. 'I thought you'd really like it.'

I took a breath and before I had a chance to turn back to Nina, my phone lit up.

Send it overnight if you can,
want to send to Richie ASAP.
He loved your first two! MP xxx

If Richie loved my first two columns, then why did he need to see a third? It was just busywork. Also, if my employee had told me she'd had a medical emergency, I'd probably ask what it was. And then I'd ask if she was OK.

'Thanks, but the one I have is fine. You can take it back.' I may as well have stamped MARTYR on my forehead. Nina let out a short, bitter laugh, dropped the box on the floor and walked into the kitchen. She returned with a glass of wine. I raised my eyebrows and saw her ignore me.

'Why are you being a dick? I wanted to do something nice for you. I know you've been having a hard time. I wanted to help.'

'Don't swear, please,' I said, knowing my voice had taken on the haughty swagger of the Self-Righteous.

Nina held up a hand in apology. 'Right, right. But seriously, George – the breast pump. I'm only trying to help. I mean, give me a break here.'

'Give *you* a break?' I asked. Then under my breath, I added, 'Your whole life is a break.'

'What was that?'

'Nothing.'

'Look, George,' she said, her tone becoming defiant. 'I'm only trying to help.'

'You want to help me? That's a laugh,' I said. Pip's eyes were closed, so I gently set her down in the bassinette. 'Where were you, then? Where have you been? I mean, let's just get all this straight. First of all, you promise to help me with Pip. And then basically every day, there's some reason you can't pick her up so I need to drop everything to go get her. Then you make me go on a date after I told you I didn't want to, and you promise to babysit and then you never even turn up. And then instead of apologising to me, you send an email. An email! Like I'm a colleague. Or a client. You couldn't even be bothered coming home to say it to my face. Do you know how hard it was for me to get out of the house? Sorry – how hard it was for me to *try* to get out of the house? Because I never actually made it, did I?'

I turned the TV off and picked up my phone, which was glowing again.

The next one should be
funny, OK? Make it funny.
Richie loves funny. MP xxx

'Then,' I said, really gathering steam now, 'I'm sitting here alone on Saturday and I honestly think I'm about to die, I have no idea why I'm in so much pain, and I call you, and you don't even answer. In fact, you don't so much as mention it until the next morning! And then – and then – you say, "Oh, is that all?"'

Pip let out a cry and I shushed her gently, rocking the bassinette back and forth. It felt very odd to be half-yelling, half-whispering and rocking a baby to sleep at the same time.

Nina frowned at me, the way you would frown at a small child who was accusing you of treating her unfairly. An indulgent, dismissive smile.

'George... I said I was sorry. And I bought you a present. And honestly... your voicemail sounded crazy. I think you overreacted. Mastitis is very common.'

'And very, very painful. I actually had never heard of it. So I had no idea what was going on. And you –' I shook my head. Nina didn't seem remorseful at all. 'I *don't* know these things, Nina. I am trying to figure it all out. On my own.'

'Look, I'm sorry, George. I'm glad you're feeling better. I'm sorry you're so upset.'

'You're sorry I'm so upset? How about being sorry for being a totally shit friend?'

Nina's face flushed. 'You need to calm down, George. Don't say something you'll regret.'

I shook my head and looked down at Pip, who was fast asleep, despite our argument. I brought the cot to a gentle stop and motioned for Nina to move out of the room.

When we got to the kitchen, Nina took the opportunity to pour herself another glass of wine. I sat at the table and Nina sat down opposite me, waiting expectantly. This was classic Nina. Stubborn was an understatement. Nina was heels-in, teeth-bared, white-knuckles stubborn. If she had been in *Titanic*, there was no way she would have let Jack go.

'Neen,' I said, 'you just haven't been here. And you promised you would.'

She raised her eyes to the roof like she was dealing with a petulant schoolgirl. 'Well, things have come up. I have a job too, you know.'

I laughed. 'Oh yes, I've heard about that. Is this the job you don't like anymore? The one you're going to quit so you can go live in an ashram or on a kibbutz or... whatever it is you're planning on doing with your life now?'

Nina's nostrils flared with anger. It felt good to be so catty.

Nina deserved this. I had trusted her. She had let me down. 'I think you're getting carried away,' she said evenly.

I smirked. 'No, you're getting carried away, Nina. This whole Jed thing has gone too far. You're too... you're too old for this.'

Nina scoffed but said nothing. She took another sip of wine.

My phone lit up again.

Just let me know your
ETA. MP xxx

'Who keeps messaging you?' Nina asked, a stab of venom in her voice.

'Nobody,' I said. She raised her eyebrows as I turned my phone off. I would deal with Meredith later. One crisis at a time.

'It's just... What I'm trying to say is, how can I trust you with Pip if you can't even turn up to sit with her for a few hours?'

Nina's eyes bulged as she gulped down the rest of the riesling. 'Are you kidding? How can you trust me with Pip? I look after Pip like she's my own child. I would never let anything happen to her. How dare you say that! How dare you say that after everything I've done for you?' She had the gall to look wounded.

'After everything *you've* done for *me*? Do you mean leaving me here alone every night while you're out with Jed watching fucking poetry slams? Do you mean offering to babysit and then not showing up? Do you mean banging on about how you're going to be a pastry chef and get a dog and find Buddha and then tuning out the minute I want to say something about my own life? Is that what you mean by all the things you've done for me?'

She stared at me.

I took a breath and quietened my voice. 'Neen. This has gone on too long. It's gone too far. You've become a different person. I mean – what is going on with you? Where have you been?'

Nina huffed. 'Where have I been? George, I'm a grown woman.'

'Yes, you are. Exactly.'

'What's that supposed to mean?'

I raised my eyebrows. 'It means that you're an adult. You have responsibilities. You agreed to be part of this, and now you're nowhere to be seen. I'm doing this all on my own and it is so –' I paused, wanting to swear so, so badly, '– so

179

effing hard, and you don't even know. You're not here. You would never know. I'm your best friend. You promised me you would help me. You said you'd pick up Pip from daycare and you've done it, like, twice. I can't rely on you. This is the hardest thing I have ever, ever done, and I need your help. And you're not here.' I wiped hot tears away.

I could feel Nina's eyes on me, trying to figure out how to respond. She sighed, sipped from her glass, and gave me a pitying smile.

'George, come on. Don't you think you're making a bit too much of this? It was one date.'

I closed my eyes and wondered if this was really happening. The old Nina would never have done this to me. The old Nina was reliable and dependable. I'd known the divorce and the grief of not having a baby would be hard on her. But she told me she could handle it, and I had believed her.

'No, I'm not.' I wasn't making too much of it. Nina had promised me. And now... what? I was supposed to do it all on my own, and wave a cheerful goodbye to her as she went out drinking and dancing every night, then welcome her home again in the morning? This was not how things were meant to be.

'George...' she began, her tone softer now. 'Hey. Come on, let's talk about this. Is it really that big a deal? Maybe you need to see someone. You know, to cope with all of this. I'm sure it's been very hard.'

My eyes stung with tears.

'It has! It has been hard! It's been hard because I've been doing it all alone! Nina, have you listened to anything I've said? It's not just about that day. It's about *everything*. Everything since Pip was born. I thought I could count on you and I can't.' I paused, staring at Nina. She looked shocked. 'I heard Jed that night, you know. I heard him ask who you lived with. You hadn't even told him about me. About Pip. I thought this was meant to be our life, together. But he'd never even heard my name.'

Her face fell. She put her hands on mine and held them. 'George, I know this must be hard. I want to be there for you. But, you know –' Nina stopped looking at our hands and lifted her gaze to meet mine. 'I have to live my life, too.'

The words stung. 'Is that what you call getting shit-faced every night and shagging a 25-year-old? "Living your life"? Who are you, Madonna? J. Lo? Hugh Hefner?'

Nina opened her mouth to say something, but nothing came out. Instead, she sighed, her shoulders falling heavily. 'Is that how you want to be with me? Really? Think about it.'

I shook my head, furious. 'You think *I* need help? You've had three glasses of wine in half an hour! I can't remember the last time I saw you without a drink in your hand.'

Nina scoffed, but cast her eyes down. 'I'm just having a bit of fun, George. Like I said, I'm a grown woman, I can take care of myself. And honestly – do you really think *you* should be lecturing *me* about drinking? Come on.'

I sighed. 'Fine. Don't listen to me. Go take care of yourself. Like you say, you're a grown woman.'

Nina squinted. 'What does that mean?'

'It means... It means I think it would be best if Pip and I lived alone.' Fresh tears sprung from my eyes as the words came out.

'What?'

I nodded, trying to back my own decision. 'Yeah. I think it'd be the best thing for all of us. You're right, you do need to live your own life. Everything's changed, I get that. But Pip needs stability, and to live in a house where she's not woken up at 2 am by drunk–'

'That happened once!' Nina stood up.

'Even so. I think this was probably a bad idea from the start. You need your space and Pip and I... we need ours, too.' I stared at the floor.

'You're serious, aren't you?'

I nodded.

'Wow.' Nina fell silent.

'So I guess I'm moving out?' she asked, finally. She didn't sound hurt anymore – she sounded angry.

I didn't say anything.

She sniffed. 'OK. Well... you just tell me what's going on and I'll... I'll get out of here, I guess.'

I gulped. 'OK.'

She took another swig of wine and turned to head upstairs. When she reached the stairs, she turned back. 'Do you really think it's worth all this, George? Do you really think we can't just work this out? Let's just talk about it.'

I sighed. And shook my head.

She set her face in a frown and sighed. 'OK. Just remember this moment, alright? I'm trying to reach out to you.'

I couldn't believe her. 'Nina, I've *been* here. I've been waiting for you. It's too late to reach out now. You just don't get it, do you? You're never here, and you don't get it.'

She laughed again, that bitter scoff, and shook her head. 'Yeah, well, neither do you.'

*

The day we'd come home from hospital – me, Pippa and Nina – had been unusually warm for May. I hadn't known what to dress Pippa in for the ride home. But Nina had brought a bag full of clothes for her – everything a baby could need, singlets and onesies and tights and the tiniest socks you can imagine. Like socks for a rabbit.

She'd also bought me a bunch of nursing tops, which I'd had no idea I would need. There were so many things I hadn't known about, so many gaps Nina filled for me. She'd picked up Lucas's old bassinette from Ellie, lugged it over to our new place and set it up in my bedroom. She'd bought a tub of formula and a few bottles, just in case Pip didn't take to breastfeeding. I had barely thought about breastfeeding, let alone the possibility that it might not take. Of course, she knew how to sterilise the bottles, too. She'd bought Sudocrem

182

and nappies and a rattle. She'd set up the wi-fi and Netflix, knowing the long days at home I'd have ahead of me. Later, she bought me a pram, and over a bottle of wine built Pippa's cot with Jase.

When she first showed me everything, I was appreciative, but I didn't have the experience to know just how much I'd use these things each and every day, or how grateful I'd be to have a friend who knew I needed them.

Eventually, on that day we brought her home, I settled on a singlet and a short-sleeved onesie for Pippa. Babies were incredibly sensitive to heat and cold, the nurses told me. They couldn't regulate their own body temperature very well, they needed help. *Oh*, I thought, terrified by my own ignorance. *How could I not know something so simple?* Every time I dressed Pip, I was panic-stricken at the thought of making her too hot or cold, horrified that my negligence or just plain stupidity might cause her harm.

The whole idea of going home was terrifying, actually. In hospital, I'd changed Pippa's nappies and simply thrown the cloth nappies into a bin outside my room for some poor nurse to deal with. I could call for help with the touch of a button. Meals were delivered and the empty trays were taken away, to be washed and cleaned by someone else, someone I'd never even see. The nurses had taught me so much in such a short space of time. *This is how you massage your nipples after breastfeeding. This is* why *you should massage your nipples after breastfeeding. This is how to swaddle your baby. This is the football hold.* There was so much I didn't know. But I suspected that, even if I'd read all the books and watched the YouTube videos and consulted the experts, I'd still have been confounded by those early days. I felt like the new guy in the office... only, the office hadn't been built yet and it was my first job and there was nobody else on my team.

At home, I would be utterly adrift, I knew it. It would just be me during the day, nobody to call on if Pippa wouldn't stop crying, nobody to help me get her latched on during a feed. As we drove to our new place in Redfern, I counted the minutes until we were home. *Nine*. That meant that, if the worst happened, if I couldn't hold it together, I could be back with the nurses in nine minutes. I could handle nine minutes.

But then, that night, Nina and I ordered a pizza and watched *Scandal* while Pippa slept. I had a shower and slipped into my own clean pyjamas and then between the fresh sheets on my bed. As I closed my eyes I started to think, if anyone can do this – even under these incredibly strange circumstances, even with the weight of grief and loss and lives turned inside out – it's me and Nina.

I guess that's why it hurt so much that she hadn't held up her end of the bargain. We'd promised. We'd made a deal.

Chapter 11

'Don't hurry back – I'll be fine,' said Jase, as I opened the freezer packed with approximately 9,000 small cubes of frozen organic purées.

'Ok, well, there's fruit purées here,' I said, gesturing to the tower of apple and pear. 'And veggies here. And these are little chicken nuggets. I mean, not real chicken nuggets, obviously –' I laughed: no mother was allowed to feed her child actual chicken nuggets anymore '– they're chicken, sweet potato and apple nuggets.' Jase stared at me blankly; he didn't get the joke.

'Got it,' he nodded.

After his park epiphany, Jase had promised to look after Pip more often. The irony was not lost on me that Jase's company had jumped at the chance to let him work a four-day week so he could take care of Pip, while Meredith couldn't fathom the idea of me leaving an hour early. Still, it was a huge relief. It took away some of the guilt I'd felt about sending her to daycare five days a week. I'd had romantic visions of Pip thriving at daycare, making little friends all of her own and learning how to French knit and possibly even make baby art installations – my very own miniature Tracey Emin. But I had quickly realised that daycare was exactly what it said on the box – a day of care. There was no French knitting and certainly no art installations – unless you counted gumming on recycled paper towel rolls. I'd hardly been surprised when I asked the centre director, Subeta, how long she'd run the place and she answered, 'Not long. We sold our hardware shop last year and thought we'd do this for a while.' As though she was a backpacker picking peaches for the summer. Only, the peaches were my child. Right.

But now Pip would only have to spend four days at daycare, not five. After failing to get my third – utterly redundant, if you ask me – column in after my argument with Nina, Meredith had written me out of her good books. Permanently, I feared. So when I'd half-heartedly asked her if I could work from home one day a week, she'd simply replied, 'Why?', as if I might be asking her to work from home so I could sunbathe or care for my axolotl. I had to explain the whole 'I have a baby' thing again. She looked like she had genuinely forgotten. When I'd finished, she simply said, 'No. We don't really do that.'

'We'll be fine, George, really.' Jase gave me a reassuring squeeze and guided me towards the door. 'Don't worry about a thing. Honestly. Claire gave me lots of tips, and I know how to change a nappy now so it doesn't leak... Really, we're going to have a great day! We're going to cuddle and read books and sing songs and... ahh, it'll be lovely.'

I took a deep breath. Of course Jase felt that way. It was the first time he had done this; it was all novel to him. He didn't have to deal with days and days of repetition on loop. I doubted Jase would ever feel the bracing panic of wondering how he'd fill all the long hours stretching in front of him.

I forced a smile. 'Great! Call me whenever. It doesn't matter. And all the emergency numbers are on the fridge. There's Panadol upstairs. Make sure you check the side of the bottle to see the dosage. And there's a thermometer – it's digital – in case she has a temperature. And remember, Ellie's home today so you can always just go over there, OK?'

Jase shot me a simpering smile. 'We're gonna be fine. We don't need Ellie to babysit the two of us.'

I waved my hand dismissively. 'I know, I know. That's not what I meant.'

Jase nodded. 'That's exactly what you meant. Now go!' he said, pushing me towards the door again.

I bent down and kissed Pip's fat cheek, cool against my lips. 'Bye, sweetie. Love you.' And then I whispered, 'You'll be fine. I promise.' Pip smiled back, a line of dribble making its way down her chin. I stared into her little face and prayed that Jase would be able to handle this. I remembered his words and repeated them to myself: *it'll all be worth it, it'll all be worth it.*

I thanked Jase as he deftly pushed me out the door, and then began my daily run-walk-check-phone routine on the way to the station. I was like an Olympic speed walker – I didn't need to look up, I knew exactly where to turn and stop.

Which is why I didn't see Nina until she was right there next to me at the traffic lights, tapping me on the shoulder.

'Hey,' she said, craning her neck to put her face in front of mine. 'Hey, George!' She'd been running; little half-moons of sweat had formed under her armpits. The last time *I*'d exercised was... well, did labour count?

'Oh, hi.'

We hadn't spoken in over two weeks. Nina had come home a few times while I was at work to pick up her clothes, but organising that had been the extent of our communication. The rest of her things: her furniture, her books, the KitchenAid that was taking up all my bench space – it was all still there, reminding me of her every day.

'How are you?' Nina smiled her big, warm Nina smile and for a second I was pulled back in. Then I remembered all the times she'd let me down, all the promises she had broken. All the times she'd been my friend in name only.

'Fine.'

'How's Pip?'

'She's good.' I didn't want to add, 'She misses you,' even though it was true. I'd caught Pip looking around, searching for Nina, a few times in the days after she'd left, though she was doing it less frequently now. 'How are you?'

'I'm good. I'm great,' she said. She looked great. She had the rosy-cheeked glow of a woman who'd recently orgasmed. Good for her.

'OK then. Bye.'

I went to walk away but Nina held my shoulder, looking wounded.

'George.' Her voice was soft, hurt.

'Neen... I have stuff to do. I have to get to work. I can't be late because I have to leave on time. OK?'

She let go of my shoulder and nodded slowly, still looking hurt. 'I just, um... look, I'm really sorry, George. I know why you're angry with me, and I'm sorry. I'm still really upset that you want me to move out, but...' she paused, shrugging, 'maybe it's for the best. But... I'm having this thing, in a few weeks, for Mum's anniversary. It's twenty years this year.'

'Oh.' The words hit me like a blow to the stomach. It was, too. Twenty years since Jan, Nina's school-canteen-running, swimming-teacher mum had died. Twenty years. I felt tears spring to my eyes and I swallowed them back. Again. Everything in me softened. 'Of course. Of course I'll come.'

She smiled. 'Thank you. It'll just be me. Jill's still in London and Dad said it would be weird... you know, with Leanne.'

I rolled my eyes. 'Jesus Christ, she's jealous of a dead chick?'

Nina cracked a laugh. 'Oh my god, George. You can't say things like that.' But she was still laughing.

'Sorry. You know what I mean.'

She rolled her eyes, nodding. 'Yeah, it's true. She's jealous of a dead chick. Anyway, I'm going to get some balloons and let them go near Bronte. She always liked to swim over there, so... I thought it would be nice. And if you wanted to bring Pip, well, I think she'd be into the balloons.'

'They're among her top five favourite round things.'

'Great. I'll text you the details.'

'OK.'

We both stood there for a second, not sure what to do next. Nina and I weren't really huggers, but it seemed weird to just walk away. In the end I sort of patted her hand, the way you would with an elderly relative you were afraid you might accidentally squash.

'Well, I should really go now.'

'Yeah, sure,' she said, nodding. 'I've gotta finish my run.'

I walked the rest of the way to the station more slowly than usual. Twenty years. Wow. I couldn't believe Nina had been without her mum for so long. And I couldn't believe I hadn't remembered the anniversary until she told me. The date had always been etched in my brain. 9 March. Usually Nina didn't do anything to mark the day, but I always sent flowers and made sure she was with someone, if she wasn't with me. How had I forgotten – this year, of all years?

When I got to the office, Meredith sauntered out and did a little, 'George is late – again' comedy bit. She was developing quite the stand-up routine.

'Helloooooo, George!' she sang out, making sure everyone on the floors above and below us could hear her bellow.

'Good morning, Meredith,' I said, at a normal volume, like a normal person.

'And what happened this morning, George?' Meredith asked, a passive-aggressive smile plastered to her face. *Don't take it so seriously!* I imagined her saying, aghast, if I actually had the nerve to call her on it. *We're all friends here! It's only a joke!*

I was tempted to tell her what had really made me late. *Well, I was showing my ex how to take care of my child, and he's taking care of her because I suddenly realised – two months in, mind you – that her daycare attendants have actually spent the last ten years selling drywall, not taking care of children, as I had rather naively hoped. And then I got sidetracked staring into my child's face, wondering if leaving her for nine hours of the day was actually worth it. And then I got delayed again when I ran into my former best friend and she told me about the anniversary of her mother's death – the twentieth anniversary – and how her father won't go because his new wife is still jealous of the old – dead, remember? – wife, and her sister lives overseas, so I'm probably the only person who'll be there, apart from her. And maybe Jed. Who's Jed? Oh, he's her boyfriend. She had a husband, but they're getting a divorce. They can't have kids. And that's sort of my fault. So that's why I'm late.*

'Train was running late.'

Meredith laughed. 'Wasn't it the bus that was late yesterday, George? Gotta keep those stories straight!'

This was typical Meredith. When we were working together, she was great. She fired off ideas and listened to mine, and we worked as a team. She was demanding and exacting, but at least she had some respect for me. But in front of everyone else, she took on the role of bemused school teacher, and cast me as the naughty student. Yesterday, when the bus had run late, she'd said, 'The bus! Nobody takes the bus, George!' and rolled her eyes, as if I'd made the whole thing up. Or she'd casually mention all the 'breaks' I took. 'Oh, you're looking for George? She's probably having a *break*,' I'd overheard her tell Neil one day. This 'break' happened twice a day, when I needed to excuse myself to pump my boobs free of milk. Terrified of people thinking I was *actually* taking a break, I'd take conference calls or answer emails with one hand as I milked myself with the other.

I sighed. 'Did I miss stand-up?'

She shook her head. 'No, no. I was running late, too, George.'

'Huh? Really?'

She nodded. 'Wasn't feeling well. Anyway, let's start, shall we?'

Behind Meredith, I saw Bea glance at me, a flash of worry on her face. Meredith was never sick.

We flew through stand-up, which was also unusual. I made it back to my desk in record time, only to be greeted, once more, by Neil.

'Hello,' he said. In the past week, Neil had taken to popping into my office, unsolicited and unannounced. Most of the time he just said 'Hello' in a sort of teasing voice, and then I told him to leave. Which I was just about to do.

'Hi, Neil. Listen, I don't really have time –'

'There's a restaurant opening tonight. Binge. In Surry Hills. Come with me.'

I raised my eyebrows and said nothing.

'Free dinner. No strings. Wine.'

'I don't have ti—'

'Yeah, you do. Come on. I never see you have any fun. Do you ever have fun?' He was only teasing, but the answer was serious: no, I didn't have any fun. Not anymore.

I laughed, a trace of bitterness coursing through it. 'Not really.'

He smiled. Mmm. Neil had a nice smile. Not cute. Nice. He looked like a man. I suddenly realised I knew nothing about Neil the Food Writer, apart from the fact that he was obsessed with something called kombucha and would probably die a little inside if he heard my Mum talk about kwin-oh-ah.

'Alright then. Come with me. We leave at six,' he said, in the same way he might have said, 'We ride at dawn.'

I laughed. 'Really, Neil...'

He flashed a furtive look. 'Listen, I'll be there. I have to go for work. If you show up, cool. If you don't...' He shrugged.

I paused, briefly considering whether to text Jase and ask him to stay a little later. Maybe I could go. After all, I didn't have to do daycare pick-up. And it wouldn't necessarily be a date. Would it?

I opened my mouth to answer, but Neil held up a single finger. 'It's OK. You don't have to decide now. But I'm fun,

George. Just come and have a drink.' And then he turned and left.

I sat down and leaned back in my chair. Grabbing my phone, I typed a text to Jase. *Going to be a little late, is that OK?* A few minutes later, I saw his reply. *Of course, no probs. Going to park. Are pram straps compulsory?* My heart jumped as I pictured the two of them: Pip hurtling down the street, entirely untethered, grinning from ear to ear as Jase pushed her racing pram down an incline, trying to see if they could set a new world record. *Just kidding, G. Figured it out. Siri helped. Jx*

I breathed a sigh of relief and opened my computer inbox. As always, there were around thirty emails waiting for me, all from Meredith and all sent overnight. They weren't really emails, in that they weren't really correspondence – more like stream-of-consciousness missives. Each one contradicted the one before it. Sometimes I just deleted them en masse – by the time daylight rolled around, Meredith had typically forgotten what she'd written – but today I decided to have a look.

From: Meredith Parker
To: Georgie Henderson
Subject: Celeste
Sent: 11.56 pm
George, back at square one with Celeste. Her aura is orange now! Orange = jealous and prone to irrational outbursts. We don't need that on the team. Let's sort this out tomorrow.

From: Meredith Parker
To: Georgie Henderson
Subject: Melbourne
Sent: 12.00 am
George, am going to Melbourne next week to do the first upfronts. Massive accounts, must chase chase chase. As face of brand, I'll need you there. Everyone will love you. Let's practise your presentation this week. Have five dot points for

me in the morning, OK, just topline stuff? George, this is a
great chance to get some more $$$. And I'll book Flower
Drum! We'll make a weekend of it.

From: Meredith Parker
To: Georgie Henderson
Subject: Celeste
Sent: 12.01 am
George, have we had your aura read yet?

From: Meredith Parker
To: Georgie Henderson
CC: Clementine Hall
Subject: Aura Reading
Sent: 12.11 am
George, meet Clementine. She's coming in to read your aura
tomorrow. Wear something neutral.

From: Meredith Parker
To: Georgie Henderson
Subject: FWD: Celeste
Sent: 12.13 am
Lee's aura was yellow. Distrustful. Scatterbrained. Highly
emotional.

From: Meredith Parker
To: Georgie Henderson
Subject: Melbourne
Sent: 12.59 am
Actually, have you been to Attica? Forget Flower Drum.
We'll go to Attica.

From: Meredith Parker
To: Georgie Henderson
Subject: FWD: Your reservation at Attica
Sent: 1.07 am It's done!

From: Clementine Hall
To: Meredith Parker, Georgie Henderson
Subject: Aura Reading
Sent: 6.17 am
Meredith, I'm on a power meditation retreat right now. Should not even be sending this email! Phones are totally banned. (But I am shagging the meditation director so fine for me. I digress.) Anyway, cannot do aura reading tomorrow. Am sensing some virtual negativity from this man George though. Thx.

First things first: I had to email Meredith and lie. I'd tell her that yes, I'd had my aura read and (a quick google later) it was vibrant red, the colour of diligence and authority. Easy.

But how to get out of Melbourne? It was ridiculous that I had to go. The 'upfronts', as Meredith called them, were merely the same old presentations we'd always given to advertisers, gussied up with an American word and some expensive pens we handed out at the end (it's difficult to overstate the power of free stationery, even among men who routinely bring home bonuses worth more than the house I live in). But gussied or not, I didn't really need to be there; Meredith could do it all. She loved the sell, the chase, the game of it all. And she was good at it. She boozed and schmoozed with the best. Me? I could barely keep a straight face as they all barrelled on about the need to 'actualise e-commerce as a viable brand focus' and 'target diversified revenue streams' and 'optimise the brand's hyper-scale agile outside-the-box thinking'.

Besides all that, though, there was no way I could go. Jase could look after Pip while I was at work, but he wasn't ready to take her for a whole weekend. He couldn't feed her, put her to sleep, put her to sleep again when she inevitably woke... I just couldn't do it. Nina was out of the question, obviously, and Ellie had her own life. And Mum... God, Pip would probably be making sugar-free cookies and doing the ironing by Sunday afternoon if I left her with Mum.

I couldn't do it.

But – how would I tell Meredith? When Lee had talked to me about coming back, it was all 'We'll fit in around you,' and 'We know Pip comes first.' But three weeks ago, when I'd asked to leave at 4 to take Pip to the doctor, Meredith asked me why the nanny couldn't take her. I explained that I didn't have a nanny.

'Oh,' she said. 'Well. If you need any recommendations–' She looked back down at her desk, where she'd been reading a copy of a rival supplement, *Weekend Style*. She gave the page her entire focus.

'Um, right. I'll let you know, thanks. But, um... about the doctor's appointment? That's fine, right?'

She didn't look up. 'Fine.'

Which really meant: not fine. So now I'd become a champion sneak. There was no hiding my late mornings, but I had persuaded Bea to organise meetings for Meredith if I needed to leave early in the afternoon. I couldn't sneak out of Melbourne, though. What was I going to do, dash to the airport while Meredith was window shopping at Emporium?

The rest of the day passed like most others – putting out small fires of Meredith's making, a run downstairs at lunch to grab a chicken salad (Meredith didn't like people eating carbs at their desks) and a cheeky trip to the salon round the corner for a quick eyebrow wax. 'Use a lot of concealer,' I warned. I didn't want Meredith – or Neil, for that matter – knowing.

I sought out Bea to ask her if Meredith had actually booked Melbourne yet. If she had, the chances of me getting out of it were a lot slimmer. I braced myself.

'Not yet,' she said, smiling slyly. 'I can hold her off if you need.' I loved the team here; we all knew Meredith was a little unhinged, and we all did our part to manage that, in small and subtle ways. Bea, like most assistants, did the majority of the heavy lifting. I once saw her hide all the scissors in the office after Meredith went nuts for a model with a pixie cut on a cover mock. We were all convinced she'd try to chop her hair off – or worse, someone else's.

'That would be great. Is she OK?'

Bea's eyes darted. 'In what way?'

'She said she was late today because she wasn't feeling well?'

'Oh,' said Bea, smiling. 'Yeah, she's fine. She just had an allergic reaction.'

'Oh really? To what?' I couldn't help myself. Part of me wanted to know what Meredith's kryptonite was.

Bea shrugged. 'A vitamin. She takes these really high-potency ones – I think maybe she gets them online, I don't think they're approved here – and sometimes she has a bad reaction.'

'Define "bad reaction".'

'She's fine, really. She went to the hospital and got a shot. She's OK now,' Bea said, smiling at me reassuringly. 'You know Meredith; she'd never miss a day of work.'

I nodded. Right. Of course not.

I closed the door to my office and set about applying some extra makeup. I'd convinced poor, perennially besieged Celeste to loan me some from the beauty cupboard, telling her I had an important meeting. Which was sort of true. A date was a meeting. Right? And I was going on a date. Sort of. I think.

I was just about to google 'contouring for dummies' when Jase called.

'George... did Pip eat anything purple this morning?'

'What?' I said, already on my feet. *Oh my god.* What was wrong with Pip?

'It's just... hold on,' he said, and I heard a faint *shh, shh* on the other end. 'She just threw up.'

'What happened?'

'I don't know. We were at the park and everything was

fine. We came home and I gave her the purée. That was about half an hour ago. I–'

'I'm on my way.'

*

Trying to get a urine sample from a small child – still in nappies – is like trying to catch a ball bearing dropped from a fair height: a little bit hilarious and a lot impossible.

Pip, not quite standing on her own yet, thought it was pretty funny to have her daddy holding her up as her mummy held a giant salad bowl under her, waiting for the much-anticipated wee. She kept kicking her legs so she'd buckle from the knees, landing in the salad bowl. Finally, she landed in the bowl and, shocked at the cold metal, let out a little wee. Jase and I looked at each other with glee – she'd done it! As I high-fived him, Pip kicked the bowl out from under her, knocking the wee onto the bathroom floor.

I slumped back on to the tiled wall. 'Shit,' I muttered. Jase laughed.

'It's alright. Let's just wait.' He flashed a sympathetic smile.

We were both Pip's parents, but this was the first time we'd really parented together. It was a relief to have someone here to help. A relief to know someone else cared this much about Pip.

The doctor had said it was most likely a UTI. I baulked at the adult-sounding illness, and barely listened as the doctor assured me it was fine. *Quite common at this age. Nothing to worry about. A small chance she'll need antibiotics.*

I'd cried a little as we left the doctor's, and Jase had put his arm around me. We must have just looked like any other family: harried, stressed mum; caring dad; baby girl dressed – inexplicably – in her pyjamas at 4 pm. Apparently Jase had 'run out of clean clothes' just six hours in. I didn't have the time or energy to question it.

'Hey, hey,' he said, 'what's up? She's going to be OK. The doctor said it was common.'

I strapped Pip into her pram and shoved the urine sample containers in the bottom, wiping away the tears. 'I know. It's just been... a big day.'

Jase rubbed my back and gave me a gentle push forward. 'Come on. Let's go home. Catch this wee.' He smiled cheekily. 'I'll make you a cup of tea.'

I shot him a grateful smile.

'Don't worry, George. It'll be fine.'

Two hours later, we finally had a wee sample and Jase ran it down to the doctor's just before they closed. For the first time, we fed Pip dinner together, laying out towels under her high chair to protect against future vomit (which – to my relief – did not come), bathed her together and tucked her in together. Apart from the purple vomit – the result of a particularly aggressively shaded tub of blueberry purée – Pip seemed absolutely fine.

Jase told me to sit on the couch as he ordered takeaway, put a load of washing on and poured me a glass of wine. It was only as he handed me the wine that I remembered what I was meant to be doing right now. *Shit*. Neil.

I grabbed my phone then realised I didn't actually have Neil's number. I sent him an email and hoped that, like any good employee of Meredith's, he checked his inbox at least every fifteen minutes outside of work hours.

Neil – so sorry. Pip is sick, had to
rush home. Was going to come.

I toyed with adding 'I swear', but it sounded a little 'methinks she doth protest too much', so I signed off and took a very large gulp of wine.

I fell back into the couch and didn't even offer to help as Jase picked up the books and toys and random clothes that littered the floor.

'Sorry,' he said, looking up. 'I don't know how it got so messy. It was perfect when you left this morning!'

I smiled. 'It's fine. That's what babies do.' I was tempted to add, *I'll clean it up later*, but I stopped myself. No: this time I would let Jase clean it up. I did manage to make myself useful and run for the door when the pizza delivery guy arrived, though. I'd started eating a slice before I'd even set the box down on the dinner table.

'Hungry?'

'Starved.' I explained Meredith's no-carbs-in-the-office rule.

'Riiiight,' said Jase, tucking into a slice. 'She sounds like a great boss, George. A real leader.'

I rolled my eyes. 'She's OK. A little highly strung, but she's good at what she does. She's kind of the best, actually, at what she does. It's a great opportunity – I'm learning a lot from her.'

Jase nodded dubiously. I checked my phone for the eighth or so time since I'd emailed Neil. Nothing.

'George, put your phone away,' Jase said, a little sternly now. 'Every time I see you lately, you're on that thing. You're worse than me!' He slid my phone to the other side of the table.

I nodded. I *was* always on my phone. I found myself 'making up' for 'leaving the office early' by checking my emails while I bathed Pip or fed her dinner. Part of the reason I was still breastfeeding was so I could scroll through my emails as I did so. I was aware – vaguely – that this was all a bit fucked up, but it also felt like I was smashing it. I could write my own productivity advice now.

'I had fun today,' said Jase. 'Really. Pip is a funny kid.'

I tilted my head, surprised. 'Oh?'

'Yeah. She's not like Thomas,' he said, referring to his nephew. 'He's boring. Pip's fun. She's got a good sense of humour.'

'Jase, you're not allowed to call kids boring.'

'What?' he asked defensively. 'Thomas *is* boring. Adults are boring and we're allowed to say so. Why not kids?'

'Because... because... I don't know,' I said, picking up the last slice and tearing it in half haphazardly, handing one part to Jase.

He shook his head and patted his stomach.

'Thank you,' I said.

'Nah, gotta keep the kay gees down,' he said.

'No, not for the pizza,' I said, savouring another cheesy bite. 'Well, not just for the pizza. For everything. I'm glad you were here today.'

He put his hand on mine and gave it a little squeeze. 'Me too. Thanks for forcing the pace.'

'What?'

'It's a cycling thing. What I meant was... thanks for making me a part of this. I didn't know how full-on it would be for you. Pip. The whole thing. I mean, I knew, but... I guess I didn't really *know*. But I'm glad you're making me a part of it. It's hard, but I like it. I really do, George. Thanks for giving me a kick up the bum.'

I smiled. 'Any time.'

Chapter 12

'George!' Meredith trumpeted as she came in to my office. She liked to announce herself, like bells on a cat.

'Hi, Meredith,' I said, and launched into my argument before she had a chance to ask. 'So, about Melbourne. I'm so sorry, but with Pip being sick, her doctor says it's best for her to stay home.'

I had worked from home the day before – I couldn't bear to put Pip in daycare when she wasn't well, even though she seemed fine. I hadn't been game to call Meredith, so I'd texted instead. No reply. An hour later, she'd emailed with a to-do list as long as Michael Fassbender's penis. Working from home really did mean working from home, as far as Meredith was concerned. Still, Pip and I went to the park, and I drank my coffee free from Meredith's harsh dairy-judging stare, and Pip slept for three hours after lunch. It was actually the best – and easiest – day I'd had in a long time, except for the fact that Meredith texted me 416 times.

Now she half rolled her heyes but held up her hands, as if in defeat. 'Of course! I understand.'

She understood? Since when?

'Oh. Right,' I said. Meredith was letting me get out of this? That was... uncharacteristic. 'Um, thank you. I can Skype in if you like, for the meetings? And you can bring me back a doggie bag from Attica!' I laughed, a little nervously, afraid of what Meredith might ask me to do in lieu of coming to Melbourne.

'A doggie bag?' Meredith squinted at me. Poor Meredith. Well, poor *rich* Meredith – she'd probably never had a doggie bag in her life. She'd probably never even been to a restaurant that offered them. Or had she? I still didn't know anything about Meredith outside of work. I knew she ate her dry veggie patty for lunch and guzzled so much sugar-free Red Bull I worried she'd have a guarana-induced heart attack. I knew now that she took vitamins strong enough to give her an allergic reaction. I knew she went to the gym for exactly twenty-eight minutes every morning, because she'd told us she 'did Kayla'. I wasn't cool enough to know what that meant, but Bea had explained. (Bea had also confided that Kendrick Lamar was not, in fact, Khloe Kardashian's husband and that I should stop referring to him as such.) She loved champagne. She never stopped working. She didn't use emojis, as a rule. And in classic eating disorder mode, I knew she loved talking about eating, just not the actual putting-food-in-mouth bit. But that was all I knew. Did she have a husband? Was she even on that team? I had no idea. She didn't tell me – or anyone, I presumed – anything about her life outside of work. Assuming she had one.

'Don't worry,' I said. 'Anyway, look, if there's anything I can do to make it easier, just let me know.'

Meredith nodded. 'No problem. It's going to be so much fun. I'm really looking forward to it.'

'Oh. Good,' I said, confused. Why was she being so chill about this?

'There might even be time to do Attica *and* Flower Drum, if we play our cards right. I'm a friend of a friend of Ben's, so... I'll pull some strings.'

I squinted. Had she not heard me?

'No, Meredith,' I said, shaking my head. 'I can't go. I can't go to Melbourne.'

She raised her eyebrows, straight-faced. 'Why?'

'Because –' I closed my eyes, trying to remember my vow to be more assertive. Being more assertive with Jase was easy, because I was constantly annoyed with him and I didn't care if he thought I was a nag. But with Meredith, I just couldn't. Although she was highly strung and probably medicated (who wasn't?), in her lucid moments, she was very good at her job. She was decisive and clever. She wasn't afraid of people not liking her. I admired her for all of those things.

And yes, I knew that, on the spectrum of crazy, she sat somewhere between Tom Cruise jumping on the couch and Katie Holmes marrying Tom Cruise. I knew that her expectations were too high, that she needed to be more flexible – with everyone on the team, not just me. But there was something in me that wanted her to think I was tough enough for her. That I could be as dedicated as she was. That I was worth having on the team. *I* wanted her to think I could have a baby and a career. Because I knew there was a part of me that didn't quite believe it either. It was precisely the reason why I needed to grow a pair and be honest with Meredith. It was the only way I could ever see this working. So I drew a breath and went for it. 'Because of Pip. She's sick. She can't go. And I can't be away from her for a whole weekend. She's too young.'

Meredith frowned. Exactly zero lines appeared on her forehead. 'Oh. I see. What about her father?'

I shook my head. 'We're not together. He hasn't spent all that much time with Pip. I wouldn't feel comfortable –'

'The nanny?'

'No. There's no nanny, remember?'

She rolled her eyes. 'Right, right. Well, you'd better bring her then.'

'No, Meredith,' I said. Was she listening? 'I can't. Pip is sick. She's on antibiotics. Her doctor said she needs to stay home, get some rest. Melbourne would be too disruptive.'

She stared at me, a cold glint in her eyes now. 'These

are very important meetings, Georgina. I would have thought you'd want to be part of them.'

I took a measured breath. 'I do. But right now my priority has to be Pip. She's not feeling well and I need to be here. Like I said, I can Skype in, or prepare something in advance for you to take with you. I'm sure you understand, Meredith,' I added, entirely sure she did not.

She tilted her head slightly, pursing her lips. 'I'm disappointed, George. I really went in to bat for you. You know, Richie was very hesitant when he heard your idea for a column, but I persuaded him to give you a go.'

'Oh... but you told me he loved it.'

Meredith's eyes darted. 'Well, he does, now, but it took some convincing. I mean – motherhood? And work? Not exactly Pulitzer Prize–winning stuff, is it?'

In another life, I might have stood up for myself. But instead I found myself, bizarrely, apologising to Meredith.

'Look, I'm so sorry, Meredith, but I really can't come. Thank you for convincing Richie to take on my column, I really appreciate it. But right now, I really just can't do this.'

'Can't, or won't?'

'Can't.'

She narrowed her eyes at me. 'You're onto a good thing here, George. But things can change. So I'd suggest you figure out a way to get to Melbourne.'

She turned and walked out of the office, barking, 'And bring a babysitter. Attica doesn't have high chairs!'

*

'Lucas! Lucas! Get down from there. Right. I'm counting! One. Two. Lucas! Lucas, I mean it. If you aren't down from there in... one... two–'

I'd only been gone for three minutes – max – but somehow, Lucas had managed to hoist himself onto the baggage carousel and was now riding atop a rather large piece of luggage.

He whooped with delight as he rode the bag around the carousel. Ellie's face was tomato red – a mixture of rage and embarrassment – as she yelled at him to get down.

'Hey! Hey, calm down,' I said, a coffee in each hand and Pip strapped to my chest. Pip looked up at me and cooed. She was so close to talking, I was sure of it. Every day, she added a new sound to her onomatopoeic vocabulary. I couldn't wait for her first word. Maybe once she started to talk, it would be easier to figure her out. Right?

It had been quite a morning. Our flight was delayed, which meant that Pip missed her nap. Not for lack of trying, though – I strapped her to my chest and made a valiant attempt to bounce her to sleep. But every time I felt her little head press closer to my chest, ready to make the leap from awake to asleep, we'd be interrupted by, 'Mrs Kylie Barnes. I repeat: Mrs Kylie Barnes. Please make your way to Gate 34. Your flight is boarding.' And then, 'Mrs Kylie Barnes. I repeat: Mrs Kylie Barnes. Please make your way to Gate 34. Your flight is about to close.' And then, 'Final boarding call for Flight 67A to Cairns. Mrs Kylie Barnes, paging Mrs Kylie Barnes.' Every time we heard Mrs Kylie Bloody Barnes's name, Pip's head jolted back, eyes wide open yet again. I must have looked like I was out of my mind: bouncing and patting the baby, giving her a peaceful *shh* every now and then, and then wringing my hands and silently mouthing, 'FUCK OFF!' every time Mrs Kylie Barnes was called to her gate.

The doctor had reluctantly told me it was OK for Pip to fly, after checking her ears for possible infection about sixteen times.

'Are you sure it's absolutely necessary to go on this trip?' she'd asked, her face full of concern.

No. No it is not.

'Yes, it is.' The truth was, I was too afraid of the alternative. Not being fired (although that would be bad, especially now that Nina had moved out and I relied on my pay cheque more than ever). No, the worst alternative was Meredith being angry with me and me having to stick around to live with the consequences.

On the flight, Ellie was adamant that Lucas was not allowed to watch television – apparently his teacher still held grave concerns for his intellectual development. So instead of letting Lucas zone out to *Thomas the Tank Engine*, he tore around the plane like a puppy chasing a ball, except without all the cuteness. Without *any* of the cuteness. I loved Lucas, but after watching him run from one end of the plane to the other for forty-five minutes, I was ready to throw him in the overhead cabin with my luggage. And a TV, to shut him up.

'What can I get for you?' the flight attendant asked, leaning over Ellie and glaring at her. I shot her a look that I hoped said something along the lines of, 'I'm so sorry this unruly child is so clearly ruining your day. Please rest assured I don't know his mother very well. Now, would you please get me a gin and tonic?'

'Gin and tonic, please.' I smiled so hard I felt my cheeks touch my eyelids.

She cleared her throat and raised her voice. 'Ma'am, under government regulations, we are prohibited from selling alcohol before 11 am.'

'Oh.' I felt my smile deflate as I flinched, sure the whole plane had heard. 'Thanks anyway.'

At least now Ellie wasn't the worst mother on the plane.

Finally, just as we touched down at Tullamarine, Pip drifted off to sleep. I couldn't believe it. I'd bounced her for an hour at Sydney! We'd been on the plane for *another* hour! And *now* she decided to go to sleep? Now? Now, when I needed to jostle for our bags and get a taxi and attempt to strap her into the car seat, which I knew she would hate as much as being strapped into the pram? Now? It was going to be a long day.

Once we were inside the terminal, Ellie announced she needed a coffee, and I started rushing away before she'd even finished her sentence.

'I'll go!' I called, over my shoulder. 'You wait for the bags. Byeeee!'

How would I get through the whole weekend if I couldn't handle TV-free Lucas for an hour? I pushed that thought aside and ordered the biggest, strongest coffees on offer, then went back to find Ellie, who was now screaming at Lucas to get off the baggage carousel before he got squashed by a fake Louis Vuitton.

'Get down, Lucas!' she shouted, stamping her foot like, well... like Lucas. Oh my god. What if Meredith saw this? She'd taken a later flight (business class had been full on my flight; sadly, it was not filled with me) and because of our delay, I was terrified she'd see us at the airport. I'd told her I had found a babysitter. I hadn't told her it was Ellie, and that she was bringing her four-year-old to stay at Crown Towers with us. I had my fingers – and toes, and legs – crossed that we could avoid running into each other. I needed to keep my two lives – work and Pip – as separate as I possibly could. I didn't want Meredith seeing the disarray that was my home life.

'Shh! You're making a scene, Ellie! Shh!'

'George, he's on top of the carousel! It's going to start moving. I need to get him down. Help me!' She stared at me in disbelief and I reluctantly put the coffees down.

'Lucas!' I called out. He looked down at me.

'Aunty Gawgee! Look at me! I'm flying! I'm the aeroplane now! *Flying high, in the sky... fly and fly and fly and fly,*' he sang, a smile breaking across his little face. If it wasn't so dangerous, it'd be darn cute.

'Oh my god,' Ellie said, burying her face in her hands.

I patted her shoulder. 'Come on, it'll be fine. Calm down.'

She lifted her head. 'It's not that. It's that song – flying high, in the sky–' she shook her head '– it's from *Peppa Pig*. My child is addicted to television. What have I done? He's–' she lowered her voice. 'He's an idiot!'

'Ellie. Enough. Your kid is not an idiot. Would an idiot know how to sneak past his mum and climb up on the baggage carousel so she couldn't get to him? Nope. Just get up there and get him, alright?'

Ellie shook her head tersely. 'I can't. He'll do a runner. He does this all the time at the park – climbs up to the highest thing and then when I go up to get him, he just runs away. It's really dangerous. The only person he'll come down for is Simon.'

'Well that's going to be a problem, isn't it? We accidentally left Simon in Sydney,' I deadpanned.

Ellie buried her head in her hands. She may have calmed down in general, but Ellie still had a penchant for overreaction in the extreme.

'Ellie, I will go find someone who works here – a man, I guess – to get him down. Stop panicking.' I lowered my gaze. 'And keep your voice down.'

Ellie crossed her arms and nodded. 'Fine. Thank you.'

As I went in search of someone to hoist Lucas down, I raced over the weekend's run sheet. Tonight, there was dinner with the agency bosses – at the much-anticipated Attica, of course. Tomorrow morning, for some reason, Meredith and I were being 'treated' to massages by the client and then we had the upfront session with them. I was prepped for the upfronts. I'd used all of Pip's feeds this week to strategise for the year ahead, sitting with my baby tucked into one arm and my iPad in the other, figuring out exactly what to say. Where would we take *The Weekend*? How could the client come on board? What could we offer that was different? You know – all that bullshit suits love.

Tomorrow night there'd be another dinner, and then on Sunday, Ellie and I were taking the kids to see The Wiggles at Fed Square. Lucas was beside himself with excitement, even though he'd already seen them seven times. Still, as he had told me in all earnestness, he'd never seen them in *Melbourne*.

Why wasn't there anyone working here? I could see people in cafe uniforms, people who worked at car rental places, Sportsgirl assistants. But nobody who actually, you know, worked at the airport. Maybe *nobody* works at airports anymore, I thought, through my sleep-deprived fog. Maybe they're like bins at train stations; one more thing the terrorists have taken away from us.

As I was walking back to Ellie, determined that we could pull Lucas down ourselves, I heard someone bark my name. Only one person barked my name.

I spun around.

'Hi, Meredith,' I said, flashing the biggest smile I could muster. But I needn't have bothered; she wasn't looking at me.

'Who's this?' she asked, as if she'd genuinely forgotten I had a daughter.

Pip cooed.

'Uh, this is... this is Pip. My baby,' I said, unnerved. Did Meredith have amnesia? Did I? Was she Drew Barrymore in *50 First Dates*? I was sure – truly, truly sure – that I had told her about Pip. Multiple times. And yet, every time Pip came up in conversation, it was as if Meredith had never before heard her name. What was going on? Was I crazy? Or was Meredith?

'Oh. Yes,' she said, nodding.

'How was your flight?' I asked.

She grimaced. 'Terrible. The vegetarian option was a sandwich. I mean, what is this, 1998?' She rolled her eyes and sighed. 'That's what I get for flying with Qantas.' She spat the name out, as if she'd flown 900 kilometres on a flea-ridden pigeon. One who'd offered her carbs.

'Mmm.' I nodded, trying to seem sympathetic. We had flown Jetstar. *We didn't get free water, much less free sandwiches.*

'Weren't you bringing a babysitter?' Meredith asked pointedly. She scanned the scene behind me.

I nodded. 'Yeah, I did. She's just, um... she's getting the bags.'

Meredith gave me the knowing nod of someone who was very familiar with the nuances of using hired help. I tried to do the same.

'Looking forward to tonight? We'll have the tasting menu. It goes for about five hours.' Meredith beamed and prattled on about something called pickled uni, which *will absolutely change your life*, she promised. But all I could think was: five hours. That really meant seven hours, minimum. Probably more like eight. I did the calculations: if we got to the hotel within the hour, I could feed Pip and then express, and maybe express again before her next feed. I would have to express again before dinner anyway, so my boobs wouldn't leak onto the navy silk dress Celeste had helped me borrow from a PR. Would that be enough milk for Pip? She nursed almost exclusively at night now, sometimes three or four times. I would really have to pace myself, wine-wise, at dinner, so I could nurse her when I got home. No more than two glasses. OK, three.

'Hello! Earth to George!' Meredith swayed her head from side to side as she sang the last three words. Realising I'd been staring into space, I looked back to her. She pointed at my chest. Where, it would appear, Pip had thrown up. Oh dear. Must stop bouncing.

'Uh, right. Gosh, sorry. Pip, are you OK?' I peered around the side of her head to see her face. Apart from a string of vestigial vom, she seemed fine. Better out than in.

I reached for the packet of wet wipes in my bag but couldn't find any. I had definitely packed them this morning, in readiness for the flight. Hadn't I?

I felt frantic. No wipes. I had never wanted to be this mum – this disorganised, flustered, out-of-her-depth mum. Meredith, a frozen smile plastered on her face, handed me a Missoni tissue (yes, they make them).

'Thanks,' I said, taking the tissue and wiping the chuck from the Ergo. There wasn't much – it was hardly a Code V. It was a waste of a $12 tissue.

Meredith seemed to be at a loss for words. 'Well,' she said, that smile still plastered to her face.

'Uh, right. We'd best be off. I'll see you tonight, at dinner?'

I smiled hopefully at Meredith. *Please don't make me do anything before dinner. Please don't make me do anything before dinner.*

She nodded, looking relieved. 'Yes. Meet me for a drink at the hotel bar and we'll get an Uber together.' It wasn't a suggestion.

I nodded. Phew. I had half-expected Meredith to spring a surprise meeting on me. Thank god. Maybe this weekend wouldn't be so bad.

*

By the time I returned to the hotel room later that night, my boobs were two concrete mounds. I could barely take my bra off, they were so swollen.

'Hi!' Ellie whispered as I cracked the door open. 'They're asleep! Shh!'

I nodded. It was 1 am. I had sort of figured the four-year-old and the nine-month-old would be asleep.

'How'd it go?' I asked.

'Good, good. They were fine. Lucas was quite sweet, actually, he helped me with Pip's bottle and patted her to sleep.'

'Oh, that's so cute. He's a good kid. Apart from the whole climbing on the baggage carousel thing.'

While I'd been busy cleaning up vomit with Meredith's Italian tissue, Ellie had eventually hailed an airport staffer who thought the whole thing hilarious and valiantly hoisted himself up to snatch Lucas down. He'd said something about how Lucas was his 'spirit animal' as he sauntered off, chuckling to himself.

Ellie nodded.

'You OK?' I asked. She looked a little wistful.

'Mmm,' she said, nodding. 'I'm fine. It was nice having the two of them. They're good together. Pip is such an easy baby.'

I stared at her. Pip? My Pip? The Pip who had barely

211

stopped screaming since she exited my vagina nine months ago?

'Are you serious?'

'Yeah, she was fine. I gave her a bottle, read her a book and she went straight to sleep. Haven't heard a peep from her since.'

I lowered my gaze, feeling my jaw drop a little. 'What time did she go to sleep?'

'7.30.'

'She's been asleep this whole time?'

Ellie nodded. 'Why are you so surprised?'

I laughed. 'Um, because she has never once done that for me. Wow. Super mum.'

Another ten points to Ellie, who wasn't just a good mum – now she was a better mum to my own kid than I was.

Ellie shot me a wry smile. 'Kids are like that. Lucas always went to sleep easier with Simon than he did with me. He knows all my buttons and exactly how to push them. Pip's probably exactly the same with you. Don't worry about it.'

I felt myself slump against the chair.

'How was dinner?'

I rolled my eyes. 'It was... fine,' I said, sighing. Like a good little Meredith acolyte, I'd waited for her outside the hotel bar until I realised she was inside and had already polished off half a bottle of Veuve while banging out emails on her iPad.

'Where have you been?' she said, pouring me a glass.

'Oh, I was waiting outside.'

She laughed. 'Oh, George,' she'd said, lightly admonishing me the way she might a three-year-old who wanted to eat Play-Doh for dinner.

The dinner was a blur of bursting boobs (mine), drunken antics (Meredith's) and a hand that lingered on my back a little too long for my liking (one of the ad execs, Jimmy's). Between courses, I rushed to the disabled toilet to relieve my engorged boobs, sure Meredith would interrogate me when I reappeared. Luckily, she was about seven sheets to the wind and could barely locate me at the table, let alone ask where I kept disappearing to.

When we were finally done with dinner, I stuck my arm out for a taxi as the others rolled out of the restaurant ready to head to the next party destination. 'Come onnnnnnn, George!' Meredith squealed as a taxi neared. 'We're all going to Peachy. Let's go! Let's go, let's go, let's go!' The five ad guys tumbled along after her as she walked towards the bar. I saw my chance and hopped straight in the waiting cab, calling out the window, 'Bye! See you tomorrow!'

In another life, I would have relished dinners like this. I would have been leading the charge, ordering the wine, suggesting dishes and frog-marching everyone to the bar afterwards. Now, it just exhausted me. I didn't want to make small talk with these ad guys, whose job seemed to consist entirely of going out to lunch and dinner and checking their phone the whole time. I didn't want to 'push' or 'live' the brand. Couldn't I just do my work?

'You don't seem to be having a great time there,' Ellie ventured.

I sighed. 'Yeah, it's... all a bit much sometimes,' I said. 'I like the work. I want to work. But Meredith can be kind of... full-on. Like, Mad Max full-on. No. Like, Furiosa full-on. You know?'

Ellie nodded slowly.

'Did you talk to her about being more flexible? Letting you work from home? Giving you some time with Pip during the week?'

I laughed. 'Yeah, I did. And she thought it was pretty funny.'

'What do you mean?'

'I mean, for Meredith, "flexible working arrangements" are a laugh. A joke. No self-respecting employee would actually invoke them, not if she wants to keep her job. Not if she wants to get ahead.'

'Mmm.' Ellie paused. 'But do you? Do you want to get ahead?'

'Of course.'

Ellie studied me. 'I guess I just don't understand why you'd want to work for this woman if she doesn't understand that Pip is your priority.'

I sighed. 'Ellie, this is my dream job. Meredith's not perfect – but nobody is. Remember Meg?' Meg, my old boss, was one of those managers who did believe in leaving on time and the occasional day from home – but she'd also practically fired me. So she wasn't exactly Employer of the Year in my books either. 'Anyway, like I told you before, I'm getting my own column. In the biggest newspaper in the country. It's a pretty big deal. Meredith gunned for me, she's looking out for me.'

Ellie opened her mouth, but then shut it again, swallowing and looking down.

'OK.' She changed the subject. 'And what about Nina? She told me she's moving her stuff out this weekend.'

I shrugged. 'Yeah, I thought it would be a good time for her to pack up. You know, while Pip and I aren't there.'

I didn't want to be there while Nina packed up her things.

'She was pretty upset when I spoke to her.'

I said nothing, just sat back in the plush hotel armchair.

'She's not moving in with Jed, you know.'

This got my attention.

'Really?'

'Yeah. She's getting her own place. Jed lives with three other guys. Nina says the house permanently smells like two-minute noodles and used boxer shorts.'

'Where's she moving to?'

'Potts Point.'

It was the Single Person Capital of Sydney. Nina would be happy there. There were approximately three Bikram yoga centres per capita.

'Cool. Well, that's great.' It wasn't great, not really. I pictured Nina setting up house on her own, sitting down at night on her own, going to bed on her own, and felt a pummel to the stomach. But then, I reminded myself, that's what I'd been doing these past few months. Now Nina would understand how lonely I was.

Ellie shot me a doleful smile. 'Time for bed. Big day for you tomorrow.'

I nodded.

Chapter 13

I double-checked the time. Eight. Eight? How could it be eight o'clock? I couldn't remember the last time I'd woken up at 8 am.

Pip. She'd never slept past 6.30. Something must be wrong.

But – miraculously – it wasn't. Pip was sitting up in her travel cot, fingering the mesh sides and gurgling away happily. She smiled up at me, oblivious to my puzzled expression.

I picked her up and she went, as was her custom, straight to the boob. I grabbed the room-service menu and the phone.

A few minutes later, eggs Benedict and coffee on the way, I checked my phone. Sixteen new messages. I sighed. One was from Ellie, telling me that she and Lucas had gone to find a cafe for breakfast at 7 am (secretly, I fist-bumped myself that *my* baby had slept longer than Lucas, before remembering that Ellie had been the one to successfully put Pip to bed last night). The rest were from Meredith: drunken early-morning missives about how I was missing out on THE BEST NIGHT EVERRRRRR, a few blurry pics, and finally a text from half an hour ago asking me to meet her in the lobby ASAP PLEASE GEORGE WE HAVE A LOT TO DISCUSS BEFORE THE UPFRONT SESSION THIS AFTERNOON.

I picked up the phone and cancelled my eggs.

*

When Pip and I got downstairs, Meredith was sipping on green tea, dressed in head-to-toe white, like she was in a laundry commercial. She did not look like someone who'd been sending bathroom selfies at 4 am. How did she do it?

'Morning, Meredith,' I said, sitting down. She looked up from her laptop but didn't smile.

'Hello,' she said crisply.

'So, how was last night? Looked like you were having fun.' Strapped in the Ergo, Pip flung her arms around like the worst sign-language translator ever.

'Yes, it was great. Lovely group they are,' she said.

I nodded. 'Yeah, it looked fun. Gosh, I can't believe how well you've pulled up today. You look amazing.'

She smiled tightly. 'Well, I know my limits.' The sentence was pointed like a knife. Was she talking about me? Was I pushing my limits by bringing Pip downstairs to plan for the planning meeting? Was she serious?

I swallowed and turned to a hovering waiter. 'Can I have a flat white please? Strong?' Screw the decaf. I turned to Meredith. 'So, uh... what do we need to plan?'

'Mmm?'

'You asked me to come down and plan for the upfront meeting?'

Meredith looked up, recognition dawning in her expression. 'Oh. Yes, of course. Listen, I think you need some guidance with the presentation.'

'Oh?'

'Mmm. I want to go over it before we present this afternoon.'

'But... I've done the presentation before. You've heard it.'

'Yes. But these are very important clients, George. You can't fuck this up.'

I winced. 'Have I been fucking it up?'

She looked – momentarily – remorseful. 'Oh. Well, not

217

exactly fucking it up. It's just that you need to be... funnier. You're so funny, George, but you don't let the advertisers see it. And they love that stuff. So be funny.'

The waiter placed the coffee in front of me. I inhaled it.

'Right, funny. OK.' I breathed out, digesting the feedback. I could be funny. Couldn't I? I tried to remember a time I'd ever been intentionally funny in front of Meredith; most of the time she just laughed at me when I said things that didn't compute in her privileged existence. Like when I told her that I took the bus to work or brought my lunch from home.

'And don't do that thing where you pause between sentences.'

'Hmm?'

'Keep going.' She made a fist and punched the air. 'People like it when you just get on with things. It doesn't have to be so dramatic, you know?'

'OK,' I said, trying to digest this 'guidance'. 'So, funnier and with less pauses?'

'Exactly! But not *too* funny. Just funny enough. I mean, it's business. We do need to be serious.'

Now I was confused. 'So... funny but also serious?'

She smiled. 'Yes.' She looked down at her laptop again, as if she'd explained everything perfectly. 'And don't forget: no pauses.'

'Right.'

'And use your hands more, OK? To illustrate the point.'

'What point?'

'Any point,' she said, her tone getting more dismissive. 'All the points.'

'Uh... OK. So... use my hands more, no pauses, funny but serious. Right. Uh, look, could you give me some examples?'

Meredith sighed deeply. 'Of what?'

'Of being funny but serious.'

She rolled her eyes. 'Oh my god, George. If I'd known you wouldn't be able to handle this, I would have invited someone else.'

I raised an eyebrow. Invited? I seemed to remember being forced to come.

'Um, OK. So... right. Funny but serious. Funny but serious.'

Meredith raised a glance at me, her head still bent over her laptop. 'Like Obama.'

'Huh?'

She huffed dramatically and gave me her full attention.

'Like. Obama.'

'*Barack* Obama?' She wanted me to speak like the leader of the free world. The most impressive living orator known to man. 'You want me to present the strategy... like Barack Obama?'

She nodded slowly, as if she'd told me to clap my hands and I couldn't quite work out how to do it. 'Yes. Can you handle that?'

'Um. I don't know. I mean... that's a pretty big ask.'

Pip started cooing at me and reflexively, I stood to bounce her. Maybe she'd go to sleep and I could go upstairs to my room to google 'how to speak like Obama'. Because at that moment, I had no idea what Meredith really wanted.

I bounced away, trying to figure it out. Maybe Obama had a good aura? Pip continued to coo, getting louder and louder. I remembered my promise to be more assertive.

'Meredith?' I ventured. 'I think I'm just going to do the speech the way I've been doing it. It's working. The other firms loved it; they all bought ads. I think it might confuse me to try and think about how someone else would do it, you know? So I'll do it my way.'

'No,' she said, her voice clipped. 'Just do it my way.'

I breathed out slowly, still bouncing, bouncing, bouncing.

What was the best way to say, 'But your way sounds weird and confusing and I don't understand what you're asking me to do, and honestly it just sounds like you want to have one over me' without losing my job I wondered?

I opened my mouth, but before I could speak Meredith spat out, 'For god's sake, stop *bouncing*.' She slammed her laptop shut.

I stopped bouncing. I felt my heartbeat somewhere around my soft palate.

'Meredith, the thing is... the upfronts are in three hours. We have to do the massage thing beforehand. I just feel like it's going to make me really nervous to try to do something I'm not comfortable with, which is totally counter-intuitive, right? I just don't know how to do it, Meredith, other than by being myself.'

She let out a little sniff, then said, for what must have been the thousandth time, 'You'll figure it out.'

*

It's an odd thing to listen to a sermon on foreign policy and the mistakes of the Iraq War as you're being pummelled into relaxed submission by an excellent Swedish masseur. But there I was, listening to the audiobook of *The Audacity of Hope* during my massage, trying to somehow glean Obama's oratorical magic by... what? Osmosis?

Even stranger still, Meredith was on the massage table next to mine. Somehow we'd ended up in a couple's massage room, and when the receptionist asked if it would still be OK, once she'd established we were not, in fact, a couple, Meredith had breezily insisted it'd be fine.

So there I was, naked but for a flimsy paper g-string, headphones in, listening to the smoothest voice in the Western world make a case for universal health care as Meredith lay next to me, similarly near-naked and emitting the occasional, disturbing 'mmm' loud enough to momentarily drown out Barack. It was about as relaxing as a bath with an alligator.

'Well!' she exclaimed, visibly excited as we got back to the change-room. 'Wasn't that amazing? Gosh, I just feel so calm. Wasn't it great?' She immediately plunged her hand into her bag and reached for her phone, tapping away at it before she'd so much as put her undies back on.

'Mmm, yeah it was... good.' It wasn't good. Childbirth

aside, it had been the single weirdest experience I'd had without my clothes on.

'Right! On to the meeting! I'm so excited! Aren't you? You're really going to kill it, Gigi. You'll smash it out of the park.'

Gigi? That was new. I squinted at her as I hooked my bra. Was she on something? Half the time, Meredith loved me, couldn't get enough. The other half, she could barely stand to look at me. What was going on? And how the hell could I get her to stop calling me bloody Gigi?

'Uh, thanks. I listened to one of Obama's books while we were in there, so I hope I'll, uh, sound a bit more like him. We'll see.'

She dropped her towel and, now completely naked, put a hand on my shoulder and looked me in the eye earnestly. 'You'll be amazing, Gigi. Don't worry at all.'

Maintain eye contact, maintain eye contact, maintain eye contact. Do not look down.

'Um, OK. Thank you.' I turned around, ostensibly to put the rest of my clothes back on, but really to avoid being confronted by Meredith's naked, entirely hairless body (OK, I looked down a tiny bit). 'Because before... you seemed to... well, you didn't seem to have a lot of faith in me.'

She gasped. I turned around. 'No! Don't be silly. Of course I do. That's why I got you on board. You're a great editor. I've told you that before, Gigi. Come on – I don't have to keep coddling you, do I?'

'No, it's not–'

'Good,' she said, grinning. 'I knew you were a tough one. And I know you'll knock their socks off.'

'Oh. OK.'

'Just be yourself.'

So... don't be Obama?

'Meredith–' I shoved my paper undies in the waste basket. 'Yes?'

'I guess... Can I ask you something?'

221

She furrowed her brow. 'Of course,' she said, not bothering to hide her annoyance. 'What?'

'Well... when it's just you and I, you're fine. You're great, actually!' I tried to compliment-sandwich it. 'But when there's someone else with us – anyone: even, like, my baby – you get a bit, er, funny. You're a bit –' *of a bitch?* '– short-tempered.'

She stared at me. 'Oh. Well.' Meredith's face fell so fast, it practically left skidmarks.

I backtracked, fast. 'It's just hard to know where I stand, I suppose.' Although right now I knew exactly where I stood: three feet away from my boss. Who was in her birthday suit.

'And, uh, I want to do a good job. You know?'

Meredith nodded. 'Mmm. You know, George, I feel the same way about you sometimes. Sometimes I feel like we're really beginning to understand each other, and that you're finally listening to me when I tell you what the magazine needs. And then you have a sick day. Or you sneak out of the office early.' Noting the alarm on my face, Meredith nodded. 'Yes, I've noticed. I also notice when you ignore my emails, and when your eyes glaze over during stand-up. And I make some allowances for you. But I'm not your mother. I'm not here to tell you what a good girl you are, or to give you a cuddle when you're not feeling well. I hired you to do a job. I believe you can do that job. Do you?'

I pulled my towel a little tighter around me and cleared my throat.

'Yes. Of course.'

'Good,' she said, brightening. 'Now let's go get a drink.'

*

Here's what it's like to have a hangover when you have a baby: it's shit. It's totally shit.

Mainly it's shit because you remember what it was like to have a hangover as a normal person, in your old, pre-baby life. You remember sleeping in until 11 am and only really waking up because your stomach was telling you it was time to seek out fried foods and possibly hair of the dog. You remember eating a bag of potato chips on the couch because you were too lazy to go get McDonald's, your heart's true desire. You remember scrolling through your phone, crossing your fingers in the hope that you didn't text your ex or post a weird pic of half of your gurning face to Instagram. You remember the relief at finding you hadn't... or the desperate shame of finding you had. Mostly you remember doing nothing at all but riding it out, waiting for your next junk food fix or nap, whichever came first.

When you're hungover and you have a baby – well, you're not really hungover at all. Hungover is too understated a word. You're totally and completely and utterly fucked, that's what you are.

And if you have to take that baby to an outdoor concert while you're hungover? The kind of outdoor concert that is for children and where alcohol is not served, when all you want is a cold Corona to wipe the previous night away? Oh dear. You, madame, are *royally* fucked.

'I think I'm going to throw up,' I said, to nobody in particular. Ellie shot me a look.

'Be quiet. You're scaring Lucas.'

I rolled my eyes. 'No, I'm not. He's watching his girlfriend.'

It was true: Lucas was in love with Emma Wiggle. On our way here, as I attempted to keep my head upright, Lucas went on at length about how, when he and Emma got married, they'd live in the Wiggle House and walk Wags and Henry every night. I asked how they would walk Henry, being an octopus and all. He raised his eyebrows and said, 'He's got eight legs, Aunty Gawgee. I think he can *walk*.'

'No, really, I think I am. Do you have a bag or something?'

Ellie huffed in disgust but rummaged around in her bag and pulled out a spare nappy bag. 'Here. What did you do last night? For god's sake, you reek. Did you have a shower?'

'Yes! Of course. And... I honestly don't remember. There were shots of Patron involved.'

'I don't even know what that is,' Ellie said, eyes squarely on Simon Wiggle, like every other female in the place.

'Keep it that way,' I said.

The night was a blur. After the post-massage pep talk, Meredith whisked me to the nearest bar, where she promptly ordered a bottle of Veuve.

'I'll just have one glass,' I warned Meredith. I had expressed that morning but I knew there was a chance I'd need to feed Pip later. That, and I would be presenting to a very important group of clients in just over sixty minutes.

She rolled her eyes. 'We don't have to drink all of it, George. Don't be such a prude.'

But we did drink all of it. So by the time we got back to the hotel conference room, I was, on the drunk scale, somewhere between flirtatiously giggly and horrifyingly lecherous. Not ideal. Meredith, however, seemed completely sober, even though she'd had three glasses to my two.

I tried my best to speak like Obama. And also to speak like myself. And to use my hands more. And to pause less. And to be serious. But also funny. The result was that everyone thought I was sending them up, making fun of their stuffy corporate world, with my speech that was simultaneously imploring, speedy and full of Italian-nonna-style hand gestures. Deep down, I think they had no idea what was really going on, so they decided to assume it was funny. I breathed a deep sigh of relief in front of them all when it was over.

'Right!' said Guy, the lead on the team. 'Off to the bar!'

I widened my eyes in surprise as everyone began to shuffle the presentation notes I'd given them and get out of their chairs. *It's over?*

Meredith motioned for me to move.

'Is it over?' I whispered. She frowned.

'Of course it's over. You did great. Well done. Let's go.'

'But... what about the rest of it? The notes? The numbers we wanted to go over? The new cover mocks?'

Meredith shrugged. 'They're sold, George. Don't question it. Now, we drink.'

So off to the bar we went. First the hotel bar, and then to the bar at the restaurant we were eating at that night. Then to the restaurant itself, where we wine-matched with our degustation, and then to the bar next to the restaurant. Then we found a club. I hadn't drunk so much since my first year at uni.

At the hotel bar, I'd gently inquired as to whether my presence was really needed. After all, it seemed to be a giant piss-up, not actual work. The media buyers had barely listened to my presentation; the gig seemed to consist entirely of getting shit-faced together, after which they'd give us ad money. They didn't care about the direction of the magazine or who we'd put on the cover or the campaigns I'd painstakingly orchestrated. They didn't even really care about their own brands, the companies they were booking ads for. There didn't seem to be any discernible reason I had to come to Melbourne to meet with these guys; a Skype date with a goon bag would have done the trick.

All I really wanted was to go upstairs and cuddle with Pip. Have our bath together, feed her and tuck her in. Watch her little chest heave gently up and down as she slept. I was exhausted. I needed to get out of my heels and drink a very strong cup of Earl Grey and lie down in one place for a decent amount of time. But more than being exhausted, I missed Pip. For the first time in my life, I didn't want to be out drinking on a Saturday night. I wanted to be with her.

I tapped Meredith on the shoulder but she didn't notice. She was busy regaling three of the guys with the hilarious story of how she'd discovered she was, clinically speaking, a psychopath. I had heard this one before.

'So the researcher says to me, you're at your mother's funeral. Sad, right?' The men nodded, entranced. Meredith had a particular power over men. She was tall and striking, but there was something more to it than that. I think they sensed her craziness, and I think they translated that into something like 'absolute demon in the sack'.

She went on. 'But you meet a man – you've never met him before – and right there, at the funeral, you fall in love. You with me?' More nodding. 'OK, so you fall in love with this guy, he's your perfect match, whatever. But you forget to get his number! You don't even know his name! You have no way of contacting him.' Meredith, ever the storyteller, gave herself a little slap on the forehead for dramatic effect. 'Two days later, you kill your sister. Why?'

The men stared at her, dumbfounded. 'Um–' one began, not sure where to start.

The other two furrowed their brows, as if deep in thought. Probably thinking how weird it was to be getting drunk with a business contact who'd posited a riddle about killing her sister.

'Can you think of why I might do that?' Meredith asked, a sly grin making her look even more sinister than usual. 'Why would I kill her?'

'Because... you're so upset that you'll never see this guy again.'

Meredith shook her head, her eyes shiny with the knowledge she held.

'Because –' another guy took a stab, 'he was your sister's husband.'

'No! Remember, you don't know him!'

The guys, one by one, began to shrug and shake their heads.

'Give up?' she asked. They nodded.

'Because you wanted to see if he'd come to *her* funeral!'

Like ceramic clowns at the Easter Show, the men all formed perfect Os with their mouths. But instead of shaking their heads, they began to slowly nod, the riddle now making sense.

'And I got it!' said Meredith, practically shimmering with

226

glee. 'I knew the answer! Isn't that amazing? Less than 2 per cent of people get it right.'

And they all went on to use their victims' skin as cling wrap, I wanted to add.

The guys laughed nervously and she tottered away, keen as ever for another drink.

'Meredith,' I asked, tapping her on the shoulder as she leaned over the bar to order more champagne. 'I think I'm going to call it a night.' It was 4 pm. We were four bottles in.

She drew her head back in surprise, and for the first time I saw the tiniest hint of body fat, the vague development of a double chin. The chub looked so out of place on her otherwise fat-free body. If Meredith were a yoghurt, she'd be Frûche.

'You want to leave?' She didn't look angry, just surprised. Maybe I'd be able to get out of this.

I nodded. 'Yeah, I think I've probably had enough to drink. I'm not exactly match fit, you know? Pip's only nine months, I haven't had this much to drink in a long time. Probably best if I head off.'

She squinted.

'And between you and me, my boobs are killing me. I really need to express.'

More squinting.

'So... I'll head out and I'll see you at work on Monday. Thanks so much for today,' I added, before I could stop myself. What was I thanking Meredith for? For confusing me? For borderline sexually harassing me? For coldly putting me in my place when I'd had the nerve to ask her what the hell her deal was? For getting me drunk before a big presentation? For dragging me across state lines for no good reason?

She laughed. 'Don't be ridiculous, George. This is part of your job. You can't leave now.' She turned back to the bar and clicked her fingers, summoning a waiter.

I stood there, open-mouthed, like a guppie. A drunk guppie.

'Um... look, Meredith, I really do think I should go.'

She ignored me, picked up the bottle of champagne and

walked back to the table, where she announced, 'George wants to do shots!' to rounds of boisterous cheers.

I'm not really clear on the details after that...

'Can you stop swaying, please?' Ellie hissed.

'I'm doing "Rockabye Your Bear",' I replied.

'That finished three minutes ago! They're doing "Hot Potato".'

'Oh.' So they were. I was still swaying. Maybe I was still drunk.

I had slept for four hours. Maybe. Once my head hit the pillow, at around 2 am, I was fast asleep. But Pip – who had slept through like such a little champion the previous night – had other plans. She woke up just as I was hitting the next REM cycle, so I pulled her into my bed to appease her. For the first time, despite my raging headache and the dread of the hangover I knew I'd have in the morning, I felt something other than annoyance that I had been woken in the middle of the night. I felt needed. I felt loved.

I felt my phone buzz inside my jacket just as 'Hot Potato' finished. I let it vibrate in my pocket, counting the number of rings. *One. Two. Three. Four. Voicemail.* I knew who it was. And I knew I didn't want to talk to her. Not right now, anyway. Whatever it was, *she* could figure it out this time.

Chapter 14

When Pip and I arrived home that night, the house seemed much emptier than when we'd left it. All the posters and art had been Nina's, so now the walls were bare – only a few stray globs of Blu-Tack remained. She'd taken her books, leaving the shelves gap-toothed. Her KitchenAid was gone, giving us back that precious bench real estate, but nonetheless leaving a hole. No more Nina.

Her room was empty. You could see from the indents in the carpet where the legs of her bed had been. But apart from that, there was no evidence anyone had lived there.

It could be Pip's room now. But even the thought of moving her cot, her change table, all her tiny singlets and swaddles from one room to another was tiring. Not yet.

We went through the usual dinner-bath-book-bed motions and as I tucked Pip in I felt a wave of fatigue. It didn't so much wash over me as crash into me. I was done. I was worked to the bone. I had not had a proper night's sleep in months. I couldn't remember the last time I had dreamed about something other than being afraid of running late.

The next round of 'upfronts' was in two weeks. This next one was a whole-day event, with lots of clients, at a fancy city hotel we'd booked for the occasion. Meredith had secured Anna Cantwell-Hart's Free Chef to do the catering, presumably for a large sum of money. Meredith had left a voicemail telling me what a 'fucking stunning' job I'd done on Saturday night, even though the majority of what I'd done was get shitfaced. I wasn't really sure what my job was anymore.

Wrapped up in bed, I scribbled my to-do list for the next day, which grew ever longer, as I never quite got time to cross off every item. I was finally ready to read 2.5 pages of my book, when my phone lit up with a message from a number I didn't recognise.

You bailed on me.

Huh? The phone shone bright again.

Not to worry. Binge was crap.
Waste of the company's money
and my time. But come to
Collard with me next week.

Neil! I texted back immediately.

So sorry. You got my
email though, right?

Between the throb of my hangover and the lure of sleep, I still found enough energy to be excited about a text from Neil.

I did. Went with
Anna instead.

Ugh. Right. So Neil was *that* guy. The one who complained about women like Anna – self-absorbed, snooty private-school girls with swishy ponytails – but then, when it came to the crunch, went right ahead and married them. Right.

Just kidding. I think Anna
would be more interested
in going to Purge. Anyway,
Binge was super-hipster. You
wouldn't have liked it. Kinda
glad you bailed, actually.

Oh. So they weren't not getting married. Right.

I think it's binge. Lower case b.

Ping!

It's b*nge.

This was fun. I fired back:

Mmm, pretty sure it's #b*nge.

Nothing. Hmm. I returned to my book, wondering if I would
ever finish it. Whose grand idea had it been to start *The
Goldfinch* two weeks into motherhood? Nine months later, I
still hadn't made a crack in the spine.

Stupid punctuation
aside... will you come on
a date with me?

I stared at the screen as I felt the excitement of having a crush
hit me. I had a crush. I was thirty-five years old, and I had a
crush. Where was Dolly Doctor when you needed her?

Yep. Let's find the most
hipster place possible.

I closed my eyes and breathed in the lovely anticipation of a date. It had been a long time since I'd felt those little flutters. The truth was, I didn't know a lot about Neil. But I knew more about him than I had about Alex. Or even Jase, when we'd first met. I knew that he wanted to date me. And I wanted to date him. And for now, that was enough.

*

The weeks after Nina left were both easier and harder than the ones that had come before. Easier because I no longer worried about where she was or if she and Jed might come home at 2 am and wake us all up. Easier because I didn't have to tiptoe around her early mid-life crisis anymore, trying not to comment on her sudden and urgent desire to adopt a French bulldog or learn how to make choux pastry or recite daily affirmations to herself. Easier because I could just Get On With It, because the equation had been simplified.

But it was harder because it was lonelier. Instead of the tantalising promise – even the barest, thinnest thread of one – of someone to talk to at the end of the day, someone to recount Meredith's latest episode to, someone to eat a tub of ice-cream with, there was nothing. Nina was not coming home. I was hit, one night, while eating that tub of ice-cream, with the thought that perhaps this was what divorce felt like. And an ironic stab of guilt twisted in my guts.

At work, I continued to award myself high-fives if I made it through a stand-up meeting without rolling my eyes (especially the time when Meredith started shouting excitedly about an interview Anna Cantwell-Hart had done with the creators of an app that summarised the plot of any book, TV show or movie in less than ten seconds. *Romeo and Juliet*: two kids fall in love, die. *War and Peace*: there's a war then there's not then there is. *Lost*: ¯_(?)_/¯ .)

I wondered whether to mention my brief textual flirtation with Neil to Meredith. Was it the professional thing to do, or would it only invite more trouble? Who could tell with Meredith? She'd either clap her hands, pop a bottle of champagne and start planning our wedding, or she'd slam her fist down on the desk, Tony Soprano–style, and demand Neil's head on a stick. Or mine. Or both.

In the end, I didn't have to decide.

'I've noticed you and Neil,' she said, not looking up from her phone.

'Neil?' I asked, as if there were several Neils on the team and Meredith could have been referring to any one of them.

'Don't let anything happen there, alright?'

'Uh...' I said, caught off-guard.

Meredith didn't look up. 'I mean it. Flirting is fine; we all flirt. But don't act on it. Understood?'

'Oh, um... I think you have the wrong idea, Meredith –' I said, trying to regain my footing.

'I don't,' she snapped. 'I know what I saw. Keep it to low-level flirtation, OK?'

'Um... sure. But –'

'Just listen to me, OK, George? Don't let anything happen.'

She walked away, phone still in her hand. She hadn't looked up once.

Later, she called me into her office, and apparently the whole thing was forgotten.

'So!' she said, clapping her hands together like an excited seal, 'I have some great news. *Media Alert* wants to profile you.'

'Oh! That is good news. Cool.'

'Good news for the brand, George. Not for you. It's not a chance to show off, you know.'

'Uh –' There she went again, pulling the rug out from underneath me. 'Yes, of course –'

'Anyway,' she said, beaming once more. 'The writer is coming in tomorrow. It's very exciting. It'll be a good chance to mention all the new directions the brand is taking – the podcast, the redesign, the new strategy, our new contributors.'

I tried to look animated but I was wary of walking into another of Meredith's traps. Meredith existed on a spectrum: there was fun, upbeat Meredith, the Meredith who was buzzing with ideas and creativity and most likely, some sort of over-the-counter narcotic. And then there was sour Meredith, dark Meredith, the one who'd walk right by you if you saw her outside of work, the one who'd stare at you blankly as you explained you needed an hour off work to fill a prescription for your sick child.

'Great! Yes, it'll be a really good chance to talk about all of that. It's such an exciting time for the brand,' I said, repeating the words that Meredith recited at least six times a day.

'Yes,' she said, smiling so wide she popped a wrinkle in her forehead. 'I'm so glad people are sitting up and taking notice of us now. We're working so hard; it's nice to be recognised.' More clapping as her smile got wider. 'I know! Let's take the team out for drinks on Friday night, after your interview! We should celebrate all of this.'

And so Fun Meredith returned. Sometimes I was more afraid of Fun Meredith: I was sure that, at some point, she'd convince me we should get tattoos of each other's faces or go to Stonewall on Ritalin and make out with gay guys. Fun Meredith was a little *too* fun.

'Sure,' I said, against my better judgement. 'That sounds like a great idea.'

*

'Just let me pop my recorder on,' said Leni. She didn't look the way I'd imagined her to. She was young, for starters – maybe even younger than Anna Cantwell-Hart. (Like a high-school frenemy or a serial killer, I could only refer to Anna Cantwell-Hart by her full name.) She was shrewd, too. I'd assumed this would be a puff piece, perhaps even something that Meredith herself had orchestrated. But Leni was a real journalist, and so it seemed *Media Alert* was going to run a real profile of me.

'No problem,' I said, trying to calm my nerves. I'd be fine with the interview if it weren't for the elephant in the room. The very skinny, very glamorous elephant called Meredith, who, like a celebrity PR, insisted on sitting in on the interview in case I 'ran into trouble'.

'Are you sure we can't get you anything?' Meredith asked for the third time.

'Uh... sure. A water would be great.'

'Bea!' Meredith boomed. Bea scurried in. 'Water, please, for Leni. Bottled. Sparkling or still, Leni?'

Leni threw her hands up. 'It doesn't matter, whatever you have,' she said, laughing but clearly over Meredith already. She turned to me. 'Geez, you guys can buy me a bottle of water? You're doing well. Most magazines I visit have sticky tape holding the carpet down.'

I laughed nervously, smoothing my dress over my knees.

'The business is performing extremely well,' said Meredith, smiling. 'Ads are up year-on-year *and* period-on-period. Circ just keeps increasing. But for us, you know, it's really about engagement. We want to reach out to our readers, make sure we're top of mind when it comes to any conversation they're having.'

Leni nodded, making notes. 'Really? Any conversation?'

'That's right,' Meredith said, barrelling on. 'It doesn't matter if it's about the new 5:2 diet or ISIS, we want them to think, "Oh, I read about that in *The Weekend*." But of course, it's not just about the magazine anymore – we're looking at a 360-degree brand experience. A podcast. A TV pilot. A series of interactive stories on –'

'Wait.' Leni held up a hand and looked at me. 'I really want to hear from Georgina. As the editor.'

Meredith cleared her throat and nodded, folding her hands in her lap. She shot me a look that said, unmistakably, *Don't fuck this up*. I pictured Obama and took a breath.

'Uh, sure. Well, Meredith's right, we want to be part of all those conversations. It's an exciting time for the brand –'

'Right, sure, but, down to brass tacks,' Leni said. 'Buzzwords and corporate BS aside, you've lost your founding editor, you've come from a women's magazine, which is totally different in terms of revenue streams, the newspaper you sit in has just made 100 staff members redundant *and* lost $5 million last year... So how are you going to make all these big plans happen? And do you have the money for it all?'

'Well, we–' Meredith began.

Leni held up her hand again and Meredith quietened. I'd never seen anyone command her like that. It was magic; I wanted to applaud.

I glanced at Meredith, whose eyes bulged at me. 'Well,' I said, clearing my throat to buy a few seconds, 'we have new advertisers on board, which is very exciting for us. We're just about to do our next round of upfronts, in Sydney, where we'll be unveiling some cool changes for the brand. The podcast, the redesign, new contributors, a new strategy. And we're doing some cross-promoting with the paper, to redirect readers to the mag.'

'What are you doing?'

'I'm writing a column, actually.' Leni looked up from her notes.

'So who's being bumped?'

'Uh... I'm not sure.' I looked at Meredith, who shook her head. She didn't know either.

'Sorry, I'm just trying to figure out how it'll work. Someone will obviously have to get bumped from the opinion pages, won't they? To make room for you?'

Oh. Oh shit. That hadn't occurred to me. I didn't want anyone to be bumped.

'I think you're missing the bigger picture here, Leni,' Meredith said, her voice taking on the strain of the Very Frustrated. 'We're taking a brand that started small and we're making it bigger. We've planted the seed and now we're watering the garden. We've got the pebble, now we need to make it a pearl. We've –'

Leni nodded and gave a half-interested, 'Mmm,' to stop Meredith from finishing her trio of metaphors (the last one was, 'We've got the grape, let's turn it into wine.').

'So Georgina, what's the biggest challenge for you?'

Meredith. Definitely Meredith, I wanted to say.

'Um... I would say the threat of digital is a challenge for us – as it is for everyone in print. But we're not trying to compete with digital, we just want to exist alongside it. People still want to sit down and read the paper on the weekend.' At this, Leni raised a sceptical eyebrow.

'Digital's great,' Meredith piped up, 'but the evidence is right there: people still want paper. They still want print. Especially for their Saturday paper. It's just not right to sit down to a tablet over brunch, is it?'

Leni nodded slowly, the kind of nod you give the stranger on your doorstep who's trying to convince you to join their church. 'Right. But you're branching out...?'

Meredith nodded coolly, her expression turned down a few notches now. Leni had not turned out to be the fluffy, fun reporter Meredith had hoped for. 'We are, Leni. It's important to diversify. And consumers love *The Weekend*, so why not offer it to them on different platforms?' She paused and crossed her arms across her chest. 'Give the people what they want, that's what I say.'

Leni nodded. 'Right. Ah, sorry, Meredith, could I have that water please? It's a little stuffy in here.'

Meredith stood up and barked at Bea again. When she didn't get a reply, she stomped out of the room in a huff to get the water herself.

Leni turned to me. 'Is she always so...?'

'Yes,' I said.

'Off the record,' she asked, 'what's she like to work for?'

'Uh... Off the record?' I glanced at the door. Open. This was a bad idea. This was self-sabotage.

237

Leni nodded, giving me a conspiratorial smirk.

'Well... not great. She's not exactly even-keeled. I mean, don't get me wrong: Meredith's great at her job. I've learnt so much from her and it really is–'

'An exciting time for the brand?'

I laughed, embarrassed. *This woman thinks I've drunk the office Kool-Aid.* I paused, and thought it over.

She might be right.

'Right,' I said, trying to figure out how to recover my composure. 'Yeah, like I was saying, it's always... interesting to work with Meredith. She works hard and plays hard.'

Leni leaned in, suddenly much more interested. 'What does that mean?'

I laughed. 'Oh, well... wait, is this still off the record?'

Leni nodded. 'Sure, of course.'

I made a little glug-glug motion and Leni's eyes widened.

'Here you are,' said Meredith, handing Leni a bottle of water. 'I don't know where Bea's disappeared to. Honestly.' She shook her head, clearly disappointed that Bea had dared to leave her desk for the first time in months.

'Thanks,' said Leni. 'So, tell me more about this podcast.'

'Yes!' Meredith said, clapping those hands again and nodding excitedly. 'We're just getting the funding approved for a studio. Eventually, it'll be a whole podcast network.'

A whole podcast network? My heart began to beat faster, wondering exactly how much more work that would mean for me. We hadn't even decided what the first podcast would be, let alone visioned an entire network.

Leni seemed surprised too. 'Big plans,' she murmured as she took more notes. She looked up at me. 'And what would you like to bring to the reader, George? Like, what's your endgame?'

Meredith went to jump in, but Leni, once again, raised a hand to silence her. It was thrilling to watch.

'Look,' I said, leaning back in my chair. 'It's not rocket science, right? I just want to give people something they can read while they're eating breakfast on Saturday mornings. I want them to be entertained, maybe learn something new. That's it.'

Meredith cleared her throat. 'If I may, Leni–' she said, flashing her best 'We're all friends here' smile, '– it's really about engaging, like I said. We want broad-spectrum, household-name engagement, and of course we also want specific recognition as an individual product. There's talk of doing a Sunday supplement, too, once we get a little bigger. And that'll help with the engagement.'

What? How would I run two weekly magazines? It wasn't possible. I spun my head to look at Meredith. She just beamed at me.

'Wow,' said Leni. 'This is all... very surprising. Most media companies are losing staff and shutting down supplements. This is very big news.'

Meredith was practically vibrating. 'It is. It's a great success story. It's foolhardy to think of your product as stand-alone these days. Readers – everyone – expects a 360-degree–'

'Brand experience?' Leni asked.

Meredith nodded and smiled indulgently. 'That's right,' she said. I knew she could tell Leni was making fun of her, but there was no way she'd ever give Leni the satisfaction of knowing she had irked her. It was one of the things I admired most about Meredith, actually. When she wasn't being so tyrannical, she was bloody amazing.

Leni smiled, bemused. 'So, Georgina, how will you handle the extra workload? Are you bringing on more staff? Opening another office?'

I laughed nervously. Was I? I had no idea. Unsurprisingly, I was yet to figure out exactly how I would handle this new supplement and podcast network, seeing as I had only heard about them, oh, sixty seconds ago.

'Well–'

'Like I always say to Gigi here,' said Meredith, her voice reaching Peak Passive Aggressive, '– she's a real go-getter,

Leni, make sure you put that in your story – what I always say to her is, "Don't worry. You'll figure it out." And you know what? She always does.' She paused to look over at me, and then smiled broadly. 'Don't you, Gigi?'

Chapter 15

'I found it,' said Neil, sidling up to me at the crowded bar.

'Mmm?' I asked, not looking at him directly. Meredith was two tables away but I suspected she'd still know I was talking to Neil. Like a dog hearing an ambulance two suburbs over, she'd pick it up, somehow.

'The most hipster restaurant in Sydney. I found it.'

'Uh-huh. Sounds good.'

Neil peered round to look me in the eyes. 'You OK?'

I nodded, eyes on my drink. As I snuck a glance at him, he shot me a confused, almost wounded look.

I whispered. 'I can't talk to you. Meredith knows.'

Watching Meredith as she liberally poured a round of champagne for the thirsty subs, I nodded for him to move outside. He followed.

The night air was bracing after the sweaty claustrophobia of the pub and I shivered reflexively. Neil moved to put his coat around me – a lovely gesture, but one I couldn't accept. I put a hand up to stop him. But before I had a chance to say, 'We have to stop all this lovely flirtation that's making me feel all sorts of fluttery feelings in my ladyparts,' Neil took my hand and pulled me along.

'Come on, let's get out of here.'

'Wait –'

He turned around and held his hand up, smiling mischievously. 'I have a plan.'

A five-minute walk later, it was clear that, true to his word, Neil had found the most hipster nonsense bullshit restaurant in Sydney. It was called blooprnt and every meal was 'carefully devolved of its whole', the waiter told us, as we nodded, wide-eyed and valiantly restraining our laughter. The waiter, who obviously recognised Neil from the food pages of *The Weekend,* attended to us like we were Bey and Jay.

'And what does "devolved of its whole" actually mean?' Neil asked, utterly straight-faced.

The waiter replied in kinds. 'Most food at restaurants is so... complete,' he said, as if what he really meant was, 'Most food at restaurants is fished from garbage bins and reassembled on plates people have wiped their arses on.'

'What we want to do, at blooprnt, is give you the *essence* of the food. We want to get back to the true nature of what eating is all about. Nothing fancy. No techniques you can't pronounce. Here at blooprnt, we're about honest food,' he said through his requisite lengthy beard.

Thirty minutes later, he returned with a bowl of raw, unpeeled carrot, to 'confuse the senses'.

Our senses already being fairly confused, we made a run for it to the nearest pub and ordered two cheeseburgers and a bottle of wine. Meredith, meanwhile, had texted me four times to ask where I was. *Baby's sick*, I replied. *Had to head home.* She texted back, *Boo. U r no fun. Why isn't the nanny there?*

I breathed out slowly, willing my fingers not to text back, *I DON'T HAVE A SODDING NANNY.*

After we got past the initial flurry of getting-to-know-you questions, Neil cut right to the chase. Between bites of fries, he asked, 'So what's it like being a single mum?'

'Oh,' I said, taking a second to think. I was feeling a little tipsy, having drunk two martinis at the pub and almost half a bottle of wine with Neil. Pretty soon – within minutes, even – I knew the truth serum effects of the wine would begin to kick in. That part of me wanted to say *it's quite hard actually*. But I knew what people wanted to hear. They wanted to hear that, yes, it was tough, and yes, it was non-stop – and they loved it when you included a hilarious and touching anecdote that demonstrated the aforementioned difficulty – but that generally, I was OK. That's what Neil wanted to hear, I was sure. I certainly wasn't about to say, on a date, with a human male, 'Well, being a single mum is basically not knowing what you're doing and being afraid every day that you're ruining not just your own life but someone else's, too, someone much smaller and way cuter than you are, and occasionally crying for no good reason, like when you hear "Cat's in the Cradle" on the radio. Also you drink a lot of wine even though you know you should cut down, and swear a lot, and hardly ever wear ironed clothes.'

'It's fine,' I lied, eating the last of my decidedly dishonest, fully constructed, properly delicious burger.

He raised his eyebrows, looking impressed. People tended to want to be impressed by mothers, especially single ones. 'Wow. Really? You seem to be handling it so well. How old is...?'

'Pip. Pippa. Philippa,' I repeated the nickname-to-real name explanation that I felt I had to give everyone who asked. 'She's almost eleven months.' The first six months of Pip's life had felt like years. Now the time was flying by like it was on fast forward.

'Cool. What are you doing for her birthday?'

I paused. What a great question. What a great question that I did not have an answer to.

'Uh... not really sure yet.' Jesus. What was I doing for Pip's birthday? It was her first birthday – it was a big bloody deal. You only turn one once, after all. I made a mental memo to text Ellie and ask her to help me. What did a one-year-old's birthday involve? Probably way too much work. I didn't have time to make 150 tiny sausage rolls from scratch (not to

243

mention the organic, grass-fed ingredients I would somehow have to procure, children these days being allergic to anything with preservatives, additives and all other -ives) only to see them end up half-eaten and strewn across the park for a lucky family of ibises. Even if I did have the time, I would never have the patience or, indeed, the inclination.

Neil nodded, mistaking my hesitation for deep thought on the matter. 'So how'd it go with the reporter today? The one from *Media Alert*?'

I shook my head and laughed. 'Uh... well, it was OK except for Meredith butting in every fifteen seconds or so. She's so...'

'Meredith?' he volunteered.

'Exactly.'

Neil laughed. 'What did she do?'

I screwed up my face. 'She pissed off the reporter. She couldn't stop interrupting. She said "360-degree brand experience" about a thousand times.'

'Oh no. Why does she say that? It doesn't even make any sense.'

I shrugged. 'I don't know. But–' I buried my face in my hands '– now I've started saying it too. Help me!'

He laughed. 'Oh man. That is bad. That is really, really bad.'

'I know. Then she started talking about how we're going to have a whole podcast network soon, and do a Sunday supplement, and–'

Neil rolled his eyes. 'Oh yeah, all that stuff. It's never going to happen.'

'What do you mean?'

He shrugged, chewing. 'Meredith has been talking about that stuff since *The Weekend* started, what... a year ago now? Actually, before that – when we first got the team together, it was "part of the plan".' He put down his burger to do air quotes.

I squinted. 'So... what does that mean? It's all just hot air?'

'Probably.' Neil kept eating as I stared at him, unsure what to say next.

I'd figured out that Meredith's emails were mostly fit to be ignored, and that she had a habit of giving me busy work and then forgetting all about it... but telling a reporter about big plans for your brand – plans that were never going to see the light of day – that was bad. That would make *me* look bad.

Neil smirked. 'Yeah. Lee never told you that? It's part of the reason she left. She was so over Meredith.'

'What? I thought... what about John's job?'

'Oh yeah, well, there was that, too. But I doubt Lee would have been in such a hurry to go if it hadn't been for Meredith. You know she told Lee she was going to get a column in the Big Paper?' He shook his head as if to say, 'Can you believe it?' I felt, quite suddenly, woozy. I gulped down the rest of my wine.

Neil smiled at me from across the table and refilled my glass. 'I guess you need to go home, huh?'

'Um...' Ellie had come to my rescue and was babysitting Pip. I glanced at my phone. There were a few selfies from Meredith, posing, alternately, with bottles of wine and Anna Cantwell-Hart. It was 10.30. 'Yeah. I should go. After this one.'

I texted Ellie. *Heading home soon.* She pinged back, *No worries, take your time. Watching* Suits. *Harvey =* 😍

'OK.'

Half an hour and a finished bottle of wine later, we left the pub and Neil stuck his arm out to hail me a taxi. When the cab pulled over and turned its light on, I made a lightning fast decision and pulled Neil towards me. He smiled, surprised, and leaned in to kiss me. Then we got in the cab.

Chapter 16

I rolled over and stifled a scream. There's a man in my bed. *SHIT*. There is a *man* in my *bed*. It took a second to remember that I knew the man in my bed. I had slept with the man in my bed. Wait. The man in my bed worked for me. *Shit shit shit*.

It all came back, albeit in pieces. Ellie's surprised, cheekily delighted face as I opened the door, revealing Neil, who was coming in for a late-night 'cup of tea'. Looking in on Pip to check she was OK and quietly shutting the door. Feeling the momentary trepidation of taking off my clothes being replaced by the straight-up need to get laid. And then getting laid.

Shit shit shit.

'Good morning,' Neil said, as Pip began to cry in her room. I looked at Neil, who did not seem at all uncomfortable that we were both naked and my child – my eleven-month-old child – was in the next room, ready for breakfast.

'Morning!' I said, trying to sound sunny and cheerful and light and not at all weirded out. 'Ah... give me a minute.'

I shot across the room to grab a robe and wrapped it around me. I opened the door to Pip's room to find her standing up in the cot.

'Pip!' I said. 'You're standing up! Good girl!' I clapped my hands together, then stopped myself. God, I looked just like

Meredith. *Don't drink the Kool-Aid, George.* I was already talking like Meredith, I didn't need to adopt her mannerisms, too.

From the cot, Pip beamed, clearly proud of herself. I picked her up and held her close. 'Good girl,' I whispered. 'Good girl.' Then it hit me – she had slept through the night! Again! Oh my god! *Ohmygodohmygodohmygod!* After that one night in Melbourne when Ellie had put Pip to bed, I'd wrongly assumed that my child had turned a corner. Not so. This was the first time she'd slept through since. I couldn't believe it. Here she was, not even a year old and already a champion wingwoman.

We sat down in the armchair in Pip's room (I had finally convinced myself to move her stuff into Nina's old room) and I started to feed her.

Neil walked in and his Mouth agog, he stared at me – boobs out, child at nip.

'Oh shit,' he said. 'Sorry.'

I covered up as much as I could, wondering exactly what the point was – he'd seen the whole enchilada – and taco – last night.

'Uh, it's OK,' I said. 'Just give me a minute, alright?'

He nodded, looking embarrassed. 'Yeah, sorry. Uh... should I go get some coffees?'

I nodded, smiling.

God. What had I done? Meredith had been clear as vodka: do not date Neil. And what had I done? I had dated Neil. I had dated Neil twice in one night. Oh boy.

Pip broke her feed and looked up at me, smiling. I let myself relax. I had dated Neil. Twice. In one night.

Oh boy indeed.

*

Are you going to Nina's mum's memorial? came the text from Ellie.

Yep, I replied.

I pulled Pip into her polka-dot romper and dabbed her face with sunscreen.

'Ready, Miss Pip? Let's go.'

I didn't know if it was the sex or the fact that autumn was here, bringing its cool, sunny mornings and giant golden leaves, but I was definitely feeling more energetic, hangover notwithstanding. It was a bright, clear day; it was time to head to the park.

My phone lit up. *What are you going to wear? Black?* I stared down at the phone. Only Ellie would have the time and mental capacity to plan an outfit for a memorial that was still two weeks away.

Don't know. Maybe.

A reply came back in seconds.

Does Pip have a black dress?
Just wondering what to put
Lucas in. Simon can wear a suit
but Lucas's tux from Hayley's
wedding is too small now
and also tux = too formal?

I rolled my eyes.

Lucas is a kid, and the memorial
is at the beach. Let him wear
shorts. Nina won't care, the
point is just to be there.

I piled the necessities into my bag: wipes, a water bottle, a snack (one for Pip, one for me), extra sunscreen, nappies. I was finally getting the hang of this. It had only taken eleven months. Pip gurgled at me and I gurgled back. She was so close to talking now – really talking, not just jumbles of sounds. I wondered what her first word would be.

We walked into the sunshine and down the street. I felt... well, I felt like a woman who had recently had three very good orgasms. It was the sort of feeling you got after being in the ocean when you lived in the city – renewed, fresh, sexy. It felt amazing.

'George!' I heard a voice from down the street. 'George!'

I turned to see who it was. Harriet!

'Hi!' I waved her over. 'We're off to the park.'

Harriet nodded, smiling. 'Us, too!' I slowed down so she could catch up.

Harriet's texts had become less frequent, but I didn't blame her; I'd rarely replied. I would see the message, get busy with something at work, forget the message was there and then by the time I did remember, usually days later, it seemed rude to reply so late. Luckily, Harriet didn't seem to be holding it against me.

By the time we got to the park, it was teeming with toddlers and babies and hovering parents and the ones who, like Harriet and I, preferred to sit on the sidelines and drink our coffees as the babies crawled in the dirt, content to play with mud instead of the state-of-the-art play equipment that had recently been installed in response to complaints about the lone swing and slide, which had been built when O. J. was still just a football player.

So as Pip and Charlie sat in literal squalor and fed each other chunks of (immunity-building, I hoped) wet dirt, Harriet and I hung by the fence, the motherhood equivalent of back-seat toughies, and caught up. Obviously, I immediately told her about Neil.

'Ahhhhhh! I am so jealous,' she said, hands to her face, doing her best *Home Alone* pose.

I laughed. 'It was pretty good.'

She screwed up her face, trying to get the whole picture. 'So you just did it, with Pip in the next room? Dev and I haven't even done that yet.'

I felt my eyes widen. 'Huh?'

She shrugged. 'We haven't had sex.'

'Since...?'

She stared at me, like I was hard of hearing. 'Since I had Charlie.'

'What?' I tried not to be judgemental, but... well, I was being judgemental. Harriet and Dev hadn't had sex in eleven months? Suddenly I felt relieved about my own relative chastity.

She shrugged again. 'It's not that big a deal. I just don't really feel like it anymore, and it's hard, you know, with Charlie. He's not–' She looked away, ashamed. 'He's not sleeping through the night anymore.'

'Oh,' I said. 'Well, he's only a baby, that's OK.'

She looked at me, doubtful. 'He'll be a year old next week. And... he was sleeping through. I don't know what happened. I mean, I've tried everything.'

It was not lost on me that Harriet seemed far more upset about her baby not sleeping through the night than she was about her absent sex life. I sensed it wasn't the time to bring that up, though.

'Oh, Pip still doesn't sleep through,' I said reassuringly. I decided not to mention that, in fact, last night she had. Maybe sex was the answer. Maybe if Harriet and Dev had sex, Charlie would sleep through. Probably shouldn't mention that either.

She shrugged and her voice took a turn for the defensive. 'Yeah, but you don't do any sleep training with Pip. And she goes to daycare for all her naps. I'm home with Charlie all day. Dev said that this year is all about me sleep training Charlie, but he's still not sleeping through, and I'm going back to work in a month. What's going to happen when I'm at work, like you?' Harriet was on the verge of tears.

I let out a little scoff that I tried to disguise as clearing my throat. 'Um, well... I don't know,' I said, looking away and trying not to be hurt by Harriet's words.

My phone pinged again. Ugh. Not another update from the Memorial Wardrobe Crisis, I hoped.

George! You missed a great
night. Did Media Alert woman
call you? She left a message
on my phone this morning.
Tried to call back but she's
not answering. WONDER
WHAT IS UP????? MP xxx

'Uh, sorry,' I said, looking down at my phone. 'Just replying to a work text.'

Harriet nodded.

Nope, she hasn't called
me. Glad you had a fun
night. Talk Monday. GH

I looked up again and clocked Pip raking the ground with her fingers, her little nails filling with mud. This was parenthood: letting your kid distract themselves with something disgusting for an hour, then spending the next two to three hours cleaning it all up. Her socks were already black, and I couldn't even imagine what the bottom of her romper looked like. Whatever: I'd had sex last night. Pip could vomit on the both of us, shit her pants and rub them all over me today and I wouldn't care. Sexy sexy sex sex.

'So you're going back to work?' I asked, keeping my voice light. The mother's group mums had been so shocked and dismayed when I'd told them I was going back to work. Harriet had been the calmest one of the lot, but even she had reacted with reservation. I had a feeling she might not exactly be creaming her jeans over the prospect of her own return.

'Yeah,' she said, with a little sadness. 'In May.'

'Oh,' I said. 'Will Charlie go to daycare?'

'Oh no,' she shook her head. 'My mum is going to look after him.'

'Wow, that's so nice,' I said.

She looked at me sadly. 'I honestly don't know how you do it, George. I mean, I just keep wondering, will it even be worth it?' She paused. 'If we paid for daycare, I'd only come out $20 ahead for the week. The whole week. It's so frustrating.'

'Mmm, but... if you love your job, maybe that's worth more than $20 to you.'

Harriet stared at me blankly as my phone pinged again. I glanced down.

Text me ASAP if she
calls you. MP xxx

'I mean... there's more to work than just money, you know?'

She frowned.

'And... it's not just you who comes out $20 ahead, that's $20 for the whole family. Right? I mean, you don't think of Dev going to work for *his* money, do you? It's money for the whole family.'

She tilted her head, frowning again.

'What I mean is... like, it's not just about you going back to work, is it? It's the whole childcare... problem. Like maybe, if it's only a difference of $20, maybe it would be better if Dev took some time off.'

Harriet shook her head.

'Dev's got nothing to do with it, George,' she said, her tone a touch withering. 'He's happy for me to go back to work.'

I realised, with a start, that I didn't even know what Harriet's job was.

'What do you do, anyway?'

'I'm a zoologist.'

I threw my head back in surprise. 'Are you kidding? That's, like, the coolest job ever. Wow. I had no idea!'

'Oh,' she said, a little embarrassed. 'Well, it's OK.'

'What? Don't be so modest. It's amazing. Wow. I'm super impressed. So where do you work?'

'Taronga.'

I felt my mouth drop open. 'Seriously, Harriet, I don't even like animals, but that is so cool. Wow. You get to work at Taronga Zoo?' I shook my head with disbelief. 'I am so jealous.'

Harriet smiled tightly. 'Yeah, it's a good job.'

'Are you excited to go back? I mean, wow.'

She laughed bitterly. 'You can stop saying "wow" now. I get it, George.'

'Oh,' I said, taken aback. 'Sorry. I just really am quite impressed. It's a seriously cool job.'

She shrugged.

'So you're looking forward to it? I know I was. It was hard to admit at the time, but... I *needed* to go back.'

'Could you drop it, please? I'm not excited, not at all. I don't want to go back to work, OK? I don't even want to think about it right now. I'm not like you. I can't just go back to work and not worry about my child, OK? Please drop it.'

Harriet was no longer on the verge of tears but actually crying.

'Sorry,' I said quietly.

She sighed deeply, as though I had said something truly offensive, like 'women aren't funny'.

'I really don't know how you do it, that's all,' she said, reaching down to scoop Charlie up.

I leaned back against the fence, watching Pip shove mud into her mouth. People had been saying that to me all year – 'I don't know how you do it' – and I'd thought they were saying, 'I don't know how you fit it all in'. But they weren't. They were saying, 'I don't know how you can be away from your baby.'

Now I understood.

Chapter 17

By Monday afternoon, if I heard Meredith say 'upfronts' one more time, I thought I might actually open the latch of her office window, push it out and hurl myself through the open space, waving my middle finger in the air as I fell.

The upfronts were next week, and Meredith was apoplectic with excitement – six-year-old on Christmas Eve excitement. Woman who's just given birth and is about to have a glass of wine and a wedge of pâté excitement. Julian Assange sunbathing excitement.

Predictably, Meredith swung between telling me I was going to completely bomb unless I listened to every specific, often contradictory instruction she gave me, and telling me how amazing I was. Today, I was amazing.

'You. Are. Going. To. Crush. It,' she said, emphasising each word with a little fist pump. 'We are going to make so much money. It's going to be so great. You are going to be so great.'

I smiled, keen to get back to the work of actually, you know, making a magazine. Sure, I wanted the business to make money, but I figured the best way I could achieve that was by making a great magazine that advertisers wanted to buy into. Not by abandoning my magazine to suck up to advertisers who really just wanted a free piss-up, anyway.

'Thanks, Meredith. I'd better get back, I need to finalise the flat plan for next week. I noticed the daycare mums sketch we talked about is on there now – is that right? Has Richard done it? I didn't brief him.'

'Oh, I did,' she said, breezily. 'It's really funny. Go have a look, it's all in the system.'

'OK, thanks. I'll let you know when the flat plan's ready to go.'

'Sure,' she said, nodding. 'I'll send you an email with my changes.'

I raised a brow. 'Changes?'

'To the presentation. I had a look last night and I need to go over some things. So I'll just send through the changes and you can make them tonight, OK? This is gonna be a big week, George!' She clapped three times, her face a tight ball of enthusiasm.

Neil was at his desk, drinking coffee and reading the paper, which struck me as a particularly leisurely thing to do at 4 pm on a Monday.

Still, he looked cute.

I resisted the urge to say anything. We'd texted over the weekend, flirtatious little missives that were like bright bursts of fireworks lighting up the sky. I was determined not to let my run-in with Harriet dampen the loveliness of falling asleep with a warm arm around me, and the texts (OK, sexts) definitely helped.

But as I walked past, he lifted his head and smiled.

'Hey,' he said.

'Hi, Neil,' I said, at least trying to sound professional.

'I need to chat to you about something,' he said, folding the paper over.

'OK. Can it wait? I need to do the flat plan–'

'No. Sorry. I really need to talk to you.'

255

Out of the corner of my eye, I saw Bea look up at us. I flushed.

'OK. Let's keep it quick.'

I turned and walked into my office, Neil right behind me. He shut the door.

'What are you doing?' I said, panicking. 'You either have to quit or tell me you're having a baby, because they are the only two reasons you would ever shut my office door. OK?'

He laughed. 'Calm down, no one will notice.'

'Everyone will notice. Open the door. Now.'

He stared at me, puzzled, then cracked a smile. 'Alright.'

He opened the door and I felt relief flood through me. What the hell was he thinking?

'Sit down,' I said, through gritted teeth. We sat on the couches in my office, two separate sofas that formed an L in the corner, and that remained partially out-of-sight to passersby.

I faced Neil. 'So?'

He leaned back into the couch, looking for all the world as if we were settling in for the night to watch *The Walking Dead* with pad Thai and red wine, not at work in the middle of the afternoon, where nobody was aware of our recently changed relationship status.

'So–' he began. 'Friday was fun.'

I nodded. 'Yep. Listen, we can't talk about this here,' I said, lowering my voice to just above a whisper.

'OK,' he said, eyes bright. 'Come out with me tomorrow night. Dinner. Drinks. We could go to a movie... or just to my place–'

I stared at him, dumbfounded. I had just told him we couldn't talk about this – whatever *this* was – at the office. It was pretty straightforward. What couldn't he understand?

'Yeah, Neil, we can't talk about this right now. OK?' My eyes bulged as if to emphasise the point.

He held up his hands. 'OK, OK. I get it.' He lowered his voice and added in a whisper, 'And it's hot.' My eyes blazed.

256

I couldn't tell if he really did think it was hot or if he was messing with me for the hell of it. 'I'll message you,' he said, as he got up to leave.

'Oh,' said Meredith, walking in. 'Hello, Neil.' Meredith's mouth drew a tight, straight line.

But Neil didn't miss a beat. 'Hey, Meredith! How are you? Had fun on Friday night. What about you? That last bar we went to was so great, wasn't it? Loved the shrubs in the cocktails. Think I might put it in the Drinks column week after next. Yeah?'

Meredith softened, and she reached out to touch Neil's arm playfully. 'Oh! Gosh, I don't even remember you being at that bar, Neil! Sneaky!'

He smiled and shot me a look as he walked out.

I tried to settle on an appropriate facial expression – mildly bored, maybe? – as my heart jumped. What was he thinking?

Meredith shut the door and turned to me.

'I'm just going to say it one more time,' she said, her face suddenly grave again. 'No messing about. No funny business. You and Neil work together. That's it. Do you understand?'

I nodded. 'Meredith, really, nothing is happening. Nothing. I promise.' Liar. Pants on fire.

She didn't blink. 'I have big plans for you, George. So don't go fucking them up, alright? Am I making myself absolutely clear?'

'Absolutely.'

She cleared her throat. 'Right,' said Meredith, suddenly sunshine and roses, 'good good. Because Richie loved your columns.'

'Oh,' I said, breathing a sigh of relief. 'But didn't he see them a few weeks ago? And he liked them then?'

A flash of annoyance briefly passed across Meredith's face, then disappeared. 'Yes, yes he did. But... uh, Richie's so busy, you know, upstairs, that, uh, he forgot he'd seen them, and then he read them again.'

Meredith looked flustered, which was odd, because

257

Meredith never looked flustered. The only time I had ever seen her look anything more than mildly perturbed was when a bartender tried to serve her Smirnoff instead of Grey Goose. And even then she'd handled it in her typical Meredith way, by coolly pouring the drink out on the counter and demanding a new one. Meredith did not get flustered. She got what she wanted.

'OK. That sounds good. You know, it would be good to meet with Richie, I think. I have this whole plan for the column. I was talking to a friend from mothers' group on the weekend, and she almost seems afraid of going back to work, and I just wanted to tell her it'll be fine.' I was aware, at that moment, of Meredith's eyes glazing over slightly, but I didn't let it faze me. 'I wanted to say, yeah, it'll be hard. Sure. Everyone knows that. But it's also great, because you'll have the best of both worlds, won't you?' By now, Meredith's eyes were so glazed over she looked like a Krispy Kreme. I barrelled on. 'You do. You get to be an adult, to make decisions, to contribute, to do something of real value and worth to the outside world, and then you get to come home and do something of real value and worth for your child. So it's great, it's just great.'

Meredith blinked at me. 'Jesus, George, I wasn't aware I was getting a lecture on leaning in.'

'Oh. I didn't mean to lecture you —'

Meredith put up a hand to signal that this part of the conversation was over. 'Yes, George. I get it. Working mothers, blah blah. Right. Anyway, speaking of, did you have a chance to look at the sketch? Hilarious, right?'

'Uh, no, not yet. Hang on a sec.'

I opened the file and took a look. I tried to refrain from gasping out loud. It was clear that Meredith had briefed Richard on the sketch. Titled 'A spotter's guide to playground mothers', it veered between cruel and downright offensive. Instead of the funny, playful sketch I had imagined, with a few knowing jokes about hypochondriac parents or parents who dressed their kids in knee pads to go to the park, this was a guide to 'IVF Mum' ('if she looks older than she should, it's because she is') and 'Formerly Hot Mum' ('has chosen her kids over her body, and it shows') and 'Stay-At-Home Sally' ('whines about how much housework she does but protests when you tell her to get a real job').

'What is this?' I asked, looking up at Meredith, who was clapping with glee.

'Isn't it funny? Richard is great. We should get him to do more of these, I think they'll really hit a nerve.'

'I agree, they will hit a nerve,' I said. 'This is horrible. There's no way we can run this.'

Meredith's smile fell. 'Why? It's hilarious. It's what you wanted.'

I shook my head. 'No. It's not. Not at all. I wanted something where everyone was in on the joke. This is cruel. You can't talk about women like this. It's offensive and hurtful. I won't run it.'

Meredith scoffed. 'Oh, George, stop it. Don't be so sanctimonious. If people do dislike it, that's fine. They have a right to their opinion, I suppose. And hopefully they'll voice it all over social media and drum up some free PR for us. There's no such thing as bad publicity.'

'There is, actually. This would be very bad publicity. *The Weekend* is meant to be intelligent and forward-thinking. This is misogynist bullshit. I'm taking it off the plan.'

'Excuse me?' Finally, Meredith looked unnerved.

'This has no place in our mag. I'll replace it with a house ad.'

'No, you won't. It's funny and topical. Like I said, George, I have big plans for you. Do you really want to jeopardise things over a bloody mummy sketch?'

I stood up and placed my palms on the table. 'Meredith, I am putting my foot down. This is not going to run. I'm prepared to fight you on this.' I took a breath and leaned back a little, trying to calm down. 'We're about to get some amazing PR from *Media Alert*. Do *you* really want to jeopardise *that* with a bloody mummy sketch?' Nervous as I was to stand up to Meredith, I was determined not to let my voice falter. I wouldn't give her that.

Meredith snickered and gave me that curt, annoyed smile she saved for when she was at her angriest.

'Fine. Drop it.'

I smiled right back. 'Already done.'

*

The next week was a blur of emails from Meredith, texts from Ellie asking about Nina's mum's memorial, and the pages of *The Women's Weekly Children's Birthday Cake Cookbook*, from which I was trying to choose a cake for Pip's birthday. The train looked way too hard, the swimming pool looked way too artificially blue, and the duck with potato chips for a bill looked way too '80s. Dolly Varden, maybe?

And Neil. There was a lot of Neil.

I had safely compartmentalised Meredith's warning way, way back in my mind. I needed this. So we went out. Jase babysat. And Pip survived. I was doing it; I was having it all; I was leaning in – and out, as the case may be.

'So you can't come into my office, OK?' I told him as we lay in bed, after an hour of leaning in and out.

He gave me that smirk that lately didn't seem quite so annoying. 'We do work together. I might have a reason to come into your office.'

'Yeah, but you can't come in and ask me on a date, alright? That's not on.'

His fingers traced the length of my arm. 'OK,' he said, not really paying attention.

I gave him a soft slap. 'Neil! I mean it. Meredith... I'm pretty sure she knows.'

'Oh yeah?' He didn't look worried.

'Yes! And she was... well, she was very clear about the fact that we're not allowed to date. So we can't let her find out.'

Neil's eyes began to close. 'That seems unrealistic.'

'Neil!' I said, playfully jabbing him with a finger, at which he jolted a little. 'I'm serious. We have to be careful.'

'Calm down, George. Come here,' he said, pulling me into his big spoon cuddle.

The next morning, as he made me coffee from his Aeropress and went on at length about how it was the best coffee maker on the market, and how it was so inexpensive when you took into account the cost-per-use, and I tried to look interested while also just thinking, *bloody hell, hurry up and make my coffee, will you?*, I looked around Neil's kitchen and saw the evidence of a life very much lived alone.

Everything had a place. Cookbooks stood in colour-coded order on a shelf above the neatly filled wine rack. The benches were bare but for the bloody Aeropress, about which Neil apparently still had more to say. Exactly three knives were affixed to a magnetic strip near the very clean stovetop. I thought about my own stovetop, with its caked-on splatters that I'd long ago made a half-hearted attempt to clean and quickly learnt to live with. My own wine rack, all but empty by now. My knife rack, safely stowed away from Pip's curious fingers. She had become a climber, which was one part cute mixed with nine parts terrifying.

Where did I fit in here? Where would Pip fit in?

Finally, Neil handed me a cup of coffee, his scruffy face breaking into a grin. 'I'm buying you an Aeropress,' he said.

'Oh, you don't have to–'

'No! I do. I've seen how much coffee you drink. You need an Aeropress.' He reached out and pulled me in for a kiss. I was still getting used to the electric feeling of it, the bolt of desire.

'OK,' I said, leaning back and making a big show of tasting the coffee. 'Mmm. Yes, definitely the best cup I've ever had. Better than an espresso in Milan. You win.' I leaned across the kitchen island to give him another kiss.

As I sat back in my chair, I saw my phone light up.

Need to see you today. SO
much to do still. Meet at
office in 30 mins? MP xxx

'Who's that?' asked Neil.

I rolled my eyes. 'Meredith.'

'It's Saturday.'

'Uh-huh.'

'What does she want?' he asked, reaching into the fridge. I took a moment to appreciate his bum – how was he a food writer and not morbidly obese, the way I surely would be if eating was a KPI? – and then replied to Meredith.

Can it wait til Monday? Not
sure I can get babysitting
on such short notice.

'She wants me to come into work.'

He turned around. 'Absolutely not. I need you right here, young lady. We have important business to discuss.' He waggled his eyebrows and I laughed.

'Well, when you put it that way–'

On the bench, my phone buzzed once more.

No. Very important.
Let's hustle. MP xxx

As I was trying to figure out a response, Neil wrapped his arms around my waist, peering over my shoulder to read the text.

'Ugh. That woman needs a life. I'd pay serious cash to see her face when you tell her you're not going in.'

I said nothing, the phone still in my hand.

'Wait,' Neil said, untangling his arms and stepping back. 'You're not going in, are you?'

'Um–' I looked down. *No. Just say no. Tell Neil you are going to spend the day in his bed, and that if you get up at*

all, you'll go no further than the bathroom or the fridge. Tell
him. Tell him you want to spend the day with him. Tell him.
Tell him right now.

I turned around, my face hot with shame. I was going to
do what Meredith told me to do; I couldn't not.

Neil's eyes bulged. 'You're going in? Seriously? I thought
we were going to hang out. I thought Jase was looking after
Pip. We have a whole day.'

'Uh, well, Meredith and I have a lot of work to do. We're
doing the advertiser presentations this week, you know, and
the mag really needs the money. So it's a big deal.'

He stiffened a little. 'Right,' he said, as I tried to ignore the
disappointment on his face. 'Right. Well, I'm not an editor.
If you have to go–'

I paused. I wanted to spend the day with Neil, I really
did. But I also wanted to show Meredith I could present to
advertisers and make her a shitload of money. Because maybe
then she'd be able to concentrate on that column she promised
me so many months ago. Sure, Lee didn't get her column, but
maybe Richie just hadn't liked her idea. He liked mine. I was
close. I was really close.

'Look, Neil... I'd love to stay, I really would. But–'

Neil dropped his head a little and sighed. 'It's fine. I'll
drive you in if you want.'

'Oh, I don't think that's such a good idea–'

Neil's eyes narrowed. 'Why?'

'Well... because Meredith doesn't want us to date. I mean,
she can't see us together at 9 am on a Saturday.'

He laughed, a big, generous belly laugh.

I waited for him to finish.

'George. You can't be serious. She can't tell you what to
do. What you do outside of work has nothing to do with her.'
He studied me, as if waiting for me to agree. I didn't say
anything. 'Right?' he prompted.

I cocked my head, ready to agree with him but also knowing
there was some sense to Meredith's no-dating rule. Part of me

was thinking, *What the hell are you doing, sleeping with your employee?* Part of me was thinking, *How will this work?* This isn't *Who's the Boss?*. I wasn't Angela. Neil wasn't Tony. Pip wasn't Alyssa Milano. Or whoever the other kid was.

'Neil, I really like you,' I said, surprising even myself as the words came out. *I really like Neil.* Oh. 'But I think she's got a point. I'm your boss. Maybe... maybe this isn't such a good idea.'

He scoffed, and that smirk came back. 'Seriously?'

I nodded. 'I just–'

He sighed. 'She pushes you around at work – she pushes all of us around, because she's so fucking insecure and anxious and probably, from the looks of it, bloody starving – and now you're going to let her push you around outside of work too? That seems sensible.'

'I'd hardly say Meredith pushes me around,' I began, but Neil cut me off.

'She's getting you to come to work on a Saturday, even though she knows you have a baby. She makes jokes about you in front of all of us. She made you go to Melbourne for nothing and made you feel like shit the whole weekend, or so you told me. And now you're saying she's got a point about us not dating? Are you really going to leave right now and not come back? Because –' Neil paused and softened his tone. 'Because I really like you, too. And there's no "but" after that. I really like you. I think you're funny and smart and a bit mad, but that's OK. I like that you call bullshit. I like that you have a baby. I like you. I don't care about Meredith because this is just a job. It doesn't really mean anything.'

'Well... it does mean something,' I said, choosing to focus on that last bit, and not the heartbreaking admission that he really did like me. Because I knew what I was going to do next. 'I mean, I've worked really hard. I studied, I've worked my way up. I've been away from my kid for months working at all of this. It does mean something – it means a lot. At least to me, it does.'

I couldn't walk away from my job – this job I had worked so hard and sacrificed so much for – just because Neil liked me. What would it all have been for if I turned around now and said to Meredith, 'Sorry, I'm shagging the food writer, see you later!'? Neil may have treated his job with a joking sort of contempt, but I didn't. I wasn't pitching stories about Manchester just so I could go and watch a soccer game; I was doing what I was goddamn told. I was working. And then, at the end of the day, I went home to my other job.

Neil sighed. 'Does it mean the end of... this?'

I opened my mouth to speak but couldn't find the words. Neil stared at me, his mouth set in a line.

'OK,' he said.

I gathered my things and went to work.

Chapter 18

The day of the upfronts, I woke, as usual, to the sound of Pip crying out for me. My movements were rehearsed and robotic now. I shuffled over and picked her up, cuddling her into me. *Downstairs. Kettle, bottle, coffee.*

My eyelids felt heavy, which seemed both odd and familiar for 7 am. As Pip and I showered, my mind raced through the day's to-do list.

Pick up dress from dry-cleaners before work

Message Harriet to say happy birthday to Charlie (even though Harriet was complete B to me last week)

Buy nappies

Pay water bill

Flatplan

Cover options for Meredith

Meredith insisted on having three different covers mocked each week, with three different celebrities, sets of cover lines and designs. One was a decoy, one would be totally wrong, and then there was the one she would actually choose. I always knew which one it would be, but she still made me do it. Getting out one cover every week was back-breaking. Getting out three was close to impossible.

And finally: *Avoid Neil*

I'd half-expected him to message or call over the weekend, apologising for overreacting. I'd wondered if he might show up on my doorstep, *Love Actually*–style, with handwritten placards explaining that he'd thought about what I'd said and now fully understood, and would happily resign so the two of us could continue sexing each other. But he didn't. I stalked his Instagram all day Sunday and saw that he was out at the pub with friends, eating chips and feeding a seagull and drinking beer, the sunlight catching bits of his hair. My heart sank.

I was rinsing the conditioner out of my hair when I looked down and realised that while I'd been mentally tallying my to-do list, and hosting my own personal pity party, Pip had been occupying herself by chewing on the bottle's lid.

I snapped out of the fog and snatched it from her, losing my footing in the process and landing clean on my elbow.

Fuuuuuuuuuuck.

Pip burst into tears at the exact moment I did. I looked down at the porcelain, sure there'd be a steady stream of blood. But there wasn't. My legs were splayed in a sort of forced yoga pose (truthfully, any yoga pose was a forced yoga pose for me), my elbow hot with pain. But no blood. OK. OK.

Pip's face was red with rage – how dare I try to prevent her from choking? What a nerve.

The shower rained down on us for a while until I mustered the courage and wherewithal to move. Fuuuuuuuuck 2.0. It wasn't so much the pain – although that was pretty bloody bad – but the realisation that somewhere, in the midst of my very busy day, I would now have to find time to go and see a doctor. Exactly how would that be possible?

Somehow I managed to hook my good arm around Pip and lift her out of the shower. I got her dry, then gingerly dried myself, trying to work out if I'd broken anything. Owing to never having broken a bone before, and also not being a doctor, I had no idea what I was looking for. I assumed it would feel like that one broken biscuit in the packet.

I chose a dress for Pip that I could slip over her head and arms, thankful that it was the warmest April in years, because there was no way I'd be able to get tights on her. There are upsides to climate change after all! My elbow pulsed with pain as I pushed the pram, but I shoved it from my mind the same way I swept magazines I hadn't had time to read off my desk. Whoosh. Gone. No more pain.

Ahahahaha.

By the time I made it into work – 8.57 (I was getting better at this whole working mother caper) – I could no longer move my arm. Something was really wrong. I would just have to get through the upfronts and then nip out to the doctor. I began to think it might actually be quite relaxing to have an hour to myself, even if it was in the waiting room of a medical centre in the CBD. The thought bordered on arousing. Yes, something was definitely wrong.

I smiled and subtly flirted my way through the upfronts. Twenty middle-aged men, barely distinguishable from each other, nodded, apparently captivated, as I walked them through our new plan for *The Weekend*, using all the 'buzzwords' Meredith had coached me on. We were taking a 'bold new direction'. It was a '360-degree brand experience'. We had 'learnt from our learnings'. Our readers were 'time-poor' but 'hungry for content'.

At 10.59, after weeks of careful planning and the whole of Saturday spent in the office, going over the minutiae of the presentation as if we were giving the State of the Union address, Meredith suddenly reared up from her chair and announced it was lunchtime, which really meant drinking time. I felt my jaw drop. Weeks and weeks of work for two hours of my time? Nobody noticed the look on my face, though, because the ad execs were all focused on Bea, rolling in a case of Mumm. They thought all their Christmases had come at once, no doubt. What they didn't realise was that, over the course of the afternoon, all their New Years, birthdays, weddings and bar mitzvahs would come too.

I was done. I seized the moment to excuse myself.

'Meredith,' I said, tapping her on the shoulder with my good hand. 'I have to go.'

She handed me a glass of champagne, grinning. She was already onto her second.

'What?' she asked. 'What did you say? Never mind – well done, Gigi! That was amazing. You did a great job. Look how happy everyone is!' She slapped me between the shoulder blades. I winced and tried not to cry as tears sprang to my eyes.

She grimaced, her mouth puckering in distaste. 'What's wrong?'

'I, uh, I slipped in the shower this morning. I hurt my arm. I think it might be broken, actually.'

Meredith raised her eyebrows in a 'You don't say?' sort of way, and said nothing.

'So, um, I just need to nip off to the doctor to get it checked out. Might as well do it now while everyone's... having a break.'

Behind me, I heard the pop, pop, pop of three bottles of champagne being uncorked at once. It was twelve past eleven.

Meredith swatted my good arm. 'I'm sure it's not broken,' she said, shaking her head. 'Maybe it's sprained.'

'Well, yeah, but even so, I should get it checked out.'

'Gary!' she yelled, looking over at one of the identical, balding, 45-year-old men. His eyes lit up as he realised Meredith 'Built Like A Supermodel' Parker was talking to him. He may have foamed at the mouth. But frankly, with the persistent blinding ache of my arm, I couldn't be sure I hadn't done the same. 'Gary, get over here!' Meredith waved at him.

Gary, glass in hand, toddled over. 'Hello, ladies. Brilliant presentation, Georgie, just brilliant. I'll take it back to the bosses, but no doubt P&G will be spending with you. And we'd love you to join us at the rugby on Saturday night if you can make it?'

I opened my mouth to say no, but Meredith got there first.

'Absolutely, we would love to. Thank you so much. Anyway, since you work at P&G, can you tell us – is George's arm broken?'

Gary raised his eyebrows. 'What do you mean?' He looked me up and down.

Meredith rolled her eyes. 'George slipped in the shower this morning and now she thinks she needs to see a doctor. But it looks fine to me. Anyway, you're the expert – what do you think?' 'Well... I work in sales. I'm not a doctor.' Gary looked hesitant about this turn of events. That was the thing about Meredith.

When she was good, she was very, very good, and when she'd had more than two glasses of champagne, she was horrid.

'Yes, but you know about this sort of thing. What do you think?' Meredith grinned wildly at him, an unleashed beast.

Gary cocked his head. 'I think you'd better go see a doctor,' he said, steering Meredith towards the open bottles of Mumm. I breathed a silent sigh of relief and made a run for it.

*

'It's broken, alright. But it's a clean break. You'll be back to normal in... oh, six weeks or so.'

'Six *weeks*?'

The doctor nodded. 'I'll pop it in a sling for you now and then we can get it cast. You'll have to make a long appointment for this afternoon. Ask the receptionist to fit you in; tell her it came from me.'

I shook my head. 'No, no. I don't have time for that. I need to go back to work. Can you just do it now, please? It's really urgent.'

I had accomplished exactly nothing on my to-do list. In fact, I had added to it: *Get cast on broken arm. Figure out how to function with broken arm.*

The doctor frowned and answered slowly. 'I have a waiting

room full of people who need medical attention. I understand you're in a lot of pain, and I'm going to help with that. But I need some time – and the help of a nurse, who is currently on her lunch break – to put your arm in a cast. So you will have to wait, Ms Henderson.'

'Fine.'

He carefully placed my arm in a sling and asked me if I wanted some painkillers. I nodded eagerly.

'Yes, please.'

'Of course. Let's get you some Endone. But be careful with it, OK? It's pretty strong stuff, and highly addictive.'

I nodded, practically holding out my hand like a kid waiting for a lolly. *Please sir, can I have some more?*

'You're not still breastfeeding, are you?' he asked, scribbling on the prescription note.

'Um. Yes.'

He looked up. 'Oh. Well, no Endone for you, then.' He balled up the note and slam-dunked it into the bin.

'What? What do you mean?'

He shook his head. 'It could be fatal to your baby. We just don't have enough data on it. Best to avoid, if you can. And there are other perfectly good painkillers out there. Panadol, hot compresses, that sort of thing.'

'Are you suggesting that a heat pack will be "just as good" as Endone for my broken arm?'

He hesitated. 'Well, no. Not exactly. It will relieve some of the pain, though. And Panadol is excellent.'

I stared at him. 'No it's not. I may as well have a Tic-Tac. Is there really nothing else?'

The doctor shot me a pitying smile. 'Well, you could have the Endone, but you'd have to wean your baby. Even then, I could only prescribe a very mild dose.'

'No.'

'OK,' he said, nodding. 'If you don't mind my asking... how old is your little one?'

'She's eleven months.'

He nodded again. 'Well, if you did want to give up, it would be perfectly fine. Your baby would be very healthy. The World Health Organization recommends mothers nurse for six months, so you're well past that window. Your baby really would be absolutely –'

'No. Panadol will be fine.'

The doctor nodded, slowly this time. 'Alright. I understand it's a sensitive area.'

It was, I thought, as I left the room, especially when doctors used phrases like 'give up'. Why couldn't they be more positive about it? Why couldn't they call it 'reaching the finish line'? Giving up sounded like failure. Giving up *was* failure. I was already failing at everything else; I couldn't fail at this.

Six weeks. How would I last six weeks with my arm in a cast? How would I pick Pip up? What about her birthday party? How would I make all those sodding sausage rolls like this? How would I fill lolly bags one-handed? How would I manage? Nina was with Jed. Jase was with Saskia. Neil hated me. Ellie had her own life. Mum – well, it would have to be Mum.

I picked up the phone and dialled her number.

'I'll be there in a jiffy, love. Just let me get my hair out of these rollers and pop on a pair of slacks.'

Chapter 19

With the help of her extremely patient daycare teacher, I managed to wrangle Pip into the pram to head home. But walking home one-armed was a struggle. We shuffled along Redfern Street at a glacial pace, the sun setting behind us. My phone kept lighting up with messages from Meredith, photos of her and the ad execs at various bars around the city.

> When are you coming back?
> Having so much fun! Heading
> to Ivy Pool soon K? MP xxx

I counted down the minutes til I could have another Tic-Tac.

Mum met me at the door, looking slightly crazed.

'Darling, what happened? Come in, come in.'

I pushed Pip's pram through the door. 'I broke my arm.'

Mum's hand flew to her mouth as if I'd said, 'I have terminal cancer'. Perhaps she wasn't the best person to call. My mum had a tendency to dramatise. She'd once made me stay up for twenty-four hours to make sure I didn't have concussion after I tripped at netball.

'Oh, darling.' Mum unbuckled Pip and set her down on the floor, where she promptly found a crayon and began to

scrawl on the hardwood. I added *Clean floor* to my to-do list.
'Are you alright?'

'Yeah, it hurts like a–' I stopped, remembering that good
mothers didn't swear. 'Yeah, it really hurts.'

'Darling, I can only imagine. Sit down, sit down.'

I did. Mum picked Pip up and went into the kitchen,
where I heard her muttering about dinner and where were
the vegetables, and would it kill me to throw out the sugar?
I closed my eyes and decided to let Mum take care of me. I
was done.

'Darling, where's your julienne peeler?' I heard her call
out.

'My what?'

Mum stuck her head around the door, Pip still in her arms.
'Your julienne peeler. I'm making coleslaw.'

'I don't know what that is, Mum. I'm sure I don't have
one.'

Mum tut-tutted and retreated to the kitchen. I sank back
against the couch and felt the hot pain course through me.

George, where are you? MP xxx

I picked up my phone and replied.

Arm is definitely broken. Dr
set it this afternoon, said I
should take tomorrow off.
Hurts like crazy! GH x

My phone rang. Shit. Mum poked her head around the corner,
eyes narrowed. 'Who's that?' she mouthed. I waved her away.

'Hi, Meredith,' I said.

'Where are you?'

'Uh... at home. Did you get my text?'

'Yes, of course I got your text. I want to know why you're
not here. Don't you know how important this is?'

Mum was still staring at me, Pip in her arms, a puréed-carrot smile on her face. 'I have a broken arm, Meredith. I'm on serious painkillers,' I lied. Technically, I *could* be on serious painkillers. 'I can't be out drinking right now.'

'George,' she said, over whoops of delight in the background, 'you don't have to drink, but you need to be here. You are the face of the brand. I can't keep making excuses for you – you're on thin ice. You've already had one day off this year. Why does this keep happening?'

Something in me finally snapped. 'Why does *what* keep happening? Life?'

'Pardon?'

'Do you mean why does life keep happening? Why have I got a broken bone and why did my daughter get sick? Why do I have to leave early sometimes and why am I late occasionally?' OK, more like *frequently*, but still. 'Because that's life, Meredith. Shit like this *happens* sometimes. It just does.'

I heard her tut-tut on the other end. 'Well, it certainly needs to happen a lot less. Do you understand? This is not a job, George. This is a *lifestyle*. You need to be here.'

I sighed. 'I can't this time, Meredith. I really can't.'

I don't know if it was the lack of Endone or the grateful look on Mum's face that made me do it, but I hung up the phone before she could answer.

*

'We remember and celebrate the life of Janice Doherty, loving mother of Nina and Jillian, wife of Greg, sister of Nancy and Donna. We honour her presence in our lives and are thankful for her. Janice, you're no longer here with us, but you are not forgotten. We love you.'

I wiped the tears away as Matt let go of his balloon. Ellie told me that Nina had asked him to come, but I hadn't expected him to do a reading, too. Jan died when Nina was fifteen; Matt had never even met her. But I saw that he, too, had tears in his eyes, for the mother Nina had lost.

Nina stood alone, a yellow balloon in her hand, looking down at the sand. Mum held Pip, who was staring, fascinated, at the balloon I held in my good hand.

'I'll be back in a sec,' I said to Mum. I made my way past Ellie and Simon, who held a sleepy Lucas in his arms, and stood next to Nina, wanting to hold her hand. I motioned to the balloon and Nina nodded. I let it go and we watched it drift higher and higher, until we could only make out a speck of canary yellow up above. I squeezed Nina's hand.

She looked over at me, her face stained with tears.

'Hi,' she whispered.

'Hey.'

'What happened to your arm?'

'Broke it. Shower. Slipped.'

'Oh shit.'

I nodded. I watched Ellie let go of her balloon, and Simon let go of his. They gave each other a hug, swallowing back tears, then Simon waved Matt over, patting him on the back and offering a grateful smile. As Matt nodded in Nina's direction, I realised Jed wasn't here.

'Do you want to...?' I looked at Nina's balloon.

'Just give me a minute,' she said, and closed her eyes.

I squeezed her hand again and felt all my anger melt away. None of it mattered, not compared to this.

'OK,' she said, and opened her eyes. 'Ready.' Lifting her head and blinking back tears, she held her hand up and gently unfurled her fist. The balloon floated away. We all watched it go.

*

'I bought something for you,' said Nina, at the pub afterwards. She set her glass of wine down on the table – the same one she'd been nursing all night – and pulled something out of her bag. A gift, wrapped in kraft paper and tied with a neat grosgrain ribbon.

'So... I've been an idiot,' she said. 'I'm so sorry.'

I smiled. 'It's fine,' I said. 'It doesn't matter anymore. I'm sorry, too.'

She pushed the present across the table. 'Here. Peace offering. Please be my friend again.'

I nodded. 'Done. But you didn't need to buy me a present.' I smiled. 'It's not a breast pump, is it? Or lactation tea?'

Nina rolled her eyes. 'Just open it,' she said, gesturing to the gift.

I nodded and unwrapped the paper.

'*Sophie B Hawkins's Greatest Hits*?'

'It's an olive branch. Plus, we don't have it.'

'How many songs does she even have? I can only think of two.'

Nina rolled her eyes and took another measured sip. 'Not the point, George. The point is, I'm sorry. I've been such a dick. I... Jed broke up with me. I'm sure you won't be surprised to hear that, but... yeah. It's over.'

Ah.

She looked down at her lap.

'I'm really sorry, George. I've fucked everything up. I can't believe you came today, I really can't. I wouldn't have. I was... I was a really bad friend.'

All my bravado, all my talk of not wanting to let Nina back in – it all dissolved as soon as I heard her say sorry.

'Ugh. I just feel so stupid. I was ready for this... this life with Jed, you know? I had all these plans for us, to travel and work overseas and... Do you know what I did? I told him. I told him all about my big plans.' She laughed. 'And he looked at me and just said, "Yeah, I need some space. I'm going overseas." It was like, once I'd actually put it into words, he just freaked out and couldn't leave fast enough.'

'Oh, hon. I'm sorry. That sucks.' Part of me wanted to say, *He's twenty-five, of course he left*, but I didn't. Obviously.

277

'That's not even the worst part, George. It's actually not even close. So then–' she paused, laughing bitterly again, 'so then I said, "I'll come with you." And he said, "No."'

'Oh.' I stroked her back and leaned into her. 'Oh, hon, it's OK. If he didn't want you to go with him, that's his loss. I mean, what a dick. *You're* the catch in this relationship, not him. He was punching way above.'

She shook her head, sniffing back a few stray tears.

'I just wanted someone different, you know?' She looked at me and I could tell she needed me to understand. 'I needed someone who wouldn't talk about babies. Who wouldn't think I had failed them because I couldn't have one. I wanted to be with someone who didn't remind me of Matt at all. I needed to have a relationship that had nothing to do with getting pregnant. I wanted to date someone who wouldn't even have *friends* who had kids, you know? I needed to get out of the dinner party circuit.'

'The what?'

'You know, the Saturday night dinner party circuit. A different couple every weekend. Sitting around at their house so they can still socialise and drink wine while their kids are asleep upstairs. I just had to get out of that whole thing.'

'Oh. Is that why...?' *Is that why you abandoned me?* I thought. *Is that why you promised to help me with Pip and then disappeared?*

'It was so hard, George. It was so much harder than I thought it would be. I'm so sorry.'

Nina looked down and closed her eyes. A tear escaped.

I held her closer. Awful, awful Jed. How dare he break Nina's heart? How dare he live up to his clichéd millennial reputation?

'It's OK. I'm sorry, Neen. I've been so caught up in my own stuff. So much has happened.'

As she finished her wine, I filled Nina in on the Neil Situation. When I got to the end, she jabbed me in the arm.

'You're an idiot,' she said.

'What?'

'This guy sounds great. You're an idiot.'

'No... it wouldn't work. Not with Pip, and Meredith–'

'Meredith? Your boss, Meredith?'

I nodded.

'George, who the hell cares what she thinks? Do you?'

I paused. I didn't much care anymore. Even though I'd hung up on Meredith, I'd half-expected her to forget about the whole thing; she'd clearly been drunk while we were talking. But no such luck. The next morning a meeting request had popped up in my inbox, titled 'THE ROLE OF THE EDITOR AT *THE WEEKEND*'. Meredith and I were due to meet about it next week. For a whole day. I couldn't wait to hear her thoughts on what my role should be. More drinking? Less editing? More flirting with media buyers? Less managing my own staff?

'Well... not really,' I admitted.

'And you like Neil?'

I nodded.

Nina raised her eyebrows. 'There you go.'

'It's not that simple–' I started, before Matt interrupted us.

'Another round, ladies?' I shook my head; I'd already had two, plus a handful of Nurofen Plus. Nina looked up and shook her head, too. 'Not for me.' She placed her hand on Matt's. 'Actually, we'd better go. It's been a long day. For everyone,' she said, nodding to Pip, sleeping in her pram as Mum, engrossed in conversation with Ellie, rocked her back and forth.

Nina turned to me. 'I'm not drinking. Well, I'm not drinking as much. I got a bit... out of control for a while.'

I nodded. 'Happens to the best of us,' I said.

'Yeah,' said Nina. 'But it all got a bit much for me. When you – I mean, no offence, but when you, of all people – called me out on it, I knew I was definitely drinking too much. Thanks for that.'

I raised an eyebrow, amused. 'You're welcome. And none taken. So uh... you're leaving with Matt?'

Nina smiled coyly. 'We're... giving it a go.'

'Really?'

She nodded. 'Yeah. After Jed dumped me, I was so humiliated. I went down to the pub, because obviously, I needed *another* drink, right? So I'm having a G&T and I think, "Oh, I should look on Tinder," even though I'd only been dumped an hour before. And guess who I saw? Guess who was in that pub on that very night?'

I knew what the answer was, but I let Neen finish.

'Matt. And then I see him come up in my matches column. And at first I thought it was a joke – like I was being *Punk'd*, but, like, ten years too late – and then I see him walk over to me. And we had a drink, and then we had dinner, and...' She trailed off, smiling broadly now. 'It's not perfect, but it's good. We're trying.'

I thought of all the years when, for Nina and Matt, 'we're trying' was followed up with 'for a baby'. Now they were trying just for themselves, just for each other.

'That's good.'

'It is good. I'm taking that year off next year. We're thinking of travelling together.'

'Really?' Matt had never been much of a traveller. He'd done six weeks of Contiki at eighteen, and then taken a few island holidays with Nina, but that was about the extent of it. 'Beirut, then? Or what about Syria? I hear Damascus is lovely this time of year.'

'Har har,' said Nina, rolling her eyes at me. 'You're not going to let me forget that, are you?'

I shook my head. 'Nope. Or the pastry chef thing. Or wanting to start transcendental meditation –'

'What? I never said that!' Nina was laughing now, the old Nina, the one I loved.

'You may as well have. You were going Full Namaste.'

She clinked my empty glass with her full one and raised it in a toast. 'Thanks for saving me,' she said, deadpan. 'Best friends don't let best friends go Full Namaste.'

Chapter 20

To: Georgie Henderson
From: Meredith Parker
Subject: Your column
Richie's given the go-ahead. First column will be May 14.
Interview with Arianna Foster.

I read over the email one more time. Arianna Foster. Arianna Foster? The name was familiar but I couldn't place it – it was like hearing an early noughties song and finally realising you heard it once on *Grey's Anatomy*. I googled the name. Oh. The soapie actress. Married to the cricketer. Wait, why was I interviewing *her* for my column?

I typed back slowly, thankful once again that I had broken my left arm. At least I could still type and scroll through my emails. And dress and feed my child, of course.

Pip would be a year old in just one week. Like every parent ever, I was contractually obliged to marvel at how quickly the time had passed, but it really was hard to fathom that she'd been here for almost an entire year. And yet, in some ways, it was hard to conceive of a time when she hadn't been here.

She was standing on her own now and so close to walking. She wasn't speaking the Queen's English yet, but she was speaking a version of it. 'Dit da' was 'sit down'. 'Oof uh' was 'good girl'. 'Uh-oh' was... well, 'uh-oh'. And 'Umma'... that was me. The first time she'd said it, I hadn't realised that's what she meant. And then she'd reached out to me, tapping me on the arm as if to say, 'Listen up, idiot. I'm talking to you.' She looked so proud, a big broad smile on her face. I cuddled her into me and closed my eyes. She threw up on me a few seconds later, but for a brief, shining moment, things were perfect.

I had assumed it'd be easier to leave her once she got older, but in fact, I was finding it much, much harder. Pip was changing so fast now, no longer a newborn ready to be shaped into the person she'd one day become. Now she was becoming that person, and I was missing it all. More than ever, I whispered to myself *It'll all be worth it, it'll all be worth it.* And more than ever, I wondered if it was really true.

To: Meredith Parker
From: Georgie Henderson
Subject: Your column
Meredith, column is meant to be about working mums, not interviews with celebrities. Not sure about this. I thought Richie loved my sample columns?

I'd envisaged my column as a chance to talk about real issues that affected working women, not as a glorified PR piece for celebrity 'working mothers'. What could the average mum – whose day likely began at 5.30 am and didn't let up until the kids were tucked in, the dishes done, the emails replied to and the lunch boxes packed for the next day – possibly glean from an interview with a rich white woman whose nanny and cleaner ensured she never had to worry about any of those things?

Meredith marched into my office, flip book in her hands. She casually tossed it onto my desk, seemingly unaware that a) it weighed approximately the same amount as my child, and

b) that she had hurled it straight towards my recently broken limb. I moved my arm just in time.

Since our showdown, Meredith had turned down her temperature from frosty to colder than a witch's tit. She'd even stopped signing off her emails *MP xxx*.

'What's the problem with Arianna? You know she's a friend of mine, don't you?' she asked.

Ah. There it was. There was no getting out of the interview now, I knew it.

'I didn't know that. Right.'

'We've been friends for years, since she was a model. I love Arianna.'

I nodded. 'Sure.'

'And you know she's launching her own line of candles, right?'

I stared at Meredith and tried very, very hard not to groan or roll my eyes or show my general contempt for candles and people who wanted to slap their name on products to make a quick buck.

'She's fascinating, just fascinating. And she has a little boy. So,' Meredith said, shrugging, 'she's perfect for your column. You wanted it to be about working mothers.'

'Yes, but... I wanted it to be about things that really affect working mothers, you know?' What I wanted to say, and did not, was: *I want it to be about women who feel the pull of home when they're at work and work when they're at home. It's for women who feel that they're slacking off when they leave on time because they have no other choice, because they have responsibilities to their children. It's for women who 'make up' for leaving on time or working three days a week by taking on extra work and staying up late at home to finish presentations and reports and answer emails. It's for women who never take lunch breaks because they don't have time. It's for women who are bloody exhausted but keep buggering on because they want to be both. It's not a place for you to publicise your friend's business. Especially when your friend is married to a multi-millionaire cricketer and probably has a sleep whisperer and a wet nurse and a Pilates instructor on call.*

And what I really, really wanted to say was: *Just fuck off, Meredith. Just fucking fuck off.*

Meredith rolled her eyes. 'Like *what*?' she asked, as if she could not possibly think of one issue that affected working mothers.

'Like... maternity leave. Like flexible hours. Like paid parental leave. Like coming back to work and feeling totally out of touch. Like wanting to be promoted but feeling out of the loop.' Like having a boss who periodically forgets you have a child, makes you work on weekends, forces you to spend weeks on a presentation that wraps up in less than half a day and then is disappointed when you can't spend the rest of the day drinking because you've smashed your arm to smithereens. Like being told that you don't have a job, you have a lifestyle. Like being sent a meeting request in all caps that promises to detail exactly what you are doing wrong and why you are so very, very bad at your job. Like that.

She made a sour face. 'Honestly... I know this will sound so mean, but... ugh, I just find all of that so boring. You have to be able to help yourself, you know? These women who find all this so tough, well... I just feel like they've brought it on themselves.'

I felt my chest rise and fall rapidly, my heart beat quicker and my face flush with rage. I had to find a way to end this conversation before I got fired or stapled Meredith's hand to the desk.

'What day's the interview?' I asked, defeated.

'Thursday,' she said, a shit-eating grin on her face.

Chapter 21

If you had told me earlier that morning that I was about to have a nervous breakdown, I... well, OK, I might have believed you.

But I probably would have thought you were exaggerating. At least a little bit.

The morning of my interview with Arianna began like most others, except for one crucial difference: Pip didn't cry when I dropped her off at daycare. When she'd woken that morning, I'd tried to feed her, but despite my best efforts Pip had all but stopped nursing now. Sometimes she'd wake up for a quick boob session in the middle of the night, but most of the time she now regarded my nipples with something like bored confusion. Like, 'Really, breast milk again? Don't you have *anything* else?' So we went through the motions of our morning routine – which now took slightly longer because I had to do everything one-armed – and got ready for the day ahead. No breastfeeding meant I was usually at work on time – more or less – but it felt like a hollow victory.

I set Pip down on the floor at daycare and gave her a board book to play with: *Oh, the Places You'll Go*. I'd loved it as a kid, trying to twist my tongue around the words. I stroked

Pip's cheek as I opened the book, showing her the pages. As I stood to leave, I braced myself for her cries. She had cried every day, without fail, since she had begun daycare.

But not today. Today Pip sat happily on the floor, her small fist flicking through the pages of Dr Seuss. She didn't even look up. I stared down at her for a second, confused, sure she would react. But she didn't. She knew I was going. She'd just gotten used to it.

I cried all the way to the train station. Later, in the taxi on the way to Arianna's, I pressed my head against the cool glass of the window, closing my eyes and thinking, *something has to change.*

*

From: Meredith Parker
To: Georgie Henderson
Subject: No worries

George, please don't sign off your emails with 'no worries.' I refer you to the instances below:

On Tuesday, I wrote: George, I won't be able to talk through cover options this morning, have a meeting.

And then you wrote: No worries.

Then yesterday, I sent you this: George, can't do lunch after all, have to head upstairs to see Richie.

And you wrote back: No worries.

George, I know that it is not a worry. I am your boss. Whatever I say, you do. It will not EVER be a worry for you to wait for me, or have me cancel a meeting, or skip something we had planned.

From now on I would prefer if you simply replied with, 'I understand.'

I tried to hit on the appropriate reaction. How I would love to reply:

Dear Meredith,
No worries,
George

My fingers hovered over the keyboard, wondering why I didn't just go for it, when Neil walked in.

'Hey, I know you're doing that interview today, but I wanted to catch you before you left.' He sat down opposite me, expressionless.

'OK. What's up?'

'I'm leaving.'

I felt my eyes widen. 'What?'

Neil clasped his hands on his lap and nodded. 'Yeah, I – uh – I'm done with this.' He gestured to the wall of *Weekend* covers opposite us.

'*The Weekend*?'

'Writing, I think. Food writing, anyway. It's a bit of a joke. I've become a joke. I wanted to write about real food stories, about climate change and permaculture and... I don't know. Important stuff. But instead I write about cronuts and freakshakes and stupid shit like that. Even the restaurants we review... most of them aren't all that great, they just have great PR behind them. I'm sick of it. I want to do something else.'

'Oh,' I said, nodding. I knew what Neil was talking about, I really did. I'd started off imagining myself on *Four Corners*. Now I drew red pen marks around the *Four Corners* hosts' thighs, asking my art director to erase the cellulite. 'What will you do?'

'I don't know. Maybe go overseas. I haven't really made plans. I just... I can't do this anymore.'

'Right.' *Overseas. Gone.*

'Well,' I said, vaguely aware of my voice breaking slightly, 'it'll be hard to replace you. Everyone will be sad to see you go.'

He smiled, that old Neil smirk coming back. 'Not everyone, I'd imagine.'

I started to shake my head. 'Neil–'

He put up a hand and rose from his seat. 'No, it's OK. I get it, George, I really do. This is your thing. This is what you want to do. I don't fit into that.' He shrugged and turned to leave. 'I'll have a resignation letter drawn up for HR.'

No! I wanted to shout. *Don't leave! This is not what I want to do! I want to do you!*

But I didn't. I smiled and nodded, and stood from my desk to shake Neil's hand, a gesture both bizarrely personal and nowhere near intimate enough. He paused before taking my hand, but when he did, I felt a surge of his old warmth coming through.

'Neil, I–'

'Bye, George.'

He left.

*

Arianna Foster and I were as different as two women could be. I knew this before I met her, in a basic sense, but now that she sat opposite me, entirely composed, wearing head to toe white (WHITE!), I knew for sure. I mean: a mother, wearing white. And absolutely zero tomato sauce stains. How was it possible?

I glanced down at my list of Meredith-approved questions (remembering with a sting the email she'd sent, to which I had replied – of course – *no worries!*) and tried hard to concentrate. *Neil is leaving. Neil is leaving.*

Arianna smiled graciously, answering my questions just as her PR firm would have instructed her. The Mona Lisa of the eastern suburbs. Her hair – my god, her hair. It wasn't blonde. No. That's far too simple a description. It was golden. It shone as she moved, as if little ripples of sunshine beamed from it. If the rest of this woman wasn't so damn beautiful, I would have been compelled to stare at her hair all the live long freaking day.

What struck me more than her beauty, though, was her... togetherness. Together was something I had not been for a very long time. Arianna looked like she had taken exceptional care of herself – always and without fail. She looked like she had never spent a night trying – unsuccessfully – to get her baby back to sleep. Like she had never felt her boobs erupt with milk, their contents seeping through her bra and top, giving her liquid headlights. Like she had never been so bone-tired that she had all but given up on the idea of looking nice. Her clothes did not bear the stains of last night's dinner, or in fact, any dinner at all. They were crisp with the recent creases of ironing. They were fashionable, on trend. Looking at her was the way I felt after visiting Ikea – surely if I just had those spice jars and that desk tray, I could achieve great things. I mean, Marie Curie certainly didn't invent radium or whatever until she had Kondo-ed her desk, right? So if I could just have a little of whatever Arianna's magic was, I could get shit done.

As it was, my clothes did bear the stains of last night's dinner. And not even my own. Pip's dinner – some sort of superfood-charged gluten-free (apparently all babies born after 2007 are gluten-intolerant) spaghetti bolognaise concoction – was splattered on my un-ironed jeans. Luckily, they were very dark (my days of wearing white jeans were decidedly O-V-E-R) so they looked OK to the naked eye. But put them under a microscope and you'd discover a Rorschach test of food stains, spilt milk and general detritus. I tried to remember the last time I had washed them. Did Febreze count as washing? Probably not.

'So, um... tell me how you got the idea... for the candles,' I said, trying to sound as interested as I possibly could. I could hardly imagine anything less captivating than discussing candles – possibly the difference between threeand four-ply toilet paper? Arianna's quiet smile broke into a fully-fledged grin. 'It's a funny story, actually,' she said, as she proceeded to tell me a dull, decidedly unfunny story about being bored at home one day (having a rich husband will do that) and thinking, 'Gee, I like candles. Why don't I buy some from China, stick my name on them and sell them to other rich women just like me?'

'Uh-huh, uh-huh,' I nodded, jotting on my pad. I wasn't actually taking notes, I just needed to appear interested. On the pad I'd written, 'YOU ARE AS BORING AS A VANILLA-SCENTED CANDLE.' I traced over and over the letters until the pen broke into the page below. 'And, uh... what are your other... plans? Will the company expand?'

'Yes! Definitely. We're launching in Singapore next month –' *more rich housewives* '– and of course, there's the subscription service. We are all very excited by that.'

'Uh-huh, sure, it's amazing.'

'It's the first time anyone has ever done anything like it,' Arianna added, as if she were talking about walking on the moon or Drake's Instagram, i.e. something of actual merit.

'Right. What's the thinking?' My recorder flashed its red light, confirming it was recording. As if it would matter. The PR company – or Meredith, for whom integrity was an optional extra, like a meal on a Jetstar flight – would change everything I'd written and replace it with a slightly more editorial version of a press release (complete with a lengthy and detailed description of what my subject was wearing and had eaten for lunch – compulsory for any interview with a woman these days).

'One candle, every month, for a year. It's the perfect gift for the woman – or man! – who has everything.'

'Except scented candles.'

Arianna beamed and nodded enthusiastically. 'Right!'

'Arianna?'

Mona Lisa whipped around to face a young, stocky woman in jeans and a paint-covered t-shirt. The Nanny.

'Yes, Robyn?'

'Atticus wants a snack.'

Arianna raised her eyebrows. 'There's plenty of seaweed in the kitchen, Robyn.'

'He's quite hungry, Arianna. I thought I'd make him a sandwich–'

Her employer shook her head. 'No. Seaweed or low-sugar fruit. Atticus knows the rules.'

Robyn opened her mouth but Arianna cut her off before she began. 'Thank you, Robyn, that'll be all.'

Robyn looked to me with a slightly aghast expression. I looked away. She left.

Arianna shook her head. 'It's only her second week. She doesn't know how to handle Atticus yet. He's quite a... strong-willed little boy.'

I nodded.

'How old is he?'

'Nine months.'

I felt my eyebrows rise quite uncontrollably as I thought of some of the crap I let Pippa eat: white bread, sultanas, the end of a ballpoint pen that had found its forever home in the bottom of my bag.

Arianna sighed. 'It's exhausting.'

I looked up.

'Being a mother. It never ends,' she continued. 'Do you have children?'

I nodded. 'Yes. One.' I smiled involuntarily, the thought of Pippa breaking through the ridiculous monotony of this day.

Arianna sighed and smiled, too. 'How old? Boy, girl?'

'Girl. Pippa. Philippa, but only on her birth certificate. Eleven months.'

She stared at me, bug-eyed. 'You must find it so hard.'

I cleared my throat. 'Well–'

'I mean, when I started working again–' *can we please not pretend that putting your name on a bunch of candles made in China is real work?* '– I just didn't have the time for Atticus that I used to, you know? The time I *wanted* to have with him. But then, a career is so important. It's so nice to have a sense of purpose outside your children, isn't it?'

Even if that purpose is filling someone's home with the scent of French pear and wild lily. Yes. Yes, I suppose that would be nice.

What *was* my purpose, exactly? Ostensibly, it was to edit a magazine, to deliver our readers news and information edited just for them, through the lenses of all the things they held important: politics, health, sport, the odd spaghetti carbonara recipe.

But when was the last time I had actually sat down and read a page of *The Weekend*, without being interrupted about a client meeting or a brand event or a 'cross-promotional integrative alignment opportunity'? When was the last time I had read *anything* at work? My job seemed to consist of putting out fires started by Meredith and spending days perfecting presentations that were over in minutes.

'So it's hard,' she went on. 'It is just so hard every single day. I don't know how you do it. Especially with your arm like that,' she said, gesturing to my broken limb. 'And with your job,' she went on, looking exhausted by my life. 'It sounds very demanding. You must have a great nanny.'

I laughed. I couldn't help it. I pictured Pip with her childcare worker – not educator, not preschool teacher – and the seventeen other kids in her class. I pictured the long days they spent together while I did something that resembled work, without the fabled sense of purpose Arianna had mentioned. I pictured Jase and my mum and Ellie filling in the childcare gaps, the times when I couldn't pick Pip up on time and had to risk the $10 a minute (!) fine to stay late at work while I asked someone else to take my baby home, feed her a bottle of my expressed milk and put her to bed without me. I pictured her crying at 10 pm as I finished my work at home, white-knuckled at my laptop and whispering to myself, 'Please go back to sleep, please go back to sleep' because I knew that if she saw my face, we'd be up for another hour. At least. And I wouldn't be able to finish my work. And the whole goddamn cycle would start over again, Pippa's cries chorusing with my own guilty tears.

'Do you want to talk about that? How hard it can be to combine work and motherhood?'

Arianna nodded with enthusiasm. 'I do. It's something I feel really passionate about.'

'Uh-huh,' I nodded, encouraging her to go on, thinking that this interview might be salvageable, that Arianna might finally give me something more interesting than the difference between soy wax and paraffin.

To be fair to Arianna, she'd started life in much the same way I had – she'd just been far luckier in the financial stakes. The daughter of a school teacher and a swimming coach, Arianna began life as most Australian kids do – lower middle-class and perfectly happy. The difference between Arianna and most kids was that she was exceptionally beautiful and had parlayed that beauty into a starring role on a hit soap opera, playing the doomed good girl with a heart of gold, Tess Wheeler. She won a couple of Logies, released a pretty bad single and dated a couple of cute pop stars. Then she got a stylist and married a cricketer with a knack for cereal commercials and the rest was Aussie fairytale history. Arianna and her husband, Chris, made headlines last year when they sold their first home, a penthouse apartment with views of the Bridge, for a record price and bought a broken-down but still beautiful six-bedroom mansion. Ten months, hundreds of hours of labour and one exorbitantly expensive mononymous interior designer later, the house was the most beautiful structure I had ever seen. For all her middle-class roots, I had to hand it to her: Arianna was classy as fuck. (Even if I did suspect that Arianna was not the name she was born with.)

'Well, I just did a shoot with Belle Maman,' Arianna began, referring to a very popular 'stylish mother' website, the kind I outwardly despised but secretly read with guilty pleasure, 'and Atticus just would not sit still.' She flushed with embarrassment. 'It was incredibly frustrating. I'm trying to work, to answer Alexandra's questions and promote the candles, and Atticus is pulling my hair – I'd just got a blow-dry for the first time in, I don't know, two weeks – and crying and just generally not being a good boy. So I was embarrassed because, well... I was not exactly being a beautiful mother, was I?'

Belle Maman was for mothers of a certain tax bracket, for whom work was a distant memory (unless they were fashion designers or children's book illustrators, in which case, they were still allowed to have their 'outlet'). It was dedicated to showing off the latest Kate Spade nappy bag, or $60 Jonathan Adler sippy cups. Ellie loved it because it felt 'real' to her. It felt like 'BS' to me – nothing about that site was real. It was full of staged, probably Photoshopped portraits of incredibly stylish mothers with their adorable offspring, neither of whom were screaming, crying, wearing day-old tracksuit pants or looking as if they'd escaped a mental asylum earlier that day. The mothers paid lip service to how 'difficult' parenting was, while thanking their various support staff as if everybody had access to personal trainers and live-in nannies. They never mentioned the thrill of watching a movie the whole way through, or the depths of misery experienced when attempting to extract snot from an infant's nose using that weird blue syringe thing. They didn't talk about the fact that sometimes it took over an hour to put your baby to bed at night, or that most days, you'd be stuck on the lounge for hours as your baby gently drifted off your boob after a feed and fell asleep, leaving you glued in your spot for the foreseeable future, without anyone to bring you a cup of tea or the remote control. They never talked about how the new highlight of your day was when the mail arrived. They never talked about getting to 4 pm and thinking, with barely restrained glee, 'It's officially socially acceptable to drink wine now!' Nope. Nope nope nope. They just talked about Petit Bateau t-shirts and how much they owed to Tizzie (the Madonna of baby-rearing, Tizzie did not require a surname) and how excited they were to have finally found the perfect organic wooden teether for their kid.

I nodded for Arianna to go on. Her shiny hair whipped about, remembering the frustration of that day.

'I mean, of course, at the end of the day, Atticus is the most important thing in my life. But I do want to make a name for myself – you know, I'd like to be remembered as someone other than Tess Wheeler – and I find it very hard to juggle my career with caring for Atticus.'

'Is that when you decided to get a nanny?'

Arianna shook her head. 'Oh no. We hired a nanny right away. It takes a village, as Chris says.'

I stared ahead blankly. Who lived in my village?

'But I'm very hands-on. We both are. I mean, I could never be the sort of mother who just drops her kid at daycare and goes to work five days a week. What's the point of having them if someone else is raising them?'

I focused on steadying my breathing. *In. Out. In. Out.*

I wanted to tell Arianna that daycare was part of the village, that mothers had enough to worry about without being afraid that they were causing their kid lasting emotional damage by being audacious enough to go to work every day. But I couldn't. Because I felt hot with shame that I was one of those mothers. I did drop my kid at daycare five days a week. I was the mother who saw her kid for an hour in the morning and an hour at night. I was the mother who couldn't make it to reading circle or playgroup and didn't know the name of Peppa's brother because we never had time to watch ABC4Kids.

'So for me, it's about balancing the time I do have with Atticus with the effort I need to put into my career. It's hard, but it's manageable if you work at it, I find.' She stopped to twirl a strand of her flaxen hair around her finger, manicured with a neutral pink shade that made her nails look like small, perfect shells. I couldn't help but notice the enormous diamond in her engagement ring, sparkling at me, taunting me even more. She took on a pensive look and delivered a final clanger.

'And, you know, I want to say to these women, "Money isn't everything".'

Breathe. Breathe, George, breathe.

I looked around. After offering me a selection of tea from her 'tea cupboard', Arianna had led me on a tour of her home – built, of course, with a shitload of money. A Brett Whiteley original stared at me from across the room. Nearby was a staircase leading down to the (fully stocked) wine cellar. Off to the side was a discreet doorway (doorknobs = poverty) leading to a soundproof media room, with a screen as big as Pippa's own bedroom. Expensive Scandinavian furniture was everywhere, sleek and starkly beautiful.

Arianna was right. Money wasn't everything. But it sure would be nice.

'Sure. But there are other reasons, besides money, to work.'

'Of course! Of course. That's what I'm saying. But you don't have to spend every day away from your child to earn a decent living. Maybe people should be content to live with a little less.'

I felt my lip begin to tremble. My mouth felt dry. I reached for the glass of coconut water Arianna had drawn from a fresh coconut after we'd finished our tea. I gulped and gulped, trying to focus on simply doing the interview, leaving and going home to see the baby I clearly did not care about, according to Arianna.

Where had my confidence gone? There was a time when I would have put this woman squarely in her place. I would have stood up for myself. Now, I couldn't. I wouldn't even be able to convince myself.

As Arianna continued to opine on the benefits of minimalism (a bit rich coming from a woman who sold $70 candles), I felt the world begin to collapse a little. There was a tremor, a break. I shouldn't have had Pip. I should never have done it.

I never wanted to have kids, and now I knew I was right. I was a terrible mother. I had fled to work instead of looking after my own child. I had put my own need to have a title, a job, an office, in front of Pip's need to have a mum.

In part, I had Pip because I was afraid that if I didn't, it would be the wrong decision. Maybe, I had thought, I had been wrong about babies. Maybe I *could* be a mother. Maybe it wouldn't be as hard or as boring or as life-altering as I thought it would be. Maybe it would be like it was in Kate Hudson movies, where she played the reformed party girl who ended up feeling right at home in the suburbs, marrying the carpenter from *Sex and the City* and making homemade Play-Doh for her three kids.

Maybe it would be good. Maybe I would love it.

I heard myself ask Arianna a few more questions, barely registering her responses as I started to scrawl again: IT WILL ALL BE WORTH IT. IT WILL ALL BE WORTH IT. IT WILL ALL BE WORTH IT. Arianna's words were on repeat in my mind. *Living with less. Money's not everything. Five days a week. What's the point of having kids?*

She was right. I was a bad mother. I didn't love spending every day at home with my kid. I wasn't built for endless trips to the park and making arrangements for playgroup and reading the same book 700 times an hour. I loved Pip, but I was shit at being her mother. How did Harriet and Jane and Ellie do it? I knew, somewhere, deep down, that it was OK to feel like I wasn't cut out to stay at home with Pip, but I also knew I should try to change that about myself. I mean, shouldn't I *want* to sing nursery rhymes to her? Shouldn't I *want* to watch Peppa Pig with her? Nina would. If Nina had had a baby, like she was meant to, she'd be doing all of those things, and probably a whole lot more – I couldn't even think of more things on account of being such a bad mother. What the hell was wrong with me?

It was getting hot. I was getting hot. Sweat began to dampen my shirt.

'Are you OK?' Arianna's voice had become distant. I was in the clouds of my own thoughts, far away from her.

'Yes, yes.'

I looked down at my notes. *IT'S NOT WORTH IT*. I let out a stifled laugh. The room was oppressively hot now; it was like Bangkok in here. My head started to pound.

'Could you turn the heating down, please?' I asked.

Arianna looked confused. 'It's not on. It's quite cool in here, actually, the air-con's on.'

That couldn't be true. It was tropical. Balmy. I peeled my jumper off, careful of my broken arm, feeling sweat on my face as I lifted the jumper over my head. I stood up and started pacing the room, as if this would cool me down somehow. There were photos everywhere, in sleek wooden frames – Chris and Arianna on their wedding day, Chris and Arianna with their famous friends, Chris and Arianna with Atticus, Atticus doing one of those weird professional baby shoots where the photographer had somehow manipulated his limbs to make it look like he was lying like a cherub, hands folded under his chin. Even in my somewhat manic state, I could tell you: no baby has ever laid in that pose naturally.

And then I realised with alarming clarity, like flipping a switch in the dark: the candles. There weren't any candles anywhere.

She's selling candles, I'm here to talk about the candles. So where are the bloody candles?

I whirled back into the room, suddenly hyper-aware.

'Arianna – can I see some of the candles? Which is your favourite?'

'Ah, well, my favourite is probably the rosemary and tuberose. It's quite, um, masculine in a way, so it's very different.' She was looking beyond me as she spoke. *LIAR!*

'Uh-huh. And where do you keep yours? I can't see any.' If I had been pulled up and away before, now I was too present, the room shimmering with colour and movement, Arianna's face twitchy, nervous. The heat continued to rise and I pulled at my shirt, now sticky with sweat.

'Yes. Well. Mainly I keep them in our bedroom.'

I nodded.

'Well, it's best to keep them away from children, you know? Some scented candles can be, er, harmful.' Arianna let out a little laugh.

'Are yours?'

'No! No, definitely not. But, um... Well, they can be a fire hazard.'

I felt like a crack detective spotting a major clue. Arianna clocked my raised eyebrows and realised she was heading down a rabbit warren of missteps.

'Are you OK?' she asked again. 'You look really pale. Are you alright?' Arianna stared at me, clearly trying to change the subject. *As if.*

'I'm fine. Never been better.'

She didn't even like her own candles. Her candles were crap, I knew it. She was cashing in on her fame with candles she didn't even want in her own house.

In my dazed yet manic headspace, I kept thinking, *I'm going to win a Walkley for this. Crack reporter breaks open the case of the missing candles. The Candle Scandal, that's what they'll call it.* I could see the headlines now.

'Well, I'd better get back to Atticus.' She stood, pushing the non-existent creases from her white jeans. Arianna turned towards the kitchen, with its futuristic fridge and polished concrete floor and perfect-looking fruit. I thought of the banana that was slowly rotting in my own fruit bowl at home, because it seemed like too much of a hassle to bin it. I couldn't even do that right.

I couldn't do my job.

I didn't do the right thing by Neil.

I wasn't a good mum.

I had ruined everything. And I couldn't see a way out.

The room spun. Suddenly I felt a surge of rage.

'You don't even like candles, do you?'

She kept walking, like she hadn't heard. Gotcha. What a fraud.

'Arianna?' I had a vague notion that my voice was getting louder – or maybe I had just, in this very second, developed supersonic hearing. The world was buzzing.

She kept walking.

'Hey! Turn around.' I was Jana Wendt, I was Leigh Sales, I was Barbara Walters. I was not letting her go. I demanded answers.

I was watching myself now, kind of awestruck that I'd had the courage to yell at this woman. And then I realised: shit, I yelled at this woman. That's not good. But also: I was reporting from the front lines now. I had to get the answers. I owed it to the people.

She turned, though, looking both sheepish and annoyed.

'Look, I'm not sure what you're talking about. I did this interview as a favour to Meredith. You're starting to freak me out a bit.'

I rolled my eyes. 'Come on, Arianna, just tell me the truth. Where are the candles? Do you even like candles? I don't think you do. Here's what I think happened,' I began, as if I were about to claim that Arianna had murdered her firstborn and buried the evidence. 'I think you got lucky. Marrying Chris, all this landing in your lap.' I gestured around the room. 'And then you got bored. Real bored. So you and your publicist thought, "Why not sell some candles?" Yeah, that'll be fun. No questions asked, right? Well I'm onto you, Foster. The jig is up. You don't even like candles, do you?'

She stared at me as if I had... well, as if I had just accused her of the great crime of not liking candles.

'I think you'd better sit down. You look... you don't look good.'

I huffed. 'No, I'm fine. I've never been better. I'm just happy I've finally gotten the truth out of you, that's all.'

'What are you talking about? Really, I think you should sit down. You look a bit faint. Do you need some water?'

I felt crazed. Really, I could feel it. It was like I'd poured caffeine directly into my veins, and it was pumping through my body like blood. Maybe this is what it's like to be on ice, I thought. I mean, not exactly a barrel of giggles, but not altogether terrible.

I refused to sit. Instead, I paced the room, peppering Arianna with questions about the sodding candles until she asked me to be quiet while she called Meredith.

'Meredith?' I asked, panicking. Oh shit. 'No! No, you don't need to call Meredith. Really.'

Arianna stared at me, phone in hand. 'I think it's probably best if I do,' she said, adding, under her breath, 'Meredith has sent a fucking loon to my house, so Meredith can come and pick her up.'

Suddenly I got a glimpse of what Arianna could see. I was, indeed, behaving like a lunatic. What was happening? How did I get here?

All of a sudden, I became aware of someone emitting a low, long moan. Everything shook. I realised I was the one groaning. *Oh god*.

Robyn, holding Atticus, rushed in, a panicked look across her face. She went to Arianna's side.

I felt my head get tighter and tighter. The world was getting too bright. I had to close my eyes. I had to get out of here. Why was it so hard to breathe? Had it always been this hard? How had I got through my entire life if it was this hard to breathe?

As Arianna, now holding the baby, backed away from me, Robyn drew closer. I think she was actually moving quite slowly, edging over to me bit by bit, the way one might cautiously approach an unknown animal, or the way I often tiptoed over to Pip's cot. But the way I saw it at that moment, she was hurtling towards me, ready to knock me down.

I ran.

*

I woke up, freezing. When I opened my eyes, the light was blinding. I closed them again immediately. Where was I?

My arm felt heavy on my stomach. *That's right*, I thought, suddenly more aware. *I have a broken arm.* I opened one eye, and then the other, slowly. I sat up and saw a curtain on one side of me.

'Hello,' said a familiar voice.

I turned slowly. 'Hi,' I said, seeing Neil. *Neil. Neil is here. Neil hates me. Neil is leaving.* 'What happened?'

He smiled. 'You're OK. They think you might have had a panic attack.'

'What?'

He nodded. 'It's OK. You're going to be fine. But uh, I'm not sure you'll be on Arianna Foster's Christmas card list.'

Oh god. Arianna. It was all coming back to me. The candles. The accusations. Arianna's self-righteousness. Atticus and his seaweed snacks. What had I done?

'Oh. Oh god. I think I yelled at Arianna.'

'Oh yeah, you definitely did. She called Meredith after she called the ambulance. She said you went nuts.'

'I did. Oh God. I'm so embarrassed.'

'Don't worry about it. Don't worry about any of it. You're going to be fine.'

'Where's Pip?' I asked as he squeezed my hand.

'She's with your mum. She's absolutely fine. Your mum picked her up from daycare yesterday.'

I nodded, trying to fit all the pieces together. 'Yesterday?'

He nodded. 'You've been asleep for a while. They gave you a sedative.'

'Oh,' I said. All I remembered was running away from Robyn, Atticus's nanny. I couldn't remember why, just the general feeling that I had to run, to escape.

'How did you–?' I asked, not quite able to finish the sentence.

'Meredith called me. After Arianna called her. Asked if I knew any of your family.' He smiled ruefully. 'You were right, she did know about us.'

I nodded, exhaustion weighing on my eyelids.

I felt Neil kiss my hand just before I fell asleep again.

*

When I woke up the next time, Neil declared the hospital's food inedible and went out to get me a cheeseburger and fries. I could have wept, I was so grateful. I had just begun to bite into the burger when the doctor came in, his face kind and concerned.

'Ms Henderson,' he said. 'Feeling better?'

I nodded.

'We believe you had a panic attack,' he said, looking at his clipboard. 'Do you have a history of panic disorders or anxiety?'

'No,' I said, shaking my head.

'Have you been under any stress lately?'

I laughed softly. 'Uh... yes.'

He glanced at me, his eyebrows rising. 'Work?'

I nodded. 'And baby. I have a baby.'

'Do you work full-time?'

I nodded.

'And you're a single mother?'

I nodded again.

He made a low whistling sound. 'Well, that's very stressful, I'd say. How'd you hurt your arm?'

'Shower. I slipped.'

'How much time did you take off work?'

'Um... like six hours?' I guessed.

His eyes bulged. 'Did you take any medication?'

'Panadol.'

'OK. And how about alcohol? Do you drink?'

I stared at him and gave a curt nod, one that I hoped would be interpreted as, 'Let's not get too specific about this.'

'Caffeine?'

More nodding.

'And how's your sleep? Are you sleeping well?'

I laughed again. 'Like I said... I have an eleven-month-old.'

'I see,' he said, nodding and making notes. 'Well, Ms Henderson, you have all the makings of a panic attack there. I'm surprised it took this long, to be honest.'

I sank into the pillow.

'You need rest. You need a lot of rest. We're going to run some tests overnight, to make sure you didn't actually have a seizure. I'm fairly certain you didn't, but we always like to make sure.'

I nodded.

'In the meantime, I suggest you sleep.'

It was just about the nicest thing anyone had ever said to me.

Chapter 22

Pip didn't have a first birthday party.

But she did have one for her second.

There was no Pinterest board, no e-vite with a birthday gift registry, no fancy layer cake – not even lolly bags, a fact that Lucas took particular umbrage with. 'Aunty Gawgee,' he said, looking confused and disappointed, when I told him that Pip was two and wasn't really at the lolly bag stage yet, 'Pip is two... but *I'm* five. *I* need a lolly bag.'

Ellie made cupcakes. Matt manned the barbecue, the one cooking job he could not fuck up (what was it with men who could use a barbecue but not a stovetop? They worked exactly the same way). Jase bought Pip a bike, of course, with pink tasselled handlebars and a basket for... what, exactly? The newspaper? She loved it all the same. Saskia came too, a new engagement ring on her hand and a slight swell to her stomach. She was due in January. Neil brought champagne and took pleasure in getting my mum ever so slightly tipsy. After I found her swatting Simon's arm flirtatiously as they chatted about their favourite *X Factor* contestants, I made Neil promise to never get her pissed again.

Pip, quite overwhelmed by all the excitement and attention, refused to blow out her candles. She sat there, frozen, as we all looked on, encouraging her. In the end we all helped and she clapped her hands in delight, then grabbed a cupcake and stuffed it into her mouth. *That's my girl.*

Pip had lengthened – sometimes, I thought, before my very eyes. Her chubbiness had faded over time, like colour from jeans. Her features were more distinct now and her hair no longer stuck up like it was shocked to see me. She wasn't a baby, she was her own little girl.

She loved colouring and biscuits pilfered from the jar Mum always kept in her kitchen (sugar apparently being acceptable if you were under five and very cute) and, somewhat regrettably, the colour pink (rationally I knew it didn't matter, but it still made me feel like a feminist traitor, like when I found myself humming 'Blurred Lines'). She sang a lot, mainly to herself, but other than that, my Pip was sort of quiet.

She was scared of the dark, and it was sort of lovely that she called out for me when she was eager for a cuddle, but also a little bit frustrating because, gosh, wouldn't a full night's sleep be wonderful?

'Nice column this week, George,' said Jase. 'The girls in the office loved it.'

'Thanks,' I said. I'd been writing my column, 'The Juggle is Real', for almost a year now. I'd left hospital after my panic attack expecting to be fired. Instead, Richie – who by that stage I'd honestly thought was a very well-developed figment of Meredith's imagination – called me. While I'd been in hospital, the *Media Alert* story had come out. The headline, 'Meredith Parker: All Hot Air?', was emblazoned across a photo of Meredith at an advertiser presentation, brandishing a microphone and stomping her foot to emphasise a point. She looked crazed, delirious, drunk on her own power. The article had detailed her empty buzzwords, her flimsy plans for the magazine, her abrupt and dismissive manner with me. It had also alluded, not so subtly, to her drinking. I was painted as quiet and slightly bamboozled, which at the time was probably quite accurate.

'Meredith's going, Georgina,' said Richie.

'Oh. Where to?' I couldn't imagine Meredith anywhere else but in her office, sugar-free Red Bull in one hand and her phone in the other, yelling at Bea to warm up her veggie patty for lunch.

'We're not sure. Meredith is... exploring other options,' he said carefully. 'What we're wondering is... would you like to take her job? Would you like to be the publisher? We've been really impressed with the editorial direction of *The Weekend*. We think you'd be a perfect fit.'

'Ah... wow. No,' I said, surprising myself. I didn't even have to think about it. No. I didn't want the job. There was no part of me that wanted it. There was no part of me that would even consider it.

'Really?' asked Richie, sounding quite surprised himself.

'Yeah. Really. But I have an idea–'

And so *The Juggle is Real* was born. It's about working parents, and it's in the paper every single Saturday. Readers – women, usually – write in and tell me about bosses who won't let them take an hour off to go to their kid's Christmas concert, or co-workers who resent the fact that they leave the office at 5.30 on the dot. They tell me about the guilt they feel when they drop their kids off and the shame of missing something important, like a school play, when they travel for work. They tell me that they love their job and they love their kids and they're just not sure how to get these two things to co-exist. I tell them, essentially, that it's OK: nobody does. It's all a work in progress. The juggle is real for all of us.

Neil moved in last month, and yes, he brought his Aeropress with him. Pip immediately picked it up, pulled the vacuum out and started using it as a trumpet. I watched the whole scene as if in slow motion, sure Neil would lose his shit. But he didn't. He got down on the floor with her, clapped along as she trumpeted away, and said to me, 'We'll get another one. That's the amazing thing about Aeropresses, they're so inexpensive. Also–'

Nina and Matt found a house swap in Provence, of which I am jealous in the extreme. Nina keeps sending me WhatsApp messages with pictures of vines and wine and plump red tomatoes from farmer's markets and little dogs with rather fetching kerchiefs around their necks. I miss her. I miss our shorthand language and the way I don't have to explain why I'm pissed about something – I just tell her the thing and she gets it. Neil's not quite at that speed yet. Last week I told him about a woman who cut in front of me in the line at Woolies and he cocked his head, unsure how to respond. Nina would have been instantly outraged on my behalf.

Neil's writing a book (which he won't let me see yet so obviously it must be a love story about the two of us), and working front of house at a restaurant. Penance, he says, for all the years he spent as a critic.

Lucas starts school this year and Ellie, while still quite concerned about the fact that he hasn't finished Proust yet (much less started, if we're perfectly honest), is looking forward to the new ways she'll be able to be Organised Mum. Shifts at the school canteen, nutritionally balanced bento box lunches for Lucas, making costumes for the school play, organising the Halloween disco, buying every teacher a Christmas present before 1 December every single year. Just thinking of those jobs brings me out in a shivering cold sweat, like an allergy, but Ellie will be so good at all of it, I just know. I've already promised to barely tease her about it.

I've only seen Meredith once since my meltdown at Arianna's house. She never called, never even sent one of her texts (*MP xxx*) to ask how I was. I had let myself feel briefly hurt by this, and then wondered why. Meredith hadn't cared about my mastitis, or Pip's UTI, or my broken arm. Why would she care if I had a panic attack?

Pip was at daycare and I had taken the train to the city for a meeting with Richie. I was walking through David Jones when I saw two little boys fighting like bear cubs in the crockery section. One of them, it was pretty clear, was about to either get glassed by a gravy boat or send his parents into virtual liquidation. Maybe both.

'Hey! Hey, stop that,' I said. They didn't look up.

A cashier appeared, tut-tutting. 'And where's the mother?' she asked, rolling her eyes.

I suddenly felt an allegiance to whoever this mother was. Maybe she was searching for a present. Maybe she was taking an important phone call. Maybe she was hiding out in the glassware section, keenly studying the Orrefors Kosta Boda just to get a moment's peace from these two animals. I know that's what I'd be doing.

'I'm sure she's here somewhere,' I said, finding myself using the same authoritative tone I'd just used on the bear cubs. I felt a kinship with this mother. Everyone's kids were total shits now and then.

The cashier, chewing gum loudly, rolled her eyes and walked away, muttering, 'You break it, you bought it,' under her breath.

'Ollie! Henry! Stop that! I said, stop that!' A voice rang out from behind a shelf.

Ollie and Henry did not *stop that*. They carried on wrestling as if they hadn't heard the woman – their mother, I presumed – and seconds later, I heard a crash as hundreds of dollars worth of china came tumbling down.

'Oliver Parker! Henry Parker! Get here this instant,' the woman barked. Oh. I knew that bark.

The woman appeared, stomping and outraged, her eyes blazing with unbridled anger. 'What are you doing? You are both old enough to know better. You are–'

She stopped all of a sudden, feeling my eyes on her.

'Oh,' she said, drawing her head back into her neck, making that double chin I always relished seeing on someone so skinny. 'Hello, George.'

'Meredith.' I paused. 'Hi.'

She smiled at me uncertainly, as if I'd walked in on something I wasn't meant to see. Ollie and Henry, for their part, were frozen on the floor, the china cracked and broken around them. The bored cashier had returned, an I-told-you-so look plastered on her face as she set about sweeping up the wreckage and adding up the damage.

'How are you?' Meredith asked.

I narrowed my eyes. *Were these Meredith's kids? Surely not.*

'I'm fine. You?'

'Good. Good.' Her bravado swept away, Meredith seemed sad and scared. I tried to picture her now, with that omnipresent can of Red Bull, marching around in her expensive high heels, and could not. Now, she looked like any other harried mother trying to get shit done. She wore sandals and jeans and a loose – though still, I noted, expensive – broderie top with the faintest coffee stain on the chest. I held back a smile.

'Are these...?'

'My boys?' She raised an eyebrow. 'Yes.'

I let out a shocked laugh. 'Really?'

'Yes. Why is that funny?'

'It's not. I'm just... I'm just surprised.'

She shrugged, pursing her lips in the old Meredith way. 'I don't know why you would be.'

I stared at her, trying to understand. 'Well... you never mentioned them. You seemed to always be working. You never seemed–'

'Like a mother?' She arched a brow.

'Uh... yeah, I guess so.'

She tossed her hair over her shoulder, considering her answer. 'Well, I didn't want anyone to treat me any differently. I'm older than you, George. I remember a time when women were quietly relegated to the mummy track once they had babies. I didn't ever want my home life to affect my career. I worked very hard to get to where I was, and I just didn't see why having children should change that.'

'But who... who was with your kids when you weren't?'

She raised a single frustrated eyebrow. 'George, would you ask a man that?'

I stopped to consider the question. Meredith was right. 'No. Probably not.'

'My husband is the boys' primary carer. And we have a nanny.'

'Right.' I hadn't even known Meredith had a husband. She'd never mentioned any of it. I thought back to her desk, filled with inspirational quotes and stacks of career self-help books. Zero family photos. Then I thought of how, gradually, I had turned my own framed photo of Pippa further and further inward, so nobody could see it but me.

'You seem surprised,' she said, her voice measured and assured as she checked the boys for cuts.

'I am. I can't believe you treated me like that when you knew exactly how hard it was for me. I guess I just assumed you didn't know, and that's why you kept pushing me.'

'I thought you were capable,' she said, brushing out Ollie's hair with her hand – still perfectly manicured, I noticed.

I smiled. 'I wasn't.'

Standing up, the boys cleared for injuries, she studied me again. 'I may have expected too much from you.'

'Maybe.'

There was so much I wanted to ask Meredith. How did she do it? How did she fly to Melbourne at a moment's notice, and stay out all night with clients, and make it to the gym at 6.30 am and not leave the office until 7.30 pm, all with these two boys at home? How did she cope with missing every sleepy morning cuddle, every bedtime story?

The boys were sitting down now, playing with their respective iPads while the cashier looked on, not even trying to hide her disdain. Meredith ignored her.

'What are you doing now?' I asked.

'Consulting, mainly. I'm doing a lot of work on new websites and podcasts – telling people what to do. You know I love that,' she said wryly. I allowed myself a small laugh at her expense.

'Right. Sounds right up your alley.'

'And you? I've seen your column once or twice. It's, uh... well, I understand people enjoy it.'

I stifled an eyeroll. 'They do. It's being syndicated now, which is great. Makes money less of a worry. And I freelance here and there. Go on TV a bit, do some radio spots.'

Meredith nodded. 'Yes, I've seen. You were right; it was a good idea for a column.'

I nodded. 'I think it's something that people relate to – the challenge of being so many things at once, to so many people. It's hard to have a child *and* a whole team of people at work depending on you. Mainly, I guess, because you want to do both, and you want to succeed at both, but something has to give.' A sense of relief washed over me. I had said it. To Meredith. I had told her – so, so long after the fact, but still – what I had always wanted to tell her. *I want to be good at my job, but I want to be a good mother, too. Why can't you let me be both?* It always struck me as supremely unfair that kids have no choice but to let their parents go to work, but the adults in charge of the parents often didn't let them go home to their kids.

'Right.' Meredith gave me a curt smile, which I chose to interpret as a level of understanding.

'I mean... How did *you* do it?'

'Do what?'

'How did you publish *The Weekend* and have these kids at home? I just... I don't understand it.'

'I loved my job.'

'Sure, but... don't you love being with your kids, too?'

'Of course. But I'm better at my job. That's the truth.'

I nodded. It took guts to admit that.

'Some people are better suited to being full-time parents, and some are better at full-time work. And we need both. That's the reality. So you just need to decide which one you're better at, and do it. I came to that realisation a long time ago. All this nonsense about "doing it all"... it's such rubbish. Just pick the thing you're good at. Play to your strengths.'

'I guess,' I said, mulling it over. What were my strengths? I still hated going to the park. I couldn't brush Pip's hair without her yelling, 'Mummy! Stop!' She still woke up multiple times a night; I'd literally thrown Tizzie's book out the window (it landed in Eileen's yard, for which I was soundly berated the next morning). But I loved watching her climb the small tree in our yard, and reading to her at night, and feeling her warm little body crash into mine when I picked her up at daycare. I still loved writing, but I didn't feel the pull of work the way I once had. I didn't need a fancy title or an office anymore. I was sure I would find another job I loved, but for now, I was OK where I was. And OK was a good way to be.

'But... how do you know what your strengths are? How do you know what kind of mother you should be?' I asked.

Meredith rolled her eyes. 'Oh, George,' she said, sighing. 'You'll figure it out.'

Acknowledgments

Writing a book is sometimes a solitary task, but it's also a team effort, and I'm lucky enough to have one of the best teams in the business. To everyone at Black Inc. and Nero – but particularly Jeanne, Kirstie, Kelly, Kate, Caitlin and Imogen – thank you so, so much. To Vanessa Lanaway, I owe you many glasses of wine and maybe a new pair of glasses. Your editing made this book what it is. Thank you so much.

To all my mum friends who very patiently answered all my nosy questions about parenting and going back to work and whether Sophie the Giraffe was a universal reference: thank you. Diya, Cindy, Jess O, Jess P, Jess I, Jo, Shivaun, Lauren, Ali, Julia, Katie and Annie – thank you for your insights and words of wisdom. I owe you all wine, too.

To my amazing family, thank you for indulging me yet again. Rob and Maryann, you're the best parents-in-law anyone could ask for. Thank you for all the babysitting and pizza dinners and bottles of NZ sparkling. Laura and Scott, thanks for being the best beta readers. Mum and Steve, thanks for everything. The list of things you do for me is too long.

And David, Annie, Buddy and Otto – thanks for being my people. I love you endlessly.

If you enjoyed what you read, don't keep it a secret.

Review the book online and tell anyone who will listen.

Thanks for your support spreading the word about Legend Press!

Follow us on Twitter

@legend_press

Follow us on Instagram

@legendpress